NICHOLAS: LORD OF SECRETS

GRACE BURROWES

GRACE BURROWES PUBLISHING

Nicholas: Lord of Secrets

This book is for everybody who knows how much love and wisdom reside in people whom the ignorant dismiss as "limited." One child's silent smile can illuminate universes, and love has a genius that soars above the pedestrian comprehension of the intellect.

CHAPTER ONE

The English peerage had come to a sorry pass when the heir to an earldom had to duck up the footmen's stairway to hide from lovely young women seeking to become his countess.

Nicholas Haddonfield, Viscount Reston, took those steps two at a time.

He emerged on the first floor of the Winterthur mansion, the corridor blessedly devoid of footmen, debutantes, mamas, or other aggravations. Nick hurried to the first door and found it locked, suggesting the evening's hosts, Lord and Lady Winterthur, were not entirely foolish. Well, no matter, the corridor was long, and there had to be an unlocked sitting room or parlor where a man could hide himself away for a few minutes of peace, quiet, and solitude.

He approached an intersection and froze.

"He must have gone this way, Eulie." The lady's tone was indignant. "The gentlemen's retiring room is on this floor, and he's too big to go missing for long."

"Really, Pamela..." The second woman's voice floated around the corner. "I know he'll be an earl, but you can't seriously be thinking of marriage to Reston? I heard him tell Lady Lavinia Gregson that he killed his mother."

The voices were coming closer. Nick spotted a door on the left slightly ajar and sent up a prayer to whatever saint looked after beleaguered bachelors. He slipped inside, finding the room dark, save for weak illumination from a fire in the hearth.

"He's likely hiding," the first woman decided. "Playing hard to get. You know when he said he killed his mother, he almost sounded as if he were serious."

Nick plastered himself against the wall behind the door while the ladies in the corridor continued their pursuit.

"Pamela, you cannot have thought what the wedding night with such a brute would involve." Just outside the door, the lady's voice dripped with distaste. "Earl or not, he's simply... well, I would fear for you, my dear."

"My mother says they all look the same in the dark." The door swung open. One of the various ladies who'd been watching Nick ever more closely as the supper waltz approached peered into the gloom, then pulled the door shut again. "Nothing in here. Perhaps he's in the gentlemen's retiring room."

As her voice trailed off down the corridor, Nick considered the intensity of his relief.

Safe—for another hour he was safe, and so damned tired that a cozy, private parlor was inordinately appealing. He moved across the room, intent on stoking up the fire, when his peripheral vision caught a pale shadow to the right of the hearth.

"I beg your pardon," he said. "I did not know the room was occupied." As his vision adjusted, Nick could make out the soft, billowy shape of a ball gown on a woman seated on a chest or bench along the wall.

"What if we each agree to be alone in here?" the apparition suggested in a voice that carried the slightest rasp.

"Suits me," Nick said, going to the fireplace. "Are you hiding or merely enjoying a quiet respite?"

"Both, I think. And you?"

"Most definitely hiding." Nick's smile was rueful. "Lady Whoever and her faithful dog Lady Simper have that let-me-be-your-countess gleam in their eyes."

"One of them sounded less than enthralled." Nick's companion spoke with a touch of humor.

"I'd wish I were a foot taller, if it would scare away more of the debutantes and their mamas. Do you mind if I sit, as we're each so plainly alone?"

"Please." The lady shifted slightly in her corner. "You are Reston?"

"At your service." Nick bowed toward the shadowy corner. "And apparently tall enough to have no anonymity left whatsoever."

"Or handsome enough. Maybe single enough?"

Nick scrubbed a hand over his face. "That too, for my sins." He satisfied himself the fire would throw off a little more heat, but resisted the urge to build it up to the point where the shadows were illuminated. Without knowing why, he didn't want to intrude on his companion's privacy. Something about having a conversation with a woman whose features he could not clearly see appealed.

He settled on a sofa facing the hearth, crossed one foot over his knee, pulled off his gloves, and slipped off his dancing pump. His companion was no heavily chaperoned schoolgirl if she could find her way to this little oasis of solitude, and he doubted she'd take offense.

"My poor, lordly, single feet are expiring," Nick muttered, massaging his arch.

"Bride hunting is work," the lady said. "Almost as hard work as being hunted."

Nick's hands paused in their ministrations, and he cocked his head to peer into the dark corner. "So are you a staked goat as well?"

"I am on my way to slaughter, I fear." For the first time, her voice had a careful, controlled quality.

She'd been crying. Nick knew it like any man with four sisters knows such things, like any man who adored women—most women, most of the time— could sense female upset.

"Your intended is not to your liking?" Nick asked, trying not to let himself care. He couldn't even see the woman, for pity's sake, though he had the sense she was as weary of the ballroom battleground as he.

"My intended is more than twice my age, and while that alone would not matter, he's spent more years being dissolute than I have breathing."

"Gads." Nick switched feet. "At least I get to do the asking. Who is this reprobate? Shall I call him out for you? Buy up his markers?"

"I really ought not to be so sensitive," the lady said with a touch of asperity, "but I do not appreciate the levity, my lord."

"Who's joking?" Nick asked, stretching his feet out toward the fire. "Tell me who he is."

"Hellerington," the woman said, a wealth of resignation in her voice.

"And you've accepted him?" Nick asked, leaning back and closing his eyes.

"I have not, but he told me at supper he would be speaking to my father, and once they come to terms, my refusal or consent won't mean anything."

Nick opened his eyes and frowned. The man's name wasn't ringing any particular bells, but then, Nick had spent much of the past few years in the country, dodging his responsibilities and larking about with friends—to hear his father tell it.

He thought of his father, growing increasingly frail, and wanted to howl at the moon with the weight of grief and guilt. Rising, he crossed the room to a decanter on a sideboard and poured two glasses.

"Dutch courage." He passed one drink to the lady. "Sip it carefully, though Winterthur will have only decent libation on hand." A graceful bare hand emerged from the shadows and took the drink. No gloves. The lady was making herself quite at home here in the dark little parlor.

"Good lord," the woman gasped, "that is potent."

"Warms the innards," Nick said, sipping his own drink. "Mind if I join you?"

"Of course not." She tucked her skirts closer to her side and scooted more deeply into her corner.

Nick lowered himself beside her, making the padded bench creak. "Have you no other prospects?" He leaned back against the wall, savoring the moment. The fire hissed and popped softly beside them, and the lady herself gave off a subtle fragrant heat, such that even sitting beside her was an odd comfort.

"I am barely received," she said. "My debut was eight years ago. I should feel lucky to have any offer at all."

"You are a fossil then, though not as prehistoric as my handsome self." And no wonder she didn't quail at sharing the parlor with him for a few moments.

Or a drink.

Or a bench in a quiet corner.

"Men do not become fossils. They become distinguished."

Nick sipped his drink. "Good to know."

"How is your father?"

The question surprised him, but if she knew who he was and that he was hunting a bride, she'd likely know why as well.

"Failing," Nick said, surprising himself with his honesty. "He's a tough old boot but hasn't lived an easy life, and seeing me married is all he's asked of me." And Nick had given his promise that before the Season was out, he'd have not just a fiancée, but a bride. The already depressing evening threatened to become downright morose.

"Parents. They excel at the gentle art of the unspoken guilt."

Understanding like that was balm to a tired bachelor's soul. "Is that why you're on your way to slaughter?"

"Not parental guilt. Sororal guilt."

"I am one of eight," Nick said, citing the legitimate total because he was in polite company. "Sibling guilt can be powerful." The guilt of a grown, unmarried son and heir more powerful yet.

"My younger sister will make her come out next year, and I must be safely away from the social scene. One wouldn't want to queer her chances by association with me."

"You are truly so wicked?" He couldn't credit that, because he knew—in every sense—the truly wicked and fast ladies of the polite world, and he did not know this shadowy creature beside him. He could not place her slightly husky voice or her lily of the valley scent.

"I was wicked," she said. "I caused quite a scandal once upon a time."

"All of my dearest friends have at least one scandal to their names." As did Nick, though he'd endure death by torture before he'd let Society catch a hint of it. He put his drink to his lips again, only to find he'd drained his glass. "More brandy?"

"Maybe just a drop. It grows on one."

He brought the decanter to her and poured them each another two fingers. "You have no brothers or aunties or grandmother who can stay your father's hand?" Nick asked as he settled beside her. He wanted to stay close to her scent and to the pleasing melody of her voice in the dark. On a night otherwise devoid of comforts, the impulse was not to be questioned.

"No aunties or grandmother." The lady did not sound forlorn so much as stoic. "Two brothers, and they have done what they could to spare me these past few years. Papa is determined to be rid of me though, so a-marrying I will go."

A-marrying, an ironic reference to a-Maying. Nick appreciated the bravado. "I am cheered, in a bleak sort of way, to commiserate with somebody else who has so little enthusiasm for wedded bliss."

"Did you really tell that poor woman you killed your mother?" The amusement was audible again.

Nick peered at his drink, watching as it caught and reflected the firelight. "I did kill my mother, in a manner of speaking. She did not survive long after my appearance in the world, which I attribute to the rigors of birthing a child who was half the size of a bull calf. Informing my various countesses-in-waiting of this fact cools their heels a bit."

"Naughty of you but not unsporting. Childbed is a dangerous place, irrespective of a lady's wealth or position."

"So I tell myself. How would your papa react were I to pay you my addresses?"

The lady beside him went still in some considering way. "You're serious. That is very kind of you, my lord."

"Not kind—it's self-serving. If I am seen to choose a prospective fiancée, then at least half of the gaggle following me from ball to soiree to Venetian breakfast will lose heart, and I'll have a little more peace for the next few weeks."

"My lord"—the lady's voice indicated she was looking at him while she spoke—"you don't even know who I am, what I look like, what scandal lies in my past."

Nick shrugged his shoulders, their width causing his arm to brush inadvertently against his companion. "Nor do I care. You are an eligible female, which makes you credible for my purposes, and you are a damsel in distress." She also had a pretty voice, wasn't the least missish, and her scent was luscious and soothing.

"Your rescue could misfire," the lady pointed out. "If Hellerington thinks you're considering me as a potential wife, he might negotiate with my father that much more quickly."

"Suppose he could." Nick felt a passing relief his impulsive offer would be rejected, though it meant weeks more of Lady Simper and her ilk. "It's still a thought."

"Generous of you." The lady touched her glass to his. "To a knight errant of the ballroom. May you find happiness, despite your apparent fate."

Nick saluted with his glass. "And you as well, my lady."

They drank in companionable, thoughtful silence until Nick spoke again. "What will be the worst part of being married to this Lord Hellerington?" He occupied himself with such dolorous musings when he contemplated his own impending marriage.

"Besides the loss of hope?"

She was silent a long moment, while Nick tried not to let that term—loss of hope—settle too hard in his mind.

"It should not bother me, for a wife must do her duty, but the thought of that man kissing me... His teeth—what teeth he has—are not attractive, and he takes snuff... And this is really more than you wanted to know. I am being ridiculous. Hellerington can't have that many years to live, after all."

Nick patted her hand. Kissing, done properly, could be more intimate than coitus. "I understand. What years you have left, you shouldn't be made to spend trying not to gag in the dark as your privacy is violated in the name of marital duty." She went still again, shocked maybe, but Nick wasn't sorry he'd spoken.

"Blunt," she muttered on a soft exhalation, "and damned accurate."

Damned. He liked her more and more.

"Shall I kiss you, my lady? I have all my teeth, and I am accounted somewhat skilled in the art. You may consider it a kiss for luck." He set his drink aside and took hers from her hand as well. He kept his movements deliberate, giving her every chance to demur, turn his threat into a joke, or slap him.

Nick was no stranger to a woman's palm walloped across his cheek, though it had been awhile. But his companion kept her silence—his liking for this woman was becoming considerable—so Nick followed her arm up with his palm until he could anchor both hands on her neck and cradle her jaw. He wanted to know the feel of her cheekbones under his thumbs, wanted to experience the exact warmth of that special, feminine place where neck and shoulder met.

"You can stop me," he assured her on a whisper. "You need only tell me."

Her breathing had accelerated slightly, though she held still and waited.

Patience in a female was a wonderful quality. Nick let his fingers tunnel carefully into the silky warmth of her hair and his thumbs slide first over her lips. Gads, she was soft, smooth, and warm. A pleasure to stroke, to inhale.

He brushed his lips gently over hers and felt her breath feather over his mouth. When he repeated the caress, her lips closed but stayed unresisting under his.

"Kiss me back, lamb," Nick whispered. "Give me something to dream about too."

She made a little sound in her throat and swayed toward him, but still Nick merely sipped at her mouth, wanting to go slowly, to savor and pleasure and share with her a few stolen moments against all the years they would both be married to other strangers.

Gently, he eased his tongue over the seam of her lips and tasted the surprise his boldness gave her. He persisted, but at an undemanding pace, one that reassured as it teased. Her lips parted, and Nick felt a lick of desire course down past his gut.

Ah, women... He sampled the plush heat of her mouth and felt a tentative caress of her tongue against his. The sweetness of the brandy lingered, blending with her fragrance and the taste of wonder. Slowly, Nick eased back, lightening the kiss gradually, reluctant to end it but knowing arousal wouldn't serve either of them when the likes of Miss Eulie and Lady What's-Her-Title were patrolling the corridors.

He kissed her eyes and her cheek, then tucked an arm around her back, drawing her to lean against him.

"If that is somewhat skilled," the lady whispered against his side, "then your version of an expert kiss would surely inspire me to swoon." She eased away.

Nick dropped his arm and passed her a drink.

His drink, if he weren't mistaken.

"My thanks, my lady." He cradled her brandy in his hands, thinking of the taste of that kiss and not of correcting his mistake with the drinks. "Won't you tell me your name?"

"Are you sure you want to know?" The question was devoid of her characteristic lilt.

"I have been advised one shouldn't go around kissing strangers."
Though he'd ignored the warning often and enthusiastically. "Based
on the past few minutes, I must disregard this guidance altogether."

"You are kind, Lord Reston. There is kindness even in your
kisses."

He wanted to touch her again, almost as badly as he'd wanted to
escape the ballroom. "Kindness? I can't say that particular descriptor
has been applied to me or my kisses." Though a lady could say far
worse things about a fellow's attentions.

His companion rose, keeping her back to him, a long, graceful
back full of resolution and sorrow. He wanted to touch her back too,
to learn the contour of those shoulder blades and the curve of
her nape.

"I will leave you here, my lord. You will wait a few minutes
before you leave?"

"Of course, but I will miss your company." Nick meant it, too, as
their odd, partly anonymous interlude had pleasantly surprised him
and put warmth into an otherwise bleak and boring night.

"Our paths might one day cross again," the lady said, "but if they
don't, I will always be grateful for these few minutes with you."

Nick kept his seat and let her move away without showing him
her face in any measurable light. She paused at the door, and just
before she opened it and slipped through, she went still again.

"I am Leah," she said softly. "My name is Leah."

Then she was gone, her name reverberating in the room silently,
the aural equivalent of a glass slipper.

~

A MAN of Nick's proportions did not fit easily into life in many ways,
not the least of which was the physical. His horse, Buttercup, was a
golden behemoth, her gender overlooked in favor of her ability to
carry such a large rider with ease. Nick's beds were built to his
measurements, and when he was forced to spend a night between

residences, he often chose to sleep on the ground rather than in beds made for much smaller people.

He ate prodigious quantities of food, and could drink more spirits than most mere mortals could safely consume. All of his appetites, in fact, were in proportion to his size. But so too were his conveyances, and thus he frequently took up his friends and acquaintances when they were in need of transportation.

Nick was in the card room, where he'd be safe from all but the oldest females, when Lord Valentine Windham found him lurking in the shadows near a game of whist.

"I am free," Valentine informed him with a grin. "What say we take ourselves off?"

"None too soon for me," Nick replied, shoving away from the mantel he'd propped his elbow on. "What are you in the mood for?" They ambled off amid cheery, drunken good-byes, and Nick knew a gut-deep sense of relief to be leaving.

"In truth?"

"No, Valentine. You are my friend, it's well past midnight, and we are both only more or less sober. Why don't you take up lying to me?"

"I'm in the mood to spend some time with that Broadwood of yours," Valentine said. "Not well done of me, I know, but as the weather moderates, your pianoforte is developing the most gorgeous middle register."

"You are incorrigible, Valentine."

"I am besotted. A good instrument is a precious find."

They fell silent as they gained the drive, the April air nippy. Nick's town coach rolled up, to Nick's eye resembling Cinderella's pumpkin carriage. The thing was huge, opulently appointed, and pulled by a foursome of equally gargantuan bay horses. It fit him wonderfully, but rendered any hope of discretion laughable.

"How many women have you seduced in this rolling seraglio?" Valentine asked, settling onto the well-padded seat.

Nick felt a twinge of irritation that his grand conveyance raised questions only about his equally grand reputation with the demimonde.

"Enough. Would you like to borrow it?"

Val glanced around as Nick lowered himself beside him. "I could fit a tidy little cottage piano in here."

"You are not right in the head, Valentine. Or in some other parts."

"I am right enough. When I first came south from wintering with my brother in Yorkshire, I tended to the obvious priorities, and now it's my music that calls to me. What about your other parts? Did you find a prospective bride tonight?"

"What do you know of Lord Hellerington?" Nick ignored Val's question. On first mention, such an inquiry deserved no consideration whatsoever.

Val grimaced. "Unappetizing shift of topics. He is often referred to as Lord Hell-raiser, an epithet he takes pride in. Old as dirt, rackety as hell, and forever trying to knock up his mistresses. Word is that various social diseases have rendered him incapable of impregnating a female, if not half mad."

Beelzebub's balls, no wonder the woman had been crying. "Wealth?"

"Enough for appearances. Nothing of great merit, or he'd have lured some sweet young thing to the altar by now."

"He's never married?"

"Three times, and wore them all out." Val paused to yawn broadly. "Why the sudden interest?"

"Somebody mentioned him in conversation this evening. Does he gamble?"

Val cocked his head and considered Nick by the passing light of streetlamps and porch lights. "He whores. He drinks to frequent excess, he duels. He abuses opium, absinthe, and women, and one hears of children coming to harm in his care. His horses are invariably crazy, or they are when he's done with them. All in all, a stunning exponent of the titled set, and he's a mere baron."

"I want his vowels," Nick said, frowning out the window. The words were unplanned, but they emerged with conviction. "I want his secrets, but I'll start with his gambling markers."

"Has he crossed you?" From a friend, the question was reasonable, for Nick was generally known for a live-and-let-live approach to his fellow man. He'd learned long ago to cultivate such a reputation, lest his peace be constantly shredded by those seeking to challenge him physically.

But what should Nick say now, when he felt the stirrings of temper on the strength of a mere passing encounter with a woman named Leah?

Who had the softest skin and kisses that tasted of wonder—and courage.

"You describe Hellerington as an embarrassment to good society in general. Perhaps I'm embarking on a public service."

"Of course. You, who single-handedly—if that's the appropriate appendage—support at least three of the best brothels in London, have taken a notion to torment one old reprobate who wouldn't be allowed through the doors of any of them."

Nick smiled slightly at his companion. "Three brothels, Valentine?"

"For now—according to rumor. You'll not be frequenting the brothels once you're married. You won't disgrace your wife that way, and you know it."

"I would not disgrace a woman I loved that way, but I have no intention of acquiring a wife for any romantic purposes whatsoever."

"Then how are you going to get your heirs on the lady?" Val shot back. "Your temperament is such that you at least like the females you bed in such quantity, Nicholas. You aren't capable of treating a woman coldly, and wives, I am told, have a habit of entangling themselves in a man's life."

"I appreciate women, Val," Nick said, but he was fatigued of the topic, of the night, and of much else in life. "That is not the same thing at all as loving one woman."

"So refine your tastes," Val suggested gently. "I know the issue is a sore one, but to see you attempting a calculating approach to your bride search rankles exceedingly."

Rankle—such a delicate term for unbridled loathing. Rather than endure more interrogation, Nick remained silent until the coach rocked to a halt.

"After you." The fewer people in the coach when Nick rose, the more room he had to maneuver. Val obligingly hopped out of the coach and waited for Nick under the porte cochere.

"You were going to finish your thought, Nicholas."

"I am going to listen to you play me a lullaby," Nick informed him, "while we both get sentimental over some of my best brandy."

"Of course. My very thoughts, but, Nick?"

"Hmm?" Nick passed off hat, cape, gloves, and cane to a footman, and Val waited until they were again alone to continue.

"You should marry only for love," Val said, oddly serious. "Another man, even I, might be able to carry off the typical cordial war that passes for a Society marriage, but it will destroy you to make such a compromise."

Nick settled an arm around his friend's shoulders and steered him toward the cozy confines of the family parlor. "Valentine, you are a dear man, with artistic sensibilities and a paucity of single brothers. Spare me your pronouncements about matrimony until the reality looms a little closer to your own experience, hmm? There's a lad, and tell me, how many bottles will it take before you play me some of that music you make up on the spot but don't write down? You've a name for it."

"Improvisation," Val said, letting Nick lead him toward the Broadwood. "Because you're being contrary and stubborn, you'll get only Scarlatti from me tonight."

"Scarlatti it is." Nick signaled his butler for an extra bottle of the good stuff anyway.

～

"DARIUS?" Lady Leah Lindsey stifled a yawn as the horses swung into a trot.

"Hmm?" Darius Lindsey exercised a brother's prerogative by yawning audibly and rolling his neck.

"What do you know of a Viscount Reston?" Leah asked, glad for the lack of light in the coach and for a brother who would join her on the forward-facing seat.

Darius peered at her with a sibling's inconvenient curiosity. "Built like a Viking, and blond like one."

"So you've seen him. But what do you know of him?"

"He's not married," Darius said musingly, "and a certain type of woman lines up to offer him her wares, according to the gossip. Some say he was rusticating for the past few years. Others say he was taking the cure for years of mischief. He has friends in odd places, high and low, and he's rumored to be looking for a bride, because old Bellefonte is approaching his last prayers. He doesn't gamble to excess, and there's no mention of public displays of temper or inebriation. Lots of speculation about the man, but little real fact."

Leah said nothing, while she privately concluded Reston must be a decent enough fellow, because as she well knew, vices were pounced upon and dissected by the gossips without mercy.

"Finances?" Leah asked, thinking of Reston's casual offer to buy up Hellerington's markers.

"Finances..." Darius tipped back his head to rest on the squabs—he was in demand as a dancing partner, and the night had no doubt been long for him. "Word when we left for Italy was that Bellefonte was all but rolled up, and with all those daughters to launch, the gossip was probably accurate. Reston is rumored to have taken over the reins and set things to rights rather quickly. He isn't seen to be in trade, so one wonders how he's done it."

"You could ask him," Leah said, sinking down a little more against the cushions.

"I could." Darius's tone was sardonic. "Just sidle up to a man who could snap my neck with his bare hands and ask how he's pulled his

family out of dun territory with no one the wiser. Do you comprehend what that question implies?"

Smuggling, at the least. "I do, though I would not for anything
risk my brothers. Still, it would be nice to know." Nice, too, to have an
excuse to converse with the man again—to kiss him again.

The thought was useless—also harmless, because there would be
no opportunity to indulge it.

Darius propped a foot on the opposite seat. "So you ask him. He's
looking for a bride, you're available, and an acquaintance between
you would not be so unusual, at least in proper social settings. I've
been introduced to him, so I can see to the proprieties."

"You said he's a womanizer. Is that whom you want me
consorting with?"

Darius's tone became lazy. "My dear, I am a womanizer. Every
man who can get away with it, practically, is a womanizer. You ladies
inspire us to it."

"Blaming the women, Darius?" Leah's tone was cool.

"Oh, now." Darius looped an arm across her shoulders. "Hellerington has rattled you. He's rattled me, too. I cannot bear to think of
you with that man, Leah."

"Then don't think of it," she said, letting her head rest on his
shoulder. Of all the considerations her brothers showed her, this one
—their casual affection— meant the most. She'd felt cast out, judged,
unclean, and unforgivably stupid as a younger woman, and Society
had done its cruel best to reinforce her opinion. Her brothers, though,
had stood by her, and eventually the scandal had been faced down.

There were good men in the world, Leah reassured herself. Her
brothers were good men.

Lord Reston... was a puzzle. His kiss lingered in Leah's memory
like a bonfire on a hill, a bright, riveting, but isolated event that drew
her attention even while she should be figuring out how to tolerate a
life as Lady Hellerington.

Reston was kind. She'd felt it in his touch, heard it in his voice,
tasted it in his kiss and in the way he'd assumed an unthreatening,

companionable honesty with her from the first moment. He was also stunningly, spectacularly masculine in that kindness. He wore some sort of Eastern scent, sturdy like sandalwood but sweetened with an exotic note of spices. His hands had been gentle, for all their size, but they'd also been undeniably knowing.

So he was kind, handsome, and single, but he was also—and most especially—wrong for her.

He would never take from a woman by plunder. He'd seduce instead, and make a lady grateful for the privilege of giving to him what he had not earned and would not treasure past a fleeting moment.

CHAPTER TWO

Nick punched his pillow, the strains of Valentine's soft music drifting to him through the darkness. Val played like this only when he was alone with a good instrument, the music flowing up from his soul, out across the keys, and off into the night, never to be heard again. Nick was in awe of such a gift, such sheer beauty from inside one generally quiet man.

And if there was a price for such talent, Nick hadn't yet puzzled it out. Usually, when Valentine conjured lullabies, sleep came to heel like a biddable spaniel.

Tonight, though, Nick was preoccupied with a single kiss.

In his thirty-some years on earth, Nick had done more kissing than he could remember. Kissing was fun, sweet, and harmless. He enjoyed it; the ladies enjoyed it; he suspected even his horse enjoyed it.

But kissing was also meant to be forgettable. No more worthy of recall than a pleasant meal, a good book, an enjoyable walk in the garden. Nick kissed his lovers, his sisters, his friends, his grandmother. Lately, he'd kissed his father a time or two, hoping each one was not a kiss good-bye. Nick kissed babies—babies were particularly fun to nuzzle and kiss and tickle—he kissed his horses and his cats and his cousins.

So why should it matter that he'd stolen a kiss from this Leah person, who was bound for holy matrimony with the odious Hellerington? He'd meant it as a little gesture of encouragement to her and himself both, a kiss for luck, as he'd said.

Nonetheless, lying in the acreage of his bed, surrounded by mountains of silk-covered pillows and the softest of linen sheets, Nick felt a growing unwillingness to let a disgusting old man have a taste of the lady, much less a husband's claim on her. From the place inside Nick that would have killed to protect a sibling or a friend, a place that had been tempted to violence on behalf of helpless animals, Nick felt a growing desire to spare the woman the fate that had moved her to tears.

His fate was sealed. He would marry a calculating woman of suitable station, and that was that.

Leah's fate, however, he could still influence.

Tossing aside the covers, Nick got up and found a dressing gown to cover his nakedness. The room was cold—Nick liked it cold. He lit some candles and found writing supplies in his escritoire. A note to his solicitors came first, asking them to attend him at their earliest convenience

Then a note to Benjamin Hazlit, discreet investigator for the privileged few who could afford him. If anyone could bring Nick what he sought regarding old Hellerington, it would be Hazlit.

Those decisions made, Nick returned to his bed and let Valentine's music drift over him once more. Val was sad about something; that was as clear as the tones of the piano's lovely middle register.

Ah, well. Nick closed his eyes. What a gift it must be, to be able to turn sadness to beauty. He thumped his pillow one last time and let his imagination conjure up the memory of a sweet, soft, lingering kiss between strangers.

~

NICK THOUGHT of spring and autumn as feminine— changeable, unpredictable, lovely—and winter and summer as masculine— entrenched, reliably trying, challenging, not for the faint of heart. April qualified as spring, and as Nick ambled along, April wore her best morning finery.

The sun shone in beneficent abundance, a hint of softness graced the air, and in the park, daffodils bloomed in profusion along with the occasional precocious tulip. The distance to Nick's grandmother's house might have encouraged another man to ride, but Nick had already taken Buttercup out for her morning hack, and he liked to move about whenever possible.

Then too, he needed time to think, to consider Valentine's question from the previous night: Were there any young ladies available this Season to whom he might offer marriage? Unpleasant topic to contemplate, but—

"I beg your pardon!"

Instinctively, Nick reached out to steady the lady into whom he had very nearly ploughed. "My apologies," he murmured, catching a hint of lily of the valley fragrance, though it wasn't coming from the petite blond squirming to retrieve her balance.

"I'm sorry, sir." The little blond peeked up at him with a tentative smile. "I was intent on getting to the ducks. I should have watched where I was going."

Nick stepped back and tipped his hat with a little bow. "I am at fault." He smiled down at her, then included the lady's maid in his smile. "I was lost in thought and cannot even claim the topic as interesting as hungry ducks."

Not a lady's maid, but rather, a youthful maiden aunt who could indulge in an alluring perfume but no longer needed—or afforded?— a fashionable wardrobe. Still, there was something about the other woman that drew Nick's interest, and not simply because she had lovely brown eyes, a bit of height, and lustrous dark hair framing a serious, pretty face.

Nick marshaled his manners. "If I may be so bold: Nicholas

Haddonfield, Viscount Reston at your service, ladies, and again my apologies." The blond glanced askance at the taller woman, obviously uncertain of the proprieties.

"Pleased to make your acquaintance," the taller woman said, her tone cultured, a little husky, and liltingly soft.

Five innocuous words, but they were enough. That soft, almost amused voice, the poise, and the charm... Nick knew immediately who she was, and drew in a slow, steadying breath. The lily of the valley scent connected with memories of their previous meeting and made the pretty day a shade closer to glorious.

"Whom was it my pleasure to nearly knock insensate?" Nick kept his smile in place, though it was arguably rude of him to ask when they hadn't been introduced. Still, he could not abide to tip his hat and saunter away.

"Ladies Leah and Emily Lindsey," the taller woman replied. She bobbed a curtsy, and her companion did likewise. Lady Leah gave not a hint of familiarity in her tone, gesture, or expression.

Not a hint of rejection, either.

"Might I impose my escort on you as far as the duck pond?" Nick offered. For good measure, he smiled disarmingly at the footman who hovered a dozen feet away. "It's a lovely day, and I would rather spend it in the presence of pulchritudinous ladies such as Mother Nature and yourselves than hurry to my destination."

"You flatter prettily," Lady Leah said, clearly more amused than impressed. "We will take pity on you." She glanced over her shoulder at the footman. "John, Lord Reston will escort us to the pond."

John nodded, apparently relieved that Lord Reston—all seventeen damned stone of him— presented no threat to his charges.

"I am on my way to see my grandmother," Nick volunteered, winging an arm at each lady. "This puts me in line for a scolding, which is what grandmothers enjoy most with grandsons like me. I've been in Town almost ten days, you see, and I've yet to call on her. What shall I say was my excuse?"

"You could tell her you're getting over a spring ague," the blond said. Lady—Nick floundered for a moment mentally—Lady Emily. "It was nasty damp until last week."

"That would serve, except she knows I'm seldom ill."

"You could tell her you dreaded the scolding and waited for a suitably cheering day to make your bow," the older sister said.

"The truth?" Nick affected a puzzled frown at Lady Leah. "With my grandmother? I will consider it as a novel approach. Do you ladies often come to feed the ducks?" He kept up a pleasant, easygoing patter of nonsense talk, something he could do without thinking. As they chatted and strolled slowly toward the water, Nick studied his companions.

In the bright light of day, Leah Lindsey was revealed to be no longer in the first blush of youth, consistent with her disclosures the previous night. There was knowledge in her eyes, of things unpleasant and unavoidable. She carried herself with a well-concealed hint of caution, her grip on his arm cosmetic, unlike her sister's.

The younger sister was innocent, Nick concluded. Probably not yet out, and happy to lark around in the park on a pretty day. This was the one for whom Leah was being sacrificed, and yet there was no enmity between the sisters. If anything, Leah was protective of her younger sibling.

Nick approved of that, though it wasn't his place to make such a judgment.

Lady Emily held out a gloved hand. "I'll take those bread crumbs now, John."

"Shall we sit?" Nick suggested to the sister still loosely on his arm. Lady Emily became engrossed in feeding the ducks over by the water, John withdrew to a discreet distance, and Nick found himself relatively alone with the lady who'd kept him up half the night.

"Let's take the bench," Lady Leah said. "This is a day so lovely one wants simply to be still and drink it in, to save it up."

"Such wistfulness," Nick said as he lowered himself beside her. "Do you fear we'll have no more of such days?"

"The future is at best unpredictable," Lady Leah said quietly. "For example, who could have predicted we'd cross paths twice in twenty-four hours?"

Pleasure—and relief—welled. "I wasn't sure I was supposed to acknowledge that other, equally delightful meeting."

"I hadn't thought to ever see you again." She was smiling as she said it, a soft, inwardly pleased curving of full lips.

Nick let himself bask in that smile and in the memory of those soft, delectable lips, until his blood began to stir in unmentionable places.

"Everybody sees me. I am too big to sneak anywhere. What you hadn't thought was to kiss me again."

"My lord." The frown was back in force. "We are in public."

"Private enough." Nick knew exactly where the footman stood, and the younger sister, and that the breeze put both upwind of this surprising conversation. "If the weather allows it tomorrow, may I meet you here again?"

"Why would you want to do that?" Her expression suggested Nick's request did not meet with her approval.

Nor his own, exactly, but he'd puzzle that out later. "I have put a few things in train you need to know about," Nick said, purposely keeping his gaze on Emily and the honking, quacking gaggle paddling about before her.

"What could you possibly be up to that would affect me, my lord?"

Nick grinned, despite his attempt to emulate a fellow just enjoying the weather. "You sound like my grandmother, all starch and vinegar. I'm will relieve you of your intended's offer."

"Has it occurred to you," Leah said, her voice very low, "Hellerington may be replaced by something worse?"

"What could be worse than being wife to a disgusting old man who will likely give you diseases you cannot recover from?" Nick's own tone had become the least bit clipped, and he was rewarded with a sharp intake of Leah's breath.

"Being his mistress," she said, so quietly Nick had to lean toward her to hear her.

Silence, while Nick considered the horror she'd just admitted. Her father wasn't content to marry her off; he must end his daughter's life in illness and disgrace as well. No man who called himself father should be free to perpetrate such misery on his daughter.

"That would be evil," Nick said. "And I shall not allow it."

~

FROM THE WINDOW of his first-floor private parlor, Gerald Lindsey, ninth Earl of Wilton, had watched his two daughters link arms and stroll off toward the park. Well, his daughter and that creature his wife had presented to him. He wasn't pleased with the amount of time Emily spent with Leah, but Emily liked her older sister, and as long as they both dwelled under his roof, it was an association the earl could closely monitor. Soon enough, he'd see Leah taken off his hands, and if he played his cards right, Leah's marriage pay for Emily's come out and settlements.

A scratching at the door interrupted his plans for Emily. "Enter."

The upstairs chambermaid bobbed a deep curtsy. "My lord."

"Well?"

"Lady Leah danced with a Lord Valentine Windham," the maid said, keeping her gaze on the carpet. "She described him to Lady Emily as tall, green-eyed, and very much a gentleman."

He was also very much Moreland's only unwed surviving son and legendarily besotted with his music. Leah would never get an offer from that one.

"What other confidences did the ladies exchange over their morning tea?"

"In the course of the evening, Lady Leah was introduced to a Lord Reston, sir. She described him as grand and fit, like an old-style Viking, and well mannered. His father is the Earl of Bellefonte, and I gather from the conversation, Reston is the heir."

"Anything else?"

"Nothing, my lord. The ladies were anxious to enjoy the sunny weather."

"Go."

The report was annoying. Nothing mentioned of old Hellerington, who was desperate enough to pay handsomely for a titled bride of childbearing age. Just foolishness about Lord Valentine and old Bellefonte's heir.

Wilton lowered himself into the chair behind his estate desk and tried to dredge up details about the Bellefonte title. All he could recall was that the present holder of the title had been a younger son, serving in the military or diplomatic corps, and not particularly concerned with the earldom. There were a fair number of offspring, like a bunch of bloody farming Hanoverians. He scrawled a note to his man of business and rang for a footman.

Hellerington was welcome to Leah as far as Wilton was concerned. Yes, the man was a dissolute, sick scoundrel, but that only made it easier to toss the ungrateful chit into his arms. Hellerington had been nothing if not patient, and in his own devious way, trustworthy. Still, business was business, and if this Reston fellow were interested, then it was simply prudent to entertain an offer from him.

Hellerington was desperate, but he wasn't particularly wealthy, and wealth was one thing Wilton respected more than he wanted free of his late wife's bastard.

~

"YOU HAVE NO SAY in the matter of my betrothal." Leah ground her words out, while the great length of Lord Reston to all appearances lounged beside her on the park bench, and Emily cavorted with the ducks like the schoolgirl she was. "And while you are no doubt well-intended, my lord, I must ask you to desist. My father will do as he sees fit. He is a peer of the realm, as he frequently reminds all and sundry. You cannot gainsay him. My brothers have tried to thwart him, and it has gone hard for them as a result."

Reston shrugged broad, heavily muscled shoulders clad in excellent tailoring. "Your brothers have to live with him. I can have you spirited off to family holdings in Ireland, and your father won't find you. How old are you?"

Damn him for the casual rescue he offered. "Five-and-twenty."

"So your father cannot tell you where to go or with whom. If you consented to some travel, it would not be kidnapping."

"I will not consent," Leah said. "Wilton has already threatened to cut off my brother without a penny and has reduced Darius's quarterly funds to a pittance, as it is."

"Let me help you." Reston shifted his tone, imbued it with a lazy sensuality that sent tremors of memory through low places in Leah's body. "I ask nothing of you, only that you let me help you, and you might as well." He stood and tipped his hat. "I intend to whether you like it or not. A pleasure, Lady Leah."

He ambled over to the water to take his leave of Emily, showing her the same courtesy he would an older lady. She blushed and smiled, flattered, no doubt, that a titled lord would pass the time of day with her. Watching the tableau, Leah had an astonishing thought: If Reston married Emily, then Leah could dwell in safety with her sister. As a member of the family, Reston would be able to provide a home for Leah, and the earl would have to allow it.

And somehow, Leah would forget that the most memorable kiss she had experienced had been with her sister's prospective spouse.

She rose. "Lord Reston!"

"My lady?" He was at her side in a few long-legged strides.

Leah glanced at the footman, who was for once keeping his distance. "If the weather is fair, I can chance to meet you again at this hour in three or four days' time. I am watched, though, so the encounter had best not appear contrived."

"Watched by the help," Reston concluded easily. "Friday then, weather permitting, or Monday. Until then." He tipped his hat again and left with a final, thoroughly friendly smile at the footman.

∾

"SO THAT WAS YOUR VISCOUNT RESTON?" Emily gushed as she and Leah sauntered toward home. "Grand, indeed, Leah. And so very well-mannered. Is he the kind of gentleman you meet at these balls and breakfasts?"

Leah smiled at her sister's enthusiasm and chose her truths, as usual. "He's larger than most and probably more charming than most. Did you like him?"

"Of course I liked him, though he is quite a specimen."

"Quite."

Emily was just a shade over five feet in her stockings, while Leah was eight inches taller. If Nicholas Haddonfield was imposing to Leah in terms of both his charm and his physique, what must Emily make of him?

"He's a mild-mannered man as well, Emily. I shouldn't think his size would matter a great deal to his friends and family."

"Perhaps not," Emily replied, then she gave a little shudder. "But to his wife?"

"He would be a gentleman, Em," Leah said. "In every regard."

Emily cast her a curious glance. "He can be your gentleman, never mine."

Bless Emily's loyalty, and drat her stubbornness. "Don't be too sure about that. He's rumored to be in the market for a wife, and he's an earl's heir. You could do worse. He'd be kind. I know he would." And his kisses would be lovely. Drat that, too.

"Kind or not," Emily said, "I've no wish to bear him his heirs. I'm sure I can find a suitable man among the fifty-one remaining candidates I've listed from Debrett's, though perhaps I'd best start making inquiries regarding height, hadn't I?"

Leah let the subject drop. Emily had been ten years old when

Leah had been whisked off to Italy, and the version of events passed along to Emily was no doubt the one that would put a girl in fear of the slightest misstep, particularly in her search for a husband.

She and Emily had never openly discussed the past, a small, curious sadness amid a sororal landscape full of them. A landscape that now included one very tall, well-mannered viscount with kind blue eyes.

And a devastating way with a kiss.

～

THE YOUNG LADY for whom Nick would cheerfully have given his last farthing and his last breath was strolling in her gardens, unaware that he watched her from the back of his mare on the grassy hill high above. Blossom Court and Clover Down were not two miles distant by the road, and the properties backed up to each other. Riding from one to the other cross-country was the work of a few minutes.

Every afternoon, weather permitting, the young lady walked outside with her companion. If the companion saw Nick up on the hill, she knew better than to wave. He paid her salary, after all, and kept the entire little jewel of a property simply so the young lady could have her peace and quiet in the pretty countryside.

Then too, if Nick's presence were discovered, he'd be compelled to join the ladies, and there would be tears and apologies and more tears. He'd already tried to explain why he could not visit as often, and why he must marry and spend more time at Belle Maison.

Explanations that had fallen on deaf, heartbroken ears.

The companion took out a book, while the object of Nick's devotion chose the location for the afternoon's picnic. She and Nick had consulted endlessly over the flowers for each bed, most of which would not bloom for weeks yet. Forget-me-nots for true love, coreopsis for cheer, a border of mint for virtue. She chose to spread her blanket near a patch of daffodils—daffodils for chivalry—that Nick had planted for her the previous autumn.

The ladies settled in for a lazy afternoon, while Nick felt his chest constricting with frustrated need. He'd give anything to be the one reading that book to her, to be the one sharing the hours with her.

He sat on his horse, savoring the simple sight of her. Sunshine beat down with springtime benevolence, while the scent of a field recently treated with the cow byre's winter leavings lent a pungent, fertile undertone to the air. Nick's mare swished her tail at some bold insect and stomped a hoof while Nick felt a yearning so old and futile it had long since eclipsed tears.

What the young lady needed from Nick was the self-discipline to turn Buttercup back down the hill and resume the search for that bride he'd promised his father. Life, Nick reflected as he trotted his horse through the glorious spring day, could be so damned brutally hard.

~

"WHAT HAS PUT you in the dismals?" Valentine asked Nick at breakfast the following Friday. "The sun is finally out, and all's right with the world."

"Buttercup and I ran into Ethan in the park this morning," Nick replied. "He is enough to put anybody in the dismals. Pass the damned teapot."

Val slid the teapot—a pretty porcelain vessel with blue and pink flowers glazed all over it—down to his host.

"I do not know your elder brother well," Val said, "but mention of him does not seem to cheer you."

"Nobody knows him well," Nick opined, stirring a prodigious amount of sugar into his tea, then a fat dollop of cream. "We used to be close."

Valentine made no reply, and Nick resented both the silence and his companion's perspicacity.

"As boys," Nick went on, "we were inseparable. I was his shadow, and we were of a size then, though he's more than a year my elder. For several years, we rode one pony, then had to have matched ponies. Ethan is brilliant—quick and smart, not just one or the other. He could devise more ways to have fun and not get caught than you can imagine. Beckman used to trail us around like a puppy, and Ethan could lose him without him figuring out he'd been lost."

"You loved your older brother."

Nick scowled mightily. "Still do." And nearly hated him too, sometimes.

"So what happened?" Val prodded, reaching for the teapot.

"An accident." Nick tossed his tea back and appropriated the teapot before Valentine could pour himself a cup. "Bellefonte was in the habit of branding his saddles and harness with an H—for Haddonfield—and we thought we'd do the same with our boots, clever lads that we were. The brand landed on my backside by inadvertence, and Bellefonte decided Ethan had done it apurpose. Before that..."

Nick poured a second cup, stirred in more sugar, then more cream.

He stared at his tea. "Before that we were brothers and best friends. After Bellefonte tore into Ethan in front of me that day, we became the bastard and the heir. He sent us to separate public schools. He no longer permitted Ethan to spend holidays and summers with us. He sent Ethan to Cambridge while I went to Oxford."

Valentine considered the teapot at Nick's elbow. "Over a stupid accident? That doesn't sound like your father."

Nick's smile was sad. "You know Bellefonte as a dear old fellow. Twenty years ago, he was up to his ears in children and responsibilities, and he was a regular tartar. Grandmother sneaked a few letters for us, but Ethan and I could not sustain a bond. After a time, I told myself it was for the best. I imagine Ethan has done the same."

"How could losing a brother and a best friend be for the best?"

Valentine had lost two brothers, one to war, one to consumption. Nick knew the question was sincere.

"I have three other brothers, and four sisters, and until my father sent Ethan away, I could barely have told you their names. Ethan and I were that close. As the heir, I needed to know my entire family, not just my favorite brother. Then too, Ethan needed to make his way, not spend his entire life protecting me and being my companion."

"I don't know, Nicholas." Val made another try for the teapot, and this time poured himself a cup immediately. "Devlin was raised with us, at least from the age of five on. Their Graces love him as if he were one of their legitimate sons. They saw to it he had the best of everything, and bought him his colors when Bart joined up, no questions asked. But he still felt second-rate, as if he were on probation..."

Valentine stopped and glared at his tea.

Rather than allow him to maunder on, Nick took pity on his friend. "Your point?"

"Your father isn't solely responsible for the fact that you and Ethan haven't made much progress recovering your friendship," Val said. "Devlin was stuck, thinking himself unnecessary to us, when he could not have been more wrong."

"But my family is not the Windhams," Nick said. "We have no duchess humanizing us, no matriarch to smooth over Bellefonte's many rough edges. Ethan is not necessary to us—he will not allow himself to be—and I'm not sure there is an us."

Val smiled, a sweet smile the ladies found irresistible. "You are ridiculous. The Haddonfields sport a great deal of 'us.' Beckman has followed you all over southern England. George and Dolph can't get a grade on an exam without you knowing about it. Your grandmother knows before your head hits the pillow exactly how many dances you stood up for and with whom. You remember every sister's birthday, and her favorite flowers and colors. What is Beckman up to, by the way?"

Nick scowled at his plate, from which a significant portion of eggs and toast had disappeared, Nick knew not how. "Still rusticating.

The earl sent him down to Portsmouth to look in on Three Springs for Grandmother. I don't think he's in any hurry to take up Town life, and I can give him one of my estates in Kent when I'm forced to reside at Belle Maison."

But not both estates. Beckman could have Clover Down. Title to Blossom Court would always remain in Nick's hands, no matter what.

"You're frowning again," Val said. "I hadn't taken you for such an introspective fellow."

"Must be the full moon. You up for a trip to Kent?"

"Of course, if there's a piano to be played along the way."

"I'll send the requisite notes to my staff." Nick felt a lift to his mood at the prospect of leaving London. "And ring for more tea, would you? Somebody drank the entire damned pot while you were nattering on."

～

LEAH DID NOT HURRY toward the park, but oh, she wanted to. She'd tossed away half the night, thinking she should send Reston a note telling him to leave her in peace. Or a note telling him today did not suit, or a note telling him...

Sending notes safely was no more possible now in Wilton House than it had been eight years ago, so she would wave Reston off in person. Emily didn't want to marry the man, and Leah had to admit her sister had a point. Reston was the largest specimen of humanity Leah had ever seen; he had muscles on top of muscles, and such tremendous height. For the first time, it occurred to her that not just her father's servants, but anybody in the park would know she'd met with Reston. Between his height, his golden hair, and his gentleman's manners, he was that distinctive.

Gads. What had she been thinking?

"Good morning." Reston's pleasant baritone sounded to her left when she'd been on the bench beside the pond for only a few minutes. "Lady Leah? Yes, it is you. We met earlier this week, I believe, along with your dear sister, Lady Emily. May I join you?"

Leah nodded and found herself once again sitting beside the compilation of muscle, charm, and masculine appeal that was Viscount Reston.

"I sent my footman off to purchase some bread for the ducks," Leah said, her tone clipped. "We haven't privacy for long."

"Then I will reserve the flirtation and flattery for later. Has Hellerington called upon Wilton yet?"

"He has an appointment Friday next," Leah said, hating the catch in her voice.

Reston stretched out long, long legs, all nonchalance and polished riding boots. "Not until then? That is all the time in the world. I might be calling on your papa by then myself."

Leah closed her eyes, the lovely day and the handsome man so at variance with the topic under discussion as to make her queasy.

"My lord, I will ask you again to desist from this course. Hellerington is devious and determined, as is the earl. They can lock me away without a word to anybody, and Wilton has threatened as much in the past."

"Was that before or after he killed your fiancé in cold blood?" Reston inquired, keeping his eyes trained on the ducks, his hands propped on the golden head of his walking stick.

The words, so casually uttered, sent a blast of winter through the spring day. "You know about that?"

"I know your brothers also got you to the Continent for a couple years while your father's ire cooled," he added. "From what I hear, the young man was of good family and had honorable intentions. There was no cause for a duel."

"Precisely. You may conclude from my experience that Wilton will stoop very nearly to murder to have his way. I do not think to thwart him with impunity."

"You've considered it, though." Reston slanted her another look.

"You've considered running away, eloping with someone else, going into service. Why haven't you done it?"

That he'd reasoned this accurately on so little acquaintance should have made Leah uneasy. Instead, it provoked her to confidences she ought not to be sharing.

"He's promised to take out any of my misdeeds on Darius," Leah said. "I don't know what hold he has over Darius, though much of it is financial, but I will not be the cause of my brother's ruin."

Reston rubbed his chin with a hand that should have been sporting gloves. Large hands but capable of a gentle touch. "I see."

"You'll leave me in peace, then?"

"My intention was never to disturb your peace, but rather to preserve it."

"That is not an answer," Leah bit out. "My lord, you are meddling with my life and the lives of the people I care about. You have no right to do this."

"And your papa has no right to sell you to that lecher," Reston rejoined, his voice losing its polite veneer.

"I am his daughter," Leah reminded him. "He has every right."

"You have attained your majority."

"I am an unmarried female. I cannot make contracts, cannot buy land, cannot hire or fire my own employees, cannot own a business unless left to me by my family. I have no saleable skills save governessing, and any family that hired me would be subject to the earl's displeasure."

Blond brows twitched closer to a lordly nose. "You have thought this through."

"He watches my pin money," Leah went on, "so I can save but a few pennies on rare occasion. He keeps the jewelry given me by my mother or brothers locked away, so I cannot pawn it. My old dresses are taken from my wardrobe, and the same with my shoes, boots, and so forth."

"You are a prisoner," Reston concluded, temper evident in his tone.

"I am a daughter who has earned her father's disfavor."

"I am holding in my left hand two gold sovereigns," Reston said, his tone of voice reverting to deceptive evenness. "When I assist you to rise, you will slip them into your glove."

Leah felt tears threaten. "My lord, don't do this. I cannot start a life on two gold sovereigns."

"You cannot," he agreed, shifting his walking stick to the side. "But you can hire a cabbie to get you to your brothers, or to my town house." He relayed his exact address to her, all the while appearing to be studying the ducks and making small talk, even as he also told her how to reach his grandmother, Lady Warne, and that he'd monitor the park Monday and Tuesday mornings.

"The day has turned a trifle brisk," he said. "I will escort you home once we dump the bread yon footman brings."

Their time was over. Leah hadn't seen the footman coming across the park, bag of bread crumbs in hand, but in just moments, he'd be within earshot.

"You cannot escort me home."

"Can too," Reston replied pleasantly. He rose to his great height and turned to offer her assistance. By putting his body between Leah and the approaching footman, he gave himself the space to grasp her wrist and arm in such a way that two gold sovereigns were deftly slipped into her glove.

And there was nothing Leah could do about it.

Worse, the cool weight of the golden coins felt good, solid, and encouraging. She closed her fist around them and let Reston draw her to her feet.

"I'll take those." Reston stretched his hand out to the footman. "And I'll assist her ladyship down to the water."

The footman bowed and surrendered the bread crumbs, retreating to a distance that might have been respectful, though the man's expression remained watchful.

"So when might Lady Emily join you for another outing?" Reston asked, and Leah took the cue to limit herself to topics the footman could overhear. When the bread crumbs were gone, Reston offered his arm and sauntered along beside her placidly all the way home. At the foot of the steps, he bowed over her hand, giving it a surreptitious squeeze before taking a leisurely departure.

Leah made it a point to frown after him, knowing the footman would report this reaction as well.

"In future," she said, "I will not be sending you to purchase bread crumbs for me. There are too many curious gentlemen in the park, and I do not like being subject to their interrogation regarding my sister."

"Just so, milady. Curious, very large gentlemen." The footman bowed and took his leave, no doubt off to report every word and impression to the earl.

Leah repaired directly to the library, hid her coins behind a ragged volume of Fordyce's Sermons, then took up her embroidery hoop and awaited her own summons from the earl.

CHAPTER THREE

Nick's grandmother, Delilah, Dowager Marchioness of Warne, had known to expect him and was thus armed with tea, crumpets, clotted cream, and jam when he showed up on her doorstep en route to another visit to the park.

"I ran into Ethan," Nick said as they were sitting down in her family parlor. "He looks thinner to me."

"You look thinner," his grandmother said. "You great strapping lads need to mind your victuals. You lose your bloom so quickly, otherwise. Have a crumpet—or two."

"I love you, Nana," Nick said as he accepted a plate of the warm, yeasty crumpets. "Ethan was his usual unforthcoming self. How does he fare?"

"As if I'd know." Lady Warne was the picture of prim disapproval, snow-white braids in a tidy coronet, blue eyes snapping with frustration. "He keeps no mistress that I know of, he does not gamble, he does not attend services, he pores over his investments and accounts, and he seldom strays from his estate in Surrey."

Nick paused in the demolition of his crumpets. "When did he start tending his home fires?"

"He purchased the place six or seven years back," her ladyship replied. "Though he's really been in residence only for the past three years or so. I haven't seen the property, but I don't think it's far from those friends of yours. At this minute, however, he isn't in Surrey but on his way to Belle Maison."

Nick set the remains of his crumpet down. "He hasn't been home since he was fourteen."

"You lectured him into it when last you bumped into him in the park, for which I can only be grateful, truth be told, though I doubt he considers Belle Maison home in any regard."

"I didn't lecture him. I offered to go with him, and he declined." Offered to accompany him so he might make his peace with their dying father.

"Well, he's going. I cannot help but think it's a good thing. Your father was at best misguided in his handling of the pair of you, and I've let him know it a time or two."

Or ten, Nick suspected. "Your efforts are, as always, appreciated, Nana."

"Good." Her ladyship smiled at him, a particularly feminine smile that hinted at the stunning beauty of her past.

"Nana, what have you done?"

"Nothing of any import, but when I found myself at yet another boring musicale on Saturday afternoon, I did contrive to sit next to Lady Leah Lindsey and her handsome older brother. That one is sadly lacking in flirtation, I can tell you."

"You flirted with Wilton's heir?" Nick didn't know whether to groan or smile.

"I did not disgrace myself, Nicholas, but I did strike up a pleasant association with the young lady and invited her to call upon me at her convenience. I am so old and lonely, and have so much time on my hands, you see."

Guilt spiked upward. Nick shrugged it aside from long practice because Nana was a shameless baggage who delighted in her machinations.

"You are dangerous, but I was about to ask it of you anyway."

"I know." Her ladyship took a dainty bite of a tea cake with lemon frosting. "You were trying to work up your courage, my boy, and I don't think the situation will admit of such leisure. The young lady looks haunted."

"She is," Nick said, leaving it at that. "I appreciate the overture, though, and she will likely need a friend. How did the brother react?"

"He's quiet. Lost a wife a year or two ago, another match that benefited the Wilton finances, but one gets the impression he misses the lady. She gave him several children in very short order, as I recall, so they must have got along to some degree."

Or had a great deal of making up to do when they hadn't got along. "I am to meet Lady Leah in the park in thirty minutes or so. I'd best be on my way." Nick rose and drew his grandmother to her feet, then wrapped her in a hug. "You must promise me to be careful, Nana. If you get to asking questions, you could raise some eyebrows."

"Oh, my stars." The marchioness drew back, and placed a hand on her throat. "And what will Wilton do? Call me out? I command more connections in this silly little town than he can imagine, Nicholas. Do not fear for me, and do not hesitate to ask if there's more I can do."

"I love you," Nick said again, meaning it with all his heart.

"And I love you. Away with you now. You've a lady to meet, and I have to change into more splendid attire if I'm to go calling before the rain comes back in."

Nick eyed the sky as he made his way to the park, willing the rain to hold off, though clouds were gathering. The bench by the duck pond was dry, thank the gods, so Nick strolled off to another bench and waited for his quarry. In the twenty minutes he was forced to wait, he tried to review what he knew of Leah's situation and found he couldn't keep his attention on the task.

He was too busy scanning the park, anticipating her arrival and fretting about what her absence could mean. Which was odd, when he had no particular personal investment in the woman but intended simply to see her safe from her father's mischief... Even if she did kiss with a memorable combination of innocence and passion.

And carry a lovely scent.

And haunt his dreams.

Nick was thus scowling mightily when he heard a soft voice at his elbow.

"Shall I interpret that look to be a comment on my presence, Lord Reston?"

Nick rose and offered his arm, hoping his smile was merely friendly and not vastly relieved. "You should interpret it as a comment on my solitudinous state. Good day, Lady Leah. May I escort you to the ducks?"

"You may." Leah tucked her hand around his arm, her footman falling in behind them several paces back.

Nick speared the footman with a look that was mostly fatuous suitor leavened with spoiled aristocrat spiced with a sprinkling of man-to-man.

"My good fellow, unless you think to insult a peer's heir, I must ask you to keep a discreet distance so I might encourage the young lady to offer me the occasional flirtatious aside. A gentleman needs every advantage when paying his addresses, hmm?"

The footman—the same beetle-browed fellow as last time—blushed, stammered his apologies, and retreated a good distance. Nick nodded his thanks and tucked his hand over Leah's.

"He'll not bother us, provided we look to be flirting. I understand you met my grandmother."

Leah frowned at the fingers he laid over her knuckles. "Your grandmother?"

"Delilah, Lady Warne," Nick said. "I am her oldest grandson, and we dote on each other ceaselessly. You can trust her." And what a solid satisfaction it gave Nick to mean that.

"You cannot think to engage that dear, elderly lady in my father's schemes, Lord Reston."

"I cannot think to keep her out of them. How are you?" He asked the question because Leah looked to him, if anything, pale and tired.

"Hellerington calls upon my father in several days," she said, not exactly answering Nick's question. "I cannot be sanguine about that."

"I call upon Hellerington this afternoon," Nick informed her, "and I will soon hold the bulk of his markers and will use them to your advantage."

"You're buying up his debts?" Leah paused to peer up at him. "Why?"

Nick resumed their progress rather than bear her scrutiny. "It's no great effort. He generally does pay his debts, if slowly, and I can afford it." He decided not to tell her that with the aid of a discreet investigator, he was also buying up Wilton's debts, not wanting to unnerve her further.

"I dislike that you would risk coin on me. I gather I cannot stop you."

"You cannot." Nothing could stop him—Nick had made up his mind on that. "When I assist you down to the water, I will slip another two sovereigns into your glove."

"My father may be on to you," Leah said as they left the path. Nick angled his body around hers, as if they were promenading, his right hand at her waist, his left gripping her left hand. On the damp grass, Leah's foot slipped.

"Oh, well done," Nick murmured near her ear. She was cast against him, momentarily leaning on his greater strength to regain her footing. Nick slipped coins into her glove, even as he took a shameless whiff of her fragrance.

"Gads, you're strong," Leah said when he'd righted her.

"Very, and you need to explain yourself." He stepped away, finding much to his surprise that he needed the distance. Her flowery scent had teased his fancies, her lithe shape felt too right against his body, and her worry was stirring his protective urges.

Well, his urges, at any rate.

"The earl is aware we've met here twice," Leah said, casting the first few crumbs onto the water. "I am to be pleasant to you at all times and keep him informed of further encounters."

Nick glanced over at her, resenting the need to use his brain, resenting the way the muddy scent of the pond eclipsed the fragrance Leah wore.

"Am I courting you or your sister?"

Leah tossed an entire handful of bread crumbs onto the water, provoking a honking, quacking stampede on the part of the waterfowl.

"If you court my sister," Leah said when the ruckus died down, "the earl will reason you can offer for her now and save him the expense of her come out."

Nick appropriated the bag of crumbs. "Leaving you at Hellerington's mercy and enriching your father to the extent of your bride price. So I had best court you, hadn't I?"

"I don't want you to," Leah said, her expression damnably serene. "You can't keep up such a farce, and sooner or later, there will be another Hellerington, or worse."

Nick tossed the bread much farther out over the water than Leah had. "What would make you happy, Leah Lindsey?"

"Happy is not a useful concept," she muttered. "Happy would mean I did not dwell with the death of a decent young man on my conscience. Happy would mean my brothers were not saddened daily by my circumstances. Happy would mean I could be completely indifferent to those who still comment on the years I spent in Italy."

Nick handed the bread crumbs back to her, his hand cupping hers briefly in the process. Leah carried more misery and heartache than he'd first surmised, and that bothered him.

"Your past is not happy," he said, watching the ducks, "but your future can be more enjoyable. I like that little fellow on the end with the yellowish wings. He's a scrapper."

Leah smiled at the little duck, who was paddling furiously after his share of the crumbs. "He's dirty."

"Scrappers are willing to get dirty in pursuit of their ends," Nick remarked, making his point, he hoped. "Which one catches your fancy?"

"That one." Leah nodded at a swan gliding along across the pond. "She could not care less for what troubles her inferiors."

"Above it all," Nick agreed. "But probably hanging about over there so nobody will hear her stomach complaining. Too proud, that one."

"I am not too proud," Leah said, keeping her voice down. "My father is not to be underestimated, and you will make matters worse with your meddling. When you tire of playing the gallant, I will be left to suffer his displeasure."

"Hush," Nick soothed, seeing she was near tears and hating the sight. "Yon stalwart footman will suspect we are not in charity. Toss some more bread, Leah, and listen to me."

She obeyed, to his relief—and did not take umbrage at his appropriation of her name.

"I will not meddle and then lose interest in your situation." Nick kept his voice low, as it had been in the darkness of the Winterthurs' parlor. "I will see to your welfare, and without bringing you further misery. You are out of the habit of hoping and trusting, and you grow frantic at the thought of the fate pressing upon you. Trust me, and I will win you free of it."

"You must not do this." She swiped at her eyes with her glove. "You must not."

"Ah, now." Nick kept his hands to himself by dint of clasping them behind his back. "I might have been talked out of it before, but I've made you cry. Shame on me, and there's no help for it now. Compose yourself." He shifted to stand behind her, not quite touching but shielding her from the gaze of the nosy footman, literally guarding her back while she gathered her wits.

"I hate to cry."

"I'm none too fond of it myself. Are we out of bread crumbs?"

"Not quite." She passed the bag back to him, and he sidled around beside her. "Aim for your friend."

"But of course." Nick spied the little duck paddling near the bank and tossed the last handful in its direction. "I'm off to Kent for the next couple of days, but I'd like you to call on my grandmother on Friday morning, and I do mean morning, not a morning call."

"I can do that," Leah said. "She invited me in my brother's hearing, and I'm not sure my father comprehends the connection. He doesn't socialize a great deal, though he is received."

"Then don't tell him, unless Lady Warne tells you to." As Nick stood close to her, Leah's fragrance enveloped him again. Lily of the valley had never struck Nick as an erotic scent, but it was winding through his senses and stirring all manner of feelings.

"Return of happiness," Nick murmured, earning him a sharp glance from the lady. "Your scent—lily of the valley—symbolizes the return of happiness."

"I'd forgotten that," Leah said, smiling at him slightly.

"I would not lie to a woman."

"You are not the typical titled heir," Leah said, her smile fading. "I could not abide you were you to lie to me, Lord Reston."

For a man to keep certain matters to himself for years on end was not lying. Nick tried to convince himself of this regularly.

"Call me Nick," he said as they regained the path. "And send a note around to Lady Warne. Be warned, though, she'll stuff you like a goose if you let her."

Leah eyed Nick up and down. "I bid you good day, my lord."

For the benefit of the footman, Nick adopted the same polite tones.

"Good day to you as well, Lady Leah." He bowed correctly over her hand. "And my regards to your dear sister."

He appropriated the bench again and watched until she'd left the park, footman in tow. The ducks set up another squawking, and Nick glanced over to see his little scrapper swimming hell-bent for the next offering of crumbs tossed forth from the hand of another pretty young lady.

Scrappers, he reminded himself, were sometimes not fussy enough about how they gained their ends; and subsisting on just any old handout could leave a fellow with a mighty sorry bellyache.

∼

THE SOLICITOR'S spectacled gaze put Wilton in mind of a rabbit tracking the location of a fox at the watering hole.

"We have yet to receive any indication Lord Hellerington's intentions are sincere, my lord. There's been no subtle inquiry, no overt interest, no draft documents sent over by mistake, if you take my meaning."

Wilton knew a spike of murderous frustration, because Hellerington's innuendo had become flagrant—and now this coy behavior. The man intended to offer for the trollop masquerading as Wilton's oldest daughter; he'd all but announced it at his club.

"You've canvassed his clerks?"

"We have, my lord. We were particularly encouraged when there was an indication of general interest in your situation, but it came from the wrong firm."

"Explain yourself." Wilton rose to pace, knowing that leaving the solicitor seated would irk the man no end. Petty, self-important little thieves they were, but necessary if business was to be done in a businesslike manner.

"A junior clerk in the firm is related to some fellow in the offices around the corner," the solicitor began, "and they occasionally share a pint and so forth."

Wilton glowered at the man, lest the roundaboutation go on all morning.

"A Lord Reston is sniffing about."

Wilton paused in his pacing. "Bellefonte's heir?"

"Nicholas Haddonfield." The solicitor shifted in his seat, keeping the earl in his line of sight. "The old earl is rumored to be in poor health."

"How poor?"

"He is not expected to last out the year, my lord. Perhaps not even the month."

"Interesting." Wilton tried to keep his pleasure from showing on his face. This was the same callow swain who'd been sniffing around little Emily's skirts this past week. "You're dismissed."

The solicitor rose and bowed without comment. In the solitude of his study, Wilton sat back in his cushioned chair and considered Reston's inquiries. He'd have to see what this Reston fellow was made of. An earl's younger son was about as high as Emily could hope to reach, but for her to become a countess...

It was fitting, Wilton decided. Emily was the product of rape, though legally a man could not rape his wife. Still, Wilton had forced himself on his errant wife, as brutally and as often as it had taken to get the faithless bitch pregnant—and it had taken years. He'd relished her resistance, and relished even more the measures taken to impose himself on her. Full of fight, she'd been, and then she'd been full of his child.

Having made his point, however, he'd turned from his countess, unwilling to risk the child in further displays of marital discipline. If Emily could be married off this year, without the fuss and bother of a Season, it would be her husband's family who bore responsibility for presenting her at court and to Society as a whole.

And if Hellerington wiggled off the hook, then other arrangements could be made for Emily's older sibling. Leah was used goods, and oddly enough, the market for used goods was more brisk than the market for their virtuous sisters. On that thought, Wilton rang for his carriage to be brought around, as a celebratory visit to the beautiful—and routinely vicious—Monique was in order.

∼

"WHO IN THEIR right mind has a ball on a Wednesday night? I thought Wednesday was for suppers and theatre outings, or Almack's —heaven spare me." Nick directed his grumbling at Valentine, with whom he was speeding through Town in the Bellefonte coach.

"Why exactly did we jaunt out to Kent yesterday?" Val asked.

Nick smiled at his friend. "To check on my holdings, to have dinner with David and Letty, and to admire their wee addition."

Val gave a shudder Nick thought only partly feigned. "To me, a child that young does look wee, but then I think a woman must actually birth that small person, and suddenly..."

"You wonder why we're not all only children," Nick concluded the thought. "One must attribute to fathers of multiple children a certain irresistible charm, I suppose."

"Or bottomless courage in their spouses. You will make a wonderful father."

Not this again. "On the contrary, I won't make any kind of father at all."

"You?" Val snorted. "If anybody enjoys the activities that lead to conception, it's you. And I've yet to see the child who doesn't love you on sight."

"And yet there are no baby Nicks underfoot, are there?"

"Don't suppose you had measles?"

"I have restraint," Nick shot back. "Not as contagious, but equally effective. So how many of your sisters are we meeting tonight?"

"Probably the three youngest." Valentine shifted into a more upright posture on his upholstered seat. "They are the most enthusiastic about this sort of thing."

"I like your sisters," Nick said, donning his hat as the coach slowed. "They are tall, but for Lady Eve, and smarter than they want you to think they are."

"You might consider wiping that look of martyred resignation off your face," Val suggested gently. "Rather defeats the purpose of attending."

"I wish there were another way to do this." Nick looked out at the street on a sigh. "Why can't a man simply take out an ad in the newspaper: Prospective earl seeks a duty-countess who will forget he ever married her?"

In the first hour of dancing, Nick stood up with three wallflowers, each chosen for her height and lack of partners, before he ducked out onto the torch-lit terraces for a breath of fresh air. The weather was moderate, which meant the ballroom was quickly heating up, and the well-spaced urns of hothouse flowers were losing their battle with the scent of overheated, over-perfumed, under-washed humans.

"We seem destined to hide in the same places." Leah's voice drifted out of the gloom to Nick's left, and he felt a lightening of both body and mood.

"My lady." He bowed over her hand, covertly assessing her appearance in the subdued light. "At least we both hide in pleasant, well-ventilated places. How fare you?"

"Honestly?" Leah peered up at him. "I was growing slightly nauseated in there. I lost Darius after the first set and thought perhaps to find him out here."

Darius being one of her two brothers whom Nick was quietly having investigated. "Darius should not have lost you. Shall I search the gentlemen's rooms for you?"

"Not yet," she said as he led her to a bench several dark yards off the terrace. "Dare lets me slip the leash on purpose. I see no evidence of Hellerington tonight, so Darius has relaxed his guard. You should not have sent flowers, by the way."

"You must not say such things, for I will send twice as many tomorrow."

"What do they mean?" she asked after a time. "The flowers you sent?"

"The snowdrop is for hope," Nick said, pleased she would ask. He'd chosen the bouquet carefully and visited more than one shop in the process. "The little sprig of wood sorrel is for joy, the wallflowers are for fidelity in adversity, and the lilies of the valley, as you know, are for a return to happiness."

"There was a very pretty blue flower as well." Beside him, she took a deep breath of the night air. "It reminded me of your eyes."

That was a compliment. Nick was sure of it, and equally sure his eyes had never received a lady's compliment before.

"Salvia," Nick said, finding himself fascinated by the rise and fall of her chest.

"It has no meaning?"

"I cannot recall at the moment." Nick shifted his gaze to the dark foliage around them. What on earth had he been thinking, sending blue salvia?

"You met with Hellerington earlier in the week?" Leah asked, leaning more closely against his side.

"I most assuredly did." Nick forced himself to attend the sense of her words rather than her scent, the pure pleasure of her voice in the darkness, or the warmth of her body next to his. "We had a delicate little exchange, with me giving him to understand I'd appreciate it if those fellows whose vowels I hold would behave in a gentlemanly fashion toward their creditors, particularly before they take on additional familial obligations."

"Did he respond to that?"

"I wish I could tell you he caught a packet for France, lovey," Nick said, "but I was firing an opening salvo, and he understood it as such. I'll next make a few pointed remarks at the club, maybe suggest something ought to be put in the betting book at your father's club, call upon the baron again, and loudly hope I need not reduce my demands to writing or perhaps seek satisfaction through other means."

Leah leaned closer still, maybe hunching in on herself but also dropping her voice to a near whisper. "What other means?"

"Typically, one offers a challenge in such a circumstance or simply beats the stuffing out of the party who's refusing to pay a debt of honor," Nick said, letting her scent come to him on the soft night air.

"Would you go that far?"

"If I say yes, you will think me a brute beast. If I say no, you will think me a bully who threatens those weaker than I then backs down at the first hint of risk."

She said nothing for a moment then surprised him. "I wish I knew how to use a gun, or that I was as big and powerful as you are." Her voice was low and bitter, a tone no lady should ever have cause to adopt.

Nick slipped an arm around her waist and pulled her gently against his side. "You must allow me to be your champion. I would meet him over pistols," Nick said, nuzzling her temple, though only once and lightly. Very lightly. "I would not raise my hand to him."

"Why not?" She sank against him easily, as if she'd been waiting for him to make the first overture.

"Murder is frowned upon," Nick said, thinking it quite the pity in this case. "He's old and sick, and it wouldn't be sporting to beat the man with bare fists." Ladies needed comfort, he told himself, and Leah was very much a lady.

Before he nuzzled her again—or worse—Nick bestirred himself to pose a question to the woman tucked to his side. "What manner of brother is it who allows you to languish here in the dark with me? I want to like the man, but one does wonder."

"Darius is the best of brothers, but he has troubles of his own. He knows if I'm languishing, it's because I want to."

"Hmm." Nick's fingers insinuated themselves over Leah's hand. "And what if Hellerington were to appear here?"

"I'd not hesitate to scurry back to the ballroom. I know his coach. I know his scent. I know him. He's not here."

"So you can enjoy yourself with me. For this one night."

"For a single dance," Leah said. "More than that will call attention."

"I hear the musicians tuning up," Nick murmured, closing his eyes the better to feel her beside him. "I must ask for the pleasure. It's an English waltz, and they are not played often enough."

Other couples moved past them over on the path, returning to the dance floor.

"I don't want to go in."

And didn't that sentiment just flatter a fellow shamelessly?

"We'll dance out here," Nick said, rising and drawing her to her feet. "My lady." He offered her the required bow, she sank into a curtsy, and Nick led her to the wide terrace that wrapped around one side and the entire back of the ballroom. The area behind the ballroom, however, was only dimly lit and gratifyingly devoid of other people.

He drew her into waltz position then drew her just a hair closer; then, when she didn't protest or poker up, he drew her flush against his body. She melted against him, resting her cheek against his chest, and Nick knew a sensation of gratitude so intense it physically warmed his heart.

The music started, a stately triple meter that let them find their balance. Nick kept his steps simple and small, and then gradually relaxed as it became obvious Leah followed him with ease. On impulse, he folded their joined hands against his chest, and their fingers linked.

To dance with Leah like this was wicked, scandalous, naughty, and intoxicatingly lovely. When the music ended, Nick kept his arms around her.

"We should go in," Leah murmured.

"We should," Nick replied, his chin resting on the top of her head. He wanted to kiss her first though, even though he knew that was a bad, ungentlemanly idea. Dancing under the stars could qualify as a shared stolen pleasure; kissing a woman who needed his help...

Leah's lips brushed against his so lightly he went still, hoping she'd repeat the caress.

Bless you, Nick thought as Leah wrapped a hand around the back of his neck, steadying herself for another sweet, slow sweep across his mouth.

"Lovey." Nick told himself to open his eyes, not close them. "Lamb, we shouldn't."

Another achingly gentle pressure against his lips, and Nick growled, settled his hands on her hips, and resigned himself to having one more regret.

For long minutes, he let her explore his features, then—bold wench—his mouth. She wasn't experienced, he could taste that easily, but she was avid, and increasingly uninhibited as Nick groaned and murmured encouragement when she came up for air. Something else was coming up too, so Nick eased out of the kiss, resting his forehead on hers while they

both caught their breath.

"You are taking advantage of me," Nick scolded. "I'm out here all unchaperoned and lonely, and you are turning my head." To his own ears, he sounded the tiniest bit sincere. "I don't want to let you go," he went on, his tone suggesting real regret, "but this can't serve either of us."

"It's only a kiss." Leah sounded as dazed and weak in the knees as Nick felt.

"You are stealing my lines as well as my breath." Nick stepped back, softening the loss by smoothing a lock of her hair over her ear.

"You've used that line frequently?"

"Countless times," Nick said, hating himself but keeping his voice as light as he could. He really did not favor lying to women, no matter what that made him in their eyes.

"I wish you weren't so honest." Leah shifted back, and Nick feared she was regretting her advances.

"I wish you weren't so pretty," Nick rejoined. "I wish you had an honorable papa. Now, how about you introduce me to your negligent brother?"

He led Leah back around to the doors opening into the ballroom, and she even suffered his scrutiny when he made her tarry under a torch. Nick prided himself on being able to kiss a woman passionately without mussing her hair, but had to ask Leah to smooth his back into place. She obliged by sifting her fingers repeatedly through his hair, until he had to straighten, clear his throat, and deliver a mental lecture to parts of him that were getting untoward ideas from even such simple, casual caresses.

CHAPTER FOUR

Nick retreated, Lady Blanche Cowell hanging on his arm as they walked away.

"So where did you meet him?" Darius asked.

"I met Lord Reston in the park with Emily," Leah said, and then because Lady Blanche's perusal of Nick had been so possessive even as she'd clung to Darius's elbow, "Where did you meet her?"

"She's frequently at the same functions you are," Darius said, delivering what Leah suspected was a lie—Darius was nigh gulping his wine. "She travels in a slightly less genteel circle."

"Lord Reston apparently frequents the same set." And that hurt, even while it also reminded Leah that Nick's aid was a product of chivalry, nothing more.

"You needn't sound so offended, Sister mine. I will run screaming into the night if her ladyship gives up the juicy prey on her arm and returns her attentions to me."

There was something off in Darius's observation, for all he'd handled the introductions with careful punctilio. "You don't like Reston?" Leah asked.

"I like him well enough, though I can't say I know him."

Ah. Darius did not like Blanche Cowell, then. When Leah and Nick had come upon Darius literally in Blanche's clutches, Darius's expression had been one of banked despair. The notion that Leah had abandoned her brother when he might have needed her was insupportable.

"Is Blanche Cowell trifling with you?"

Darius scowled at her. "I refuse to dignify that, unless you want to tell me if Reston is trifling with you. Shall I lead you out or find you a place to hide?"

"Leave me in peace." Leah wasn't up to concealing her emotions from her brother, but knew if she went home before supper, her father would be railing at her, reminding her he didn't spend a fortune on ball gowns so she could hide away at home night after night.

"Keep an eye out for Hell-raiser," Darius warned. "If you see him, find me or Lord Valentine, or even your new friend Reston."

Leah waved him off with a flick of her fan and sank onto a bench nearly obscured by potted plants. She loved her brothers, and she owed them more than she could ever repay, but Darius of late had been more than a little trying. If she did see Hellerington, she was under strict orders from Wilton to be pleasant to the man, just as she was supposed to be pleasant to Reston.

And look what had come of that.

She blushed anew at her forwardness and at Reston's careful retreat. He was trying to help her, for pity's sake, and she had to behave like the strumpet her father believed her to be.

A ruthlessly honest part of her had to admit, though, that strumpet-hood had never been so appealing. Reston's scent was divine, and dancing with him... When Nick Haddonfield held her, she felt protected, cherished, understood, and treasured. When he kissed her, she felt all that, and so much more that was wicked, wonderful, and hopeless.

"Pining for me?" Reston's mellow bass-baritone startled her out of her reverie, only to be followed by the surprising bulk of him settling in beside her on the bench. "I feel like a bunny rabbit, peering out from between the fern hedges. You have a knack for finding hiding places. Still no sign of Hellerington?"

"My lord." Leah's tone was cool, which seemed only to amuse him.

"Reston?" Nick arched an eyebrow. "At your service, and so forth? Will you make me start all over with the elementary civilities like an errant schoolboy who's offended teacher at the dame school?"

"I am not up to your humor, my lord."

Nick surveyed her with a thoughtful frown. "You are not out of charity with me because of the time I spent with you on the terrace, though you should be, but you are out of charity with me because I rescued your poor, beleaguered brother from Lady Blanche's clutches. Am I right?"

Rescued Darius? Perhaps he had, but still... "She was familiar to you. Familiar with you."

"Leah, I am a single young man of good fortune and rank, and that makes me part hound. The Lady Blanches of this world consort with dogs like me according to very well-understood and sensible rules. I am not proud of such associations, but I am capable of treating decent women decently. Blanche is a dog of a sort herself, and you should not envy her."

Leah liked that he was honest with her, more honest even than her brothers could be. "I am to feel sorry for her?"

"You really should. She is lonely, mean, pathetic, and headed for a miserable existence. Warn your brother off her if you get the chance. Now, the supper waltz is coming up, and you owe it to me to let me prove I can behave. Will you do me the honor?"

"I'd rather not." She wanted to; she wanted to so very badly, which meant she ought not.

"If I'm to credibly court you, lovey"—Nick bumped her shoulder gently with his own, which was rather like being nudged by a well-mannered horse— "you must be seen with me, and supper will start the tongues wagging nicely. Now don't be difficult. There are always sacrifices to be made in the course of being rescued."

"You won't jolly me out of this," Leah said, though she was feeling unaccountably more sanguine. Nick smiled over at her, a smile full of flirtation the likes of which Leah hadn't seen since, well, ever. A smile like that made a woman wonder if she might show off just a hint more of her bosom, or perhaps tap the handle of her fan against her lips.

Slowly. Repeatedly.

"You remind me of my grandmother again." Nick rose and extended a hand to her, the same hand that had cradled her jaw so tenderly. "This is a great compliment, I assure you. I am not asking you to forgive me my private associations, Leah, just tolerate a few minutes in my company for a good cause."

"Oh, very well." Leah rose without his assistance just to make her point, but let him stand up with her and lead her in to supper. The dance was different, of course. Nick held her at the proper distance, though he twirled her down the room with the same sense of utter competence she'd found so appealing on the darkened terrace. On one or two turns, he did pull her in a little too closely. Leah had the impression he was doing it to maintain appearances, that it was expected that Lord Reston part hound—couldn't help but flirt with whatever lady was to hand.

How utterly not flattering.

"And now we line up at the trough with our fellow shoats," Nick leaned down to whisper in her ear. "May we return to your hedge-bench to eat in relative peace?"

"You are flirting," Leah whispered back. "It's tiresome."

"It's expected." His nose bumped her temple— which had to be an accident, didn't it? "Of both of us, if I might remind you."

He was right, damn him and his canine attributes. Leah arranged a smile on her face, and let Nick fill up her plate and one for himself as well.

He leaned in again to speak close to her ear. "Now we make our escape, or Lady Blanche will find me unprotected and start pestering me."

"Poor Nick." Leah's voice dripped with irony. "Too bad for her she doesn't have a papa like mine."

Nick bent close, maybe too close. "She did. That's how she ended up with her current spouse. He's not a bad sort, but he's hardly a young girl's dream. Still, he had the title, you know?"

"Papas are the very devil," Leah allowed on a sigh, but she'd used Reston's name—just like that, and it had come easily and it fit him and she wanted to say it again to herself, over and over.

"Papas, brothers, nephews, all the very devil," Nick said as he got himself arranged with Leah on their bench, plates on their laps. "I'm a neighbor of your brother, by the way. Would you like a strawberry?"

"I adore fruit," Leah said, glancing at his plate. "You didn't tell me there were strawberries."

"I took enough for both of us. Here." He held up a strawberry, not to pass to her plate, but rather before her mouth, for her to take from his hand. She watched his eyes, and the teasing she'd seen there earlier shifted, first cooling then heating to a silent dare.

Holding his gaze, Leah leaned forward, touched her tongue to the succulent red berry, then took it between her teeth.

"My thanks." She chewed slowly then swallowed. "Delicious."

Nick, looking gratifyingly disconcerted for once, simply passed her his plate and surrendered the rest of his strawberries.

❧

THINKING OF YOU.

Blue salvia, Leah learned from a book her mother had given her as a child, meant "thinking of you."

How interesting, and how odd that Ni—Leah caught herself —*Lord Reston* had included it in his bouquet and conveniently forgotten its significance. In the long-dormant part of her soul from which feminine intuition sprang, Leah suspected he'd known good and well what the flower meant, and he'd included it on purpose.

And forgotten its meaning with the same sense of purpose.

Reston had chosen his bouquet with care and an unerring sense for what was lacking in her life.

"Pretty," Wilton remarked, eyeing the bouquet as he sauntered into the family parlor. "I have to commend the man for showing some strategy."

"I beg your pardon?" Leah resisted the urge to get to her feet. Wilton might interpret it as a sign of respect, though more likely a sign of weakness.

"Reston is courting your sister," Wilton said, touching the little white snowdrops. Why didn't they wilt on contact? "He's scouting the terrain, forming an ally, gathering information before he tips his hand."

"No doubt."

Wilton eyed her pensively. He was a good-looking man, tall, trim, with even features and a full head of white hair. His smile, when he produced one, gave Leah chills nonetheless.

"Perhaps he thinks to take you off my hands," Wilton said. "I cannot credit his taste, but his coin will spend as easily as the next man's. You'll have him, if he offers."

"He won't offer for me." Leah bent to her book, turning a page as if in idle perusal.

"You will do nothing to deter him from that possibility," Wilton informed her icily. "Your sister can reach higher, but you will take what's offered and be grateful."

"Aren't we being premature, my lord?" Leah strove for an indifferent tone. "One bouquet does not a courtship make."

"One bouquet, a supper waltz, several meetings in the park," Wilton shot back. "Don't think you're ever far from my sight. Your brothers can't hide your comings and goings, and neither will you, if you value their happiness."

"I value their happiness," Leah said, and thinking to offer a placatory display of submissiveness, she added, "and if Reston offers, I will accept him."

"Of course you will. If he's stupid enough to make that mistake, I will not preserve him from his folly."

Having left the requisite ill feeling and discontent behind him, Wilton stalked out, calling for a footman. His footsteps had barely died away before Leah looked up to see the bouquet with its blue salvia directly in her line of sight. By the time Wilton had slammed out the front door, she felt the first tear sliding down her foolish, wretched cheek.

~

COLONEL LORD HARCOURT HADDONFIELD, fourteenth Earl of Bellefonte, had not enjoyed a decent bowel movement in weeks, by which evidence he concluded that death was indeed stalking him. He had some time, maybe even weeks, before the filthy blighter actually took him down, but when a man couldn't preside competently over the lowliest throne in the land, what dignity was left in living?

Neither one of his deceased wives would have understood that sentiment or appreciated its vulgar utterance even in private, which thought provoked a faint smile. Good ladies they had been, but ladies through and through.

His heir shared his appreciation for the fairer sex, which was a bloody damned relief, as that George, the third boy, was a nancy piece. Beckman was deuced independent, and Adolphus, who aspired to professordom, would be unlikely to marry young.

"My lord," Soames intoned, "a Mr. Ethan Grey to see you. He did not leave a card."

Soames had been with the earl for only ten years and could be forgiven his ignorance. He could not be forgiven for sneaking up on his employer.

The earl turned a glacial blue eye on the hapless man. "Soames, if you have to pound the damned door to sawdust, you do not intrude on your betters unannounced, and you do not intimate I am going deaf, when I can hear every damned footman and boot boy sneaking about and pinching the maids."

"Profuse apologies, my lord." Soames bowed low, his expression betraying not a flicker of amusement or irritation. "Shall I show the gentleman in?"

"The gentleman is my firstborn," the earl said more quietly. "Of course you show him in, but give me a minute first, and hustle the damned tea tray along, if you please."

"Of course, my lord." Soames bowed again and glided out.

The earl waited, wondering what one said to a wronged child grown into a wronged man. He'd kept track of Ethan, of course. He'd also paid his bills through university, managed his late mother's little property, managed the modest sum he'd set aside for the boy, and was managing it still, as the cheeky bastard—well, no, probably not the wisest word choice—the cheeky devil wouldn't touch a penny of it.

"My lord." Soames had on his company face. "Mr. Ethan Grey, late of London."

"Thank you, Soames." The earl waved him off and took in Ethan's appearance. He'd most recently caught a glimpse of Ethan three, maybe five years ago, and in the intervening years the last vestiges of the youth had been thoroughly matured out of the man. At thirty-some years old, Ethan was quite tall, like all the Haddonfield men, with golden-blond hair, arctic-blue eyes, and a damned good-looking bas—fellow to boot. He had a little of Nick's aristocratic features, too, but more hauteur than Nick aspired to and a leaner frame.

"Ethan. I would rise, but lately I cannot even attempt that without assistance. I suppose your arrival confirms my impending death—you, and a lamentable lack of intestinal regularity."

"My lord." Ethan gave him the barest nod, his expression so disdainfully composed the earl wanted to laugh. Ah, youth... Except behind the boy's monumental cool lurked a significant hurt, for which his father knew himself to be responsible.

The earl waved him over to the massive estate desk. "You can glare at me ever so much more effectively at close range, sir." He waited until his son had prowled away from his post by the door. "One of the advantages of age is I no longer have to hear or see so much of this benighted world, but upon inspection, I must say you are looking well."

"And you are not," Ethan said, taking a seat across the desk from his father. Rude of him to appropriate a seat unbidden, but the earl was certain his own wretched appearance had sent his son to his figurative knees.

"I look like hell. The divine wisdom therein is that all and sundry will be relieved when I shuffle off this mortal coil, because if I get any uglier, my own daughters will be unable to stand the sight of me."

Ethan smoothed a wrinkle on a perfectly tailored pair of riding breeches. "You don't seem particularly perturbed at your approaching demise."

"I'm not." The earl smiled. "I've lived my three score and ten, and eked out more besides. The earldom is in good condition, thanks largely to your brother, and my children are provided for. One grows tired, Ethan, and the indignities of great age are every bit as burdensome as you suppose they are. The alternative, however, ceases to loom as quite such a fearful option. Why are you here?"

"Because you swived my mother."

Truly, a son to be proud of. "You always were the quickest of my children." The earl's smile widened, but he held his verbal fire until the tea tray had been set on the desk. "You'll have to pour, lad. My hands shake too badly, and I can barely hold up the teapot. My cup should be only half full, and cool it down with some cream, for I'm likely to spill it."

Ethan flicked a glance at his old papa spouting off so cheerfully about his egregious infirmities, and then his eyes shifted to his father's hands, which the earl could not have rendered steady had he wanted to.

"You've learned a little restraint," the earl decided as his son poured for them both. "Can't say as I ever got the knack, myself. The ladies despaired of me."

"Was it lack of restraint that caused you to send me off in such disgrace?" The desk was so large Ethan had to get up, walk around it, and hand the earl his half-full, heavily creamed cup of tea. The earl knew a moment of something—shame, relief, glee... gratitude?—when Ethan wrapped his father's cold fingers around the warm cup.

The earl carefully—and shakily—brought the teacup to his mouth.

"Used to like it hot," he sighed, "but a lapful of hot tea modifies one's priorities. Now..." He turned his gaze on his firstborn and saw a handsome man in his prime, completely composed, shrewd and patient enough to wait him out. But approaching death had only heightened the functioning of the earl's bladder, so waiting all afternoon wasn't an option.

"The disgrace was mine," the earl said, looking his son straight in the eye. "I know full well you did not attempt to burn your brother with that iron."

Ethan took a delicate sip of his tea. "Were you merely being petty and tyrannical then, when you turned the little thugs and perverts of Stoneham loose on me?"

"Perverts." The earl tasted the word, found it foul. "Interesting choice. I'd discovered you asleep in Nicholas's bed just the night before, and not for the first time."

"Of course I was in his bed," Ethan scoffed, "or he was in mine. How else were we to stay up half the night whispering without waking the younger boys?" Ethan's anger swam much, much closer to the surface, so close the earl perceived that the frigid cool in Ethan's eyes was not impatience, annoyance, nor anything else half so tame.

A betrayed boy yet lurked in the man who'd come to call. A devastated, betrayed boy.

"I comprehend now, Ethan, that you and Nick remained innocent of the most lamentable adolescent behaviors. It took some time, Lady Warne's incessant carping, and raising several more boys before I understood my mistake. By then, you were no longer speaking to any of us, save Lady Warne, and things turned out for the best."

Ethan took another measured sip of his tea, then another, clearly trying to absorb the explanation the earl offered, but no doubt stumbling over the emotional enormity of the wrong done him, and not for the first time.

"In what manner," Ethan spoke very softly, "do you consider things turned out for the best?"

"The two of you were entangled. You protected Nick. He protected you."

"Is that not what brothers do?" Ethan asked with chilly civility.

"Not when one will take a seat in the Lords and the other is merely an earl's by-blow. Sooner or later, you and Nicholas had to face facts. I did neither of you any service by letting you get so close in the first place."

The earl reassured himself of this version of the past regularly. Things had worked out for the best—or they would soon.

"So having made that mistake," Ethan said, "your only recourse was to compound it by separating us the way you did, bellowing accusations, and setting us against each other?"

The earl let his teacup clatter unsteadily onto its saucer. "I've said I was wrong, both in what I did and how I did it. I am not a perfect man, as you well know. But admit to me, please, that both you and Nicholas thrive, and despite my errors, you are both people to be reckoned with, capable of standing on your own two feet."

Ethan rose to those two feet with an ease the earl tried not to envy. "You think old age alone has impaired your hearing and vision, sir. I can assure you, your faculties have long been wanting, else you would have realized Nick and I have always been capable of standing on our own two feet, regardless of our relationship as brothers or friends. Good day."

He departed in a few brisk strides, closing the door with enviable decorum.

Round one to the pup, your bloody uncrapping lordship. The earl sat back with a sigh, sipping his cooling tea disconsolately. God willing, there would be a round two.

~

VALENTINE TOOK a seat at Nick's Broadwood and folded down the music rack, then petted the instrument as if it were an obedient mistress.

"So tell me what you seek in a wife, Nicholas. The hunt doesn't seem to be progressing, and the Season doesn't last forever."

Satan's hairy testicles. "This line of questioning— upon which you seem fixated—does not bode well for our friendship, Valentine."

There was no heat in Nick's reply. He'd never go a round of fisticuffs with a friend whose hands were so very talented. Instead he went to the sideboard and poured them each a brandy. "Any woman who marries me has to understand it will be a marriage for the sake of appearances only, and leave me in peace for the rest of my days."

Val's opening flourishes at the keyboard came to an abrupt pause. "In God's name, why?"

"Why what?" Nick set Val's drink on the piano's lamp stand.

"Shame on you." Val moved the drink to a little music table. "Why would you, of all the randy creatures on God's earth, marry a woman with no intention of taking her to your bed?"

Nick lowered himself to the sofa and regarded the drink he really did not want. "Firstly, I don't need to marry to find women by the pairs and trios in my bed. Secondly, I do not intend to have children with my wife, because my size makes me poor breeding stock. Thirdly, I will not take advantage of some sweet young thing by bedding her, then tossing her over while I look for livelier game elsewhere, thus precipitating endless painful and avoidable scenes involving many damp handkerchiefs, broken vases, and hurt feelings."

"You are full of tripe," Valentine said calmly. When he resumed playing, the clever bastard chose a lullaby. Sweet, lyrical, and perfectly suited to coaxing confidences from unsuspecting friends. "First, you adore women and invariably make them happy, at least bed-wise. There are witnesses to this, Nick. Eyewitnesses. Second, you are superb breeding stock, being handsome, intelligent, prodigiously healthy, and, for want of a better word, lusty. Find a great strapping country girl and space your children, but do not tell somebody who is only a bit shorter than you that size makes you dangerous to your wife. Third, even you have lost your appetite lately for the easy conquests, if you can call them that. You are posturing to take a real wife, my friend."

The little song lilted along, while Nick considered firing a pillow at Valentine's head.

"I am posturing to court the semblance of a real wife." Nick stretched out on the long sofa, his drink resting on his chest. "The fiction must be credible, at least until one of my brothers can go about the business in earnest."

"You are serious about this," Val said, frowning over the lid of the piano at Nick.

Nick waved a hand. "I killed my mother, you know."

Val didn't dignify that with a rejoinder, and the music grew even softer. "If you were to marry in earnest, what sort of wife would you seek?"

Nick didn't answer. He kept his eyes closed, let his breathing slow and deepen, let the music wash through the melancholy Val's choice of topic left in his heart. What sort of wife would Nick choose, if he had any sort of meaningful choice?

A woman who could love him, of course. A woman who didn't care that he'd be an earl, who didn't care that he was too damned big to fit even in a ballroom, who didn't care that the one thing he must never do was attempt to secure the Bellefonte succession.

~

"LEAH DANCED the supper waltz with Reston again," Darius said as he appropriated a drink from his brother's decanter.

"And that's good?" Trenton Lindsey, Viscount Amherst, watched his younger brother pour, thinking Darius's eyes held a hint of something desperate.

"It's good. She seems to like him, and he's not Hellerington. The talk about Reston seems harmless enough—he enjoys the ladies of a certain reputation, but nothing more condemnatory than that. Have you seen Reston?" Darius tossed the drink back and punctuated the question with a glower.

"I doubt it. I do not circulate, to speak of, unless I'm escorting Leah. You know that."

"He's big," Darius said. "Enormously tall with the muscles of a stevedore."

A hazy impression tried to coalesce from the swampier regions of Trent's memory. "Blond? Like Wotan or Thor in evening dress?"

Darius eyed the sideboard, his expression shifting to include a touch of consternation. "Berserker of the Bedroom is one of his nicknames. Biggest damned peer of the realm I've ever seen."

Trent ran a finger over the sideboard and found a smudge of dust accumulated on his fingertip—a metaphor for his memory, perhaps. "I have met him, at Tatt's. Reston seemed genial enough."

"Always. He pulled me aside tonight and warned me very pleasantly that one of my female associates tried to threaten him when he'd parted from her."

Female associates. A prudent older brother didn't touch that with a garden rake in one hand and a bullwhip in the other. "What kind of lady would threaten that much man?"

"She is no lady at all," Darius said on a sigh. "Why do you think I found her of any interest? Reston backed her down somehow, though."

Interesting word choice. Rather than dwell on the implications,

Trent took the empty glass from his brother's hand and set it on the sideboard. "One wonders, Darius. There are naughty women, and then there are mean, wicked women. One should distinguish."

Darius picked the glass right back up. "And their characteristics are always easily discernible across a ballroom?" "Perhaps not." Trent smiled in response. "But across a bedroom, one's instincts are usually reliable."

"Across a bedroom, it's usually one's instincts getting one into mischief." Darius made short work of a second drink and set the empty glass down.

"Valid point." Trent's smile faded. "Darius, I can't help but renew my expression of concern for you. Whatever is amiss, I wish you'd tell me."

"Nothing is amiss." Darius clinked the stopper into the decanter then did it again. "Nothing more than usual, anyway. My thanks for the brandy. You're managing well enough?"

"Anytime, and yes, I'm managing," Trent murmured, watching the way his brother's eyes strayed to the darkness beyond the window. They were lying to each other, and Trent felt despair taking up residence beside the permanent sadness in his gut. "Come by in the morning, and we'll look at Leah's schedule. You need some decent rest, and I can be her escort."

"It will be afternoon before I can get here," Darius said, hand on the door latch. "Mid-afternoon."

"Until then." Trent watched his brother silently slip out into the darkened corridor, even as he wondered what could possibly be worth remaining out and about for what little remained of a cold, dark night.

CHAPTER FIVE

"Did you know your father is selling off property?" Nick passed Leah the bag of bread crumbs and kept his gaze on the swan coming closer to their side of the pond. When Leah tossed a handful of crumbs onto the water, the swan retreated, while the ducks swarmed down the bank, honking and flapping with no dignity whatsoever.

"I am not in Wilton's confidence regarding financial matters," Leah said. "Regarding any matters, really. What is he selling?"

"The smaller of the two estates in Surrey." Nick turned slightly to admire Leah's profile. The breeze was such that her scent drifted over to him, redolent of lily of the valley, and he was struck by the simple beauty of her features on a lovely spring day.

"We used to have four estates, total." Both her tone and her expression were... sad. He wanted, badly, to make that sadness go away. "Wilton would go to Trenton, of course, and then Ambrose Place to Darius. The two little properties were to be Mama's gifts to Em and me, for our dowries. But when Darius escorted me to Italy, the earl sold Ambrose Place."

"There's a path around the pond," Nick said. "Shall we stroll?"

"I'd like that."

"The lady and I will stroll the path around the water," Nick informed their liveried watchdog, who was at the ready up on the gravel walk. "You need not accompany us."

Wilton's minion nodded, though his expression was disgruntled.

"Come." Nick winged his arm, then tucked his hand over Leah's and led her away from the footman. "And walk slowly, if you please. I've been in want of your company."

"I've danced with you twice this week."

"That is your presence," Nick said. "I miss your company." He let a comfortable silence stretch while they put some distance between themselves and the footman. When they had wandered out of earshot, Nick bent down and unabashedly inhaled Leah's fragrance.

"I don't believe I've encountered lily of the valley on another woman. It suits you wonderfully."

"I like your scent as well. Sandalwood, but something else too."

"It's blended exclusively for me. I didn't want it too sweet, but sandalwood alone can be cloying. Now, why would your papa be selling an estate that should have been held in trust for you?"

"Because he does not consider himself under any obligation to provide a dowry for me," Leah said. "I am fallen, and thus not worthy of such an honor." The sadness was muted behind a mask of composure, while hurt lingered in her eyes.

"Just how fallen are you?"

This silence was not quite so comfortable. The answer was none of Nick's business, and yet, he wouldn't withdraw the question.

"You ran off with that young man," Nick guessed, "because you allowed him liberties."

"I did," Leah said, gaze fixed on the flat surface of the water. "Liberties only a husband should be allowed."

Nick hurt for her, because she'd thought to gift her lover with something irreplaceable, only to have the lover taken from her permanently. But another part of Nick, the part that panted and wagged its tail, was relieved. Exchanging stolen kisses with a woman of experience was not quite so reprehensible as exchanging those same kisses with a lady who had little knowledge of men.

"Few brides speak their vows from a place of ignorance," he said, "and many a wedding night would be more pleasant if fewer still wed in ignorance."

She moved along for a few steps, showing no reaction to his words. Nick realized belatedly that speaking from experience on this topic was not quite gentlemanly of him—for all it was honest.

"I should not have eloped," Leah said. "But Wilton told Aaron he would not provide me a dowry, though he also said he would not withhold his blessing on a fait accompli. Aaron was convinced the earl was telling us to elope. Eloping would provide an explanation for my lack of dowry that Polite Society would accept without censuring my father."

Something about this recitation did not add up. "You were intimate with Aaron Frommer, then he asked for your hand, and the earl told you to elope?"

"I was not intimate with Aaron until we had eloped. Aaron asked for my hand then met with the earl to gain his blessing. The earl said he would not dower me, that he expected Aaron to be able to support a wife without needing additional funds. At that point, Aaron believed the earl was telling him to spirit me away, and alas for me, I believed the same thing."

"So you thought you had Wilton's tacit approval," Nick said. Perhaps some fathers were that subtle—his certainly was not. "Could Frommer have been that mistaken?"

"I've had a long time to consider this." Leah leaned more heavily on Nick's arm as the ground became slightly uneven. "And no, I do not think he was mistaken. Younger sons tend to be shrewd people, and Aaron was a very intelligent young man. I believe the earl intended to be rid of me, but then changed his mind for some reason, came after us, and called Aaron out."

"What could have been worth murder?"

"Dueling is frowned upon," Leah said, "but illegal in a technical sense only. For the most part, if discretion is observed, it's tolerated."

"Let's pause here," Nick said as the path wound through a stand of willows leafing out in gauzy foliage. The swaying boughs formed curtains of soft green that hung to the ground when the breeze was still.

"Come." Nick shifted to grasp Leah's hand in his. "We can appropriate some privacy." He parted the feathery green boughs and drew her under the canopy of a large tree, effectively screening them with new growth on all sides.

"And why do we need privacy?" Leah asked, even as she did not withdraw her hand from his.

Nick smiled at her over his shoulder, then stopped and faced her. "Because I need to hold you." He drew her close, and a sigh escaped her. She relaxed against him while his hand settled between her shoulder blades, pressing her nearer.

"The more I learn of your situation, Leah"—Nick rested his chin against her temple as he spoke—"the less I like your papa."

"Good," Leah said, her cheek on his chest. "Don't like him. Don't trust him. Don't underestimate him." The feel of her quiet in his arms was enough to make Nick lose the train of the discussion entirely, which would not do when time was limited and dire consequences threatened. She had seemed to him in need of a little affection, not a mauling in broad daylight.

"Why would Wilton change his mind about letting you marry Frommer?"

"I have suspicions," Leah said. "I think Mama's settlements specified that the Surrey estate was to come to me upon my lawful marriage. I don't think the earl realized this, at least not until after Aaron and I had departed for Manchester."

"Manchester? Why not Scotland?"

"There was need for haste regarding the nuptials." Leah rubbed her cheek over his shirt like a tired child might. "Aaron got us a special license. His brother went to school with the man who held the living at a town on the way called Little Weldon, and we planned on having the ceremony en route."

"I see." Nick's hand on her back started a slow, easy stroking over her shoulder blades, more to soothe him than her. "Do you know who Aaron's seconds were?"

"A friend," Leah responded, her voice sounding sleepy and distracted. "Victor someone. I forget the other one. A brother, maybe."

"Who would your father's seconds have been?" Nick asked, thinking they could be having this discussion while they walked, though he didn't want to move from the spot—ever. Leah's weight leaning against his length so trustingly made his chest feel strange, even while it settled something inside him too.

"I don't know who his seconds were." Leah pulled back to peer up at Nick. "Why is this ancient history relevant, particularly when anything that discredits the earl will discredit Emily?"

Nick guided her head back to his chest. "Let's hope the earl recalls that if the time ever comes to discuss the past with him. I would really like to know who the seconds were, though."

"Trent might know, or Darius."

Nick reluctantly loosened his hold on her and grasped her hand once more, leading her back to the path. "You don't think Trenton was your father's second?"

"I do not. Trent approved of Aaron, and so did Darius. Mama liked him too."

"And you loved him."

Leah nodded then tipped her gaze down, and Nick knew he'd again summoned her tears.

"I am so sorry," Nick said in the same quiet voice. "Sorry to make you talk about it, sorry you had to go through it."

"I wasn't *in* love with him," Leah said. "Though I loved him, and he said that was enough. The rest would come in time. He was a good man, and he did not deserve to die for me. I was just so eager to leave my father's house..."

"You loved him," Nick reminded her, "and you've said he was a shrewd young man, and he knew you weren't in love with him. You were honest with him, and you were prepared to give him your entire future. That was enough for him. It would be enough for any man who loved you." Honesty being a precious necessity in any true union.

Nick kicked the thought away.

For Nick, the conversation regarding Leah's elopement brought a greater sense of concern regarding the Earl of Wilton. Wilton hadn't been a papa enraged to find some young scoundrel had spirited his daughter away. He'd been instead a calculating, scheming spider, who spun a web of circumstances around his daughter and her intended, until one was killed and the other run out of the country. In all likelihood, only the hovering presence of Leah's brothers had stayed the earl's hand from further mischief against her.

Words formed, and Nick let them pass from his brain out into the pretty spring day. "I think I had better offer for you."

Leah stiffened but didn't break contact with him.

"Hear me out," Nick said, glancing up to find they were more than halfway around the pond. "I do not intend that you be stuck with me, but I do want your father to believe his interests are better served by keeping you in good health, rather than by allowing harm to come to you."

"This offering does not contemplate marriage," Leah replied. She was preparing to argue, when Nick really and truly wanted her assent. "If I must cry off, my chances of ever being married will be reduced if I jilt you."

"When you cry off," Nick said, "it will not be as great a problem as you foresee. I will commit some outrageous act of philandering, and you will be pitied by Polite Society. You will be more greatly esteemed for putting me in my place, not less."

"I am not willing to cost you your good name."

"I am not willing for you to be at risk of harm under your father's roof," Nick said.

"I could be your mistress."

Nick stopped in midstride and peered down at her. By St. Michael's mighty sword, she was serious. The hound in him was barking approval of her mad scheme before he could toss the damned beast into the nearest horse trough. He closed his eyes, the better to obscure his wayward impulses from Leah's notice.

"Lamb, you would disgrace your siblings by becoming my mistress, and it's well known I do not keep a particular mistress. I am rather thought to be a connoisseur of variety."

"Oh." Leah's face flamed, and Nick felt awash in contrition.

For not agreeing to ruin her?

"Leah"—Nick's tone took on a cajoling note—"you were casting about for a solution, tossing out any idea, no matter how unlikely. I comprehend that, and let's keep thinking, though I refuse to ruin you, delightful as the process might be for me." Delightful, captivating, pleasurable, exhausting.

Nick swatted his internal hound on the backside.

Leah looked off into the distance, where a nanny and her charge were throwing a ball for a brown-and-white spaniel. "It was just a thought."

He leaned down to speak directly in her ear. "A wonderful, scandalous thought. You should never have put such an idea in my head."

"What other ideas can we come up with?" Leah asked, eyes front, shoulders back.

The ideas that came to mind were not constructive, not in the least. "You could get engaged to someone else," Nick suggested. Ethan might do it, provided the engagement were temporary. Beckman was another possibility, though he'd have to be retrieved from Portsmouth first.

"An engagement is not a permanent solution," Leah said, "but I'd take it, if it were the only option."

"Engagements can last months, years even. If you were engaged to my brother Beckman, the earl will no doubt soon be casting our family into mourning. That would buy you a year."

"That is ghoulish, Nick, to use your father's death that way, to buy me time to escape Wilton."

Impossible woman—not that Nick particularly liked the idea of even a temporary engagement between Beckman and Leah. "I can get you to the Continent. You could go back to Italy and wait Wilton out. He won't live forever."

If anything, her pretty mouth became more grim. "I will not become your dependent, though Italy has a certain appeal. I was happy there, all things considered. I would be there without a brother or father, though, so it could be more difficult than it was years ago."

"Would your brothers help you leave the country?" This was an obvious solution, one Nick should have thought of sooner. "You are not a minor, so you should be free to leave, and you already know the language, I presume?"

"I do. It isn't so different from Latin, though I'm rusty, of course. I think supporting me would be a hardship for Darius and Trent though."

"Why is that?" Nick slowed his steps as much as he could, because they would soon come back to their starting point.

"Darius has tied his coin up in that place in Kent," Leah explained. "When Ambrose Place was sold, Darius took what little my mother left him and sank it into his own property. He gets a very small stipend from the Wilton estate, but Trenton and I are both puzzled as to how Darius supports himself. I don't think Darius has coin to spare, and Trenton is in much the same boat, because his funds are derived from those of his children."

"Unfortunate. We will continue to think on this, though. I cannot accept your present circumstances, even if—and you will note the conditional—old Hellerington's guns have been spiked."

"I will brace my brothers on the prospect of a return to Italy."

"If it's a matter of passage money or a stipend..." Nick began.

"No," Leah said firmly. "You have tied up too much coin buying Hellerington's markers, in the first place. In the second, you will marry soon, and you cannot support me while you are waiting at the altar for your countess."

A logical woman was an abomination against the natural order, or at least against Nick's protective intentions.

"Do you think I wouldn't be supporting a mistress if it pleased me to do so?" The question was out, a function of how rattled Nick felt at the prospect of Leah having to leave the country again to escape her father's scheming.

"You will not keep a mistress once you've chosen your bride. You would not dishonor your wife that way."

She was as bad as Valentine. "I keep no mistress because I enjoy variety, not because I entertain any notion of being faithful to my countess."

Now, now when they must part in moments, she beamed a smile at him. "Tell yourself that, if you must. You are not that hard of heart, Nicholas."

Bother that—though he loved hearing her use his name to scold him. "How did you enjoy your visit with my grandmother?" Nick knew it was a maladroit change of subject, but a gentleman didn't argue with a lady, and Leah was just so... wrong.

"Lady Warne is a delightful woman. She asked to call upon me tomorrow."

"Be warned," Nick said as they approached the waiting footman. "I might join her."

"That would be lovely." Leah gave him a smile that reached her eyes, and Nick searched his mind in vain for the reasons he wouldn't take her on as his mistress.

"I will make a point of it then." Nick smiled back at her, knowing the footman's eyes were goggling out of his head. Nick bent over Leah's gloved hand and rose without turning loose of her. "And that other matter I raised with you? We'll both put our minds to it, and I'm sure a solution will present itself. My thanks for your company, my lady, and until next we meet, may you keep well."

Before swanning off with Wilton's spy in tow, Leah bobbed the requisite curtsy, and waited that extra beat of the heart for Nick to release her hand. Nick watched her go, thinking he usually engaged in flirtation and innuendo without thought, but in this instance, he sincerely hadn't wanted to let her hand go.

Try as he might, he could not come up with a credible reason he shouldn't marry her, but Leah as his mistress? No. Not now, not ever, not even if she begged him, naked on her knees between his...

"Heaven help me."

~

EMILY SMILED over at Leah from between the pages of a small volume. "I am enjoying this book to no end. Miss Willers claims she does not know the language of the fan or the glove or the parasol, but the way she says it makes me think she simply disapproves."

Leah glanced up from her needlework and kept her voice down. "She is not a finishing governess. It's very likely she doesn't know, Em. She's taught you a great deal though. And a decent girl hardly needs to be sending coy signals with her fan, her parasol, or her gloves."

Though a decent girl might dearly wish to send those signals.

"My French is wonderful," Emily said, "my Italian passable, and my manners impeccable. I can do fetching needlepoint, I play the piano a little, and I know how to seat any dinner party of up to thirty if the Regent and his Princess are not both attending."

"I don't know who could solve that particular puzzle. You do not seem very proud of your accomplishments."

"I've been at lessons for ten years, Leah." Emily used a feather as her bookmark, a pure white quill about six inches long. "What do a few words of French or Italian matter when it's my face and my fortune that will decide my future?"

What was this about? "You'd be surprised how handy some foreign languages can be, but you have a point. Your skill at academics should not entirely decide your future, nor should your face and fortune."

"What does that leave, if you discount funds, brains, and appearance?"

"Your heart, little Sister. Your inherent virtue, your goodness or lack thereof, your humor or kindness or graciousness toward others. Those things should count for something with the man who seeks to marry you."

Emily's expression became solemn. "I do not mean to be unkind, Leah, but you chose a man based on such qualities, and look what befell you. I do not want to end up like you."

"Well said." The Earl of Wilton stepped into the room, his smile of approval for Emily only. "Your older sister was selfish, foolish, and properly made to suffer for her sins. You will be wiser than she, and life will reward you for it."

"I hope so, Papa," Emily murmured, careful not to look at Leah.

"Excuse us now, Emily," the earl bade her.

Emily was out the door before Leah could blink, for which Leah could not blame her. With Wilton looking on, Emily did not dare show Leah too much deference.

"You think to corrupt your younger sister, miss?" The earl remained standing, his hands tucked behind his back while Leah sat before him.

"I think to encourage her to be happy." Leah bent her head to her embroidery hoop rather than yield to the urge to cringe.

"Your example has proven instructive," the earl said, beaming a malicious smile. "It did not occur to me you would have value as a cautionary tale, but it appears you do. I bring you words of caution as well, Leah."

Leah raised her gaze to his and felt her chest constrict at the hatred she saw. "I am listening."

"Hellerington rescheduled his appointment with me last week, but today I have his note postponing the meeting indefinitely. This tells me you have failed to secure the attentions of even such a one as he, who would at least have taken you off my hands and perhaps paid modestly for the privilege."

"I'm sure you're disappointed," Leah said.

"Sending you into his waiting arms would have had a certain appeal, and you might yet end up there," the earl replied. "Without benefit of matrimony."

"You would condemn me thus?"

"Happily," the earl snapped. "And when I hear you spouting off to Emily about choosing a man for his character... Your days under this roof are numbered, miss. I will choose Emily's husband and the terms upon which she weds, make no mistake about that. I had hoped... well, no matter. I've had indications this Lord Reston might be seriously interested in you, and because he is soon to assume his papa's title, I will take some time to consider the matter of your future. You, however, would be well advised to flirt your way into some man's affections sooner rather than later. I care not whether it's Reston or some wealthy merchant. Consider yourself forewarned."

He left, sparing Leah the effort of a reply.

He'd warned her, at least. She could be tossed into the streets, her only recourse to impose on Trent, or perhaps to retreat to Darius's little place in Kent. As her options were truly narrowing, Leah felt the foreboding in her chest congeal into dread. To be not merely a spinster daughter, but a poor relation cast out of her own home...

God in heaven, what had she done to deserve such a fate? And God in heaven, what was she to do? She had four sovereigns to her name. What in the world was she to do?

~

"SIR." The butler waited until Ethan Grey looked up from his ledgers. "A gentleman to see you."

Ethan waved the salver away. "Tell me who it is."

The butler, without raising a brow, read the card. "A Lord Reston," he pronounced, "and the corner is bent."

"Ah, Jesus." Ethan sat back and saw the usual sea of ledgers, correspondence, and documents covering his desk. First that audience with Bellefonte, now Nick knocking at his door—in person—when there was work to do.

"Show him in." Ejecting Nick would take more footmen than Ethan wanted to spare. "Bring us a tea tray with whatever the kitchen can add to it that's passable."

"Very good, sir."

Nick was here, at Ethan's town house, and Ethan knew damned good and well who had given him the address.

"Ethan." Nick breezed in, his blue, buff, and cream riding attire showing his phenomenal physique to excellent advantage. "My apologies for not sending a note, and my thanks for your willingness to receive me."

"I've always been willing to receive you." Ethan frowned, for Nick looked harried. Nick never looked harried. He was the quintessential self-possessed, easygoing charmer. Ethan was the one who couldn't manage to get enough done in a day. Nick looked to be dropping weight as well, and Ethan's characteristic irritability ratcheted up a notch. Nick was not allowed to be worn and tired. Nick's job was to be happy, amiable, and bustling around in a fog of randy contentment, flirting his way from one merry widow to the next.

"Tea's on its way." Ethan shoved out from behind his desk and extended a hand. Nick's expression showed momentary surprise, but he shook solidly then tossed himself down into a sturdy cushioned chair.

"Thank the gods for a man who appreciates real furniture." Nick dragged a hand through his golden mane. "How was your trip to Belle Maison?"

Amiable and very, very direct.

"Trying," Ethan said, lowering himself into the other chair and realized that Nick—and probably Nick alone—was someone with whom he could discuss the trip.

"He really is dying," Nick said softly. "Doesn't seem right, doesn't seem like it's time, and it doesn't help that he's ready to go."

"He is, isn't he? Miserable old pestilence."

"I think he is miserable," Nick said. "Angry and ashamed to be old and sick, and ready to get on with being remembered fondly."

"By most."

"But not all," Nick agreed, smiling slightly. "I gather you did not grant him pardon, absolution, and remission of all sins?"

Nick's directness on that issue was oddly welcome, even though it reminded Ethan starkly they'd once been able to read each other's thoughts and had Bellefonte to thank for the distance between them now. "I could hardly stand to be in the same room with him."

"One doesn't need to bear a grudge against the man to feel thus."

A soft tap on the door, and both men fell silent as the tea cart was rolled in.

"You pour." Nick closed his eyes and leaned his head back. "I am damned sick of being my own hostess."

"You're soon to acquire a countess, though, aren't you?" Ethan asked as he peered at the tea. "It's middling strong."

"Let it steep," Nick said, eyes still closed. "Did you put the earl in his place, Ethan?"

As if one could. The Lord God Almighty would probably be hard put to do as much. "I left in a temper. I did get something like an explanation from him, though."

"Did you now?" Nick opened his eyes and sat up. "The grim reaper must be stalking him in earnest."

"Or his indigestion was plaguing him. All those years ago, Bellefonte found you and me in the same bed."

"Of course he did." Nick looked puzzled. "Else the little boys would have heard all our secrets. As it was, every time Dolph had a nightmare, he was in with us as well."

"But his lordship thought we were inappropriately attached to begin with," Ethan said, "and when it became obvious we often bunked together, he decided we were engaging in perversions with each other."

There was a beat of utter silence, then another, followed by a roar.

"He thought *what?*" Nick shot out of his chair and rounded on his brother.

Ethan remained seated, peculiarly gratified by Nick's indignation. "He thought we were lovers, or the adolescent male variation on that theme."

"God's eternal balls," Nick swore, pacing off. "Jesus George Christ Almighty in the Clouds. I cannot believe this. I will kill the misguided old goat and make it hurt. He cast you away because he thought we might have been a little too close? A little curious with each other? Jesus."

Nick came to a halt, breathing deeply. Ethan watched, knowing he'd just seen Nick come as close to losing his temper as Nick ever would.

"I walked out," Ethan said, "if that helps. Left him wheezing in his chair while I headed blindly for the stables. I ran into Nita there, and that distracted me temporarily."

Nita had been a girl the last time he'd seen her, a pretty little girl who'd once told him he was her favorite brother.

"Nita would distract St. Peter. I am disappointed in our father, Ethan. I was disappointed in him for separating us in any case, but over nonsense like this... Disappointed and disgusted. Had you any clue?"

"No." Ethan held out Nick's teacup to him. "Not really, though we probably should not have been quite so cozy that late into boyhood."

"That is utter tripe!" Nick shot back. "You left, so you have no idea what transpired as our brothers grew older, Ethan. I can promise you George and Dolph were up to no good with each other, and Beck use to pleasure himself as he spied on me with the dairymaids. The earl had a randy damned pack of sons, and you and I were not the worst of the lot."

Nick's casual recitation of fraternal prurience hit Ethan with a curious blend of revulsion, humor, and relief. "I'll take your word for it, though I doubt you are paying me the signal honor of a call after all these years to rehash ancient history."

"I am not," Nick admitted, looking at the teacup in his hand dazedly.

"Sit you down, Nicholas. We can talk more later, if you find you want to. I'm not sure I do. State your business."

"I can hardly recall my business," Nick growled.

Ethan waited him out.

"I need help," Nick said at length, his tone truculent.

Not at all what Ethan had expected—though he wasn't sure what he had expected. "What manner of help?"

"I've been called to Belle Maison, but there's a young lady here in Town whose safety I have pledged to ensure."

With Nick, it was ever a problem with the ladies. This predictability also gratified. "What manner of young lady? I've no need to take on one of your lightskirts, Nicholas."

"She's a decent woman. I've asked Grandmama to invite her to Clover Down for the week, or until I can get free of Bellefonte. Her dear father, the Earl of Wilton, seeks to wed her to Hellerington, or somebody of that ilk. If she can't secure such a match, the old man might procure a different sort of situation for her."

"You appear to have taken up the shining-armor business, Nicholas."

"I have not, but neither can I leave somebody who is essentially helpless in harm's way." Nick's pronouncement was made in tones of self-disgust, which Ethan allowed to remain unremarked.

"What am I supposed to do? Wilton is a nasty bugger, Nick, and I am nobody's heir."

"All I ask is that you escort Lady Warne and Lady Leah out to

Clover Down," Nick said, "and hang about until I come back from Belle Maison."

"I can do that." Ethan was surprised to see the depth of the gratitude in Nick's eyes. "Christ, Nick, are you really so alone as all that?"

Nick's gaze slid away, and Ethan had his answer. "Your ladies will be safely tucked away in the country. Is there more you would ask of me?"

Nick was silent, and Ethan reached over and plucked Nick's empty teacup from his hand.

"This is me, Nicholas," Ethan said in low, impatient tones. "I accidentally branded your bony little arse, I was the first person to get drunk with you, and I wouldn't know how to read if you hadn't taught me my letters. What?"

"Come to his funeral," Nick said, his gaze on his empty hands. "Not the service, if you don't want to, but to Belle Maison."

Ethan rose and ran a hand across hair slightly darker than Nick's. "I did ask." He turned his back to Nick, staring into the fire as a plethora of emotions rioted through him—resentment, surprise, and something else. An elusive little bolt of warmth Ethan wasn't about to examine too closely. Nick needed him, and for the first time in more than ten years, Ethan could help. The sneering, righteous rejection he'd practiced off and on for all that time was the last thing on Ethan's mind.

"You don't have to." Nick rose as well. "I'm presuming, to put such a request to you."

Ethan half turned and regarded his younger brother—his harried, tired, worried, very large younger brother who had gone into the shining-armor business, whether he admitted it or not.

"I'll go. I'll escort Lady Warne and your damsel, and when Bellefonte goes to his reward, I'll at least put in an appearance, if you're certain you will want me there when the time comes."

"I am quite certain," Nick said, eyeing him grimly. "Beck is lying low in Portsmouth, Dolph and George will probably be skipping around from one house party to the next, you'll be easy to reach, and…"

"And?"

Nick slapped riding gloves against his thigh in a slow, solid rhythm. "And of real use. To me. To the girls. They've missed you."

Ethan said nothing rather than remark on all the letters he'd never received from his devoted sisters.

Nick turned his back and reached for the door latch. "God knows I've missed you too."

And then he was gone.

~

"WILTON HAS MADE it plain that I'm to secure Lady Warne's sponsorship for Emily, and that's the only reason he's allowing me to accept this invitation." Leah ambled along on Nick's arm at a decorous pace completely at variance with the panic building inside her.

"What aren't you telling me, Leah?" Nick's tone was pleasant, a gentleman escorting a lady on a casual ramble by the duck pond on a spring day.

She wasn't telling him that she was scared nigh to death, wasn't telling him she needed his embrace with a desperation that qualified as pathetic.

"Wilton's growing worse, Nick. He no longer seems to care what befalls me or who learns of it."

Nick's hand closed over hers in a warm, reassuring squeeze. "In two days' time, you'll be ensconced at Clover Down. Because I must away to Belle Maison, my brother Ethan will escort you, and you can pry all my boyhood secrets from him. We were incorrigible, of course…"

She let the soothing patter of his voice wash over her, let herself believe that a week in the country would work some miracle where Wilton was concerned. She also let Nick draw her once again into the privacy of the willow bower on the far side of the pond.

"You are pale, lovey," Nick said, wrapping his arms around her. "Your eyes are haunted, and fatigue shows around your mouth." He bent his head and brushed his lips over her mouth. "You must not fret. All will be well."

When he held her like this, Leah could believe that—Nicholas seemed to believe all would be well, but then, his father hadn't murdered his intended, and all but promised to deliver him, bound hand and foot, into a life of abject depravity.

She let herself cling to Nick for just a few more minutes, storing up the sandalwood scent of him, the heat of his tall body, the solid muscles enveloping her, and then she forced herself to step away.

"For two more days, I can manage, Nicholas. I'm not usually inclined to such dramatics."

The look he gave her was searching, far more serious than his usual genial expression. Leah was struck in a whole different way with how very attractive he was. The woman he married had best guard her heart and guard it well.

The breeze stirred, teasing a lock of blond hair across Nick's brow. They were still in the sheltering embrace of the willow branches, so Leah allowed herself to smooth that errant lock back into place.

"Two days, lovey, and then Ethan and Lady Warne will kidnap you from your tower. Wilton won't risk anything drastic when he knows you're expected by a dowager marchioness at week's end. Be strong for two more days."

He kissed her again, a sound smack on the lips. One of his kisses for courage—though what did it say about her, that she was starting to catalogue the kisses of a man whom she had no intention of marrying?

CHAPTER SIX

Leaving Clover Down without stopping in at Blossom Court nearly killed Nick, but he'd learned years ago that Leonie was a creature of routine. She loved him, and he loved her, but that meant if she wasn't expecting him, he could disturb her peace by just dropping by.

When he did reach his father's side, he was glad he hadn't tarried on the way.

"What took you so infernally long to get here, boy?" Bellefonte's voice had lost volume but not bite, Nick noted as he mentally armored himself for this interview.

"One doesn't leave Town in the middle of the Season without having to send out regrets, confer with solicitors, and make other arrangements." The old man was losing ground, and that, not the earl's temper, his displeasure, or his infernal meddling, was what bothered Nick most.

I'm losing him. Nick wandered around the overly warm, camphor-and-books-scented study, the better to avoid looking at his father.

We are losing him. Nick would never again be a little boy who could throw himself into his father's arms and feel small and protected, knowing a robust, if irascible, father would defeat all dragons and slay all demons.

"Perhaps one doesn't." The earl's scowl eased. "You're too skinny, Reston."

"Too much dancing."

"Not enough dancing. You've brought me no sweet young thing for my approval."

"I'm considering a few possibilities," Nick said, "but I know you're too stubborn to die until I find the right lady, so there is no real hurry."

"Cheeky." The earl grinned. "You get that from me, but don't be too cocky, my boy."

"Of course not." Nick forced himself to take a seat opposite the desk that now seemed to dwarf its owner. "I want this marriage business over with probably more than you do."

The grin evaporated. "You don't make sense. Of all my lusty boys, you are the lustiest of the lot. Word is you'll swive anything in skirts—unlike your nancy brother, George, by the way—so what's the delay in finding a countess?"

"In the first place," Nick said pleasantly, "I do not swive anything in skirts, but am, rather, very choosy about my partners. In the second place, keep your beak out of my personal business, or I'll dawdle until June to make a selection and let her choose the wedding date. In the third place, not just any woman could take on the family you've created, my lord, much less your rather generously proportioned heir."

The earl waved a bony, mottled hand. "Marry some bovine parson's daughter. You know I believe in the occasional outcross."

"I will consider that advice." And reject every word of it.

"See that you do," Bellefonte snapped. "This dying business is tedious. I do not relish becoming an ugly, odoriferous old stick, and I would be done with it sooner rather than later. Your dithering wears on me, sir."

Nick suffered that hit, as it hid a genuine plea for haste and for understanding.

"So how fare you, Father?" Nick asked, all hint of posturing gone.

Bellefonte smiled thinly. "I do not suffer, particularly, except that indignities bring a pain all their own. I am not bedridden yet, though, so you have some time. I truly do wish only to see you happy."

"One would never accuse you of having any other motivation," Nick drawled, returning the smile.

"And as to that brother of yours." Bellefonte shoved the momentary sentimentality aside with another dismissive wave of his hand. "I have formally acknowledged him."

Nick went still, not having seen this pronouncement coming. "You haven't told Ethan," Nick surmised. "Don't expect me to tell him. This is between the two of you."

"Don't preach to me, Nicholas. I know how to deal with my own children."

"By sending them all away," Nick said. "You wanted to spare us the ordeal of watching your decline." A final, poignant display of patriarchal kindness.

"And spare myself the pleasure of being watched as I decline," the earl added. "I've unfinished business with you and your brother."

Your brother, Nick noted, meant Ethan, as if those other three young men were something else.

"So finish it." Nick fell silent, waiting and wondering what in the world his father had to say to him. In recent years, they'd grown more skilled at bickering, taunting, and insulting their way through difficult matters, such that what needed discussion was in some-wise discussed. So what did that leave?

"I owe you and Ethan an apology," the earl said, spearing Nick with a glare. "I was wrong to separate you all those years ago, and more wrong for how I went about it."

"Apology accepted," Nick heard himself say, though a shivery feeling came over him. "Will you be joining us for dinner? I've brought one of Moreland's sons with me from Town."

"Bother that." Bellefonte rummaged in a drawer of the desk. "My hands shake so badly, eating is no longer pretty, if it ever was."

"You had exquisite manners," Nick said softly, knowing his own delicacy at table had been gained by following his father's example. "Is this why you're turning into a shadow?"

The old man banged the drawer shut. "Assuredly not. I'm fretting over the succession, you insolent, thoughtless, self-centered puppy."

Only his father had ever called him a puppy and managed to make him feel like one.

"Of course." Nick rose, his smile genuine. "Then you won't mind if I have a word with Nita and the cooks regarding your menus."

"Listen, pup." The earl struggled to rise, and Nick let him. Pure cussedness got the old man to his feet, and love of a good scrap had him leaning over the desk, bracing himself on gnarled knuckles. "You will not go telling Cookie to feed me beef tea through a damned straw. The day I can't chew my own food is the day I stop eating."

Nick's smile broadened, knowing his father's display of temper had been for his benefit. He sidled around the desk and bent to kiss his father's cheek.

"I love you too, Papa," he said before sauntering off, knowing the earl was grinning like a lunatic at his retreating back. Over his shoulder, Nick called, "And see that you finish your pudding. I have my spies too, and locating a worthy countess may yet take some time."

~

"YOU SENT FOR ME?" Leah joined Nick in his study at the back of the Clover Down manor house. She'd left the door open, of course, but when Nick silently padded across the room and closed it, the anxiety she'd carried with her everywhere of late congealed low in her belly.

Since his arrival the previous day, he'd been distracted and distant, though never rude. As much as she studied him, as carefully as she'd tried to pry details from Mr. Grey or Lord Valentine, Nick's present mood was a mystery to her.

"Please have a seat, Leah. We have matters to discuss. You are enjoying your stay here?"

"Very much." She settled on the couch rather than one of the huge reading chairs. She'd sat in one for much of the previous morning, reading and enjoying its subtle hint of Nick's scent—and feeling utterly dwarfed by its dimensions.

"Ethan has behaved?"

"Your brother was slow to warm up," Leah said, watching Nick as he paced the room, "but he has proven to be charming company."

"Good." Nick stalked over and seated himself beside her, taking her hand in his. His hands were warm and callused across the palms and pads of his fingers. Not exactly a gentleman's hands, but capable of tenderness.

"I want you to hear me out," he said, glancing at her then at their hands. "I have a proposition for you—a proposal, really—but it won't be what you want or what you deserve."

"I'm listening."

Nick ran his free hand through his hair. "Christ's blessed, hairy..." He dropped her hand and rose again, tramping the length of the room like a stall-bound horse.

Leah rose and stood in front of him where he'd paused at the window. "Whatever it is, just say it. I know you have many responsibilities, and I am a passing obligation you've taken on out of the goodness of your heart. I will always be grateful to you."

"Grateful. God's holy... drawers."

Leah raised herself up on her toes and brushed her lips over his. "Grateful," she repeated with soft insistence.

"Oh, hell and the devil," Nick muttered, his arms going around her, pulling her snugly into his body. Leah felt something in him ease, or possibly give up as his chin came to rest on her crown. "Lovey— Leah, *my lady*—we need to have a somewhat awkward discussion."

What she needed was to remain right where she was, wrapped in

Nick's embrace, reveling in his warmth and the way their bodies fit so wonderfully together. Nick's physical power was only part of what made him attractive. He also exuded a sense of masculine competence that revived Leah's flagging spirits like all of her brothers' long-suffering devotion had not.

And yet, they were to discuss something awkward.

Leah burrowed closer. "I'm listening."

She felt his lips brush against her temple. "I'll have you know, my lady, I had no intention of worrying about you. You were safe, I knew that, and yet—"

Another soft brush of lips and nose, this time against her brow.

And yet, he'd appeared at Clover Down a day earlier than planned. Leah began to hope that in Nicholas Haddonfield's lexicon, a proposal of marriage was an awkward topic.

"I missed you too, Nicholas." She kissed him for emphasis, right on the mouth. He'd consumed a quantity of ginger cake at breakfast, and Leah could taste the spice and sweetness on him. "And that wasn't in my plans either."

He growled and wrapped her closer. "We should not—"

Leah arched into him, finding evidence of his arousal rising against her belly. Rather than listen to his infernal, misguided, male should-nots, she resumed kissing him.

She had been the object of a passionate young man's fancy and had concluded with some puzzlement that while marital intimacies had the potential to be pleasant, the poets (being male) were given to exaggerations regarding the whole business.

Nick Haddonfield in a kissing mood was not pleasant. Whereas Leah's earlier experiences had been accompanied by hesitance, shyness, and a quality of reverence, Nick's approach to intimate matters approximated the arrival of a gale-force wind, knocking Leah's sensibilities end over end. His tongue swept over her lips, bringing heat and spice, and igniting a conflagration of wanting below the pit of Leah's stomach.

She got a hand wrapped in his hair and drew her slippered foot up the back of his riding boot, as if she'd climb straight up him. "Nicholas, I want—" *You.* She could not quite say that, not yet.

"I want you too, lovey, but we mustn't—"

We mustn't was worse than we shouldn't, and Leah might have spared some concern over whatever was troubling Nick, except she had missed him, missed not only the pleasant gentleman and handsome escort, but the lusty, sexually astute, desirable man who made Leah feel, for the first time in her life, that being a woman was a lovely, wonderful thing.

A gift.

"Hold me," Nick coaxed, startling a squeak out of her as he hoisted her raised leg even higher, up around his hip. "Hold tight."

His strength was such that he could easily take her weight with his arms, and he hiked her up, so through the layers of their clothing, her sex was pressed against the surprising length of his arousal.

"Nicholas." Leah gasped as her body reacted to the pleasure—and frustration—of his proximity.

"Hang on to me." Nick took a few steps and settled her back against the wall, leaving him free to hold her in place with one arm while his other hand brushed down over her breast.

This was what the poets had been blathering about; this was passion, madness, pleasure, and desire all rolled into one experience, and Leah wanted as much of this experience with Nick as she could get. She used the wall at her back for leverage and arched forward, such that a particular, hot, female part of her body pushed directly against the rigid length of his arousal.

The pleasure of that boldness, even through their clothing, was startling—and inspiring. She did it again, then again, and then felt Nick's mouth covering hers, his tongue sweeping forward, and bliss rising up to eclipse worry, misgivings, common sense—everything.

~

"SWEETHEART, SLOW DOWN," Nick rasped. "We shouldn't..."

Leah arched against him, her thrust having enough determination to be almost angry, and Nick's ability to speak was swamped by the pleasure of her writhing in his arms. All he knew was that she felt right. Not too small—many women were too small—but not too large, not that sturdy rural denizen his father had urged on him. She felt womanly and good and pleasurable.

He should stop, Nick knew that, just as he knew the royal succession from generations before the doomed Harold Godwinson on down to the Regent. Stopping was sensible, but Leah's breast had found its way into Nick's hand, and the sensation of that soft weight arching against his palms...

"Ah, God." Nick closed his eyes and lifted his mouth from hers long enough to bury his lips at her neck, inhale the fragrance of her, and gently, gently, palm the weight of that lovely breast again.

"Nicholas..." Leah's voice saying his name with need, and desire... He applied the least hint of pressure to her nipple, and covered her mouth with his own while he pressed his cock tightly against her.

He could come like this. He could make *her* come like this. Those notions illuminated his awareness between one breath and the next, a delightful, intoxicating couplet of pleasure that had him going still, debating logistics—he'd pleasured more than one woman against a stout wall—and trying to recall if he'd locked the library door.

"Ah, Nicholas..." Leah sighed, and her body imperceptibly softened, yielding to him, enveloping him in feminine acceptance while Nick contemplated greater naughtiness. She signaled, with that bodily sigh, that she trusted him, trusted his ability to pleasure her and to protect her as well.

And her surrender got through to his flagging common sense like his own clamoring conscience hadn't. Like a bucket of cold, filthy water. She would let him take her like a doxy against the wall while she was a guest under his roof—under his protection, for God's sake.

"Hush." Nick eased his body away from her slightly, enough to let her foot find the floor again. Self-disgust made him want to wrench away, but something stronger kept him close to her. "Just hush." He brushed his hand over her hair and hung there, braced over her by his arm against the wall. He shifted, hiked her against his chest, and carried her to the couch.

"I did not mean for that to happen," Nick said, setting her down gently then pacing off a few feet to regard her. Hysterics on her part were not out of the question; a scathing scold was easily possible. The outcome that made him truly uneasy was the prospect of her tears.

"Neither did I," Leah replied. "I am not sorry we are passionate with each other, while you clearly have regrets."

Nick watched while Leah's arousal and anticipation faded, leaving her features impassive. He deserved a verbal birching, and she apparently meant to deny him that penance.

"I'm sorry." She gained her feet with exaggerated dignity. "I should not have importuned you."

God spare me from martyred women whose lips are still damp from my kisses. Nick's hand circled her wrist. "It is I who owe you an apology. Will you sit?"

She resisted by not looking at him—Eurydice in the underworld came to mind—but she let him tug her down beside him on the couch.

"I am sorry for what just passed between us," Nick said. "Very truly sorry, because it makes what I have to say much more difficult."

His lapse in self-restraint also left him feeling stupid, disgusted with himself, and bewildered, particularly when he'd never once in all his years of disporting with women lost his head like that.

"Stop dithering, Nicholas."

Dithering. He was becoming skilled at dithering.

Perhaps he was the one at risk for strong hysterics. "Promise me something first." Nick laced his fingers through hers, hoping she'd slap him before she tossed his offer back in his face. "Promise me you won't reject what I say out of hand, but take a few days to think about it first. Talk it over with Lady Warne, with your brothers, even with

Ethan or Lord Valentine, or my horse, but don't just toss it aside as a foolish notion."

"I'm listening, Nicholas."

He loved hearing her say his name, even in that starchy, wary, put-upon tone. "Your promise first."

"I promise."

"I believe your father, or Wilton," Nick corrected himself, "truly wishes you harm, Leah. When I discussed your situation with your brother Trenton, Lord Amherst, he characterized Wilton's dealings with you as not sane."

She gave him the barest nod of agreement, and her fingers closed more tightly around his.

"I can offer you safety as my wife, but that's all I can offer you. You will have safety, and a place in Society if you want it. My family will accept you, and my title and wealth will be yours to share."

She swiveled her head to regard him, confusion and hurt lurking in her eyes. "I don't understand."

"You won't have *me*," Nick said, hating himself, hating the way the hurt gained ground at those words.

"What does that mean?"

"We will have a white marriage, Leah," Nick said gently. "I do not want children, not with you. The only way to absolutely ensure I have no legitimate issue is to abstain from relations with you."

"Relations?" She made the word sound putrid.

"Coitus," Nick clarified. "I will be your husband, not your lover."

"Ever?" Leah's expression was suffused with bewilderment. "I truly don't understand."

"I did not expect you would," Nick said on a sigh. At the present moment, his own comprehension was dodgy at best. "And I did not want to put you in this position, but it seems the best I can do."

"But you..." She waved a hand toward the wall, a world of accusation in the gesture.

"I desire you, yes." Nick's middle finger traced the edge of her hairline. He hadn't planned to touch her, though she didn't stop him.

"I'm sorry for that. A gentleman would have kept his prurient interest to himself."

Now she swatted his hand away. "It didn't feel prurient."

Nick wrapped her hand in both of his. "I am sorry for the way I acted just now. It was badly done of me."

Terribly, horribly, egregiously badly done. Nick did not let his gaze stray to the decanter, but it was calling to him loudly.

"I am confused, Nicholas. You desire me, but it shames you. You want to protect me, but you do not want me to be your countess in truth."

Argument was good. Argument would give Leah some purchase on her self-possession. "Firstly," Nick said, "I want to keep you safe from Wilton's schemes. Marriage will do that. Secondly, I want to keep you safe from me. Abstaining will do that."

She folded her arms, the drawbridge going up on the citadel of her dignity. "What on earth can you mean?"

Nick took her right hand, brought it to his lips, kissed her knuckles, and then tucked her hand back into her lap—all without the least clue why he'd provoke her further.

"I did kill my mother," he said, rising and turning his back. "No woman should have to bear my children. I'm larger than my father, and you are not larger than my mother."

"That hardly means we'd have to abstain. We'd have to take precautions."

Nick was quiet for a long time, wishing to hell and heaven both she'd just accept his proposal and let them get on with the business— and how did a decent woman know of precautions, anyway?

"That's not it, is it?" Leah guessed, crossing the room to face him with a swish of skirts signaling unstoppable female determination. "There's something else, isn't there?"

She deserved the truth, but silence on this issue had been a habit for so long Nick couldn't bring himself to have mercy on her. He held her gaze, willing her to see what he couldn't tell her, knowing he was being a coward.

"You love another," Leah decided, her tone ominously calm. "You love a woman you cannot marry, and you've promised her your marriage will be in name only. I'm not sure if your behavior is chivalrous or deranged."

Nick blinked, realizing in an instant Leah's hypothesis was a version of truth, and—more important— credible to her.

"I've promised my father a countess. I've promised you safety, and you've promised me you will think about this before you answer." The pseudo-syllogism pleased him, bringing order to a difficult situation.

"Do you want me to hate you?" Leah asked, incredulity seeping into her words. "You offer me safety and the daily insult of knowing your promises to another woman preclude you from giving to me that which you've already assured yourself—assured us both—I could desire passionately."

"It isn't like that." It was exactly like that. "I cannot risk having children with you, Leah. If what you want is easing of your needs, I can do that without taking my clothes off."

It would kill him to attempt it, and yet—

"Nicholas"—Leah's voice was very soft—"I've given you my word I will consider your offer, and I will keep my word, but right now, I do not understand you. What you've offered is the first indication I've had that you are capable of unkindness. I am disappointed, and will take my leave of you."

She turned to go. Nick's hand on her arm stopped her. "I am sorry," he said, searching her gaze for some hint of common ground, of understanding. "If there were another way, if you find another way, I'd offer you that instead."

"That provides a great deal of comfort, Nicholas." Leah's voice was still soft, but her eyes narrowed slightly, and she didn't give Nick time to react before she brushed a kiss across his lips.

Her pace was dignified, her spine straight as she took her leave. The door closed quietly behind her, leaving Nick, two fingers against his lips, staring at the closed door in miserable silence.

~

"I'M off to the arms of my muse." Lord Valentine bowed to his companions and slipped out the door, the ladies having already vacated the dining room to retire above stairs.

Ethan eyed Nick from across the table. "Do we get drunk here or in the study?"

Plain speaking, for which Nick was grateful. "We'll be closer to the piano in the study," Nick said. "Am I that obvious?"

"Not particularly." Ethan shoved to his feet. "But between you and Lady Leah, there was a certain lack of conversation. Did you upset her during that tête-à-tête you had earlier today?"

"Royally." Nick followed Ethan out the door. "And she deserves better."

"Has it occurred to you to offer her better?" Ethan asked as he pushed open the door of the study and headed to the decanter.

"You don't know what I did offer her," Nick said. "Don't skimp on the brandy, Brother. I have serious matters to regret."

Ethan handed him a half-full glass. "Not you too."

"Me too." Nick nodded his thanks and lowered himself to the sofa. "I've spoken with Leah's brothers, and something must be done, sooner rather than later."

"Speaking of Lady Leah's brothers"—Ethan slid down on the other end of the couch—"I was out riding this afternoon and came across Darius Lindsey. He was in the company of that dreadful Cowell woman. The one who likes to rouge her nipples under her silks."

"The lovely Blanche. I'm supposed to warn him off of her, so to speak. I didn't realize he was rusticating, but without Leah to squire around, I don't suppose there's any need for him to be in Town." Nick closed his eyes and toed off his boots, then propped his feet on the low table before the sofa. "I did something stupid today, Ethan."

"If we're to imitate the Papists, the proper introduction is 'Bless me, Father, for I have sinned,'" Ethan replied. "Are you sure I'm the one you want to talk it over with? Windham is the nonjudgmental sort."

Nick smiled slightly. "Valentine can be a bloody Puritan, and I'll no doubt hear from him directly, in any case."

Ethan got up with the air of a man resigned to a long-suffering fate, and brought the decanter over to the table. When he sat, he chose the center of the couch, not touching Nick, but not as far as he could get from Nick, either.

"Tell Papa Ethan what wickedness you've been up to, though if it involves whips and blindfolds, I refuse to listen until we're halfway through this brandy."

"That would bother you?"

"No," Ethan said. "Well... maybe. I did brand your ass, you'll recall. Wouldn't want to think your early experiences gave you a taste for the unusual."

"Perish the thought." Ethan was stalling, perhaps as nervous about hearing Nick's confidences as Nick was about imparting them. "I offered Leah a white marriage."

There followed a considering sip of libation.

"So you do have a taste for flagellation. Interesting. There are professional establishments that cater to such whims, you know."

"Ethan, I'm serious."

Ethan shifted down the couch to Nick's side, bringing the decanter with him. "This has to do with Leonie, doesn't it?"

"You remember her name."

"Of course I do." Ethan propped his feet up on the low table. "How is she?"

"Sweet," Nick said, smiling at his brandy. "Dear, more lovable than any female has a right to be."

"It isn't a matter of either a wife or Leonie, Nick," Ethan replied, his voice containing a hint of sympathy.

"For me, it has to be."

"I have wandered this wicked world for the past fourteen years,

Nicholas, searching in vain for a force equal to your stubborn will. Alas, you see before you a disappointed man."

From Ethan, this was commiseration.

"We've wasted years, Ethan," Nick said quietly. "I'm sorry for that."

"Spare me." Ethan sipped his drink with exquisite indifference. "Lest I confess to the same regret."

They fell silent, though Nick considered they were making progress.

"You ought to just tell Leah about Leonie," Ethan said. "Leah's a tolerant woman and would understand. Other men have mistresses, by-blows, entire second families."

"I more or less did tell Leah." Nick doubted he'd fooled Ethan. To a brother's ears, "more or less" left acres of room for prevarication. Entire shires and counties, in fact.

"What did Leah say?"

"I hurt her feelings, offering her only appearances when she knows my caring for another prevents me from offering more." Nick frowned at his empty glass. He passed the glass to Ethan, who obligingly refilled it. "Leah didn't reject the idea of marriage to me outright, but she still might. Don't suppose you'd be interested?"

"Are you procuring for Leah now too?" Ethan asked pleasantly.

"That was mean, Ethan. Any husband will do for her. It doesn't have to be me."

"No woman should have to find herself wed to me, Nick. I have no title to pass along, and my wealth is all a product of that dreaded scourge referred to by your kind as trade. Leah is an earl's daughter, and she could do better than me."

Nick shook his head, which made the room swim a bit, though not unpleasantly. "No, she can't. Her father will not dower her, she is plagued by old scandal, and she is too formidable for the average prancing ninny in search of a sweet young thing. Leah has been through too much to sit docilely stitching samplers while her husband gambles the night away."

Ethan bumped Nick's shoulder gently. "Correct me if I'm wrong. Isn't that exactly what you've asked her to do, except—let's not forget the details—you'll be heating the sheets with your lightskirts—while Leah is stitching the night away?"

"I hate you, Ethan." Nick slouched down, sprawling against his brother . "I really do."

"Drink your brandy," Ethan said softly. "I've missed you, too."

CHAPTER SEVEN

Inbreeding being undesirable beyond a certain point in any species, Nick had agreed to exchange bulls with his neighbor, David Worthington, Viscount Fairly. While Fairly's bull was a mature gentleman content to propagate the species wherever the duty arose, Nick's bull was a strapping young fellow of four, and while not mean, Lothario was obstinately attached to the herd Nick had first put him to as a two-year-old.

Lothario was also, fortunately, attached to the man who had hand-fed him as a calf, and thus it became necessary for Nick to personally escort Lothario two country miles to Lord Fairly's estate.

Ethan had cheerfully declined his brother's invitation to share the errand.

"Something amiss?" Ethan asked as Nick slammed into the front hall looking once again harried.

"Oh, please." Nick bounded up the steps. "Aggravate me all you dare, Ethan, for there's nothing I'd like better than to pound on somebody for a bit."

"Didn't enjoy your constitutional with Lochinvar?" Ethan drawled, grinning.

"It's Lothario," Nick shot back. "And no, for your information, waltzing with a lovesick bull who's trumpeting his woes to the neighborhood is not how I'd like to spend a spring morning."

"The lovesick debutantes being so much better company?"

"At least they smell better, and when they step on my feet, they do not imperil my delicate bones."

"But you and Lothario seemed so comfortable with each other," Ethan went on blithely, because whether Nick admitted it to himself or not, he needed someone other than any old fellow to imbibe with of an evening. He needed—after all these years, still—a brother. "You and the bovine struck me as kindred spirits, hail fellow, well met, and all that."

"Bugger off, Ethan." Nick glowered as they reached his room. "I got a damned note from Mrs. Waverly at Blossom Court."

"And she would be?" Ethan closed the door behind them. A huge copper tub sat steaming by the hearth, and Nick began to wrench at his cravat.

"Leonie's companion," Nick bit out, scowling.

"You're knotting the cloth tighter." Ethan batted Nick's hands away. Nick never did think clearly when he was worried. "Chin up and stop glaring daggers at me. What did the note say?"

"Leonie recognized the horses Valentine and Leah rode earlier today, and she is quite out of sorts to know I am entertaining a lady here and I have not bothered to call upon her to explain."

Ethan stepped back and went to Nick's wardrobe, where he began assembling a fresh set of clothes while Nick stripped down to his skin.

"So you hadn't told Leonie you were here?"

"I'm trying to ease her into seeing less of me," Nick said, heaving a martyred sigh as he lowered himself into the water.

"Is this attempt at self-restraint because you're contemplating marriage?" Ethan brought Nick a bar of hard-milled soap and set it on the stool beside the tub. The soap smelled of sandalwood, and Ethan made a mental note to take a bar of it with him when he left.

Nick sniffed the soap and scrubbed up a lather between his hands. "Marriage has nothing to do with it. Almost nothing. I've seen less of Leonie because our father is dying, and I will soon be called upon to manage the bloody earldom, and take my bloody seat in the Lords, and live at the bloody family seat... And I am bloody whining." He fell silent and leaned back in the tub, closing his eyes on another sigh.

Ethan draped clothes over the foot of the enormous bed then drew a hassock up to the tub. Nick was not merely worried, he was overwhelmed and alone with it—also confused regarding a matter of the heart, and that last inconveniently and irrevocably resurrected all of Ethan's fraternal instincts.

"You already manage the earldom," Ethan reminded him, "and you won't have to take your bloody seat until you've put in a period of bloody mourning. You can live anywhere you please, Nicholas."

"For now," Nick agreed, not opening his eyes. "Eventually, I won't be able to spend as much time here as I'd like—hell, I can't do that now—and with Leonie, changes that do not suit her are best introduced in the smallest, least noticeable increments."

"Probably a sound strategy with any lady."

"Speaking of ladies." Nick squinted at his brother. "What are you doing for companionship these days?"

"I hardly have time to worry about it," Ethan replied, realizing he was—somewhat to his surprise— telling the truth. Well, in for a penny, in for a pound. "You're an uncle, you know."

Nick's gaze whipped to Ethan, who sat on his hassock, examining his hands.

"You have a child?"

"A couple of little boys," Ethan said, still studying the same hands he'd had for more than thirty years. "They live at Tydings, raising hell, climbing out their bedroom window, harassing the daylights out of their tutors."

"And when," Nick asked quietly, "did you plan to introduce me to my nephews?"

Ethan rose from the hassock and paced off to gather up the clothing Nick had cast to the compass points. "I hadn't really planned on it."

"I suppose you haven't told Bellefonte he is a grandfather twice over?" Nick sounded angry, but Ethan could hear the bewilderment beneath the indignation.

"I did not tell him," Ethan said, wishing Nick hadn't been so quick to spot this very oversight. "I thought I'd start by telling Lady Warne."

Nick ducked his head under the water, came up, and began lathering his hair. "Did Lady Warne get an invitation to your wedding, Brother? Doubtless, I must have misplaced mine, for I do not recall attending."

"Nick..." Ethan eyed his sibling, wondering why they were having this conversation now, when Nick was at his bath. Perhaps such a moment should have put Nick at a tactical disadvantage.

"Explain this to me, Ethan." Nick went on scrubbing his hair, his voice deceptively casual. "Even given our estrangement, you could not drop me a note? Not when you got married, not when you had your firstborn or your second?"

"How do you know I married?"

"You would not sire a bastard, much less two," Nick said, dunking again and coming up, sloshing water all around the tub.

"I did not sire bastards, but neither am I married as we speak."

"You lost a wife," Nick concluded, staring straight ahead and frowning mightily. "You did not think to inform me of this either?"

Ethan crossed the room and picked up one of the two pitchers of warm water sitting beside the tub. "Close your eyes," he ordered then poured both pitchers over Nick's hair.

Nick rose out of the tub and took the towel Ethan passed to him. "Talk to me, or so help me God, Ethan, I will start pounding on you, and pounding hard." For some reason, that Nick offered this threat while very casually naked, his every bulging muscle in plain sight, made the menace more believable.

"I had a mistress," Ethan said, running a hand through his hair, "a perfectly mundane business arrangement with a woman suited to that purpose. She conceived, and because my dealings with her were exclusive, I married her to prevent my child from being illegitimate. Once married, a second child came along directly. When Joshua was two, and Jeremiah three, their mother succumbed to typhus."

Nick scrubbed his face dry but stood for a long moment, naked and dripping all over the hearthstones while he clutched at the towel and stared at his brother's face.

"How long ago did she die?"

"Several years. Several years this summer."

"Did you love her?" Nick's tone was puzzled.

"By the time she bore the second child," Ethan said wearily, "I hated her, and she hated me."

"I'm sorry," Nick said, looking like he meant it quite sincerely. "I am not sorry you told me, though, and it goes without saying I would like to meet—I would like to *know*—my nephews. I can promise you the rest of the family will feel the same."

Ethan nodded, wishing to hell he'd kept his mouth shut, for there was a damned uncomfortable ache in his throat.

"Lady Warne doesn't know?"

"I haven't told her." Ethan lowered himself back to his hassock, the scent of sandalwood wafting around the room. "I didn't want to put her in a position of having to keep a secret from you, though she somehow got wind of my marriage."

Nick stalked over to the bed and surveyed the outfit Ethan had assembled for him. The selections were tidy, conservative, and altogether appropriate for a social call on a lady. Ethan watched as Nick transformed himself from a gloriously naked male animal into a properly clad gentleman. He finished the ensemble with a sapphire pin for his cravat, then fished a comb off his vanity tray.

"My damned hair is too long," he groused, combing the hair straight back from his face.

"You look dashing and fresh from your bath."

"Leonie likes me clean and sweet smelling," Nick muttered, regarding himself in his full-length mirror, then splashing on some scent. "I'm forgetting something."

"Your jacket." Ethan picked it up from the bed and tossed it to him.

Nick shrugged into it. "I still don't feel quite dressed."

"So stop in the garden and pick a bunch of posies. They are the perfect accessory for a gentleman with awkward explanations to concoct."

"Pick some yourself, then," Nick suggested, spearing Ethan with a look. "I can appreciate now is not the time to interrogate you regarding your sons, Ethan, but when you're ready for the telling, I want to know why you'd keep them from us for years. Bellefonte did not do right by you when you were a boy, but those children are our family, and I would not have them think otherwise. I want to know who they are, what makes them laugh, what gives them nightmares, and what they do that reminds you of us when we were their ages."

Ethan nodded, not knowing how to reply. If anybody had told him today was the day he'd tell his brother about his family, he would not have found the accusation amusing. But then, Nick was a tolerant man whose own sins were legion, at least by the lights of some people. Perhaps Nick had been the right family member to tell first.

"Ethan?" Nick's tone gentled when he paused by the door.

"Nicholas?"

"Whatever your reasons for guarding your... privacy," Nick said, "I trust they were important to you at the time, and you were thinking of your sons' best interests. As their father, that is your prerogative, and your duty. I do think, though, Bellefonte would want to know, if he doesn't already."

Ethan nodded, but the ache was back in his throat, so he let Nick leave without another word, then crossed the room to sit on Nick's great bed.

The proverbial cat was out of the bag, and the world hadn't come to an end. Nick had offered condolences, in fact. One upset female clamoring for his attention, another female trying to deny herself his attentions, and Nick himself probably both hurt and bewildered, and yet Nick's first impulse had been simply to acknowledge his brother's losses.

Ethan sat on the bed for a long time, waiting for the ache in his throat to ease and recalling the sympathy in Nick's blue eyes.

$\sim$

"WHAT CAN HE BE DOING?" Leah asked Lady Warne.

"Nicholas Haddonfield is a law unto himself," her ladyship said, pursing her lips as she joined Leah at the parlor window. "It appears he's selecting flowers for a bouquet, but why he'd include something with thorns is beyond me."

"What's the hyacinth for?" Leah asked, dreading the answer.

"Sorrow," her ladyship replied, her tone puzzled. "He's also conveying remorse, which is what the raspberry is about, affection, declarations of love, consolation, and I didn't see that last little green sprig—the one from the shrubbery tree."

"Arbutus," Leah said, thinking back to her blue salvia—*I think of you.* At least he hadn't put that in this bouquet. "What does arbutus mean?"

Lady Warne continued to visually follow Nick's progress around the gardens. "I love only thee."

Damn him. Damn him for being so attentive to a woman he'd loved long before Leah's stupid difficulties had landed at his feet.

"He has a mistress," Leah said, the words making her heart ache. "He admitted as much, and he loves her, and yet he thinks to oblige his father by making a white marriage with me."

"He thinks to protect you by marrying you," Lady Warne said, watching her grandson. "If Nicholas thinks he can sustain a white marriage, he's deluding himself."

"Why do you say that?" Lady Warne spoke with firm conviction, and her thoughts seemed to echo comments Mr. Grey had made to

Leah when they'd been out riding. Comments about marriage being fraught with opportunities for an enterprising wife, regardless of the terms her husband thought he'd struck at the outset.

"Nicholas is as lusty as a billy goat, my dear," Lady Warne said with a smile, "and he comes by that honestly. More to the point, he is not in the habit of denying himself what he desires most, and he desires you."

Leah marveled at her ladyship's indelicate speech, even as she resented the notion Nick could be reduced to the motivations of a barnyard animal.

Resented that too. "He desires her more." Much, much more. Enough to promise the woman fidelity for all the rest of his days.

"For now, perhaps, but you've known him, what, weeks? And she's been part of his life probably for years. Still, you would have the advantage, as his wife, because you will be in his life for the rest of his days—and nights."

"That is not the point," Leah said, temper fraying as outside in the garden Nick took a moment to arrange his bouquet just so, then trimmed up the end of each stem with a folding knife. "I refuse to compete with some doxy for my husband's affections. I do not want Nick to marry me out of pity, or because it's convenient for his purposes, or it's the only way I can be free of Wilton."

Lady Warne turned, planted one fist on her hip, and shook an elegant finger. "Listen to yourself, my dear. I can understand resenting a mistress, but as for the other, you are not using your head. Pride will be no comfort when Wilton's schemes have landed you in Hellerington's bed, or somewhere worse. Do you know there are men who enjoy—enormously, erotically—beating women, hurting them, making them bruise and cry and bleed?"

"My lady!" Leah was horrified to hear such ideas coming from the mouth of a refined elderly woman. Worse yet was the simple content of her ladyship's warning.

"There are still those who traffic in female slavery, as well," the marchioness went on. "Then too, men carrying diseases are a menace of a different class, and you are upset because Nick will never put you at risk of same."

One did not clap one's hands over one's ears in disrespect of one's elders. "You are trying to frighten me. I am not wrong to want my husband's respect."

"No, you are not," Lady Warne conceded as Nick sauntered out of the garden, "but Nick does respect you. If he didn't, he'd be leading you a dance, flirting up a storm as only Nick can flirt, and enticing you into his bed, as only Nick can entice."

"What do you mean?" Leah wanted to despise Nick—and call him back, finery, flowers, and all, to tell him so—though Lady Warne was suggesting she should not have that comfort.

"Nick isn't using his head either, my dear, or he'd realize you and he will be expected to dwell under the same roof for at least the period of the earl's mourning, and that will be a very long year, indeed. He'll have to bide at Belle Maison, too far from Town to make coming and going frequently easy. When he takes his seat, he'll be scrutinized from every angle, and this profligacy he's so casual about now will be frowned upon by those whose vote he might seek for this or that reason."

Leah's brows knitted as Nick disappeared from view. "You are saying he won't be able to avoid me as easily as he thinks."

"He won't be able to avoid you," Lady Warne said, "and he won't be able to indulge in many of his usual diversions."

"That doesn't mean he'll become a husband I can live with."

Lady Warne's blue eyes softened. "Love frightens most men. They come to it kicking and bellowing, all indignation and wrath to hide their confusion and the fear that they'll misstep. Women, by contrast, know little else but to seek it, and you and Nick are no different."

Seeking love came at a price in Leah's experience. "My father has never wanted me," she said. "My brothers are burdened by my situation, though they do care for me. I do not want to be simply an obligation for a husband who cannot care for me." The truth of that sentiment, the longing to be wanted and cherished by a particular, worthy man, hit with a stark pain.

"Then be useful to Nick. Run his households, grace his arm in public, be his friend, give him time, and accept what he can give you in return."

"You are asking me to be patient," Leah said, "and reasonable, and adult."

"I know this is difficult. It's difficult for me most days, and I've been practicing a great deal longer than you. Imagine how hard it would be for us were we men."

A small, hesitant smile bloomed at this sentiment, and in the place in Leah's heart that had been missing her mother for long, long years, warmth kindled. Lady Warne wrapped her in a hug, and in those moments, the horror of being Nick's countess didn't loom quite as painfully or as immutably.

Nick was just a man, as Lady Warne had pointed out. Leah would consider in the coming days if she could resign herself to marriage with him, with all the attendant frustrations—and hopes?—that might entail.

~

"TOO LATE, Nicholas Haddonfield, you've been spotted by the enemy's pickets." Leah addressed him crisply, though her tone was laced with humor, and she didn't make any move to leave her post at the kitchen's worktable.

Nick took another two steps into the dim, cozy confines of the kitchen, both relieved that Leah was speaking to him and wary that he'd been caught in a female ambush.

"I'm easily spotted, another burden of my excessive height, but nobody's firing on me yet. What brings you down here at this hour?"

"I couldn't sleep," Leah said, rising and fetching the kettle from the hob.

"Tea won't help with that." Nick reached up to a high shelf that ran around much of the kitchen. "This might."

"Brandy?"

"Brandy," Nick confirmed, getting down two glasses and pouring a healthy slosh into each one. "I'm also in search of victuals. To your health."

"And yours." Leah saluted with her glass and sipped her drink.

"Are you hungry?" Nick wrestled a wheel of cheese from the larder and then commenced plundering in search of a loaf of bread.

"I am. Just a little."

"I'll eat with you here then, while Valentine assaults our ears with his infernal finger exercises."

Nick shaved off slices of cheese then sliced bread as well. A hungry man needed meat—and Nick needed to puzzle out Leah's mood—so he put the bread and the cheese wheel away, and carved off slices from a hanging ham to add to a growing platter of food.

The season was too early for strawberries from the kitchen garden, so Nick put two Spanish oranges on the plate and grabbed two linen serviettes. After an instant's hesitation, he decided the enemy picket was in a friendly mood, so he scooted onto the bench beside her.

"I am pleased you did not flounce out of the room upon sighting me," Nick said as he passed the platter to Leah—an appetizer of honesty. "Eat, for I'll gobble up all you do not take."

More honesty, because he was famished.

"What about Lord Valentine?" she asked, arranging cheese and meat between two slices of bread. "This needs butter, my lord."

"You are my lording me," Nick said, getting back up. "Though we do need butter." He rummaged in the larder and emerged with a dish of butter, sniffing at it delicately. "I've warned my steward every year since I bought this place not to let the heifers into the upper pasture until the chives are done, but he ignores me, and we get the occasional batch of onion butter."

"This passes muster?" Leah asked, accepting the butter and a knife from him.

"It does." Nick resumed his seat on the bench beside her. "Will I pass muster?"

"Are you referring to your proposal?"

He watched while Leah put a generous amount of butter on her bread. "I am." Nick took the knife and butter from her. "You are not afraid to use enough butter so you can taste it."

"I like butter." Leah considered her sandwich while Nick built his own. "And as much as I want to be upset with you for the terms you offer, I like you too. Then too, marriage is still considered by most titled families to be a dynastic undertaking. Other things—love, passion, personal preference—are not of great moment."

They were of great moment to Nick, and yet her words nourished his hopes in a way having nothing to do with food. He studied his sandwich. "You'll have me then?"

"I'm not sure. I need a little more time to think."

Damn the luck. "That's my lady." Nick patted her hand. "If I'm offering you half measures, then you should at least make me sweat for it."

"Are you serious, teasing, or complaining?"

"I'm serious." Nick bit into his sandwich and chewed in thoughtful silence for a moment. If he were to start in complaining, he'd be at it until autumn. "If I could offer you more, Leah, I would. Or I think I would."

"Thank you, I think," Leah replied, her tone ironic. "You're prepared for the fact that I have no dowry?"

"I am." Nick felt an odd lifting in his chest. She'd meant it when she said she liked him, and whatever temper he'd put her in yesterday, she was navigating her way through it.

"If I'm not to provide you the services of a wife in truth, much less progeny, then I at least want to earn my keep."

"You don't need to earn your keep, Leah." Nick scowled over at her as she munched her sandwich. "For God's sake, you're a lady."

"How many estates do you control?"

This was not a question from a woman who intended to reject a proposal, so Nick launched into the litany, including the continental properties.

Leah grimaced. "That must keep you busy."

"Endlessly, and I hate it, but Beck is entitled to ramble around until he wants to settle down, because he has already traveled for us extensively, and George and Dolph are still at university."

"If I were your wife," Leah said slowly, "could I offer you some help with it all?"

"What kind of help is there? An avalanche of correspondence lands on my desk in English, French, Spanish, and Portuguese and it all must be dealt with posthaste if civilization is not to topple on account of my neglect."

"How is your French?"

"Spoken?" Nick shot her a leer. "Adequate for my purposes, but written? Deplorable. Spanish and Portuguese, similar."

"My French is excellent," Leah said. "You should either hire a factor on the Peninsula who can communicate in English, or hire a secretary to come in one day a week who can manage the Iberian languages, if not those and the French."

Nick paused in the assembly of a second sandwich and stared at her. Lady Warne had probably told him the same thing, though he could not recall exactly when. "Suppose I should at that."

"Hiring such a person is easy. If you mean to take your seat in the Lords, you'll need a parliamentary wife."

Which was something else Nick hadn't wanted to think about. "My stepmother excelled at that. Bellefonte would have been useless without her."

"You will never be useless," Leah scoffed, reaching for an orange. "You will enjoy the intensity of the political process."

Nick hadn't considered he might enjoy any part of it. "Not the tedium. Not that at all."

"How active was your father?" Leah asked, tearing a strip of rind from the fruit. The explosion of scent and juice had her bringing the orange to her nose for a long whiff. She closed her eyes to sniff the zest, then opened them slowly and blinked at him.

What had she asked? "My father was very active in politics," Nick said, "until he fell ill a few years ago. Will you inhale that thing or finish peeling it?"

"Maybe both." Leah smiled at him over the ripe fruit. "I can probably also be of use to you with regard to your siblings, Nicholas."

He could hardly focus on her words, so aware had he become of Leah's physical presence beside him. It was that damned orange, the way she looked when she closed her eyes, and the knowledge that under her night rail and nightgown, she was likely naked.

Her skin would bear the scent of the household's guest soap, redolent of roses and lily of the valley.

"Here." Leah passed Nick three sections of orange, stuck together. "Your disposition looks like it needs sweetening."

"I am merely tired. I need an infusion of Valentine's music to soothe me."

"He plays so well," Leah said, popping a section of orange into her mouth. "I've wondered what it feels like, to have such talent literally in your hands."

"It's in his heart too," Nick mused, watching as Leah licked orange juice from her thumb, then reached for the second orange.

"I am already a sticky mess," she said, "let me peel this one for you." She took the second orange and made short work of it, while Nick watched and tried not to let the words "sticky mess" play havoc with his brain.

When she was done, she split the entire orange in half and put each half on the empty plate, save one section. The last one, she passed to Nick, but rather than put it in his hand, she brought it directly to his lips, as if she fed large, hungry men from her own hand every evening. Nick accepted the morsel, chewed, swallowed, and kept his eyes on her as she rose to wash her hands at the sink.

Marriage to this woman would flay his wits, incessantly. "My thanks, Leah. How much longer will you need to consider the possibility of marrying me?"

"Not long. Will you speak to my father?"

"Not until I have an answer from you. I've already spoken to Amherst, and he favors the match, guardedly."

Leah's brows shot up—she had the most graceful arch to her brows. "Guardedly?"

"Your older brother is a romantic. He wants you to have a knight in shining armor, one smitten with your charms and swooning at your feet." Nick wanted her to have the very same things, which was a bad joke of divine proportions.

"Heavens. I'd settle for an occasional heartfelt sigh."

"Amherst will settle for letting me keep you safe," Nick said, noting for the first time how red her hair looked by subdued light. "I hope you do as well."

"We'll see. Can you give me a week? I'm sure you want an answer sooner rather than later, but I really do need some time."

Her tone suggested she was considering whether to add another hat to a collection already grown too large, nothing more.

"Why?" Nick, having ingested half the orange sections, sat back, and crossed his arms over his chest. "My offer will not change."

Leah dried her hands on a linen towel, briskly, as if concluding her interest in the topic of marrying him. "Mustn't be petulant, my lord. I can, however, see that your father's situation makes you impatient, and understandably so. I expect if we do become engaged, you will want to marry by special license."

"You're willing to forgo St. George's and the whole...?" Nick waved his hand in upward spirals.

"My past is scandalous," Leah replied, "and my father unwilling or unable to bother with settlements. You promised your father not a fiancée, but a wife. Then too, should something befall me while we're engaged, you'd be obliged to start hunting all over again, and there's no need for that."

"Suppose not." Watching Leah move around the kitchen in her

nightclothes, Nick abruptly wanted to get the actual wedding over and done with. She was right: the expedient course was the only sensible one.

"Good night." Leah bent and placed a lingering kiss on Nick's cheek. "My thanks for your company, Nicholas.

You'll talk Lord Valentine into playing us some lullabies?"

Lily of the valley, roses, and female warmth wafted to Nick's nose.

"I will," he managed, utterly stunned by that innocent little kiss on the cheek. Good heavens, did she have to smell so delicious when they were all alone in the damned deserted kitchen? He watched her disappear up the back steps and forcibly shifted his thoughts from the view of her retreating derriere.

~

NICK SAW his brother off to Belle Maison, and though Ethan's errand was sad, the idea that Nick would join him at the family seat in a few days was comforting. Those logistics, however, meant that Darius Lindsey would be pressed into service to escort the ladies back to Town.

Nick proposed that he and Leah call on her brother in person to request his aid.

"If you were my countess, you would acquire a passel of family," Nick said as he boosted Leah into the saddle. "I have four sisters and three more brothers besides Ethan. They are placing bets on what kind of woman I will marry."

"Bets?" Leah asked, frowning as Nick swung up onto his mare.

"Mostly the betting is divided between will she be short or will she be tall," Nick said, "but the sisters are more concerned about will she be mature or a simpering little twit from the schoolroom. Della, my youngest sister, is voting for the twit. She claims any woman of sense would not have me."

Their talk moved forward on the same lines, with Nick

describing each sibling in detail, along with stories of that brother or sister's childhood, or recent antics. He spoke lovingly of all of them, as well as about his late stepmother, hoping the picture painted with words would increase the attractiveness of his proposal to Leah.

But gradually the talk slowed, until they were ambling along in silence.

"Penny for them?" Nick asked as they approached the gate to Darius Lindsey's drive.

"Nicholas, I am not at all sure I have the fortitude to be your countess."

"Fortitude?" Nick's brow shot up. "I won't pester you for your favors, Leah."

"And that's part of the problem," she said gently. "I will want a kind of intimacy I can never have with you, and I know from experience what it's like to yearn that way."

Nick cocked his head in puzzlement, because this was female logic, and thus, a contradiction in terms. "You miss Frommer that much?"

"I miss Aaron, but mostly I feel crushing guilt for his death. I don't refer to him, though, so much as I do to being raised by a man who cannot abide me. I wanted my papa to love me, Nick, to approve of me. As far back as I can recall, I was consumed with being as good as I could be, as smart, as demure, as tidy, as quiet—whatever I could imagine him wanting me to be. I tried to excel at that. And he has never, not once, suggested he's proud of me or pleased with me. He is burdened by the fact that I draw breath."

"I see," Nick said, bringing his horse to halt. To keep Leah safe, he would have to break her heart. This was not fair to him, and it was grossly unjust to her.

"I don't know if you can see." Leah's gaze traveled over her brother's dwelling, a modest Tudor edifice some would say was too humble for an earl's spare. "I could not be what Wilton wanted, and he has grown to hate me."

"You think I'll hate you?"

"No, Nicholas," Leah said as grooms approached to take their horses. "I'm afraid I will learn to hate you."

Nick said nothing to that, as resentment was something he'd anticipated from her. Resentment not for withholding sexual intimacy, but rather because he was rescuing her from her father. Damsels with backbone, wit, heart, and dreams did not like needing rescue from their distress.

Hatred was a significant remove from resentment though, and the thought gave Nicholas pause. Leah assumed he would not be faithful, and Nick wouldn't argue her conclusion, but with her—with this whole business of acquiring a wife—he was at sea, and in too great a hurry to have the uncertainty end and the marriage get under way.

They collected Lindsey's agreement to escort the ladies back to Town two days hence, and Nick was soon riding around the curve in Lindsey's lane with Leah perched on the sedate mare at his side.

Nick paused as a noise came to them from the direction of Lindsey's stables.

"What is that?" Leah asked, patting her mare. "The horses heard it too."

"Just a child," Nick decided. "A happy child, based on the glee in that shriek."

"You know a happy child when you hear one?"

"I do. Or I know if you can't tell if it's a happy shriek, then it is, because an unhappy shriek is utterly apparent, painfully so."

"Hmm."

Nick slanted her a curious smile. "What does that mean?"

"For a man averse to siring children, you are certainly discerning about them." Leah nudged her mare into a relaxed canter, sparing Nick the effort of a reply.

Which was a good thing, because he hadn't one.

CHAPTER EIGHT

"You could stop pacing a hole in Lady Nita's carpets," Ethan suggested amiably.

"I can't help but feel I should have escorted the ladies back to London," Nick grumbled. "If Wilton means Leah harm, her brothers can offer her only limited protection."

"Wilton will not touch a hair on her head," Ethan replied, "if he thinks she's about to bring a baby earl up to scratch."

"And a particularly brawny baby earl at that," Valentine added from the piano bench. "Besides, we're going back to Town tomorrow, so sit you down and stop distracting me."

"Ethan?" Nick aimed a look at his brother. "You coming with us?"

"I am. Nita is ready to roll us up in a carpet and toss us to the tinkers."

"Your business with the earl is satisfactorily concluded?" Neither Ethan nor the earl had said a word to Nick, suggesting Ethan had been afflicted with a case of the dithers too.

"It is not. If I make plans to leave, then I'll see to it."

"You've just made plans to leave."

Ethan scowled at him. "Nicholas, you are being irksome. I'm off to see the earl, and if I don't emerge whole within the hour, fetch the surgeon and the vicar, for one of us will need same."

He sauntered off, his casual tone belying the serious nature of his errand.

Valentine watched as Nick resumed his perambulations about a parlor that was larger than most but felt no bigger than one of the loose boxes in the stable.

"What troubles you, Nicholas?"

"I wish I knew." Nick lowered himself beside Val on the piano bench. "What are you playing?"

Val shrugged. "Just notes. You may chime in, I'll stay below high G."

"Shameless." Nick sipped at his drink. "Now you are attempting to trifle with me."

"Dodging, Nickie dear," Val murmured, "prevaricating, weaseling..."

"I think I am more distracted to be away from Leah than to be away from my usual consorts. I'll want to leave early tomorrow," Nick said, rising from the bench. "You're welcome to sleep in and follow with the coach. I've no idea what time Ethan will rise, but I plan to head out at first light."

"Why?" Valentine brought his piece to a gentle close and rose from the bench, rubbing his backside with both hands. "London isn't going anywhere, and you should at least eat and rest before making a journey."

As if Nick would be able to sleep or have any interest in food. "I am to meet Leah tomorrow afternoon in the

park. She's promised me an answer to my proposal."

Val left off rubbing his delicate fundament. "Are you more concerned that she'll have you, or that she'll reject you?"

And why did Valentine choose now to focus on something other than his music? "God help me, I do not know. I simply do not know, but in my gut, I cannot like that I let her return to Town without one of us to keep an eye on her."

"Lady Warne will man the watch tower," Val reminded him, crossing to the sideboard, "and Darius and Trenton Lindsey can spike Wilton's cannon for a day or two. Speaking of Darius..."

"Yes?"

"Have you ever seen such a collection of misfits as he has staffing his estate?" Val poured a half portion of brandy into Nick's glass, and a full measure for himself. "I hadn't pegged him as the charitable sort," Val went on. "Those females on his arm suggest he's more the type to play hard and fast."

"I tried to tell him Blanche Cowell would eat him alive, but he merely laughed." Nick frowned in thought. "Not a happy laugh, either. At first I thought he was simply being foolish, but I do not take him for a fool upon closer inspection."

"Can't his brother talk sense into him?"

"Amherst is up to his ears in small children, and both brothers fret over Leah."

"Which brings the total to three," Val said, "because you fret over her too."

"I do," Nick conceded, though fret was too mild a word for the roiling panic in his gut. He was tempted to ride out with the moonrise, so intense was his unease. "I'm going upstairs to pack."

"I'll probably see you back in Town, then, because there's more I need to say to my muse tonight, and she to me, I hope." Val sat back down on the piano bench. "May I assume the hospitality of your town house is yet available to me?"

"You may," Nick assured him. "In fact, I will insist on it, if you like. Your company..."

"Yes?" Val paused and glanced over his shoulder.

"I've enjoyed your company. Even if you do make a great lot of noise at all hours."

"Love you too." Val blew him a kiss then brought his fingers crashing down on a resounding chord that heralded the introduction to some rousing Beethoven, the title of which, Nick could not for the life of him recall.

~

ETHAN WATCHED as his father was assisted into a voluminous blue velvet dressing gown. The color of the robe accented the degree to which age had leached the brilliance from the blue of the earl's eyes, and the way it hung loosely on him revealed how much weight and muscle a once-impressive man had given up.

"Will you stand there gawking," Bellefonte asked when he'd batted his manservant away, "or come sit in the light where I can pretend to see you?"

"I'll stand," Ethan said, but he moved closer, understanding that his father was constitutionally incapable of asking for consideration.

"Suit your arrogant self." The earl balanced carefully on the desk and slowly lowered himself onto his chair, landing with a soft plop and a sigh. "Now then, why have you come here, robbing me of my slumber, when we both know we'll end up yelling and wishing this might have kept for later?"

"You are running out of laters," Ethan said, trying to keep his tone brisk. "One must accommodate this inconvenience."

The earl grinned, making his drawn features look skeletal. "So accommodate, and tell me why you've come back. I know you've been lurking about the place for the past couple of days. Nita has been looking like the cat in the cream pot to have you underfoot."

"Matters between you and me need further resolution."

"You want to bellow and strut and reel with righteousness?" The earl waved a veined hand. "Well, have at it. I can't hear or see to speak of, so you'll only be wearing yourself out, but I suppose you're entitled."

"Why would I be entitled?" Ethan pressed, the injured boy in him unwilling to give up his due.

The earl met his eyes squarely. "Because, lad, I made grievous, compound mistakes with you, for which I am sorry. There, can we dispense with the tantrum now?"

Ethan lifted an eyebrow. "That is a declaration of remorse, which does not quite rise to the level of an apology, but no matter. I've a modicum of remorse of my own."

A large modicum, if there was such a thing.

"Oh?" The earl's tone was a masterpiece of indifference, but he sat slightly forward, and his eyes tracked Ethan's expression like a sinner eyed salvation.

"Oh." Ethan lowered himself into a chair opposite the desk and crossed his ankle over his knee. "Their names are Jeremiah and Joshua, and they are your grandsons, born to me and my late wife, five and six years ago."

The words started up that damnable ache in Ethan's throat. The boys would not care that the earl was old and skinny and grumpy. They would love him for the stories he told and his sly, irreverent humor.

They would have loved him.

"No matter my quarrels with you," Ethan said more quietly, "I should not have kept your only grandsons a secret from you. To do so was to commit a version of the same folly you visited on me when you sent me away."

For long, silent moments the earl said nothing, merely held his peace and kept his head down. Were he a younger man, a healthier man, Ethan knew he'd be indulging in a tantrum, roaring and reeling and making the servants shudder with his outrage.

But he was old, frail, and dying.

"I am too damned tired to rise from this chair for something as petty as a display of pique, which would impress you not one bit. Have you miniatures?" the earl asked.

Silently, Ethan passed two gold-backed miniatures across the desk, then slid a candle nearer to the center of the desk as the earl peered at the likenesses.

"You will have your hands full with these two," the earl said.

"They have your stubborn chin, Ethan, and the same light of mischief in their eyes you used to sport. Tell me about them."

When the earl ran out of energy to ask further questions, he sat back, still studying the little paintings. "I'm glad you told me. If Lady Warne or Nick knew, they kept your confidences."

"Nick did not know."

The earl nodded. "Good of you." He pushed the miniatures back across the desk, straightening with effort.

"Keep them," Ethan said, leaving unspoken what they both knew: The miniatures were a loan, to be redeemed after the earl's death.

"Believe I shall," the earl said. "And I shall extract a price for guarding them for you."

"Oh, of course." Ethan felt humor and an oddly welcome respect for his father's wiliness. "Name your price."

"Your brother informs me of his intent to ask for this Lindsey girl," the earl began, all paternal nonchalance. "Will she do?"

That Bellefonte would seek this information from Ethan was touching. That Ethan would provide it, proof the age of miracles had not entirely ended.

"I like her," Ethan said. "More to the point, she likes Nick and doesn't view him as just a means to a title. He doesn't scare her or awe her or sway her with his charm."

The earl frowned. "And Nick? Why is he choosing this one, when her past is checkered, she's not young, and he can't dazzle her with his usual weapons?"

"I think he trusts her. Trusts she will be grateful enough for his protection to keep her vows and take his interests to heart."

"So she's honorable," the earl concluded. "That will have to do, but, Ethan?"

"Sir?"

"I fear in my dotage, or perhaps in anticipation of an interview with St. Peter, I am growing difficult. I have pushed your brother mercilessly to find a bride before I die, when I myself did not marry until I was older than Nick is now."

"You were a younger son." The defense came out unbidden, though it was the simple truth.

"And Nick has three other brothers, though we can't really count on George to contribute sons to the House of Haddonfield, can we?" the earl groused. "I did not have to demand so vociferously that my heir take a bride, and now that Nick's marriage is close at hand, I am wishing Nick had chosen for himself, not for me."

And thus, the ground became boggy with conflicting loyalties. "I don't think Nick regards himself as very promising husband material. Had you not cornered him with a promise, I doubt he would have chosen any bride at all."

The earl smiled. "There is that. The boy is a damned stallion with the ladies."

"He has that reputation," Ethan said. "He's curbed his enthusiasm while he's seeking a bride."

"Maybe. Nonetheless, I want to extract the proverbial deathbed promise from you, Ethan." Never was such an endeavor so gleefully posited.

"You may try," Ethan replied coolly, knowing the earl expected no less of him.

"Resume the job I took from you in your youth."

"What job would that be?"

"Guard your brother's back. If I know him, he's charging into this marriage headlong, with all sorts of fool notions and no clear sense of the institution's proper purpose. Keep him from making a complete hash of it, would you?"

"I made worse than a hash of my own marriage, ergo, this is not a promise I feel qualified to make."

"You married the wrong woman," the earl concluded dismissively. "This Lady Leah has potential, as does Nick."

"So I'm to what?" Ethan shoved to his feet. "Serve as some sort of Cupid? A fairy godmother to my little brother in his Society marriage? You know I can't promise any such thing. Nick has more experience dealing with ladies than I will ever have."

Than Ethan ever hoped to have, come to that.

"You are simply to be his friend," the earl said, sitting back with a sigh that was the embodiment of subtle parental histrionics. "Don't let the estrangement I created keep you from each other, not when Nick will be dealing with my death, his eternally dear but squealing sisters, a new wife, and that pack of buffoons we refer to as the Lords. Nick will find a title brings with it a peculiar brand of loneliness, and he'll need you every bit as much as he did as a boy."

The earl's words held no posturing or attempt at manipulation. He was just a papa, trying to see to his children's happiness in a future they would face without him. And in truth, the earl had read both sons accurately.

"I will be Nick's devoted brother, to the extent he will allow it."

"Perishing lawyer." The earl scowled at his son with what Ethan knew damned well was affection. "Fair enough. Now go scare him and tell him I want to see him, and I don't have all night."

"Pressing engagements?"

The earl grimaced. "Wait until you are old, boy. You'll learn the tyranny of the chamber pot, see if you don't."

And now, Ethan did not want to go. Not even so far as the comfortable chambers down the hall. "I'll be leaving in the morning."

"Off to Town, no doubt," the earl said briskly.

"Would you like to be closer to the fire?"

"I would. Why don't you bring the fireplace over here?"

"That would likely be less trouble than getting you to accept assistance," Ethan muttered. "Up you go." He took his father's arm and boosted him to his feet with a hand under the opposite elbow, then kept his arm around his father's waist as the old man tottered across the room.

"There is no accurately conveying the bitter depths of the indignities that befall a proud man in old age," the earl said, pausing before the cushioned chair at the hearth. "I know I should be grateful for each day..."

"But it's a qualified gratitude," Ethan suggested. "Like many of life's blessings are qualified."

"Just so." The earl weaved a little on his feet and clutched Ethan's hand. He weaved more and reached his bony arms around Ethan's waist. "But don't worry about me, boy, and don't worry for yourself. You'll do fine in this life, and I am proud of you." He held on in Ethan's embrace with a ferocity belied by his frailness, before repeating, "You'll be fine. I know you'll be just fine."

"Guard those miniatures for me," Ethan said, carefully lowering his father to the chair.

"Oh, of course." The earl wheezed a laugh. "With my life, you may depend upon it. My very life. Now be gone, and fetch our Wee Nick."

"Good night, Papa."

The earl's lips quirked as he withdrew the miniatures from his pocket. "Good night, Son. Safe journey."

∾

NICK AND ETHAN pushed the horses, and they made Town by early afternoon, bringing the sun with them, much to Nick's relief. He declined Ethan's invitation for lunch and barely tarried in his own mews long enough to pass the reins of his mare to a groom, before taking off at a brisk pace for the park.

He would be at least an hour early for his appointment with Leah, but he needed the time to gather his thoughts. At his town house he would find correspondence to answer, bills to pay, petty squabbles to sort out between the maids and the footmen, menus to look at, invitations to sort, and God knew what other trivialities to take up his time and clutter his mind.

Leah would put him out of the misery of his uncertainty one way or another, and he needed to think.

Nick found his usual bench and settled himself upon it. His favorite duck waddled over, honked at him, and waddled away in disgust when it became apparent no food would be forthcoming. A breeze stirred the water, the swan glided by, and gradually, impression by impression, the peace of the day seeped into him.

There were nice spring days, and then there were glorious spring days. Somewhere between Kent and London, the day had turned glorious. The temperature was perfect—neither hot nor chilly, but just comfortably, agreeably right. Colors were brilliantly clear, in the flowers, the shimmery green expanses of lawn, the reflections on the pond, the greening trees. No creature could dwell in such a day without feeling blessed.

Nick's gaze fell on various aspects of his surroundings—children chasing a ball, a loose dog chasing the children, governesses in their drab attire trying to visit while keeping their eyes on their charges. He shifted to take in more of the passing scene and became aware of something not quite in harmony with the tranquility of the whole.

A woman was walking across the green from Nick's bench—though she moved too quickly, her head down, her body radiating tension. She was well dressed, but on either side of her were men garbed in the rough wool of the working class, each man with a hand clamped on the lady's upper arm.

Trouble in paradise, Nick thought, just as his mind registered what his eyes were trying to tell him:

That woman was Leah. He was on his feet, bellowing, pelting across the grass and turning all heads. Anger that Leah should be handled roughly warred with gut-clenching fear that Nick wouldn't reach her in time.

The men trying to drag Leah with them stepped up their pace, but hearing Nick's voice, she began to resist more strenuously. He reached her just at the gate nearest the street and hooked a massive arm around the neck of her closest assailant.

He would not do murder while Leah looked on, but it was a near thing.

"Don't make me break your bloody neck," Nick hissed, heaving the man away, leaving her only one escort to wrestle with. Nick clipped the second man in the jaw and sent him crashing to the walk, then turned on a third man—a simian specimen who'd come lumbering forth from the trees—trying to hustle Leah toward an unmarked town coach.

"Not bloody likely," Nick muttered just as the idiot backhanded Leah and attempted to toss her over his shoulder. Nick grabbed the brute by his shirt and walloped him in turn—right off his feet. Two more men came racing up from the coach, and Nick went into a crouch, fists raised, body slightly turned to present a smaller target.

"Leah," Nick growled, "get behind me and start screaming."

She scrambled to comply, emitting a series of ear-piercing shrieks. The reinforcements eyed Nick and the shrieking woman behind him, and stopped in their tracks.

"You get Ollie," the larger of the two said, "I'll get Sykes and hope that big bastard don't give chase."

The big bastard couldn't give chase, because he knew damned good and well Leah would be left undefended. As their attackers scrambled off and disappeared into the town coach, Nick turned to wrap his arms around Leah.

"You're safe," he said, though his own heart continued to pound. "You're safe, Leah. They're gone."

She was weeping and shaking too hard to even clutch Nick's handkerchief securely, so he scooped her up and carried her to a bench in the shade.

"They tried to take the lady's purse," Nick explained to the milling onlookers, "and were threatening her person. She'd appreciate some privacy."

It took a few minutes, but the crowd dispersed, leaving Leah sitting beside Nick, pale and weepy. He kept an arm around her shoulders, despite their public location, because he was haunted by the same thought Leah no doubt was: What if he hadn't been there? What if he'd said one more farewell this morning to his father?

Lingered over a pot of tea, hoping the clouds would lift?

Heeded Ethan's suggestion that they share luncheon before parting?

"God's hairy toes." Nick wrapped his arm more tightly around her. "I'm taking you home with me." This merited him a shaky nod of assent. "I'd like to carry you, but you'll feel better if you can walk. We'll move as slowly as you need to."

Nick stayed glued to her side, her left hand in his left, his right arm anchored snugly around her shoulders.

"Nick?" Crying had left her voice husky.

He bent his head to hear her, even as he kept them moving. "Lovey?"

"Th... thank you." A shudder passed through her, and right in the middle of the walk, Nick stopped and wrapped both arms around her again, resting his chin on the top of her head. He held her tight. She clung to him too, until he felt her breathing calm and her tremors cease.

"I'm all right now," Leah murmured against his cravat.

"I am not," Nick said, but he resumed their promenade nonetheless and felt marginally better when they'd gained the busy streets and left the open spaces of the park behind them. As he escorted Leah the several streets to his town house, his nerves did calm somewhat, coalescing into unshakeable resolve.

She would marry him, and she would be safe in his care. No other outcome was acceptable. None.

And threading through that resolve, in the aftermath of battle, was an incongruous arousal. Possessiveness played a part, as did animal excitement, but Nick's reasoning mind could barely wrestle into submission the heat under his skin and the urge to lay Leah down and cover her body with his own.

When he'd closed the door of his home solidly behind them, Nick was in no condition for Leah to plaster herself against his chest, grab him by the back of the head, and drag his mouth down to hers.

"For the love of God, Nick," she groaned against his mouth. "Please... just..."

He gathered her close, bent his body over hers, and fused his mouth to hers. She tightened the grip of her fingers in his hair, and Nick felt her breasts straining against his chest. Simmering lust exploded into the full-blown need to spend as Nick sent his tongue plunging into Leah's mouth.

"Not here," he muttered against her lips. "Not..."

Then he realized what he'd just said. Not here, *not anywhere*, for the love of God. He groaned and gentled the kiss, though the shift in intensity took torturous seconds to register with Leah. When she drew back to rest her forehead on Nick's chest, her breath was heaving in and out, and her hands were shaking again.

"I'm sorry," she whispered.

His arms settled around her gently, and he angled his body slightly away from hers, so the evidence of his arousal wasn't as apparent.

"I'm not," Nick countered, rueful humor in those two words. "I believe we experienced the same impulse that sends soldiers pillaging through conquered cities after a battle." He stroked his hand slowly over her hair, willing them both to calm, to find some peace and sanity. To be so close to her was absolute hell, but to let her go would be worse.

"If you will steady me," Nick teased gently, "I think I could get as far as the family parlor."

She nodded, keeping an arm around his waist even as his arm stayed across her shoulders. A startled footman met them outside the parlor. Nick ordered tea and a late lunch, and asked that the running footman be sent to him, as well as a groom. Nick dealt with the groom first, scribbling a note and directing him to make all haste to Willow-brook, the Marquess of Heathgate's estate. As the groom decamped on his appointed task, another knock sounded on the door.

Nick sent the runner off to the fashionable address of investigator Benjamin Hazlit, and from there to the houses of Lady Warne, Darius Lindsey, and Trenton Lindsey, specific messages memorized for each. The tea tray arrived shortly thereafter, followed by a cart laden with food.

All the while, Nick stayed seated at Leah's hip. "Drink, lamb," he urged, putting a cup of tea in her hands and wrapping her cold fingers around it. "And blessed, benighted Jesus, we need ice for your jaw." He went to the door and bellowed for shaved ice, arnica, and a towel.

"You have ice?" Leah asked, though to Nick it was a curiously mundane thing to focus on.

"It's not yet May. Of course we have ice. I have Jennings's warehouse deliver it. Drink your tea, to settle my nerves if nothing else."

Leah sipped obediently, her expression disturbingly blank.

"Talk to me, lovey," Nick said, putting all the reassurance he could into his voice. "Say anything. Tell me about your journey from Kent, what you had for breakfast, what you were doing in the park so much before the appointed hour."

He reached over and stroked her back in slow, rhythmic circles. She might not have been aware of his touch for all she seemed to heed it, but touching her soothed Nick.

Leah cocked her head. "It wasn't before the appointed hour. You sent a note telling me when to meet you."

"Did you see the note?" Nick asked, his hand going still between her shoulder blades.

"I did not. William told me a boy brought it to the kitchen door, though he thought it was from Darius. But you're telling me you didn't send it?"

"I did not," Nick said, his hand moving over her back again. "Who knew you were going to the park, Leah?" His tone was curious and relaxed, but inside his skin, he felt the urge to bellow with rage. Leah's disclosure eliminated any possibility the attack had been random mischief.

"Emily knew, Darius, and my lady's maid, who reports directly to Wilton. Anybody those people talked to, you, whomever you told, and Lady Warne. I'm always strolling there. The park is the only place where I can think in peace."

"Drink your tea," Nick said, downing his at one gulp. "I cannot like this, Leah. It implies somebody in your own household colluded to have you attacked. I don't want to let you go back to Wilton's household." Her father might be behind the attack, a notion that acquainted Nick with the sensation of his blood running cold.

"I don't want to go back there."

"Leah, tell me what you're thinking."

"Those men told me that where I was going I'd be taught respect, because the rough trade was always eager for haughty bitches like me, even if I was slightly used goods."

Nick's voice was much steadier than he felt. "I want to hold you, but I also want to treat the bruise on your jaw. I'm sure there's ice and arnica waiting just outside the door, and you will bruise less and hurt less if we see to you now."

"All right."

"There's my lady." Nick gave her an approving nod—though she wasn't his lady, wasn't his anything, yet—and rose to fetch the ice. "If you'd sit on the table? You are lucky," Nick said as he hunkered before her a moment later. He had the towel over his shoulder, the bowl of ice in his hand. "This could have easily laid you open."

He blotted some cold water on a corner of the towel and dabbed carefully at her chin. "You will be sore. The bruise is rising from here"—he grazed the point of her chin with his finger—"to here, and then back along your jaw to here."

"Soft food," Leah said. "Soups, fresh bread and butter, and willow-bark tea for the ache."

"And ice," Nick reminded her, gently applying the freezing towel to her jaw. He rose and stood beside her so she could lean against his hip while he held the ice against her face. "I am sorry," Nick said. "So sorry, Leah."

"You didn't cause this."

"We will find out who did. That's a promise."

A knock on the door interrupted his assurances but didn't move Nick from his post. "Enter."

Benjamin Hazlit walked in, taking in the scene with a frown. "I beg your pardon, Reston." His dark gaze shifted to Leah. "Lady Leah, I presume?"

"Hazlit." Nick didn't move away from Leah. "I am pleased to see you."

Hazlit smiled sardonically. "And astonished, no doubt. While I will invariably ignore a summons, I will honor the occasional request, particularly when violence to innocent ladies is involved. How are you, my lady?"

"I have all of one bruise," Leah reported. "Nicholas, would you introduce us?"

"My apologies." He would have danced on his head and spit pennies had she asked it, though how the civilities would add to the situation, he did not know. "Lady Leah Lindsey, may I make known to you the Honorable Benjamin Hazlit. Hazlit, Lady Leah."

"A pleasure." Hazlit bowed. "Even under the circumstances."

"Likewise."

"I took the liberty of intruding on Reston's home because I wanted to discuss matters before your memory of them has faded." He glanced at Nick, who gave tacit assent to an interview. "May I be seated?"

"Of course. Nick?"

"Five more minutes," Nick replied, moving the ice a little against her jaw as he glanced at the clock. "Help yourself to tea, Hazlit, and we ordered a late lunch, but the lady wasn't equal to that challenge. It will go to waste otherwise, and I've graced your table often enough."

"My breakfast table," Hazlit allowed, pouring himself tea. "Lady Leah? Can you tell me what happened?"

He let her get through one telling of the entire story, addressing her need to put the sorry business into words, then he went back and began to color in the gaps: Did her attackers have any accent? Did she notice any particular scents? Did they address each other as familiars or by name?

On and on he questioned, drawing from her things she no doubt hadn't realized she knew. He'd begun making notes, and somewhere during the interview, Nick had brought a rocking chair for Leah and lowered himself to the arm of the sofa so he didn't quite sit beside her but remained propped near at hand, keeping silent watch.

In truth, Hazlit's arrival was an unlooked-for blessing, because his calm, methodical questioning was creating results Nick, in his anger and upset, could not have.

"And what did you see of the coach?"

"Was there a tiger holding the leaders?"

"Were the wheels painted any particular color?" Hazlit went on in the same fashion then shifted to put his questions to Nick, who was surprised at what he knew but hadn't been aware of: How tall the men had been, their ages, the color of their clothing, hair, eyes. The type of boots they'd worn, the color and condition of the horses pulling the unmarked coach.

"So what do you think, Hazlit?" Nick asked almost two hours later.

"These were not common ruffians," Hazlit said. "Not just fellows hired for a morning's lark. You're dealing with somebody of means, who can keep a matched team of decent coach horses, frequent the more expensive houses of vice enough to know which ones are procuring, and use not just two, but five men to subdue a single woman."

"Wilton," Nick hazarded. "Or Hellerington."

"We'll start there," Hazlit agreed, "and it shouldn't be hard to find somebody who knows something, then too..."

"Yes?" Leah prompted.

"I always have eyes watching the park," Hazlit said. "A great deal goes on there, right under the nose of Polite Society, that you wouldn't suspect. Lovers meet, illicit notes are passed, purses snatched, crimes negotiated, blackmail payments made. The park is a busy place and worth keeping an eye on."

Nick regarded his discreet investigator with no little respect. "You scare me, and I'm glad you're not my enemy."

Hazlit looked Nick up and down. "I'm glad we are not competing for the favors of the lady, for I rather enjoy having my teeth and the ability to walk upright. I'll report back as soon as I know something. Lady Leah." When he'd bowed his farewell to her and left them alone, Nick hunkered on the low table and faced her, his splayed legs falling outside of hers.

"He's a useful fellow to know," Nick said, "and I like him."

"I did too, but I think you have the right of it. His enemies had better run fast and far, and hide well."

"You want to run and hide too," Nick said. "Why? I want only to keep you safe."

"I had planned to refuse your proposal today." She smoothed the pleats of her walking dress down but could not hide the slight tremor in her hand. "I want a real marriage, Nick, not some polite caricature of the institution. I want all the foolish, romantic, impractical things I realized five years ago could not ever be mine."

"They aren't foolish, and you deserve them."

Nick could be patient and reasonable, despite the panic Leah's words set off, because she'd used the past tense in a conditional sense. She *had planned* to refuse his proposal, and this alone gave him the resolve to keep his wayward embraces to himself.

Still, he had to be sure. "You had planned to refuse me," he said, "but you won't now—will you?"

CHAPTER NINE

"My lord." Nick's butler tapped on the door but did not open it. "Lord Amherst and the Honorable Mr. Darius Lindsey, come to call."

About damned time. "You aren't going anywhere," Nick said. "I will not have it, and you don't want to go. Leave your brothers to me."

Leah said nothing, and then Trenton and Darius Lindsey joined them in the library.

"Gentlemen," Nick offered in greeting.

"Leah." Darius held out his arms to her, and Leah was in his embrace in two quick strides.

"My sister has a bruise on her jaw," Amherst said with quiet menace. "Leah, tell us you're well, save for that."

"I'm well enough," Leah managed, though her words were muffled against Darius's coat. "It's only a bruise, and I'm otherwise fine, now, but oh, Trent..."

Before she could start crying again, and reduced three grown men to blithering imbecility, Nick summarized the events of the afternoon, the threats made to Leah, and the steps he'd already taken to track down the culprit.

"Leah and I had made arrangements to meet in the park at three of the clock." The day was temperate, but Nick had had a fire lit. He stabbed at it with a wrought-iron poker as he spoke. "Wilton's footman told Leah a note had been delivered to the kitchen, asking her to come to the park at two, though the note was not signed. Had I not gone to the park quite early to enjoy the day, this kidnapping might well have been successful."

He crossed the room and passed a brandy to Leah, making sure their fingers brushed. Her hand was ice cold, but her eyes lacked the bruised, wary look they'd had two hours ago.

"That doesn't prove Wilton's involved," Amherst observed, sipping a brandy.

"It doesn't," Nick allowed, "but neither did he require that a footman attend Leah on this outing, when he has on every previous one."

Leah spoke up. "Nick is right. I was so preoccupied with my own thoughts and pressed for time to make the earlier hour, I left the house without an attendant. Though I doubt a single footman would have been a match for five brutes intent on mischief."

"I suppose we must wait to hear more from your investigator," Amherst concluded, "but Leah can stay with me until we have some further word. Even Wilton would not object to her spending some time with my children."

The look of relief on Leah's face sliced at Nick's composure. He told himself her brothers were not kidnappers, and yet the fire received another assault with the poker.

"I cannot permit that," Nick said, "for several reasons. First, if somebody means Leah harm, then you are bringing that danger to a household with small children. Second, Wilton's guilt is not something you want to see objectively, my lord, and nobody can blame you for trying to think the best of your father. Third, both in my considerable person and in the bachelor nature of my household, I have more strong arms and hard heads with which to protect the lady."

"That is logical, Trent," Darius said. "Wilton makes a bitter enemy, as I well know. You and I can't afford to antagonize him, and Reston can. I don't like it, but I like even less what would have happened to Leah had Reston not been with her this afternoon. Then too, from my perspective, Hellerington is sniffing around Leah's skirts because Wilton encouraged it, and to that extent, Wilton is complicit in this mischief if Hellerington is behind it."

"What do you mean 'if'?" Nick pressed.

Darius shrugged. "Frommer's family might have learned Leah was to make a match, and taken steps to obstruct the marriage. Wilton might have made an enemy who seeks to take from him his most saleable asset and make him look like the miserable excuse for a father he is. Leah might have offended somebody who thought to set her cap for you, Reston. Desperate women are a force to be reckoned with, occasionally a deadly force."

Nick recalled Leah's comment that younger sons tended to shrewdness. "I will pass these thoughts on to my investigator. You make sense, Lindsey, though I wish you didn't."

Darius drew Leah against him, pressing his lips to her temple and closing his eyes. "If anything had happened to you, Leah, I don't know how I would have gone on. You'll stay with Reston? He'll have Lady Warne here in no time, I'm guessing, and it won't be forever."

"I will stay here," Leah said, "with Nick and Lady Warne."

"What do we tell Wilton?" Darius asked, turning Leah loose.

"I sent him a note," Nick said, "telling him Leah had run into Lady Warne in the park and would be taking a late tea with her."

"Believable," Amherst said, "so why not throw Wilton off the scent further by sending another note saying she's with me, visiting the children for a day or two?"

"That will serve," Nick agreed, though he could see that matters were moving too quickly from Leah's perspective. He was not kidnapping her. He was keeping her safe. "Leah, can you live with this plan?"

"I can live with it," Leah said, "but then what? I can't hide here forever."

"Let's handle this one day at a time," Nick suggested. "We are all tired, upset, and flustered. Gentlemen, can I offer you sustenance?"

"I think not," Amherst said. "I've seen with my own eyes that Leah is safe, and we've made interim arrangements. If Leah might be visiting me later in the week, I'd best return home and alert the staff."

"I'll take my leave too," Darius said, "and go about my usual haunts this evening. There's always talk, and I can listen for it in a few low places that might yield some useful information."

After Leah's brothers had hugged her tightly, Nick walked them to the front door, though leaving his intended alone for even those few minutes flayed his nerves.

"No brooding," Nick chided when he returned to the library. "Talk to me, lovey. Tell me what's on your mind."

"I am upset," Leah said, getting up to pace. "I am not keen on being alone, but I don't want anybody to hover. I feel angry, but also tainted, and I am tired, Nicholas—tired to my soul—of feeling like an embarrassment, a useless, shameful appendage to my family. My brothers don't know what to do with me, society doesn't know what to do with me, and my father's plans for me don't bear mention."

"And then there's me," Nick added, sensing the direction of her ire. "I want to marry you, but only by half measures."

She crossed her arms. "You mean to give me refuge from what my life has become, but it doesn't feel like that, Nick. I wish it did, but it doesn't."

He wished it did too, but the only thing he knew to do—take her in his arms and kiss her witless—was a direct road to disaster.

"I will order you a bath," Nick decided, rising, "and send you up a tray, from which, Leah Lindsey, you will eat something. Valentine will be here soon, and he will play you lullabies before I send him elsewhere, and when I've set a few more wheels in motion, you and I will talk."

He waited for her to protest, but she dropped her arms. "A soaking bath would be appreciated."

"If you want me, you need only ring, or just yell. I won't go out again tonight."

He gave her another up-and-down look, assessing and weighing what he saw. "Come. I'll take you to your room and show you where Lady Warne will be staying." And he did, ensconcing her in a lovely, airy guest room, right across the hall from Lady Warne's quarters—and around a corner from Nick's own suite. "Anybody seeking to travel the corridor you and

Lady Warne are in has to pass my room. Your bath should be here in a few minutes. Turn around."

"I beg your pardon?"

"Please turn around," Nick said. "I have one very matronly housekeeper, who has retired for the day, and a cook who has likely nodded off over her sherry. I seek to unhook your gown, and then I will take my leave of you."

He did his best to look entirely sincere, maybe even a trifle testy. Leah turned around and bowed her head, offering him her nape.

The pose was erotic, at least in the estimation of certain parts of Nick's anatomy. He gave himself about two seconds to envision kissing her nape, and in those two seconds he caught her floral scent. He'd never unhooked a gown quite so quickly. While he was in the neighborhood, he made short work of her stays then stepped away.

"You'll find a vanity behind the privacy screen," he said, "and you can change there while the water is brought in. A few of Lady Warne's cast-offs are hanging on the hooks, and the maids will leave you towels and soap." He regarded her closely, fisting his hands to keep from touching her. "You'll be all right?"

She nodded, looking to him forlorn, bruised, and much in need of tenderness rather than solitude.

"Then I'll leave you for now," he said. "Soak until you pickle, and I'll come back later for further discussion."

∼

LEAH FELT Nick's absence keenly.

Nicholas Haddonfield, she realized as she finished undressing, was a toucher. He gathered information with his hands, with the embrace of his body, with his skin and his nose and his senses. He conveyed information by touch too, conveyed caring and competence.

Without his presence, Leah felt every raw edge on every nerve and emotion.

Climbing into the steaming, fragrant water helped settle her though, at least enough that she could consider her situation. Nick was coming back to her room to finish the discussion Darius and Trent had interrupted in the library. She had yet to accept Nick's proposal, and watchdog that he was, he would not rest until she had.

She scrubbed herself from head to foot, then scrubbed herself again. The day's memories would not wash away, but bathing helped put them at a slight distance. Then too, Nick's tub was nigh large enough to swim in and shaped to encourage a lady to repose at her bath, and even to close her eyes.

"Lovey." Leah heard a sound like a chair scraping. "Leah? Sweetheart? Lamb?"

She opened her eyes to find Nicholas Haddonfield looking large and concerned from his perch on a stool by the tub. His sleeves were rolled up, suggesting he'd been sitting there for more than a moment.

Gracious. "I fell asleep," she murmured—inane comment. She had sense enough not to sit up, but realized the fading bubbles provided her only so much camouflage.

Nick smiled at her with only a hint of innuendo. "As long as I'm here, shall we wash your hair? I promise not to peek, and your bubbles hide the best parts anyway."

He sounded as if he were inviting her to stroll his back gardens or take tea on the terrace. Such was the savoir faire of the man who'd proposed to her.

"For now," Leah muttered. It wasn't right, how tempting it felt to be with him under such circumstances. It should be shocking, upsetting, wrong... not reassuring, not comforting. Sitting in the warm water, seeing the concern in Nick's blue eyes, Leah realized something else: She would marry him.

"You'll have to take down my hair."

He shifted his stool to sit behind her, giving Leah a measure of privacy in which to grapple with the truth of her realization. Downstairs, she'd told herself marrying Nick was the sensible, safe course. A good match, a friendly match, one she could accommodate if she dwelled on the things Lady Warne and Ethan Grey had suggested about propinquity and happenstance.

Here in Nick's house, with him so casually at ease with a significant intimacy, accepting the notion of a white marriage with him took on bodily ramifications. They would occasionally share a bed, or at least a bedroom. She would see him in casual dishabille. He'd know when her monthly plagued her with cramps.

Nick's fingers in her hair were deft. He stacked her pins neatly on the vanity and tugged her hair down over her shoulders in long, unfettered skeins. He'd undone many a lady's coiffure. The knowledge left Leah more sad than angry.

"Down you go, lovey. All the way."

She submerged completely, a baptism of sorts into a marital reality she had yet to inform Nick she'd accepted.

"Now close your eyes," Nick instructed, "and lean back." He used both hands to lather her wet hair, taking the weight of her head in one broad palm and massaging soap into her scalp with the other. The sensations were novel, both soothing—to be cared for—and arousing—to entrust her welfare literally into his hands.

The arousing part, she'd have to learn to deal with.

"I've always liked your hair," Nick observed conversationally. "My sisters are all fair, save the youngest, and so many of the blushing little debutantes aspire to that pale-English-rose sort of beauty. On most of them, it's insipid and childish. You have color and substance. Your hair is full of fiery highlights, and it always smells lovely."

"You notice too much," Leah murmured, eyes still closed.

"Dunk." Nick's voice held a smile. To Leah's pleasure, he lathered her hair again and finished with several thorough rinses with warm water.

"My thanks." Leah sat up, blinking water out of her eyes. "I'll ring for you when I'm through."

"Not so fast." Nick rose from his stool and retrieved a bath sheet from the wardrobe. "We have matters to discuss."

"We can discuss them when I am dry and decently covered," Leah replied. If the bath water weren't cooling, though, she would have been just as happy to drift off and talk in the morning—or never. Once Nick was assured they'd be marrying, she doubted there would be any more cozy baths.

Which might be for the best, drat the man.

"Out you go, lovey." Nick averted his face and held the sheet wide. "I won't peek, if you'll recall."

He would not be nagged into leaving, and Leah was too tired to argue with him. Then too, she was hardly a blushing virgin, and he was no callow youth. She wanted him to peek, though, which made the sadness harder to ignore.

"Close your eyes, Nicholas."

He did, and she rose, stepping carefully from the tub, and backing into the bath sheet to wrap it around her. Nick's arms finished the task, enfolding her in clean, soft toweling and his fleeting embrace.

That simple hug had been nice—also heart wrenching.

"I'll hang your robe behind the screen," Nick said. "When you're decent, I'll start on your hair."

"There's no need for that."

"Can't have you taking a chill," he replied, the soul of equanimity. He probably bathed women regularly, the wretch. When Leah had retreated to the screen, Nick bellowed for the footmen to remove the bath, and by the time Leah emerged, it was gone.

And Nick was sitting on her bed.

Maybe her husband-to-be had a cruel streak? "Why are you still here, Nicholas?"

"Because we need to talk, lovey." Nick's tone had lost its teasing quality, and Leah knew a sinking dread in the pit of her stomach.

"I'm too tired for this," she said, crossing to the bureau and retrieving a brush.

Nick rose and padded across the room to her. "And yet we do need to have a very personal conversation, Leah, and sooner rather than later. I would spare you this if I could, but soon Lady Warne will arrive, and until such time as you are my countess, she will afford us little real privacy."

"You will bully me into marrying you," Leah said, lowering herself to the thick rug before the hearth. She arranged her robe so she could sit cross-legged, and started on her hair with the brush.

"I would never bully," Nick said, folding his long frame down behind her, "but I will attempt to persuade. No matter what scheme we concoct, Leah, you will not be safe as long as your father is in authority over you."

"He won't live forever," Leah said, giving up the brush without a fight. Nick put it aside, using a strong grip to twist lengths of her hair with toweling to wring out the moisture.

"You shouldn't brush your hair when it's wet," Nick chided. "And while your father will not live forever, he could live for a long time. Rather than coming up with schemes to buy you time, Leah, we need to discuss what about marriage to me makes the idea so objectionable." He wrung the rest of her hair to dampness with the towel, then added, "I want you to be honest."

Leah drew her knees up and rested her forehead against them. The honest truth was that she was likely to desire Nick, to harbor an attraction to him, for all the rest of her days.

"This topic is hard to even consider, Nicholas."

"All the more reason to broach it now, when we have time and privacy."

Leah's throat constricted, and a wave of homesickness washed through her—but homesickness for where? Not Wilton Acres, though the green terrain of Hampshire had seen most of her childhood years. Not the sterile, tense atmosphere of the earl's town house, and not even Italy, where she'd known some happiness and much pain. Maybe she missed her mother, but in truth, that lady's life had become so circumscribed by bitterness and disappointment, her death had been a blessing.

"I am tired of being an outsider, Nick," Leah said, raising her face from her knees. "You want to keep me at arm's length in this marriage."

"I want to keep children at arm's length," Nick replied, unwrapping the towel from her hair and taking up the brush. "Have you set your heart on children, Leah? Is that why my conditions are so unbearable?"

"One cannot set one's heart on children," Leah observed wearily. "They come, or not, as God wills." They also left, as God willed. "But yes, given my preferences, I'd present my husband with heirs."

Nick sighed mightily behind her. "I do not give one goddamn which of my nephews inherits. I love all my brothers and will be proud to call any of their sons my heir."

"Fine for you, Nick," Leah said, feeling honesty about to gallop past her common sense. "While I gain significance from what, exactly? Running into all the Society ladies you've taken to your bed in my place? Not asking where you go when you are from home night after night? Not allowing myself to drive past the house where I've been told you keep your current mistress? I watched my mother suffer torment upon torment at Wilton's hands. She went into her marriage hoping for the best, offering that man her heart. She ended up bitter, hurt, and as mean to him as he was to her. And supposedly, at one time they cared for each other."

Nick drew her hair over her shoulders in a slow, soothing caress, proof positive that some men had more courage than brains. "I can promise never to take a mistress."

"Nicholas," Leah said in weary disgust, "you said you'd never taken a mistress because you prefer variety, remember? Don't think to fence with me then ask that I, alone, be honest."

Memories of Nick plucking a sprig of arbutus jabbed at Leah's composure. Perhaps the lady was something beyond even a mistress to him.

"You don't want us to end up hating each other," Nick said, his tone aggravatingly reasonable, "and you do want to bear my children. I don't want you to hate me, either, but neither do I want to think of you naked, handcuffed to a bedpost, while some deranged old man takes a riding crop to you and beats out of you what self-respect you have."

Leah shuddered at his graphic description. There were rumors about Hellerington...

"I'm sorry. That was not helpful." Nick fell silent again, and Leah felt him dabbing at the end of a handful of hair with the brush. He was suited to the task, working his way slowly, slowly up each lock, dealing patiently with each little tangle until her hair was drying in smooth, shining waves. He'd do the same with her arguments, parse them one by one, until her resistance to his offer was obliterated.

"What would help?" Nick asked, putting the brush down and drawing Leah back against his chest. "What would make marriage to me less unattractive to you?"

Less unattractive. He did not know what he asked. Leah remained against him, holding herself away from him even as their bodies touched.

"You use the word attraction," she said, "but you don't want to be attracted to me, and you want to pretend I am not attracted to you. That is the problem in a nutshell, Nick. I need you to protect my very life. You need me merely for the sake of appearances. Our stations are unequal. In any marriage, a man and woman are of unequal station, but an earl's daughter— even under Wilton's roof—is raised to expect her consequence, her household skills, and her willingness to secure the succession can even the balance and allow her to hold her head up. Those assets allow her to expect her husband's protection, respect, and affection."

"You have those things from me," Nick said. "And I am attracted to you."

"Nicholas," Leah said with pained patience, "the first time you kissed me, you couldn't even see me. How can you be attracted to someone you can't see? And yes, I comprehend that when we are affectionate, your body responds. I am not a virgin, and I understand men are prone to such reactions. That is not the caliber of attraction I would hope for from a husband."

"You think I become aroused for just any woman?"

"You've said as much, Viscount Variety, and you can't tell me you are attracted to me in any personal way, and then tell me we won't be intimate. You are frighteningly intelligent, Nicholas, and you would not put yourself in such a position for the rest of your life, wanting what you cannot have, and yet you expect me to step gladly into such a role."

Leah was making herself upset with the extent to which she could assure herself of misery in this marriage, and yet... chained to a bedpost, naked, the sound of a riding crop slicing through the air above her...?

She would marry Nicholas Haddonfield and be grateful for the privilege.

"I did not say we would not be intimate," Nick replied, his voice a whisper against Leah's neck. "I said I would not risk conception with you."

"You split hairs, Nicholas." Leah tried to keep her voice level, but the sensation of Nick's lips grazing along her neck was infernally distracting.

"How much of a non-virgin are you?" Nick murmured, nuzzling the other side of her neck.

"I am deflowered," Leah said, and now she did shiver. "Aaron and I both considered that was exactly what Wilton was encouraging."

"So you've had one encounter?" Nick asked, his tongue lapping at the pulse near the base of her throat.

"Th... Three. What are you about, Nicholas?"

"I am making a point," Nick replied, biting her shoulder gently. "You think I do not suffer attraction to you, but I intend to convince you otherwise. Relax, Leah."

Suffer attraction to her, like a disease or an excess of drink. "This cannot be a good idea," Leah said, unsure whether she was trying to convince herself or Nick.

"It's a splendid idea," he assured her. "My best idea yet." He shifted, then scooped her up against his chest and carried her to the bed.

Just like that.

Leah had known he was strong, but gracious, to be handled like so much eiderdown... Nick sat her on the mattress at the foot of the bed and peeled the covers back, then laid her on the sheets.

"The night robe goes, Leah."

"I am not ready to go to sleep, Nicholas." Leah tried to sit up but got caught in the curling masses of her hair, and Nick's hand on her chest gently pushed her back down to the mattress.

"We won't go to sleep just yet." Nick pulled his shirt over his head and toed off his house boots. "Not if my arguments are persuasive." When he was standing beside the bed clad only in his breeches, Leah stared at his naked chest then closed her eyes.

A few moments later, she opened them again, and Nick was still standing by the bed, his chest still magnificently bare.

CHAPTER TEN

Thank you, merciful powers, Nick thought, sitting at Leah's hip and reaching forward to undo the ties of her night robe. He knew when a woman was interested, and Leah Lindsey—soon to be Haddonfield—was far more interested than she wanted to admit, maybe even to herself.

"Nicholas Haddonfield." Leah's gaze was glued to his chest. "What are you doing?"

"Unless you object, we shall be intimate," Nick replied as he divested her of the night robe. He liked the sound of his own words: He would be intimate with her, give her all manner of pleasure. "But we shall not copulate. You have my word on that."

"And if I want to *copulate?*"

Despite her bravado, Nick knew she'd never said the word aloud before, probably never heard it spoken either.

His countess was a brave woman. Nick left his hand resting on Leah's abdomen, one thin layer of cotton between his palm and her skin.

"I cannot allow it, and I will not ask it of you ere you consent to be my countess, in any case."

"You and your allowing. Can't you see that's the very thing I object to most strongly?"

His countess was also stubborn. He liked that about her too.

"You do not have enough information on which to base your decision, lovey." Nick's hand trailed down, so that his thumb brushed over the crests of her hip bones, then back up, to trace her ribs. "You see us, nodding politely when we pass on the dance floor, and that isn't how it has to be."

She watched his hand follow the same pattern, again and again, without pausing. Then, while Leah's frown had shifted to a look of bewilderment, Nick lifted her against his chest with one hand behind her back. With his free hand, he gathered her hair and collected it to one side, his fingers brushing her neck, her collarbones, and the soft curve of her shoulders.

Oh, yes, they would be intimate.

"I have tried to consider how I might be your friend." Leah fell silent, a single sentence apparently the limit of her oratory.

Nick felt a gratifying sense of progress. "I would like to be your friend too," he murmured, easing her down to the bed again. "Tell me how to do that."

"You can't," Leah said through clenched teeth. Nick trailed the backs of his fingers down her bare arm, from her shoulder to her wrist and back up again. "You are too cuddly."

Cuddly. Nobody had accused him of this quality previously. He rather liked the notion, coming from her.

"This is a problem, how?" Nick asked, stroking her arm.

"You are always touching people," Leah said in a rush. "You hug, and pet, and kiss, and clasp hands..."

"I do like to touch." Nick leaned down and brushed a kiss over Leah's forehead. He sat back up and smiled down at her in the waning firelight. She looked vaguely puzzled and disoriented. Like she was trying to recall what, exactly, had been coming out of her own mouth.

Nick smoothed her hair back and kissed her again, this time on the cheek. "You smell good," he murmured. "Like spring."

"That's another thing. You always smell delicious, better than a man should, and it isn't just your shaving soap."

"No?" She spouted the oddest, most endearing notions when she was flustered.

"No. You are clean about your person and in your habits."

"And this disqualifies me from friendship?" Nick queried, his lips landing on the unbruised side of her jaw, slowly working their way up to her cheek before he lifted back up to sitting position.

"You smell too good to be merely my friend," Leah informed him desperately. "You kiss too well, your touch is too... too..."

"Yes?" He pressed a chaste kiss to her lips and retreated one half inch. "You were saying?" Lazily, he brushed her hair back again, his gaze following the caress of his fingers.

"Kiss me, Nicholas."

"What are friends for?" Nick whispered, claiming her lips gently. He plied her with easy, relaxed strokes of his tongue, burrowing his hands under her shoulders and bracing himself on his forearms. He nibbled, he tasted, he teased until Leah's tongue entered the lists and her fingers winnowed through his hair, and her body began to shift on the bed in slow, needy undulations.

"Please, Nicholas... Yes, more..."

"Easy, lovey," Nick crooned. "We have all the time in the world." They did not. If she didn't cease moving against him, if she didn't stop touching him everywhere he'd exposed his skin, he would soon lose his wits entirely.

Leah whimpered into his mouth and half rolled to hook her leg over his hips.

"What, lovey?" Nick murmured. "Tell me."

"Come. Here." Leah's hands went dodging south, to try to encircle Nick's waist and drag him over her, but fortunately for his flagging self-restraint, she got distracted on the vast plane of his chest, delineating slabs of muscle, ribs, sternum, and... nipples.

"Easy." Nick tried to catch one of those hands as it skimmed directly over a nipple, paused, and returned for closer investigation.

Leah left off plundering his mouth long enough to gaze up at him. "Will I hurt you? Here?" Another feathery, shivery brush of her fingers.

"Never. Not ever." Though she would kill him dead, dead, dead with her explorations. He closed his eyes and waited for her to set her hands loose on him again. She used both hands, and Nick lifted a few inches to allow her free run of his chest. Kissing paused as the fascination of caressing and being caressed became too absorbing, then too frustrating.

"Nicholas, get in this bed, please."

He knew a moment's indecision—did he get under the covers with her? Try for the nightgown now? Peel off his bloody, bedamned, infernally too-tight breeches?

No, not that, because the sight of his erect cock would give her the vapors, virgin or not—and do nothing to calm the insurrection in his body. He stood, lifted the covers, and budged in as Leah obligingly shifted to the center of the bed.

"Better," she muttered, turning her face into his biceps.

"Let me hold you." Nick smiled at her shyness, having already seen enough—felt enough—to know he could coax her past that and have a wonderful time doing it, too.

"No." Leah kept her nose pressed to his arm. "I want you to..."

"You want me to what, lovey?"

"Here." Leah threaded an arm under his neck and pulled at his waistband until she conveyed her general intent. "Over me. Please."

The last was whispered against Nick's collarbone, but he heard her, oh yes, he most assuredly did. Slowly, he let her tug, pull, wiggle, and whisper him into position over her, his weight braced on his knees and forearms.

"This is where you want me?" Nick asked, crouched above her. He kissed her forehead again, needing to kiss her somewhere. Anywhere.

"For now," Leah replied, her tongue running along his jawbone. "Don't worry that you'll crush me."

"I'm tangled in your nightgown," Nick said, his frustration real. He bunched the cotton in one hand and drew it up to Leah's hips. "Lift up, Leah, it's coming off."

"But then I'll be naked."

"You'll be naked under the covers," Nick reminded her, not sure how that made things any better. "I can't see you, and I can't get tangled in your nightgown."

She lifted her hips, and the nightgown went sailing to the foot of the bed. Nick's reward for this bit of swashbuckling was to feel Leah's naked chest pressed to his, and to watch his control go careening across his mental decks like so many loose cannon.

"Kiss me, Nick," Leah ordered, her mouth seizing his.

Too late, Nick realized he was in bed with that most voracious and fascinating of creatures, the near-virgin. Leah had lost her reputation when she'd run off with Frommer, but she had by no means appeased her curiosity. She was already deemed lost to propriety, and she'd been royally cheated of the pleasures such a sacrifice should have gained her. She was bent on making up for lost time, and Nick was the lucky, bedamned man in her bed when her passions slipped the leash.

"Leah." He lifted up then rested his cheek against her temple, caging her with his body. "We are gobbling up our pleasures. Please, may I savor you for just a bit?"

"This is as much frustration as pleasure," she said, accusation in her tone, and Nick considered she might not like that she wanted him, but she wouldn't lie about it or linger over it.

"You will be more comfortable soon," he promised, wishing the same could be said for himself as he shifted carefully to his side. "Let me touch you now. Your only job is to enjoy what I do, or tell me to stop if you don't like it."

Leah nodded against the pillows, her expression guarded and impatient.

"Close your eyes." Nick leaned over to nuzzle her neck. "And keep them closed, the better to focus on my touch." He ran his nose the length of her collarbone, and God's unmentionables, she smelled divine. "Your skin is the softest thing I've felt in ages. Every inch of you begs to be stroked, petted, nibbled, and caressed. I need more hands, the better to enjoy you."

He went on like that, half musing to himself, touching her with languid indulgence as he spoke, his tone admiring and his touch purely reverent. She was exquisite, she was passionate, and she was his to pleasure and protect.

Truly, truly, seducing his countess was his very best idea ever.

∼

THIS IS *how he does it*, Leah thought in some detached portion of her mind. This is how Nick Haddonfield charms his way into any woman's bed, offering her all the pretty words and pleasurable touches she's always craved, as if he could read her most secret, unacknowledged dreams or see into her heart.

He must have sensed the direction of her thoughts, because he chose then—right then—to drift his mouth down over her throat, pausing to push his tongue against the pulse at the side of her neck. He nuzzled the juncture of her neck and shoulder then curled lower against her, so his cheek rested on her sternum.

"Your breasts," he whispered, "are so lovely, so beautifully, abundantly womanly. I am aroused just looking at them, Leah, and now, you will please allow me to touch you, touch your breasts."

She'd been peeking, watching him in the dim firelight, but when he announced this intention, she closed her eyes and held her breath.

"Or maybe," Nick mused, "I'll simply taste you and indulge one of my most fervent wishes." He let several beats of silence go by, looking at her, no doubt, and then Leah felt a little warm flick against her nipple. The sensation returned, soft, wet, warm, and then cool. Her hands threaded through his hair, and without her intending it, Leah's back arched, and she offered herself to his mouth again.

"You like that," Nick concluded, the conclusion a little smug. "I like it too, lovey." He got down to business, settling his mouth over her nipple and introducing her to the use of a skilled tongue on a very sensitive part of a lady's body. When he finally drew on her, Leah knew the urge to clutch at him—his hair, his head, his shoulders, any part of him, just to convey her desperation.

He shifted again on the bed, crouching over her, and Leah found that helped her growing sense of restless unease. When he used his mouth on her breasts, uncomfortable feelings stirred beneath the pit of her stomach.

This was arousal; she didn't have a lot of experience with it, but recognized it, and both marveled and cringed at its intensity.

But twining through the arousal was something darker, an empty ache, a forlorn, homesick quality that was anxious, needy, and unwelcome. Having Nick once again over her, surrounding her with his weight and scent and muscle, helped with that hollow ache.

She arched up, wanting to be closer to him. The hard length of his arousal, evident through his breeches, brushed against her stomach before Nick could crouch back out of range.

"Don't do that," she muttered, her fingers going to his falls. "Let yourself touch me."

"I want to lose these breeches, but you mustn't look," Nick admonished, humor warring with sternness in his voice. "Promise me, Leah."

"You are worrying for nothing, Nicholas," Leah said, her fingers stroking over his hair. "I am not a virgin, and you have assured me we will not copulate. But if it's important to you, then I will not press you on this, particularly when my interest in lengthy discussions is not now at its greatest." She kissed his cheek, and Nick let out a sigh.

"You are hairy," she went on, her lips pressed to his throat. "Like a golden lion. I like that you are different from me."

And she wasn't done with him. He wanted intimacy, and by

heavens, she'd oblige him. "But your chest is smooth, with only a little hair on your stomach. I wonder"—Leah's tone became teasing—"if your body is as sensitive as mine." She recalled her previous interest in his nipples, only this time, she angled her body so she could get her mouth over one of his.

"I am your willing servant." No lazy seduction warmed his words. They sounded tight, bitten off.

"Take your breeches off, Nicholas. Please." Leah planted one hand on the small of his back and eased it under his waistband, a suggestion of the pleasure he'd feel were her hands anchored on his muscular fundament.

"No peeking," he admonished.

She peeked as he rolled to his back, unfastened about half the buttons on his falls, and jerked the last of his clothes from his body. They joined Leah's nightclothes at the foot of the bed, and then Nick was positioned back over her, giving her no opportunity to inspect what he was so intent on keeping from her view, the dratted man.

She would not suffer him to frustrate her curiosity entirely. "Closer, Nicholas, let me feel you."

Tentatively, he gave her contact with his chest then wrapped his arms around her and held her to him, a sort of static body caress that let his tremendous heat seep into Leah's joints and bones.

To be this close to him was pleasurable, to know he would not join with her was torment. The greater torment was Leah's sense that Nick hadn't been honest with her regarding his reasons for his self-enforced limits.

"So is this what you wanted?" Leah asked when Nick eased his hold and shifted off to her side. "Is this what we'll share besides a passing nod on the dance floor?"

"Not quite," Nick murmured, shifting to his side. "There's a bit more."

Leah yawned, and slid a hand down over his buttocks. She didn't come right out and tell him to be about it, though she gently squeezed a handful of taut male muscle.

"You trust me?" Nick asked, brushing the hair back from her forehead.

To break her heart and keep her safe while he did it. She squeezed him again. "In bed, I trust you."

"Spread your legs a little," Nick suggested, his hand stroking the center of her chest. "You'll be more comfortable, and please recall"— he pressed a kiss to each of her closed eyes in turn—"you are to relax and trust me and not peek."

He covered her mouth with his, and while his tongue teased at hers, that hand gently palmed the weight of each breast. He glided his fingers teasingly over her nipples, and gave her just the weight of his hand resting over her.

Leah arched up, trying to inspire Nick to greater activity, but he growled a warning and let his hand drift down over her ribs, then her stomach. He stroked his fingers over her navel, evoking surprising sensations from a place on Leah's body she had never really considered. Then he paused again, while Leah experienced the warm weight of his hand on her naked belly.

"Nicholas, must you be so...?"

"Tender?" he suggested. "Careful... deliberate... enthralled... enchanted...?"

"Aggravating." Leah landed on the word with relish, because Nick was wandering about her body as if the growing restlessness inside her were pleasurable, and to Leah, it was increasingly bothersome. Aaron had not left her feeling like this, had not taken more than a few minutes of kissing, poking, and apologizing, then heaving about and making the bed creak.

"Can't have my lady aggravated." Nick brushed the backs of his fingers over the down on Leah's mons. "Eyes closed, lovey." Nick bent his head over her breast. "Legs spread a little."

He settled his mouth over her nipple just as his hand began to stroke her thighs, and this time when he suckled, Leah growled. Behind her closed eyes, colors were dancing and surging. Her body felt similarly full of heat and color and odd, novel sensations.

When Leah felt Nick trace up the crease of her sex with a single finger, her hands found his shoulders and gripped hard.

"Easy, lovey," Nick murmured between kisses. "Move if you want to, against me."

He pushed gently against her mons, and she pushed back, slowly but not so gently. The undulation of her body eased her and made things worse, too, but she was helpless to stop as Nick's deft fingers delved gently into her folds.

"You are growing eager," Nick whispered as his fingers slipped higher. "Your body grows slick in anticipation of your pleasure."

"God above, Nicholas..." She clutched at his thick wrist and stilled his hand. "What was that?"

"What was what?" Nick didn't remove his hand.

"You touched me, and it felt like I rapped my elbow, but much, much worse."

"You'll grow accustomed to such sensations," Nick said, his words laced with amusement, "and they'll become more pleasurable if you'll be patient with them." He moved his hand again, with her fingers still circling his wrist, but this time he used a more definite pressure on the apex of her sex.

"Ye gracious gods..." Her grip loosened, but still she didn't let him go. In silence, he touched her for long, fraught moments only there, letting her focus on that one source of sensation until she was breathing heavily and moving against his hand in slow, powerful surges of her hips.

"Nicholas...?" She wet her lips with her tongue, her arousal and bewilderment ringing in his name.

"Trust me," Nick reminded her, dipping his head to brush his lips over her nipple. "Trust me and take your pleasure, Leah."

Pleasure took *her*, as tight spasms seized Leah from the inside, turning her into a thrashing, keening, mindless wanton, her nails digging into Nick's wrist, her body moving desperately to accept what he was giving her, her heart pounding with the sheer, terrifying glory of it.

"Too much..." she panted, and then Nick drew on her nipple, and the too much redoubled to be more than too much for long, shuddering moments.

When the sensations ebbed, she lay on her back, body slack, mind slack, her only thought gratitude for the comfort of Nick's hand, still pressed firmly against her sex. If he moved, if he moved even one inch, she would dissolve into fairy dust and drift away up the chimney.

He did move, but not that hand. Instead, Leah felt Nick's other arm burrow under her neck and wrap her against his chest. That brought comfort, but not as much as when Leah shifted herself more closely still, hiking a leg over Nick's hips and wrapping an arm around his waist.

She was profoundly grateful not to have to ask that he hold her. He seemed to know what she needed, and to know how to go about it, enfolding her snugly against him, but not so tightly she felt smothered.

Gradually, as the tumult in her body eased, Leah became aware of Nick's erection. It lay along her stomach now, thick, hard, and hot, a discordant note of rigidity in a soft tangle of bodies. Tentatively, Leah reached between them and brushed her fingers across the plush head of his member.

Dear God. Aaron had not at his most passionate been possessed of such dimensions. She fitted her hand over him, testing his width and length in slow, careful movements. As intimately as they were embracing, Leah felt the stillness in Nick's body, heard his sharp inhalation. She tucked her face against his chest and waited for him to dissuade her.

But he remained still, waiting, and so Leah followed the urge to explore him.

She traced her fingers over his stones then teased through the hair at the base of his shaft. When she circled his shaft with her fingers then stroked the length of him, he hissed and pushed into her hand. She repeated the stroke, and he pushed more strongly.

"Show me," she whispered. "Nicholas, I don't know how... Show me."

He wrapped his hand around hers and tactilely explained the rhythm, the grip, and the stroke, then left her to it as he held her tightly, tucking her leg up over his hip.

"Tighter," he whispered, moving more quickly. "You won't hurt me, I promise. Beelzebub's cockstand, yes, that's it..." A few more moments of that, and he gently disentangled her hand from him, so he was thrusting against her belly. Gripping her buttock, he held her to him, and in the seamless seal of their bodies, Leah felt a spreading warmth as Nick pulsed against her.

"Oh, lovey..." He tucked her head against his chest and kept her there, where she could feel his breath soughing in and out, and hear his heartbeat as it gradually slowed beneath her ear. "I hadn't meant to do that," Nick said, stroking a hand over her hair. "Are you all right?"

Leah nodded, his words striking hard against an ache that had been building in the pit of her stomach. He hadn't meant to do that? Hadn't meant to share pleasure with her, as opposed to visit it upon her unilaterally?

As desire ebbed and fatigue reasserted itself, Leah's previous sense of loneliness stirred back to life too. Except it wasn't as simple as loneliness. Her throat constricted around a sharp ache, and what she felt in that moment was desolation.

Hopelessness.

Which made no sense. She was wrapped in Nick's arms, he'd just shown her more spectacular physical pleasure than she'd known existed, and he was promising her more of that as part of her due as his wife. He had even let himself find pleasure as well.

As the first tear squeezed its way past Leah's closed eyes, she knew a despair so great that if Nick hadn't been holding her, she might have physically flown apart. This closeness Nick was willing to settle for, it wasn't enough. For all Nick's tenderness and consideration, it was without love, a subversion of the intended purpose of marriage, a parody of the union Leah had longed for.

He did this with many other women, and did more than this too.

Nick shifted carefully, bringing her over his body to sprawl on his chest. "Tell me again that you are all right, lamb."

He'd felt the heat of her tears, no doubt. Leah furtively wiped at her cheeks where she was curled against him.

"Here." Nick reached out a long arm to the nightstand and retrieved a linen handkerchief. He dabbed gently at her cheeks, then when she shifted up, mopped at their bellies.

"We're not quite spotless," he said, "but the linens are safe. Now come here, let me hold you, and tell me what bothers you."

"You mean well," Leah allowed as she eased down against him on a tired sigh. "But you can't repair my feelings, Nick. I do not believe I will be availing myself of this aspect of your marital offer."

His hands, which had started stroking her back, went still, then resumed their steady, gentle caresses.

"You are not all right," he concluded. "Talk to me, Leah." He drew the covers up over her back and wrapped his arms more securely around her. "Please, talk to me."

She wrapped herself around him, pushed the pain away from her heart, and prepared to be honest, as Nick had insisted she be.

"I bore Aaron Frommer a son."

CHAPTER ELEVEN

"I'm listening, lovey." Nick angled his head to kiss Leah's temple.

Those three words were offered in what had to be the gentlest, kindest tone Leah had ever heard, and her resolution faltered.

"Aaron was a good man," she said, "but he had not one tenth your skill with the ladies, Nick. He cared for me, though, and so I was pleased to find I carried his child. He would have been pleased as well."

Nick apparently divined the argument she was about to make. "While I can't be pleased to think my child might cost your life."

"I carried my son easily, Nick, and bore him easily as those things go. I labored but a few hours, and he was born with a perfect complement of fingers and toes."

"Where is your child now, Leah?" Nick asked, his hands moving again, more slowly than ever.

"In heaven." Leah took a shuddery breath. "He caught a fever when he was little more than a year old. I went into town to fetch the doctor, the midwife, the healer, anybody who might be able to help. My Italian was far better than my brother's, and when I returned a few hours later, my baby was gone. Darius gave me some time to grieve, but brought me back to England shortly thereafter. My mother was asking for me, and I did very much miss her."

"I am so sorry." Nick gathered her close, rolled, and blanketed her with his naked body. "I am so very, very sorry."

He stayed over her, sheltering her and holding her until Leah was holding him in return and letting tears long repressed pour forth.

She clung, and cried, and clung some more, until her grief was spent and her body too wrung out to cling anymore.

"I'll be right back." Nick kissed her nose and eased from her embrace. He brought her a glass of water, watching while she drained about a quarter of it, then helped himself as well. He set the glass aside and turned serious blue eyes on her.

"You will marry me?" he asked, expression pensive.

"I will. But there won't be any of this pleasuring, Nicholas."

"Move over." He climbed under the covers. When Leah kept to her own space, Nick flopped to his side, curled his body around hers, and wrapped her in his arms.

"You did not enjoy what we did?" he asked, his cheek resting over her temple.

"My body was very favorably impressed," Leah said, glad he could not see her face. "I've never known such sensations, Nicholas, and for that, I thank you."

"You're thanking me, and now you're willing to marry me, but you do not want to repeat the experience?"

"I do not."

"Was it... me?"

"Nicholas?"

He gathered her closer, his nose against her nape. "I've been told stallions are less vulgarly crafted than I am in my aroused state."

"God above, Nicholas." Leah glared at him over her shoulder. "You are the envy of every man, of this I can be sure, and you are the most magnificent dream of any honest woman. But in a sense, it is you that troubles me."

He huffed out a sigh against her neck. "You want more from me than pleasuring."

"I *have* more from you. You've told me I have your respect, your affection, I will have your title, and I do have your protection."

"So what does that leave? And for the love of God, don't reply that if I have to ask, you won't tell me the answer."

"I'm not sure," Leah said, and she wasn't being coy. "But whatever it is, it is important, and it was missing from this demonstration of your very impressive bedroom skills."

"And it wasn't missing with Frommer?" Nick asked, his voice betraying his frustration.

"It very likely was, but I had not the sense or the experience to know it."

She drifted off to sleep while Nick pondered in silence. As sleep tugged at his brain, Nick tried to reason out why he should take a minuscule comfort from her words.

Leah had been willing to settle for Lord Aaron, merely to escape her father.

Not quite. Nick reconsidered.

Leah had been willing to settle for Lord Aaron *on Lord Aaron's terms*. Eloping, anticipating vows, risking scandal, and more scandal with the duel with Wilton.

She was willing to marry Nick and accept his protection, but not on Nick's terms. Nick eased into his slumbers with the sure conviction that this somehow put him not merely in a different class from the sainted Lord Aaron, but in a better class.

❧

NICK WAITED in the Earl of Wilton's library, his thoughts focused on the upcoming interview with his prospective father-in-law, and on the marriage contract drafted and copied for Nick by his solicitors. He tried to mentally rehearse what needed to be said, but thoughts of Leah kept interrupting.

Dear God, she'd borne and lost a child, and lived with the secret of her grief for long, silent years.

That sorrow explained a lot, Nick reflected, as he inspected weighty tomes likely chosen for display rather than the earl's personal tastes. A mother's grief illuminated Leah's reserve, gave ballast to her sadness, and helped explain why putting up with Wilton since her return from Italy had probably been a bearable annoyance.

After losing a child, alone and in a foreign country, Wilton's petty tyranny was simply another variety of suffering. More puzzling was why Leah had bothered to survive, and where she'd found the courage to endure what she had. Nick paused on that thought, and it occurred to him that refusing to give Leah children was probably the one thing he could do to most effectively add to her pain.

Jesus on a donkey.

The stinging lash of Nick's conscience was stilled by the approach of footsteps in the corridor. Nick schooled his features to those of an anxious suitor, one who could be written off as big, slow, and harmless.

"Reston." Wilton stopped halfway across the room, forcing Nick to come to him.

"My lord." Nick returned the greeting with a bow and what he hoped was a suitably hesitant and hopeful smile.

"Shall we be seated?" Wilton gestured to a pair of padded gilt chairs Nick might easily have snapped into kindling. "The tea tray will be along presently."

Wilton was a handsome specimen. Tall, lean, and sporting a full head of white hair, about which he was probably vain. His eyes were pale blue, though something about them put Nick in mind of a hungry reptile.

"I must say, Reston, you don't waste time."

"I appreciate your directness," Nick replied, thinking a modicum of civilities would have been appreciated more. "Bellefonte is not enjoying good health, and I've made my papa a promise I intend to keep."

"Never knew your father well," Wilton mused, smiling at nothing Nick could discern, "but you have my wishes for his speedy recovery."

"Thank you, my lord." Nick let his gaze travel around the room, unwilling to launch his campaign until the tea had been brought. "You have a lovely home."

"It's comfortable," Wilton allowed dismissively. "The ancestral pile is far more grand."

"But your children and grandchildren are ensconced in Town, so you maintain a residence here."

Wilton shrugged. "Needs must. One has parliamentary obligations."

Nick had seen the barest hint of a flinch at the reference to the grandchildren, reinforcing Nick's sense the earl was prone to vanity. The tea tray arrived in decorous silence, and Wilton suggested Nick pour, which was ungracious, and a tacit way to put Nick in the female role.

So Nick took his time and made an elegant business out of it, like the docile son-in-law he would never be.

"Your note suggested you had something personal to discuss," Wilton prodded, sipping his tea and frowning.

Nick had jotted off several notes last night while waiting for Leah to complete her bath. "Urgent and personal. To be very direct, my lord, I wish to court your older daughter."

"Why?" Wilton's question was offered in such puzzled tones, Nick feared it was sincere.

"I am in immediate need of a countess. I promised my father not merely a fiancée, but a countess before his demise, and I have run out of time."

"Why Leah? You could have your pick of heiresses, debutantes, titled widows, and the rest." The question might have been from a concerned father watching out for his daughter, but the glint of condescension in Wilton's eyes suggested he was simply looking for leverage.

"I am at a disadvantage when courting a wife," Nick said, which was mostly true. "My size alone means the more diminutive women are of no interest to me, nor I to them. Then too, I have a certain reputation for trafficking with the demimonde, and protective parents would not turn a sweet young thing over to my keeping. I need a woman who is practical, and experienced enough in the ways of the world that my peccadilloes will not dismay her. She must be of suitable rank and willing to marry immediately. I believe Lady Leah meets those criteria, and we appear compatible in the ways that matter."

Wilton laughed shortly. "If you think so, I'll not dissuade you."

"You'd accept a match between us?"

"You are in a hurry, aren't you?" Wilton took a leisurely sip of his tea, pinky extended just so.

Go ahead, fool, enjoy your moment of power. "I made a promise to my father. He has been patient with me for years, but his health is precarious, and if I delay now, there will be mourning to observe."

"Are you asking for not only permission to court, but also permission to marry?"

Nick studied his hands. He wasn't quite up to making them tremble, except possibly with the need to choke the life from Wilton in the next two minutes.

"I am asking for both, if the lady will have me."

"Her wishes are of little concern to me," Wilton said, "but trouble yourself over them if you must. What terms do you have in mind?"

"Given the haste with which I make this request," Nick said, "I suggest we get down to specifics now. I might be called to Belle Maison at any moment." *Forgive me, Papa.*

"What specifics do you offer?" The earl arched an eyebrow, and Nick conceded the man had balls.

An apologetic smile was Nick's next feat of histrionics. "I believe a dowry is customary?"

"Oh, really, dear boy." Wilton let go the most irritating laugh. "You cannot expect me to *pay* to solve your little problem, not when

I've been keeping a roof over her head these many years long past her come out?"

As if Leah's brothers hadn't supported her in Italy out of their own pockets, as if she hadn't served as Wilton's unpaid housekeeper, as if Wilton hadn't begrudged her every groat...

"There are many ladies who do not find a match in their first few years in Town," Nick pointed out. "I was under the impression Mr. Darius Lindsey had taken some interest in his sister's welfare."

"A jaunt to Italy." Wilton waved a hand. "What makes you think I wasn't footing the bill for both of them?"

Offensive in every sense of the word, but the earl posed a question and therefore did not quite a lie.

"I cannot claim to have any sense of your family's personal arrangements," Nick said. "Are you suggesting Lady Leah is to have no dowry?"

"She most assuredly is not," Wilton snapped. "I am guessing, Reston, that your father's circumstances have robbed you of the natural prudence a man in your position should show. Let me speak to you as a father, though, when I tell you she forfeited her dowry years ago, when she brought scandal and shame to this family. She made her bed, so to speak, knowing full well I could not countenance the option she chose. If you want her, you're welcome to her, but you will pay for the privilege."

"I will pay?" Nick knit his brows in the expected display of consternation, and he took a long, perhaps worried-looking sip of his tea.

"You shall. You've boxed yourself in with your promise to your papa, young man, and Leah can get you out of that box, if I allow it."

Beelzebub's pizzle, the man was unnatural. "So what are your terms, my lord?"

"Your own finances are reputed to be improving, Reston." Wilton's pinkie finger was back in evidence. "If you are provided an instant countess, your funds will likely continue to grow, particularly as you take your seat and gain influence in government. For that privilege and Leah's role in it, you will compensate me a certain sum."

He named a figure, and Nick rendered in return a virtuosic display of restrained, gentlemanly dismay.

"If I provide that sum," Nick said after a suitably awkward silence, "you will approve of a marriage by special license?"

"If you provide the sum prior to the wedding, yes."

"I see." Nick nodded, and nodded again as if thinking furiously. "Well..."

"Well." Wilton rose. "Why don't you have your solicitors get to work on it, and when you have a draft of something suitable, have them send it along to mine. I really cannot spare this interview a great deal more time, my lord. Your suit will stand or fall exclusively on the basis of your ability to meet my terms."

Because Leah's happiness meant nothing to this man.

"It is fortunate," Nick said, keeping his seat, "that my solicitors, in view of my unseemly haste, have already been busy." He withdrew the sheaf of papers from his breast pocket, reached across Wilton's desk for a pen, and scribbled a figure onto the document in duplicate. "If you'd take a moment, my lord, you'll see that your terms are met herein."

Wilton resumed his seat, but not before Nick saw a flicker of surprise and avarice in the earl's eyes. Nick passed him both copies of the contract and sat back, keeping a guardedly hopeful expression on his face.

By tremendous effort of will.

"How ill is your father?" Wilton asked as he perused the contract.

"Mortally."

Wilton glanced up fleetingly, but with enough arrogance that Nick could see what the earl thought of sons who valued deathbed promises over money and freedom.

"The terms appear to be in order, Reston." Wilton sat back. "I'm impressed."

"So you'll sign that contract?"

"When you produce the required consideration, my boy. Once I sign this, she's yours, and you have what you want. I don't get what I want until you provide the funds."

"If I provide those funds, you'll sign?"

"With enthusiasm. Lady Emily deserves to have her sister away from this household before she makes her come out next year."

Nick withdrew another sheaf of papers from his breast pocket. "Then here is your consideration, my lord."

"That hardly looks like the sum you've agreed to," Wilton observed, but his voice shook a bit, enough that Nick knew the element of surprise was working in his favor.

"The contract calls for funds, as cash, drafts, or other negotiable instruments, at my discretion, provided they find their way to your hands prior to the day of the ceremony. I have here bank drafts, my lord"—Nick paused and tossed one across the desk—"in increments of a thousand pounds, some cash, some bearer bonds, and other negotiable instruments, exactly as the contract specifies."

Wilton picked up the draft and studied it. Nick tossed him another bank draft but added a sardonic arch of his eyebrow, indicating that even Nick, on bended knee, would not tolerate a gross insult to his honor.

"You have to be the most eager bridegroom to grace the kingdom in years."

"I am," Nick said as Wilton picked up a pen. "But not so fast, my lord."

Wilton dropped the pen and eyed Nick speculatively.

"We need witnesses, sir. If you can trouble yourself to share another cup of tea, I'll send around to my town house for my man, and perhaps you can provide a second witness?"

"On such short notice?"

"Very well. I can provide two witnesses. Shall you pour?"

Wilton barked for his running footman, and Nick spent a very tedious half hour drinking tepid tea with his future father-in-law. The longer the earl nattered on, the less Nick had any use for him. His conversation was a string of criticisms aimed at his older daughter, his sons, his Regent, his neighbors, the French, the Americans, and by the time he started on the Irish, Nick was ready to kiss the butler for interrupting.

"Callers, my lord," the butler said, and something about his manner, a panic behind the reserve of an upper servant, must have communicated itself to Wilton. "The Marquess of Heathgate and Lord Valentine Windham."

Wilton's eyebrows shot up, and he swung his gaze to regard Nick closely.

Good. Even a rabid fox should be able to perceive when the hounds were in full cry.

"What would Heathgate be doing lounging about your town house with a duke's son?" Wilton asked.

Nick shrugged and prepared to lie through his teeth. "They are acquaintances and probably thought to take me up in anticipation of lunch at the club. I assume they volunteered for this duty out of respect for me, and my father's expected passing. Will they do?"

"They'll do," Wilton said, the only answer he could give. To refuse men from two families that outranked his would be to offend them both, and Nick as well.

Even to Nick, though, Heathgate's presence was a surprise. The second witness arranged the previous evening would have been Valentine's older brother, Gayle, Earl of Westhaven.

"Lord Heathgate." Wilton bowed. "Lord Valentine."

Around his betters, Wilton's manners improved. He briefly, and with every appearance of respect, explained the need for witnesses, and presented the documents to his guests.

"This is a happy occasion, Reston," Heathgate remarked. Big, dark-visaged, and taciturn, the Marquess would scare small children when he was in a foul mood—and grown men as well. "You are satisfied with the terms you've struck?"

Nick permitted Heathgate his posturing, as it was all for the cause. "I am, though the earl has driven a hard bargain."

Heathgate grimaced as he glanced over the documents, no doubt seeing that the earl had in fact required coin to part with his daughter, a display of disrespect for the lady, if nothing else.

"Unusual terms. And you, Wilton? Are you satisfied with these terms? They hardly devolve to your credit."

"They devolve to my benefit," Wilton corrected him evenly. "And with all due respect, Heathgate, you need not consider the particulars of the document. Your role is to verify the parties are signing the agreement freely and voluntarily."

Heathgate's arctic-blue eyes bored into Wilton's, and Nick considered the stage had lost a talent when Gareth Alexander ascended to his title.

"You sign this freely and voluntarily?" Heathgate asked.

"I most assuredly do," Wilton said with a touch of hauteur.

"Shall I review the consideration offered?" Heathgate asked. From Wilton, that question would have been rude. From Heathgate, who was unapologetically up to his lordly elbows in trade, and whose rank was superior to Nick's and Wilton's, it was simply playing by the rules.

Wilton nodded. "If you please."

Heathgate prowled to the desk, took the stack of money and notes from Nick, and sat down, leafing through item by item, until he looked up and arched an eyebrow at Nick.

"You're short by two thousand pounds, Reston." Lovely bit of histrionics there. Wilton handed Heathgate the two bank drafts Nick had passed to him earlier.

"That completes the sum. There is here consideration in cash and commercial paper worth the total agreed to in that contract."

"I am satisfied," Wilton said, as he bent over the contract and signed both copies. Heathgate passed them to Nick, who appended his signature, followed by Valentine, then Heathgate himself. Wilton sanded both copies and passed one to Nick.

"Now then?" Wilton gave Nick an expectant look.

Nick let relief show on his face. "The ceremony will be tomorrow at Lady Warne's town house, two of the clock, sharp. I'll send my carriage for you and your younger daughter. Leah will stay with Lady Warne prior to the ceremony.""Tomorrow?" Wilton's surprise was visible. "I realize time is of the essence, Reston, but surely, you haven't anticipated your vows?"

"I will ignore that insult to my future countess."

Heathgate speared Wilton with a look. "Let me suggest that the earl and his daughter accompany me tomorrow in my town coach. My marchioness has warned me Lady Emily will be very much sought after next year, and asked that I make the young lady's acquaintance."

Wilton's eyebrow rose again, as if he weren't sure he was hearing correctly. Heathgate, after years of cutting a broad swath across Society with all manner of vice on his mind, had settled down and taken a nobody for a bride. His wealth and influence were undisputed and far-reaching, but in the years since his marriage, his marchioness had shown little interest in using hers.

Clearly calculating the enormous benefit to Lady Emily, Wilton graciously accepted and sprang the trap Heathgate had so generously set for him.

"We would be pleased to join you," Wilton replied, his smile for once devoid of malice.

"I'll call for you at half past," Heathgate said. "Reston, I believe we've an appointment at my club."

"I'll take my leave of you, my lord." Nick bowed formally, keeping his expression as grave as a young man's in anticipation of marriage should be. "We will not start the ceremony without you."

Valentine, assigned the role of the silent observer, followed Nick and Heathgate to the door. When they reached the street, Nick steered them to the park and made sure they were not being pursued.

"I'd like to visit a friend," Nick said as they ambled along the walk. "If you gentlemen wouldn't mind joining me?"

Valentine exchanged a look with the Marquess as they strolled through the park, a display of lordly pulchritude that turned the heads of the governesses and shop girls enjoying the spring day.

"Where did you get that?" Val asked, staring down at the crumpet in Nick's hand.

"Pinched it from Wilton's tea tray for my friend." They approached the duck pond, and only when they were off the path and away from prying ears, did Nick speak again. "My thanks, gentlemen, and you in particular, Heathgate. I wasn't expecting you, but you have hidden thespian tendencies."

"Wilton is an ass," Heathgate spat. "Are you sure you want to marry into that family?"

"Leah likely isn't related to him," Nick said, "but yes, I am sure, though I wish I could see the expression on dear Papa-in-law's face as we speak."

"He should be leafing through those IOUs by now," Val mused.

"Those are negotiable instruments," Nick said. "Ask any barrister, and because half of those IOUs are Wilton's personal markers, and the other half Hellerington's, I don't see how the earl can make a fuss."

"Not accepting his own vowels in payment for a debt?" Heathgate mused. "That would be a novel way to impugn one's own character."

"Are you ready for the wedding?" Val asked.

"Now that Heathgate has agreed to dragoon the doting papa," Nick said, "I believe I am. Leah and I will be well and truly wed with a half-dozen titles on hand to make the union proper and unassailably binding."

Heathgate .treated Nick to an assessing glance. "You sound pleased about that. Is this your friend?" He gestured toward the bold, dirty little duck waddling over to investigate Nick's boots.

"My friend. He chaperoned some enjoyable encounters with my future countess." Nick tossed a shower of crumbs to the duck. "I hope you both know how much I appreciate your assistance today."

"I don't mind in the least assisting," Heathgate said, "but I am off to other appointments and will see you both tomorrow."

"You will go through with this wedding," Val said when Heathgate was out of earshot. "It's happening rather quickly, Nicholas. Are you sure this is the best course?"

"Brave of you," Nick mused as they took the path circling the pond. "Trying to talk me out of this at the eleventh hour."

"So you have an hour to reconsider," Val said. "Leah can be kept safe simply by an engagement."

"She can be kept safer by a marriage," Nick retorted. "Much safer."

"From her father, but what about from you?"

"What is that supposed to mean?" Nick resisted the urge to stop dead on the walkway, grab Val by his brave, well-intended lapels, and heave him into the pond.

"You are the terror of the demimonde, Nick," Val said gently. "At least by reputation, though I know not all the talk can be true."

"Leah knows what my reputation is, and she has accepted my terms."

"For now, she likely has, but what about five years from now?"

"What is your point, Valentine?"

"You have the capacity to hurt her badly, Nicholas, and that will be unfortunate, when—not if—it happens. But Leah strikes me as a resilient woman, as most females tend to be, so that leaves me with you to worry about."

"Whatever are you prosing on about?"

"I am your friend," Val said, his gaze traveling around the lovely spring landscape. "As a friend, I am telling you that when you break her heart, you who will suffer more than she will."

"I'll suffer guilt. I'm prepared for that. Guilt and I are old acquaintances. You can't cut the swath I've cut without having some regrets, Val."

The mother of all understatements, that.

"I'm not talking about guilt, Nick." Val's smile was pained. "I am talking about having your very large and tender heart broken."

Valentine sauntered off, leaving Nick to realize his scrappy little friend was honking indignantly around his boots, demanding even the crumbs remaining in Nick's pocket.

~

"GREETINGS, LADIES." Nick walked through the parlor door, looking relaxed and pleased with himself. He kissed Lady Warne's cheek, then surprised the stuffing out of Leah by stealing a quick kiss on the lips from her.

"Shame on me." Nick smiled down at her. "But forgive me too, for I have irresistible provocation in the person of my bride. Grandmama, if you would excuse us, I have matters relating to Leah's family I would like to discuss with her."

Lady Warne wagged a finger at him. "You want to kiss her again, young man. Don't think you'll be fooling me when you do."

"Of course I want to kiss her again, just for starters, but if you don't trust me, you can leave the door open."

"As if the threat of discovery would slow you down," her ladyship huffed, letting Nick draw her to her feet. When she swept from the room, he settled beside Leah and tucked a lock of hair behind her ear.

"You are bearing up?" he asked, his gaze traveling over her profile.

"Lady Warne is good company and very generous. She truly loves you, Nicholas."

"And I love her."

"But you don't love me," Leah reminded him, standing abruptly. "I know that, Nicholas, so you don't have to pretend otherwise for the sake of appearances."

"I do care for you, Leah." He rose and wrapped his arm around her gently. "I know you don't believe me, and it would be easier on us both were it not true, but I do. You care for me as well, and I'm inclined to think caring is a better foundation for marriage than many other emotions." He rested his cheek against her hair. "Tell me about your dress."

He was cozening her. With his affection and amiability, with reason, and with his sandalwood scent. Leah told him about her dress anyway, reluctantly at first, but because she hadn't had a new gown in ages, much less one designed to make her look her best, she grew enthusiastic in the telling. Then too, Nick's big hands were tracing slow, warm patterns on her back, and then her neck. When she fell silent, he buried his hand in her hair, and urged her head against his chest, then massaged her scalp while she closed her eyes and rested against him.

He explained to her that he wanted the wedding to be unassailably proper, unlike the wedding Frommer's family had ignored after the fact. He went on to give her some of the details of the wedding contract, duly signed by the parties and witnessed by men of impeccable standing.

For a wife Nick wouldn't permit to bear him children, he'd gone to a lot of bother in a short time—a minor consolation.

"You will be quite dashing tomorrow." Leah smiled at the thought. "Knee breeches, and satin, and all the finery a gentleman is allowed."

"I will attire myself as befits a man marrying his countess," Nick said. "I don't want to give you ammunition for regrets."

"Regrets." Leah ruminated on the word. "I don't have regrets at this stage, Nicholas, so much as I have misgivings."

"You think those are unusual?" His words were those of a man who sniffed a swamp on either side of a poorly lit trail but wasn't about to back up.

"No, I suppose not. You?"

"I should tell you I have them," Nick said, "so you won't feel so alone with your doubts. In truth, I cannot admit to many, and none about you. You will be an outstanding Countess of Bellefonte, Leah, and my family will love you. Lady Warne and Ethan are much taken with you already, and Valentine has nearly threatened to steal you from me."

Honesty. He could cozen her with that too. "What doubts do you have, Nicholas?"

"I worry what I offer won't be enough for you." His hand on her nape slowed. "I can keep you safe, I am confident of that. Wilton is a bully and unlikely to trouble himself with you once you're under my protection. I saw my man of business this afternoon."

"What mischief did you get up to with your man of business?" Leah asked, allowing his maladroit change of topic. Much more of his honesty and she'd be back to doubting her ability to be his countess.

"We've sent to Italy to see about bringing little Charles home," Nick said. "The whole business will take weeks, of course, because the mails are slow and the weather uncertain, and there are documents needed all around, but the process is started."

"Ah, Nicholas." Leah buried her face against his shoulder. "And you wonder if you have appeal beyond your muscles, your charm, and your title."

He hoisted her against his chest and sat, cuddling her in his lap. Leah looped her arms around his neck, giving her more to add to her list of the myriad ways he cozened and charmed.

"Lady Warne will be scandalized at our lack of dignity, Nicholas."

"Hardly. In fact, it was she who suggested you bide here again tonight."

Leah pushed images of enormous, steamy tubs and rose-scented bubbles from her mind. "She'll chaperone, of course."

Nick shook his head. "No, she will not. We'll put your cloak on old Magda, pull the hood up, and bundle Magda into Grandmother's coach after dinner, once it's dark."

"Who's Magda?" Leah closed her eyes and felt the slow, soothing beat of Nick's heart.

"My grandmother's familiar below stairs. She's been with my family since my father's salad days. When I'm in town, Grandmother sends her here to spy on me and poach brandy from my cellar. The other servants love her stories about me, Grandmother, Bellefonte, and the rest."

"A fairy godmother. Every handsome prince needs one."

"And she's tall enough to pass for you," Nick said, "and happy to perpetrate subterfuge if it means keeping my princess safe."

Leah said nothing. The sound of his voice, the feel of his embrace, the soft, steady thump of his heart was enough to convince her she was safe.

"Sleep, lamb." Nick's lips feathered across her forehead as he gathered her more closely.

Leah let herself drift, never having had the adult experience of falling asleep in arms determined to keep her safe. It was dear, and reassuring, and at some point she would find it frustrating as well.

But not today. She simply didn't have it in her to protest this luscious pleasure today.

CHAPTER TWELVE

"What do you think of this marriage?" Trenton asked his brother. For once Darius was actually sitting, not pacing around the library like a predator held captive in a menagerie.

"I thank God for it," Darius said, accepting a glass of brandy. "That was a very bad business in the park, Trent. If Reston hadn't happened along, I hate to think what might have happened."

Trent sipped his drink and took a place beside his brother on the sofa. "If it had been just you or me, or even you and me against five determined miscreants, we would not have fared as well." The wording was intended as a sop to fraternal pride wherever it might arise.

"You can accept Reston as a brother-in-law?"

"Of course I can." Trent's lips curved up slightly. "He's devious. Got Wilton to sign a marriage contract, then paid dear Papa off with his own gambling markers. Had the Marquess of Heathgate and one of old Moreland's sons on hand to witness the settlements, all legal and binding. Dear Papa is still fuming and trying not to shout. I rather enjoyed it."

Darius smiled as well. "That's not devious. That's sheer genius on Reston's part. You have to respect a fellow who can orchestrate such doings on short notice."

"Respect him, hell, I'd kiss him on the lips at Almack's for what he's doing for our sister."

"Interesting offer. One hears many things about Reston, but not that particular penchant, and you a father of three."

"Shut your mouth, baby brother." Trent paused to yawn and crack his neck. "Speaking of penchants, when will you stop keeping the company of discontented wives and gamblers?"

"There is gain to be had in such company," Darius said, "and you of all people know I am motivated to garner coin when and where I can."

Trent fell silent upon that observation, considering his drink, his circumstances, and his little brother. "Reston might be able to help."

"It isn't Reston's problem," Darius said, but without heat.

"Leah is our sister, but she'll be his countess. I'd say that gives him an arguable interest in your situation."

"So you'd make Reston privy to the things we perpetrated years ago and haven't found a way to apprise her of since?"

Trent was silent a long time, feeling Darius shift beside him and tug off his boots. Well, good. It had been forever since Darius had spent more than an hour under Trent's roof, and Trent missed him.

Worried about him.

"It's like this, Dare." Trent leaned his head back and set his drink aside. "I have to admit what a bloody relief it is to be out from under the guilt of failing Leah, and the strain of trying to convince myself I haven't."

"Now, now," Darius said gently, "we got her to Italy, and she was reasonably content there. The talk died down, and Frommer's people were decent about it, too."

"I suppose." Decent enough to ignore a woman who'd legally become part of their family. "But back to my point."

"Your confession, rather."

"Fine, call it a confession, because that's what it is. I am relieved to pass Leah off to Reston, and I did much less for her than you did. I would like to pass the rest of our family's situation along to him as well, just not quite yet."

"I'd prefer to do that before the ceremony, not after, but I can't argue with you as strenuously as I ought," Darius said. "Leah deserves to know the truth, and like you, I want to be out from under the deceptions of the past, but we need to take Reston's measure first. Let him and Leah get used to their married state and perhaps bury the man's father."

Trent ran a hand through his hair. "Hadn't thought of that. Suppose that will be a bit of a distraction."

"Suppose. You ready for another drink?"

Trent hesitated. He was trying to moderate his drinking, which was growing steadily greater in quantity. "Half," he said, reluctant to leave his brother drinking alone.

Darius nodded, leaving Trent with the conviction Darius saw more than he let on.

Leah would hate them. There was no way on earth the truth could come out without Leah being mortally put out with both of her brothers—and that would kill Darius more quickly than any penchant for vice and debauchery.

When Darius brought the decanter over, Trent grabbed the neck of the bottle and held it above his glass until the tumbler was full to the brim.

~

LEAH DRIFTED IN A COMFORTABLE, contented fog, the rocking of the carriage and the warmth of her husband's embrace soothing her into a drowsy, post-wedding lassitude. Nick must have been dozing as well, for he'd gone silent before they'd even left Town, and as darkness had fallen, he'd kept his peace. Leah could not quite sleep, but because the seat was well upholstered and considerably deeper than any she'd seen before, she was content to doze. Her brother Darius's words of parting after the wedding breakfast kept ringing in her memory:

Reston is a damned decent man. He could love you, if you'd allow it. Really love you, not just use you to thumb his lordly nose at his indifferent papa.

Had that been the sum total of Aaron's interest in her? Leah told herself it wasn't, that Aaron had been genuinely fond of her and as considerate as a very young man could be. But Darius—damn his too-knowing brown eyes—had a valid point as well. Aaron Frommer had been fond of dramatics too, and of feeling victimized by his place as a marquess's fourth son. He had been making a play for his father's attention by riding to Leah's rescue, trying to assert his independence while proving he'd not achieved it, in truth.

She curled down onto Nick's chest more snugly, thinking this was an admission she could make to herself because Nick had married her, and married her knowing her past and accepting it.

Accepting her.

"Penny for them?" Nick's hand came through the darkness to rest on her cheek. "I'll light the lamps, if you insist."

"I'm fine without them. I was thinking you are uncharacteristically silent."

"Tired," Nick said softly, his fingers feathering over each of her features in turn. "And worried about my father."

"You felt his absence today at the wedding," Leah guessed, closing her eyes beneath Nick's explorations.

"I felt that, and his presence, his approval. He would like you, Leah. Approve of you. He will like you."

"You say that as if you're sure." Leah turned her head so Nick's fingers could wander more easily.

"I didn't realize his approval was a factor until Ethan pointed out Bellefonte would get on with you swimmingly."

"What are you doing?" Leah asked, stifling a yawn.

"Touching my wife's face. You met Magda. She's older than she looks, older than Lady Warne. Her parents lived into their nineties."

"I've never met anyone who lived so long."

"Her father lost his sight early in life," Nick went on, "and she used to tell me about him touching her mother this way. Magda said she was closer to him as a child, because he could tell her mood by the way her feet hit the stairs on their porch, by the way she came through the door, by the feel of her hand in his, or the sound of her exhalations. I've been fascinated by that, by the thought that her father knew his daughter so well."

"A blind hound often does well enough, provided he had some sighted years first."

This was a new facet to Nicholas Haddonfield, this thoughtful, quiet man with excruciatingly gentle hands. Leah tried to tell herself it was yet more of his cozening, but the notion simply wouldn't wash.

Nick's thumb brushed over her lips. "Maybe someday when I am an old, blind hound, I will know your moods by touch, sound, and instinct, Leah Haddonfield, and perhaps you shall even know mine." In the soft darkness of the spring night, Nick sounded so wistful, and his hands were so tender as they skimmed and caressed and danced across her face, she felt a lump constrict her throat.

Maybe Darius had been right, and this misbegotten union might flower into something real and lovely and permanent.

"I would like that, Husband." Leah turned her cheek into his palm and kissed the heel of his hand. "I would like, someday, to know you by instinct."

Leah drifted off, content in Nick's embrace, and did not wake up until he was hefting her into his arms and trying to extricate her from the coach without disturbing her.

"Nicholas, I can walk."

"Nonsense," Nick said, shifting as he freed her from the coach. "I will carry you over this threshold, for it's one we own. Belle Maison, thank God, is still in my father's hands."

Leah did not protest, though she wanted to. With his talk of blind fathers, dying fathers, and thresholds that "we" owned, he was looping one thread of longing after another around Leah's heart.

"My lord, *my lady*." An old fellow standing by the mounting block bowed and picked up his lantern. "Congratulations, and welcome to Clover Down. The lad will light your way."

Nick nodded his thanks as the coachmen steered their conveyance around to the carriage house and a young footman held a second lantern up to illuminate the front steps of the manor house. The butler opened the door, offered them congratulations and welcome, and was quickly waved off to bed. Leah gained her feet only when Nick had deposited her in the master bedroom, which to her surprise boasted an enormous tub of steaming, rose-scented water.

"A lookout was no doubt posted," Nick said, "and the water kept heating in the laundry until we were spotted. Your staff wants you to feel welcome."

"I most assuredly feel welcome. Perhaps you'd like to go first?"

"We can share. Because this is our wedding night, I will be your lady's maid."

Leah turned and offered him her back, thinking how odd it was, to be so casually intimate with Nick once again, and how nonchalant he seemed with the whole business.

"I feel as if I'm watching some woman who looks like me embark on her married life with a man who resembles Nicholas Haddonfield," Leah said, her back to her spouse. Nick's fingers made short work of the myriad buttons on Leah's wedding dress.

"Maybe married life, if it's to be successful, is no different from the rest of one's life, or it shouldn't be."

"This feels different," Leah decided, "but not strange." She turned, the back of her dress gaping, and lifted her hands to Nick's chin. "Hold still," she said, unfastening his sapphire pin and untying the elaborate knot in his cravat. Without pausing, she undid the buttons of his waistcoat, and then relieved him of his sleeve buttons, which also sported inset sapphires. "You do clean up well, Nicholas."

"You mustn't stop now. I am hardly ready for my bath."

He was teasing, so Leah humored him. Many married men had

no valet, and this was something she could do for him as his wife. She undid the buttons at the knees of his satin breeches and the garters to his stockings, slipped off his shoes, then took another step back. Nick reached forward, turned her by the shoulders, then eased her gown down to her hips and unlaced her stays. Leah balanced with a hand on Nick's shoulder to step out of her gown and found herself facing him in chemise and petticoat.

He smiled down at her. "Now we're getting somewhere." He knelt to deal with her stockings, garters, and slippers, then unfastened the tapes to her petticoats, gathering the entire frothy pile and dumping it on the couch that faced the hearth.

He padded barefoot across the room, and it was as if with each piece of clothing they shed, Nick became more himself and less that polite, well-dressed aristocrat she'd married hours ago.

"You are looking at me, Wife. I like that."

"You are rather hard to miss."

Nick walked right up to her and gathered her close. "I will blow out all the candles, sleep in my clothes, pledge to leave you in peace, but on our wedding night it will be expected that we share a bed. I'll sleep elsewhere if that's what you prefer."

Nick, in his boundless kindness and perceptivity, was offering her a reprieve. "Let's begin as we intend to go on," Leah said, though she could only manage that declaration with her cheek resting against Nick's chest. The fine linen of his shirt lay beneath her nose, and below that his beating heart. She pushed his shirt aside, put her ear over that heart, and listened to its steady rhythm while Nick's hands caressed her back.

"As you wish." He rested his cheek against her temple, and silence spread around them until Leah planted a tasting kiss over his heart.

"Lovey?"

"Nicholas?"

"What are you doing?"

Such a careful question. She dropped her arms from around him.

"I honestly don't know, though of this much I'm certain: I am not enamored of what passed between us earlier, when you pleasured me and I allowed it. We are to be married, though."

He remained unreadable, watching her as she visually took in the tub, the bed, the flowers in a vase on the windowsill—red roses, of course, with maidenhair and baby's breath.

"We are married," Nick said, as if picking up the conversational shuttlecock and batting it to her.

Leah had thought about this, after he'd left her aching in her bed, when she'd dressed in her wedding finery, and on the coach ride out from London. Her husband was a stubborn, independent, shrewd rogue of a man, but he was also kind and the closest thing Leah had to a friend. She hadn't been at ease with what had passed between them, but neither was she ready to toss all intimacies with him aside.

Which left only one course: "Nicholas, will you teach me what pleases you?"

~

NICK COULD NOT FORM AN ANSWER, for his mind was whirling, robbing him of coherence.

Why, why in the name of sweet, squalling baby Jesus, did his wife have to be the first woman to ask him how she might please him?

Women who were intimate with Nick were safe with him; they could take and take and take to their hearts' content, and that was how he wanted it. He'd learned, to his eternal heartache, that when he took, misery followed.

So he gave generously and skillfully, and found his pleasure that way.

He wanted to give to Leah—had planned on years of that very martyrdom—and here, she wanted to give as well.

For the first time, he experienced the subtle rejection of the pleasured by the pleasurer who would not yield to her own desires. She sought to make love *to* him, not *with* him, and the distinction made his heart shrink even as his cock began to stir.

And between bewilderment and arousal, fear licked through Nick's veins.

He would not be able to keep his distance from Leah, to offer her pleasure and companionship and the kind of fondness he offered most any woman who sought it. She would wind herself around his body, and around his heart, and he'd be reduced to begging, breaking a promise he'd made to himself on Leonie's behalf, and regretting and regretting and regretting.

God help him, if he wasn't careful he'd be falling in love with his own wife.

"Nicholas?" Leah peered up at him, concern in her pretty brown eyes. "Are you all right?"

"I will be fine, though tonight would serve us both best if we used it to get some rest," he said, his voice sharper than he intended.

Leah stepped away. "If you say so. The day has been long."

Before the hurt in her gaze had him howling on his knees for forgiveness, Nick ducked into the adjoining dressing room.

"Here." He held out a blue velvet robe, the smallest he had, though it still pooled on the floor at Leah's feet, leaving inches of hem trailing on the ground. Leah shrugged into the robe, regarding him with puzzlement.

"Thank you." She belted the robe as best she could. "Shall we to bed?"

He would rather have crawled over hot coals. "A capital notion." And worse than hot coals was the uncertainty he'd put in his wife's eyes. "The footmen will deal with the tub tomorrow."

"A cricket pitch of a bed," Leah remarked, eyeing the vast, dark, canopied wonder where Nick slept. "Do you prefer one side or the other?"

"I sleep in the middle. But we're both probably so tired we won't know we're sharing. And tomorrow night, your things will no doubt have arrived in your chambers."

"So we are not to share a bed regularly?" Her tone was perfectly casual; Nick wasn't deceived for a moment.

"Our bedrooms adjoin," he said, moving around the room to blow out candles. "I will be happy to accommodate you when you desire my attentions, Leah."

"I see." Leah's voice radiated with suppressed hurt. Nick steeled himself against it and faced her in the dim light

He would burn in hell for this day's work. Slowly, while every neglected wife in the realm jabbed at his parts with hot, rusty pitchforks.

"Shall I pleasure you now, Wife?" he asked softly.

"I think not. Fatigue is catching up to me."

"As you wish." Nick took a candelabrum down from the mantel and blew out the last of the lit candles. He cursed himself for hurting his new wife, cursed her for being so damned desirable and good and lovely and married to him. He cursed marriage as an institution and the Creator for making conception so pleasurable for the child's father, and he cursed himself again, because he hadn't seen this disaster looming.

Nick eased the robe from Leah's shoulders then accepted her chemise when she pulled it over her head. She paused for a moment, naked beside his bed, illuminated only by firelight.

"In you go," Nick said. "I could lend you a shirt, but it would likely strangle you." He did not dare pat her bottom, lest he then tackle her and doom them to further miseries.

Leah climbed on the bed, and Nick tried to recapture the admonition Val had left him with— something about Nick's heart breaking when he disappointed Leah.

"You don't sleep in a nightshirt?" Leah asked as Nick moved around to the other side of the bed.

"Typically, no," Nick said, unbelting his robe. His cock was still more than middling interested in the woman sharing his bed, and so Nick mentally cursed his simple-minded organ for good measure too. "One of the characteristics of great size is an ability to conserve heat, so I'm more comfortable without yards of nightshirt around me."

"Well, then." Leah let out a soft, gusty, unhappy sigh. "Good night, Husband. Thank you for marrying me and keeping me safe from my father."

She sounded so forlorn, Nick's chest began to hurt.

Damn it, damn it, damn it...

"Good night, Wife. Thank you for marrying me and allowing me to keep my promise to my father." And thank you, he silently went on, for even asking what pleases me. He shifted on the bed, and with one more hearty curse directed at his whole, stupid life, Nick linked his fingers through Leah's and gently squeezed.

He fell asleep like that, cock throbbing, heart aching, fingers entwined with those of the wife he would protect with his life, but whose body he would never fully know.

～

ONLY SLIGHTLY COMFORTED by the feel of Nick's fingers closed around her own, Leah struggled with her thoughts long after her husband had drifted off. What had she said; what had she done? Something had put Nick off, had shifted his mood from playful and intent on marital intimacies of some kind, to remote, annoyed, and out of sorts.

At least Nick didn't intend to torment her by sleeping beside her each night. No doubt, this initial night of sharing a bed was for the sake of appearances, to further ensure their marriage was unassailably valid. Leah eased her fingers from Nick's.

This marriage would be lonely, probably for them both. She'd be safe from Wilton, at least. But his pure, unrelenting malevolence was a simple source of pain compared to the complication that was Nick's version of wedded bliss.

Morning arrived with sunlight streaming through the bed curtains and a pervasive warmth flooding Leah's awareness. Nick's scent enveloped her, bringing with it associations of safety, affection, and... frustration. Opening her eyes, Leah examined the room where she'd spent the night. The world's largest tub in the middle of the room was the only jarring note in an otherwise elegant and luxuriously appointed bedchamber.

Nick's scent, Nick's house... Nick's *bride.*

"You're awake." Nick's voice rumbled from behind her, and Leah realized she was wrapped in his arms, tucked on her side against his chest. His lips grazed her neck, and then she felt those arms withdraw. "I've been down to the kitchen." He bounced over to the far side of the bed. "Our breakfast is being brought up. This is the smallest shirt I could find." He passed Leah a linen shirt that could have fit four of her inside it, and lifted his velvet dressing gown from the foot of the bed.

"One doesn't want to scandalize the help," Nick said, shrugging into his dressing gown while he presented Leah with a fine view of his muscular backside. "Do you need help with that shirt?"

"I can manage," Leah reported just as her head emerged from the shirt. "But if for any reason I can't locate my arms, please notify them that a search has been started."

Nick smiled and tugged the shirt down. "Arms in sight, and all is well."

Their eyes met, and Nick's unfortunate word choice reverberated in the silence.

He sat back. "About last night?"

"What about last night?" Leah tied the shirt closed at her throat, but it still dipped below her collarbone.

"I have a very clear idea how I do not want to go on with you," Nick said slowly. "But that doesn't tell me much about how we should go on, or what you'll need to be happy as my wife."

I need you. Leah wondered where that ridiculous sentiment came from. Nick was providing her safety in exchange for an untroublesome, virtually white marriage. They could be friends, eventually, if she were very determined and Nick amenable.

"What is it that you don't want?" Leah asked, but Nick's answer was preempted by the arrival of breakfast and a parade of footmen intent on draining and then removing the great round tub.

"Gentlemen." Nick raised his voice slightly. "If you could wait until my wife and I have absented ourselves from the chamber?"

"Very good, my lord." The head footman bowed and waved the other three away.

"They all wanted a peek at you," Nick groused when the room was once again devoid of servants. "Let me prepare you a plate. Cook sent up more food than Napoleon's army needed to reach Moscow."

"As much as all that?" Luscious, bacony, toasty breakfast scents assaulted her nose, and her stomach reminded her audibly that she hadn't eaten much on her wedding day.

"Eggs and toast," Nick said, "bacon, ham, butter, jam, fresh oranges, forced strawberries, kippers, sweet rolls, muffins, and what's this? A pot of chocolate for my lady, and perhaps for my lord, if my bride is willing to share. How shall you break your fast?"

He was back to being his smiling, charming, agreeable self, but something about the performance was off. For this was a performance, a very good one, in a role Nick adopted as easily as a second skin, but a performance nonetheless.

"Let's start with bacon and eggs, toast with butter, and some of that chocolate," Leah replied. "What will you have?"

"All of the above." Nick filled a plate for her, the portions generous but reasonable. "And some ham, and an orange or two, as well as the inevitable cup or three of tea."

Leah built her breakfast into a sandwich. "I take it," she began between bites, "we shared this bed last night to create the appearance of consummating the marriage?" Her tone was casual, but she had the sense it took Nick a heartbeat or so to comprehend the substance of the question.

"Just so," he said, studying the chocolate pot. "I trust my staff, but they do gossip, and Wilton can hire spies as well as the next person can. I wouldn't want Wilton using any doubts to his advantage."

"If I am asked," Leah said, pausing in her consumption of the sandwich, "I can honestly say I made love with my husband."

Nick bristled beside her, the chocolate pot returning to the tray with a sharp little clink. "Meaning?"

"Aaron Frommer assured me he was my husband in fact," Leah said. "I made love with him, or consummated the marriage, in the necessary fashion." She took a sip of her chocolate, keeping her expression placid. "I think every marriage takes some getting used to, just like the first time you ride a new horse or sail a new boat. I will not render all you've done for me pointless, Nicholas."

"Nor will I allow my efforts to keep a promise to my father be shown as an empty exercise," Nick said. "So like the good English folk we are, we will maintain appearances, but, Leah?"

She was Leah this morning, not lovey, not lamb, not sweetheart.

"I hope we can do more than that," Nick said. "I don't know how, not when the entire business of the marriage bed will be complicated, but please know I want us to be at least cordial."

"Cordial." Leah blew out a breath, hating the word. "I can manage cordial, if that's what you want."

"I think it for the best. Shall I peel you an orange?"

A cordial damned orange. Despair reached for Leah's vitals with cold, sticky fingers. The sandwich she'd eaten abruptly sat heavily in her stomach, and the chocolate less comfortably still.

"No, thank you," she said, feeling her throat constrict again. She didn't cry, as a rule, not when Wilton insulted her before guests, not when her brothers lectured her about finding a husband, not when Emily was thoughtlessly cruel in her parroting of Wilton's positions and sermons and criticisms.

She hadn't cried when her mother died, hadn't cried when her father warned her Hellerington would offer for her.

If she cried now, Nick would hold her and stroke her back gently and murmur comforting platitudes, all the while oblivious to the fact that he was breaking her heart with his very kindness.

"I suppose our dressing rooms connect?" Leah asked, her voice convincingly even.

"They do," Nick said, watching her from the corner of his eye as he buttered a slice of toast. "And you have a sitting room between your bedroom and the corridor, though I do not. I had my bedroom redesigned to encompass my sitting room as well."

Always helpful to know the architecture of one's husband's rooms.

"I think I'll be about sorting through my trunks, then." Leah tossed back the covers and threw her legs over the side of the bed. "I can't very well review the staff in your shirt."

She managed to get free of the room without facing him. The next challenge was closing two doors quietly, and then the third challenge—barely any challenge at all for her—was to sob out her heartbreak without making a single sound.

CHAPTER THIRTEEN

When Nick knocked on Leah's door, she was dressed, thank the gods, and sitting at a vanity, plaiting her long hair. He watched in silence as she wound the coil at the back of her neck, jabbed pins into it, then rose, a faint smile making her look tidy, capable, and self-contained.

And not at all like the well-pleasured bride she should be.

"Are you sorry you married me?" The question came out of Nick's mouth without his willing it into words, and Leah looked to be as surprised by it as he was.

"No," Leah said at length. "Not yet. In any marriage husband or wife or both succumb to momentary regrets, or second thoughts, but you were very clear about what you offered, and about what you did not. I am very relieved to be free of my father."

"That's... good." What had he expected her to say? Leah wasn't vicious, and she'd had few real options.

"May I escort you downstairs?"

"Of course." She smiled at him, but her smile had turned tentative, and Nick's silence as he led her through the house was wary, and their marriage had indeed begun the way Nick intended it to go.

He pushed that sour thought aside as he introduced Leah to each maid and footman, the senior staff, and the kitchen help. From there, they moved to the stable yard, where the stable boys, grooms, and gardeners presented themselves. When the staff had dispersed, Nick led Leah through the gardens, where the tulips were losing their petals, the daffodils were but a memory, and a single iris was heralding the next wave of color on the garden's schedule.

On a hard bench in the spring sunshine, they decided to tarry for two weeks at Clover Down before presenting themselves at Belle Maison. The earl had sent felicitations on the occasion of Nick's nuptials, and yet Nick felt an urgency to return to his father's side.

"Has your father asked you to join him at Belle Maison?" Leah's hand was still curled over Nick's arm, though they sat side by side.

"He has not, and he has told me on several occasions not to lay about the place, long-faced and restless, waiting for him to die. He's sent my sisters off to various friends and relatives, all except Nita, that is. George and Dolph are similarly entertained, and Beckman is away to Portsmouth to see to my grandmother's neglected pile."

"What does Nita say?"

"I hadn't thought to ask her. I'll send her a note today, but I should also consult with my wife. How do you feel about traveling to the family seat when death hangs over it?"

"I have no strong feelings one way or the other," Leah said. "When your father dies, there will be a great deal to manage, and I suspect Nita will appreciate some help then. I might be more useful if everything isn't a case of first impression for me."

"True," Nick said, realizing he hadn't thought matters through from the most practical angle—the angle the women would be left to deal with when Bellefonte went to his reward.

"Two weeks then," Leah said, "and you'd best let Nita know that as well. We'll likely leave here before the neighbors start to call, and that might be a good thing."

Which meant what? Nick didn't dwell on Leah's comment, but instead drew her to her feet. "I've something I want to show you."

"I am at your disposal, Nicholas." As they made their way

through the stables, the feed room, and the saddle room, to a space tucked against the back wall of the barn, Nick reflected that he liked it better when Leah called him Husband.

"This is a woodworking shop," she said, scanning the tools hung neatly along the walls and the wood stored and organized by size along another. "This is yours?"

"It is. I have one in the mews in Town, and another at Belle Maison."

Leah picked up Nick's bare hand and peered at it. "I've wondered what all the little nicks and scratches are from, and this is why you have them, isn't it?"

"Mostly." Nick eased his fingers from hers. "I like to make bird-houses." He pulled a bound leather journal down from a high shelf. "I can show you some of my designs, if you like."

He pulled up a stool, and Leah had to scramble a little to take her seat. Everything in the room was scaled to Nick's size—the stool, the workbench, the drafting table, even some of the tools were proportioned to fit his hands.

And yet, Leah looked as if she'd been made to fit in this room with him, on this fine mild morning, sharing a part of himself he hadn't shown to anyone else.

"This is one I made for my stepmother," Nick began, opening the book. He'd drawn sketches, and then colored illustrations all over the pages. Leah studied each one, asking questions as if birdhouses mattered.

"This is lovely." She traced the lines of the birdhouse on the page. "It looks like a garden house, a little hanging gazebo, with trellises and flower boxes. How could you even see to make such things?"

"I wear magnifying spectacles," Nick said. "The next one was for my papa, though a birdhouse is hardly a manly sort of present. I was eight, though, and had found my first personal passion."

"Eight is a passionate age," Leah murmured as she followed his castle with a finger. "This is quite fanciful."

"I only had illustrations in my storybooks to go by, but it was my version of Arthur's castle. My father loomed in my awareness with all the power and mystery of the legendary king, of course." And now his father lay dying, and Nick's birdhouse had weathered to a uniform gray where it hung outside the earl's bedroom window.

He would repaint Papa's birdhouse when they repaired to Belle Maison. He should have done it sooner.

They spent most of the morning in Nick's shop, the time passing pleasantly. Nick showed Leah sketches of the current work in progress, the birdhouse intended for Ethan.

"I have kept you out here much longer than I meant to," Nick said. "Shall we return to the house for a noon meal?"

As Leah slid off the high stool, she linked her arm through his. "Do you ever miss your mother, Nicholas?"

"I never knew her, but yes. I wish I'd known her. Do you miss your mother?" Nick posed it as a question, but any woman would miss her mother at the time of her own wedding.

"I did," Leah said. "When I went to Italy, I missed her terribly, but it was her idea that I go. And as to that, she proved prescient. When I left England I didn't realize I was carrying a child. I was twenty and figured my body was just upset, which it was. Darius guessed before I did, and thank God he was his usual blunt self about it, or I might have done something stupid."

"Something stupid?" Nick stopped short in their progress past the single iris and stared down at her. "You would have taken your own life?"

She bent to sniff the iris. "Young people can be dramatic when they think they are in love."

"Irises symbolize messages," Nick answered her unasked question. "You would really have taken your own life, but for your pregnancy?"

"I don't know, Nicholas. My father had killed my husband, and there was to be no recourse. I could not prove we had married, because Aaron had taken charge of all the formalities. I was alone, disgraced, deflowered, and not even afforded the status of widow or access to such funds as a widow enjoys. Then too, my mother's health had failed, and I foresaw the rest of my life, alone in that house, with Wilton's criticisms and castigations my daily fare."

Nick's hands slid to either side of her neck, and he leaned down to rest his forehead against hers. He showed her a few birdhouses, and she trusted him with her darkest memories.

"Promise me"—he gripped her gently but quite firmly —"promise me no matter what happens between us, Leah, you won't let this marriage make you so miserable you think of taking your own life."

She laid her hands on his and peeled his fingers away. "I was young, feeling sorry for myself, and grieving. I promise you, I will not contemplate such measures, not as a function of being married to you."

"Not as a function of anything," Nick shot back. "You are too... You just... It wouldn't be right."

"I agree," Leah said, resuming their progress. "I saw that when my son died. Life can be difficult, but death is difficult too. Had I taken my life, all of my brothers' sacrifices and risks would have been for nothing. My mother's heart would have been broken, my sister disgraced by my suicide. I had no right to hurt the people who loved me like that. Worse, at least at the time, taking my life would have proved Wilton's assessment of my flawed nature all too true, and that, more than anything, dissuaded me."

"And who raised this most convincing argument to you?" Nick asked, letting her draw him along beside her.

"Darius. Sometimes his ruthless streak is really a strength."

"May I ask you something?" And, please God, change the subject?

"Of course."

"Has your brother ever given you the impression that he has unusual personal tastes?"

A moment of considering silence followed, in which Nick congratulated himself for at least shifting the topic.

"Not exactly," Leah said, "but it's as if Darius associates with a fast set despite his own preferences."

"A very fast set," Nick concurred. "The question is, why?"

"To disgrace my father? Or because that's all Darius feels he deserves in this life? Because it's a way to be different from Trent, who can be a dull boy indeed? I don't know, and it's not something a sister should know about her brother."

"Maybe not in your family," Nick said as they gained the back steps. "My sisters seem to know every lady to whom I've given a handkerchief."

Leah fell silent, and just like that, they were surrounded once again by a marital bog, one enshrouded in a miasma of hurt feelings and miscommunication.

And yet, Nick had to try. "I didn't mean that I'd... I meant, literally, a clean handkerchief. I always carry at least two, you see, and... You don't believe me."

"I believe I have enjoyed spending time with you this morning, but it's past noon, you have to be hungry."

"Excellent point," Nick said, wanting to kick himself. "Shall we go in?"

They ate companionably enough, the conversation turning to which neighbors lived where in proximity to Clover Down.

"What will you find to occupy you this afternoon?" Nick asked as he topped off Leah's teacup.

"The rest of my things have arrived," Leah said. "I'll see them situated and start exploring the house."

"Sounds productive. I will go for a ride. The trusty steeds in yonder stable are getting fat on spring grass, and this I cannot allow. I'll be back well before supper, and look forward to seeing you then." He rose, brushed his lips across her forehead, and took his leave.

Leah would notice that her new husband hadn't invited her to join him on his ride. Nick knew that, hated it, and headed off to the stables at the most decorous pace he could manage. Once there, only a gentleman's unwillingness to spook the horses stopped him from slamming both fists into the wall, repeatedly.

~

SO THAT'S HER.

Leah had taken herself out walking in the afternoon sunshine as soon as her meager wardrobe had been set to rights. The weather was lovely, and she had had little opportunity to move around the previous few days, so she'd struck off through the gardens and aimed for the hill behind the stables.

The acclivity was crowned with trees, a pretty copse not quite leafed out, the occasional patch of bluebells dancing at the foot of the trees, as if laughing in the dappled sunlight.

Leah took a seat among flowers nearly the color of her husband's eyes, intent on enjoying the view of the surrounding neighborhood. Clover Down, neat and tidy, spread before her to the left. On the right, another estate, just as tidy and still generously dressed in tulips, graced the view. Whoever lived there was also unwilling to waste the lovely afternoon, and was moving into their garden.

Leah made out a man and a woman, both blond, their arms linked while they looked for a spot to make use of the sketch pad the man carried under his arm.

She was struck first by the companionability of the couple. Though the lady was tall, the man's head was bent to catch her every word, and when he seated his companion, he settled in right beside her, still listening intently. Even seated, though, the man was quite a bit...

Taller—Leah's heart lurched, a painful, aching dislocation that did not ease as her eyes confirmed what her mind had already deduced: That was Nick, that tall, blond, so-considerate escort down there in the distance. That was her husband, kissing the woman's temple, hugging her... Oh, God.

As Leah sat in abject misery amid the flowers and the dancing sunlight, Nick made his companion laugh frequently, and each time the lady laughed, Nick smiled down at her.

Leah was too far away to see details of Nick's expression, and the breeze blew in the wrong direction to carry their words to her, but she knew from the angle of his head and the worshipful way the woman beamed back at him, that he loved her and she loved him. Still, Leah could not bring herself to leave until Nick had escorted his hostess back inside.

He will ride home and take tea with me, asking about my afternoon and pretending to care. He won't be honest, but he'll be as kind as he can be.

And sitting alone on the hill, Leah hated him for it.

For all of about three minutes. Sustained ill will toward Nick would have been quite handy, except that he had been honest when it counted. He'd never lied to Leah about his availability as a husband, never tried to convince her she held his heart or he wanted to hold her heart. Nick was as much a victim of circumstance as she was, and there was nothing to be gained by dramatics.

There never had been.

Leah had no recollection of returning to Clover Down, but as she made her way down the aisle in the stables, petting velvety equine noses and carrying a fat yellow tomcat purring against her middle, she heard Nick's voice in the yard.

"Greetings, Wife." Nick handed the reins off to a groom and strode over to Leah's side. He bent down to kiss her, but she shifted to let the cat go at the last instant, so Nick's lips landed on her cheek rather than her lips.

⁓

"GREETINGS, HUSBAND." The words were prosaic, and Nick's wife uttered them in the most unremarkable tones, but still, *Husband...* He was a husband, and being labeled as such left an odd ache in Nick's chest. And he wasn't just any husband, he was *her* husband. Leah Haddonfield's husband.

"Did you have a pleasant afternoon?" his wife asked.

"The day is pretty, and I ran into some neighbors." The pleasant glow of time spent at Blossom Court faded as Nick eyed Leah's profile. He knew women, and his instincts warned him something about Leah was off. Then again, he'd also just told a half-truth, and the guilt was no doubt making him jumpy.

A quarter truth, he corrected himself, then sighed.

He'd misrepresented entirely. "What did you find to do in my absence?" he asked, wishing his conscience would just shut the hell up. He was doing the best he could.

"I sorted out my wardrobe and poked around the house," Leah replied, letting Nick take her arm and steer her down the barn aisle. "I also established menus for the next week with your housekeeper and put my seal of approval on the organization of the pantries. Very impressive staff you have, Lord Reston."

Her voice had taken on a brittle quality, not quite ironic, but not... Not his usual Leah.

"Lovey?" Nick peered over at her. "Are you feeling all right?"

"No, actually." She paused in her progress toward the house. "I did not sleep as well as I would have liked last night, Nicholas, and I might be developing a headache."

"Understandable," Nick said, wanting to be relieved, though she'd slept like a new recruit after a forced march. "Lady Warne pulled me aside at one point yesterday morning and told me surviving the wedding is harder than surviving the marriage. Shall I escort you up to bed?"

"That might be for the best," Leah said, relief lacing her tone even to Nick's ears.

"I want you to feel comfortable here, to consider any residence of ours your home," he said as he held the back door for her. "You needn't soldier on for my sake when you're in pain, and I certainly won't be putting on airs before you, of all people."

Lying through his teeth, frequently, but never putting on airs.

"I'll..." Leah paused, and while he watched, swallowed and looked away. "I'll try to recall that, Nicholas."

"I can have a tray sent up later, and I'll check on you before I turn in if you'd rather not come down for dinner." He brushed a kiss to her forehead, wanting to touch her, though he didn't deserve to.

"You might consider getting to bed early tonight yourself, Nicholas."

Nick lifted a hand to her shoulder, contemplating adding an embrace to that prosaic, stolen kiss. An embrace intended to comfort a new wife in a new house—and to comfort a new husband too.

But Leah whirled before Nick could get his arms around her and left him standing alone in the corridor.

～

OVER THE NEXT FEW DAYS, Leah's heartache grew worse. Nick insisted on showing her his progress with Ethan's birdhouse, and walking with her in their garden, and asking her to help him with French correspondence.

She tried to think of him as a benign, charming cousin or brother-in-law. A man she might know fairly well, and whose company she could enjoy, but not *like that*.

And her self-deception worked adequately, until Nick would touch his thumb to her lower lip and ask her, "Why so grave, Wife?"—his expression likely the same worried, tender gaze he'd turned on their blond neighbor.

Or until he'd bring Leah breakfast on a tray, then sit on her bed and feed her as he asked her about her plans for the day or her correspondence from her siblings.

Or take her hand and lead her to the kitchen, there to share a late-afternoon cup of tea and a crumpet pilfered from the pantry. Leah bit into her buttered crumpet then watched as Nick brought it to his mouth and nibbled off a bite from the same spot.

Nick put the crumpet down. "You look so forlorn I am about to cry. What can I do to please you?"

"You are a good man, Nicholas," she said, "but being married to you on the terms you've set is harder than I ever imagined. Much, much harder."

Nick regarded the single bite of crumpet left on his plate. "How is it difficult?"

"I am falling in love with you, and I don't want to."

The kitchen clock ticked softly, the kettle on the hob gave off a low, simmering hiss, and the last of the kindling used to heat the burner shifted in the stove.

"I don't know what to say," Nick replied, coming around the table to sit beside her. He reached for her hand, and she closed her eyes, but made no move to withdraw her fingers. Nick was a toucher. He would not understand that what he sought to give as comfort couldn't always be appreciated as such.

"You don't have to say anything, Nicholas. You can't help that you are so naturally affectionate, or that you are charming and kind and considerate. You can't help that you are handsome and so gloriously well made. You've been honest with me, as honorable as circumstances allow. I'm just..."

"I've been trying not to hover," Nick said, stroking the back of her hand with his fingers. "I am somewhat at a loss as well."

Leah opened her eyes to frown at him. "Please be as blunt as you know how to be, Nicholas. I am not good at reading subtleties from a member of the opposite sex."

"Keeping my distance from you is difficult," Nick said on a bewildered sigh, "but I think I should. I'm not sure why I think that, when you've never been anything other than welcoming and accommodating, but the feeling is there, that if I'm to be a husband only by half measures, I should leave you entirely in peace."

Leah remained silent, and then, perhaps because he was possessed of a certain recklessness, Nick spelled it out for her. "I should leave you in peace, but I don't want to."

"This is a dilemma," Leah said, closing her fingers around Nick's hand. "How long do you think we can endure this situation, before we begin to hate each other?"

"I cannot hate you." The words held relief, topped with a dollop of sadness. "I can hate the part of me that has no conscience and wants to pleasure itself in your body regardless of consequences, but I cannot hate the lady who consented to spend the rest of her life with me, knowing how little I can offer her."

Heat flooded Leah's face. "That is impressively blunt, but, Nick, where do we go from here? We're tied together at the ankle by this marriage and will have to spend some time together at least for the short term. I do not like feeling I'm mooning after a man who doesn't want me, and you cannot enjoy my longing glances and maidenly sighs."

He did not smile. "Of course I can. I am a man, Leah, and all the practical considerations in the world won't change that. Glance and sigh, and I'll strut and paw. It's the way the animal is made."

"Would we be better off apart, Nicholas?"

Panic or something like it flared in his blue eyes. Whatever it was, Leah assured herself it wasn't relief.

"Leah, I haven't been with another woman since I met you."

∼

IN THE BIBLICAL SENSE, Nick could tell his wife he'd not strayed. Marriage was turning him into a barrister, though, because he'd spent the entire afternoon in company with a female he never intended for Leah to meet.

And maybe Leah sensed the prevarication, because she would not meet Nick's gaze.

He wasn't ready to let her go. Worse, he could not envision the day when he would be ready.

Booted steps sounded swiftly above, and then on the kitchen stairs. Nick exchanged a puzzled look with his wife—his sad, cranky wife—but admitted relief that the conversation had been interrupted.

Leah's courage had towed their discussion out to deep, dangerous waters, and shoals lay all around them.

"Nick?" Ethan's voice rang with anxiety. "Where the hell are you?"

"Down here," Nick bellowed, rising from Leah's side, "and I'll thank you not to shout when in the presence of my lady wife."

A dusty, road-worn Ethan thumped down the stairs, and Nick's good cheer evaporated. "Papa's gone?"

Ethan gave one tight nod.

Nick stood in the middle of the kitchen, the reality of the moment imprinting itself on his mind: the ticking clock, the low song of the simmering kettle, the lovely spring sunshine pouring in the open kitchen windows, the breeze bringing with it the scent of garden flowers, turned earth, and the stables.

This is the moment when I become an orphan. When my brother and all my siblings and I become orphans. A chasm opened up in his chest, bottomless and yet filled with pain, sorrow, and bewilderment. Wordlessly he held out an arm to his wife, who was beside him in an instant. The other arm went out to Ethan, who joined them in an odd, three-way embrace.

"Let's sit," Leah suggested a few minutes later. "Ethan, your horse?"

"The lads are walking him out," Ethan said as he led Nick to the table and slid onto the bench next to him.

"You probably haven't eaten today," Leah said, frowning at Ethan. "You will eat, Ethan Grey, and don't even attempt to argue. Nicholas?"

He turned to her, trying to fathom her meaning, as though plain English had suddenly become a foreign language at which he had little proficiency.

"I will feed your brother and have some provisions packed for us." Leah spoke slowly. "I will also have some clothes packed and

send word to my brother I'll be leaving with you this evening for
Belle Maison."

Nick nodded, unable to get his voice to work. If he said something, anything, he'd lose his composure, and he could not allow Leah
to see that.

Leah knelt beside his chair. "I'm coming with you to Belle
Maison—if that's what you want?"

He managed another terse nod and barely resisted the compul-
sion to drag her against his chest. Leah rose and moved off. Nick was
aware of her bustling around the kitchen, aware of his brother looking
haggard and weary, and aware that Papa—the earl, his lordship, the
only person standing between Nick and a miserable damned title
—was gone.

When Leah put a tray of sliced beef, cheddar, sliced bread, and a
peeled orange before Ethan, she kissed Nick's cheek—even her scent
helped Nick breathe— then took her leave.

Nick started on the sad, predictable questions. "When?"

"Late last night," Ethan said, making no move to eat. "He just
slipped away, Nick. He was breathing one minute, and then he did
not breathe again. Nita and I were there, and he was asleep."

"You rode here from Belle Maison," Nick observed, stupidly. Of
course Ethan had ridden from Belle Maison. Ethan's arm circled
Nick's shoulders. "I'll go back there with you. I promised you
I would."

"I need to send word to the others," Nick said, lowering his forehead to his folded arms. "The funeral can't wait."

The practicalities, Nick thought vaguely. Leah has foreseen a
need to deal with the practicalities.

"We can have a memorial service next month if we can't all be at
the funeral," Ethan suggested.

With a sigh, Nick nodded and pushed to his feet. "Eat, or Leah
will know the reason why. Your horse can stay here, and you'll travel
with us in the coach."

"If you wish," Ethan said, regarding Nick.

"Leah did say she'd come with me?" Nick ran a hand through his hair, embarrassed to have to ask but needing the reassurance. Needing his wife.

"She did. You told her it was what you wanted."

"I do want that," Nick said. "Give me an hour to jot off some notes and confer with Leah and..." His voice trailed off, and Ethan waited. Eventually, Nick figured out something to say to his brother. "Thank you for bringing me this news, Ethan. I would not have wanted to hear it from anyone else."

"Not that you wanted to hear it at all, and not that I wanted to bring it. I'll meet you in an hour."

What Nick wanted was to find his wife, bury his face against her neck, and let his sorrow overtake him. Instead, he went to the library and penned notes to his solicitors, to his siblings, and, after an attempt at deliberation that ended up being a spate of staring at a blank page, to Leonie.

LEAH'S HUSBAND was being stubborn, in what she suspected was venerable tradition for the earls of Bellefonte.

"Leah, I do not want to put you through this."

What Nick clearly did not want was to burden his wife with further evidence of his grief.

"Nonsense." Leah kept her voice down, though the corridor outside the small parlor housing the old earl's remains was deserted. "I've seen bodies before, Nicholas, and I've also not seen bodies."

He looked haunted, glancing up and down the carpeted hallway. "What does that mean?"

"My Charles wasn't buried until I'd had a chance to hold him one last time," Leah said, "though Aaron was taken back to his father's house after the duel. I was not permitted to see him before they buried him. Both are equally dead, and I felt equal sorrow to lose them."

Nick grimaced and scrubbed a hand over his face. "I have unpleasant associations with this sort of thing. When my stepmother died and my uncle..."

He was not only stubborn and grieving, Leah suspected he was also intimidated by the role he expected himself to fulfill. The idea that Nicholas, the most singularly self-possessed man she'd ever met, should face such a moment alone was untenable.

"What lies in the parlor is not your father, Nicholas. It's a body that houses no life. You need not go in there."

He searched her gaze, probably looking for tacit judgments. He would find none, not about this. He shoved away from the wall.

"I'm his son. His heir."

She took his hand, as he'd so often taken hers, and willed him to feel all the reassurance and support within her. When Nick escorted her through the door, she saw that the parlor was awash in lilies, though thank God somebody had also opened the windows.

Nick's grip on her hand was tight, probably tighter than he knew.

"He's... dead," Nick observed softly after a few silent moments. "There is no mistaking that pallor and that stillness."

"He's at peace," Leah countered. "His body is dead."

Nick's grip eased, but she did not allow him to drop her hand. While Nick made his final farewells to his father, Leah stood beside him and took courage from sharing the moment with him. For all their problems, they were man and wife. If Nick allowed her to remain by his side now, perhaps it boded well for their future.

"He would not want to be seen like this." Nick sounded so sad, so lost.

"He is disporting with his wives and mistresses, or so you told me."

A ghost of a smile passed over Nick's features. "Come, else I shall weep like a small boy missing the only person who could ever make me feel like a small boy, regardless of evidence to the contrary." And yet he didn't move and he didn't give up Leah's hand. "I don't want to be Bellefonte," Nick said softly. "I never wanted to be the earl."

And maybe there was guilt here, for not wanting what his father would bequeath to him. That would be utter male nonsense, of course, but because it was Nick's male nonsense, Leah shifted to embrace him.

"No loving son wants his father's title, Nicholas, unless it's to spare his father a longer sentence in a painful existence."

Nick's arms came around her slowly, maybe reluctantly. "Papa didn't want the title either, and yet he was a fine earl, all things considered. A very fine earl."

That was not nonsense. That was something Nick could hold close, as Leah held her husband close.

He shifted, so his arm was draped over her shoulders. "Come upstairs with me?"

As if she'd drift away from him now? "Of course." And yet, "upstairs" held a curious development. Being newly wed, Leah and her husband had been housed in Nick's bedroom. Both of their trunks were empty and sitting open at the foot of Nick's enormous bed.

Well, they were married—and the earl's chambers would require airing and possible redecoration. Perhaps it simply hadn't occurred to Nick to direct that Leah be quartered elsewhere. He was that distracted by his bereavement.

Leah sent up a silent prayer of thanks to the late earl.

"I'm of a mind to take a nap," Nick said, sitting down and tugging at his boots. "If you'd join me, I'd appreciate it." Leah glanced at the bed and then back at Nick, but she couldn't fathom the motivation for his request. Maybe it was as simple as Nick being tired and unwilling to be alone.

Or perhaps he was aware, as Leah was, of how close they had come to declaring their marriage over before it had begun.

"A nap sounds good." Leah crossed the room and sat beside Nick, turning her back only when he'd finished with his boots. His fingers made short work of the hooks on her dress and the laces of her stays, but then he slid his arms around her waist and held on, a shudder passing through him, then a sigh.

"Off to bed with you," Nick said, rising and drawing her to her feet. "I'll be along shortly."

Leah stripped down to her chemise while Nick undressed himself, but when she saw he intended to come to bed naked, she paused. What was this, and what did she want to do about it?

"I'm merely getting comfortable," Nick said, climbing onto the bed. "You could fill this bed with naked women, Leah, and at present, I could do justice to none of them."

He was both rejecting her—not that she'd offered anything—and accepting her. She decided to focus on the acceptance, whipped off the chemise, and joined Nick on the bed.

Though that left at least five feet of cool mattress and bedding between them.

"Meet me in the middle?"

He was asking her for something, or maybe admitting that in these circumstances, he was entitled to the comfort of having a loyal wife. After a moment's hesitation, Leah crab-flopped herself over a couple of feet and lay back, letting Nick take her hand in his.

"Let me hold you, Nicholas," she said. "I just... I don't want you to be alone in this bed, not today."

He was in her arms in a heartbeat, his cheek resting against her breast, his thigh hiked over her legs. He let out the sigh to end all sighs, and closed his eyes, his lashes sweeping against her skin.

"How will I last until Friday, Leah?" Nick asked softly. "The neighbors will swarm, as will the well-meaning friends. The house will be full of people, when all I want is to be alone with my family. I comprehend now why there is always libation at wakes and viewings and funeral buffets."

Leah tightened her hold on him, feeling the kind of ferocious protectiveness she'd directed previously only toward her son. Nick might not know it, but he trusted her the way a man ought to trust his wife. With painful certainty, Leah realized she did not want to lose him. Whatever their marriage could become, she did not want to lose this trust and closeness.

"We shall contrive. Nobody will stay for long, or your countess will make them sorry."

Nick raised his head, his expression guarded. "You'll stay?"

A thousand retorts circled in her brain: I'll stay as long as you need me. Why wouldn't I stay with my husband? And then: Nicholas, you need not be always so alone.

He'd leave the bed if she said that.

"Of course I'll stay." For as long as he'd allow it, she'd stay, and hope that the painful, impossible topic they'd raised in the kitchen at Clover Down was never, ever raised again.

CHAPTER FOURTEEN

"The kitchen isn't keeping up with the guests at the buffet." Lady Nita Haddonfield drew a black handkerchief from her sleeve, a warning to any of the neighbors thronging the house nearby not to approach.

"I'll get the footmen moving," Leah said. "Nicholas is in the parlor with your sisters, and probably passing out his handkerchiefs."

"Oh, my poor Nicky." Nita bustled away, her expression determined, which left Leah wondering where Ethan had got off to. She found him in the kitchen, sipping a cup of tea, effectively hiding in plain sight. Her first task was to find the head footman and put the fear of hungry neighbors in him, and then she made directly for Ethan.

"How is Nick doing?" He moved over as Leah sat beside him.

"He did not enjoy seeing his father's corpse," she said, stealing a sip of his tea. "And he's resting more than I've known him to rest, actually spending time in his bed. But other than that, I think he's managing. He's glad you're here, but why are you dodging your siblings, Ethan Grey?" Leah stole another sip of his tea. "Gracious, that is good. Is the kettle on the hob?"

"Cook is keeping a pot going for the servants," Ethan said. "I pinched a cup by special dispensation."

"Nick will appreciate a cup. Shall I send your sisters down here for you to receive them?" She rose, determined that this day should pass with a minimum of difficulty for Nick.

"I..." Ethan dropped his gaze to his nearly empty teacup. "I haven't seen them for years, Leah. My brothers, I'd run into in Town, but the ladies... there's such a crowd up there, all curious, no doubt, and I don't want my sisters to have to ..."

"All right," Leah interrupted. The late Earl of Haddonfield's sons were a surprisingly shy bunch—shy and considerate. "I'll send them to you in the music room, how's that?"

When she half expected him to bolt, he set his teacup aside. "That will serve."

Leah eventually shooed the siblings who were present into the music room, and had a tea tray sent to them laden with all manner of appealing food, as well as a brandy decanter. She was directing the restocking of the buffet when the head footman found her and drew her aside.

"Lord Reston..." The man paused, cleared his throat, and started again. "*The earl* is asking for you, my lady. He's in the music room, and he said to tell you..."

"Yes?"

"You need to take a break, my lady, and get off your feet for a few minutes. His lordship's exact words." Leah did not need a break, but Nicholas might need her by his side. She gave a few more instructions and found her way to the music room. She slipped inside and saw the family was assembled, seven tall blonds bearing a strong resemblance, and their youngest, Della, petite and dark-haired.

Because Ethan was in the middle of a story about Nick as a child, Leah took a quiet seat at Nick's feet. His hand settled on her nape, and his brandy glass appeared before her eyes. She took a sip and passed it back to him, enjoying the smooth burn of the alcohol and the smoother heat coming from Nick's fingers caressing her neck.

When Ethan finished, Nita spoke up, reminding them of an occasion when the earl had been spectacularly in error and held accountable by his second wife. Leah felt a draft and looked over to see that another handsome, strapping blond had slipped into the room.

As discreetly as she could, Leah caught Nick's eye and nodded toward the door.

Nick rose and crossed the room. "Now we are complete." He drew the fellow to the center of the room and slid an arm around his shoulders. "Our Beckman has come home."

Beckman was not as tall as Nick or quite as handsome. He had something of Ethan's sharper features, and yet in his height, blue eyes, and blond hair, he was unmistakably a Haddonfield.

He scanned the room as Nick's arm slid from his shoulders.

"We're all home," Nick said, "every one of us, and it's about damned time."

The room went silent as Beck's gaze fastened on Ethan, who was blinking at a portrait of a young blond man in old-fashioned regimentals.

Young Della held up her brandy.

"Here's to family," she said, "reunited, and isn't Papa just laughing his harp off to know he's the reason."

~

THANK GOD and all his angels, Della's toast had broken the ice, because Nick hadn't known what to say. Nothing and everything. Love for his siblings swirled through his grief, through his marital woes, through his dread of assuming responsibility for the earldom, and all of it seemed to impair both his ability to speak and his ability to think.

As Beckman wedged into a place beside Ethan, the room once again settled in to storytelling, reminiscing, the occasional teary aside, and more frequent laughter. When Nick resumed his seat, he arranged a leg on either side of Leah's perch on the floor, and drew her back to lean against his chair. His hands caressed her neck and shoulders, not idly, but because it soothed him to touch his wife.

Nick leaned down, his lips near her ear, his nose buried in the lily of the valley fragrance of her hair. "Your behind has to be getting numb," he whispered. "I'll trade you."

A man could say such a thing to his wife, and watch for the way she tried not to smile.

"Why don't we shoo the last of the guests away and arrange for a late supper on trays in here for the family?""You shoo, Wife. I'll get word to the kitchen."

Leah shook her head. "You're the earl, and I'm sure your letters patent spell out very clearly that you are in charge of shooing on all occasions of state. Come along like a good earl, lest I report you to the Regent."

Oh, how he loved her, Nick mused as he trailed her from the room. Then his steps slowed and faltered as he realized exactly what he had admitted.

God in heaven, what he'd tried to characterize as fondness, protectiveness, and sexual attraction was much worse than all those combined. All odds to the contrary, he loved his wife, and he'd not even truly become her lover. Nor could he, ever.

"Nicholas?" Leah eyed him curiously. "Are you coming?"

"Yes, lovey." Nick took her hand and linked his fingers through hers. "A-shooing we will go." They passed the family parlor, and Leah paused to close the door. Across the hall, neighbors were still eating, drinking, and visiting the day away, leaving Nick to frown in consternation.

"How exactly does this shooing work?" Because Leah would know.

"You find the vicar or the mayor or the local magistrate," Leah said, "and ask them to clear the room as politely as possible. Their consequence will demand they see to it with all dispatch."

"I did not learn this at university," Nick muttered, his eyes lighting on the vicar. In five minutes, the crowd was thinning, his neighbors and friends offering final condolences, until he, Leah, and the servants were the only ones left.

"God's hairy b—beard." Nick looped his arms over Leah's shoulders and drew her close. Time enough later to ponder the disaster looming for a man in love with a wife he could not have. "This has been a long, long day."

"You're managing wonderfully," Leah murmured against his chest, "but the brandy is catching up with me."

"Was that you who sent the decanter to the music room?" Nick asked, his cheek against her temple. "Little Della was in alt to be taking spirits, but George surreptitiously snitched most of her portion."

"I am the culprit. Ethan did not want to greet his sisters in public, and the best part of any funeral is the stories."

"I wasn't aware funerals had a best part," Nick said, though the memory of Leah curled at his feet while his siblings laughed and cried together was precious, if not without pain. "Nita was wise to put the actual service off for a day. We will want tomorrow to recover from today."

"Can we have the body sealed into its coffin now?" Leah asked, stifling a yawn.

"We can. You are so matter-of-fact, using words like body, coffin, and burial. I did not know I married a woman of such ferocious courage." And she would need more courage yet, given his feelings for her. "There's still some daylight. Will you walk with me?"

"Of course." Leah slipped her arms from his waist.

The head footman was smiling at them, the maids were trying to look interested in packing up the food, and the junior footmen were trying to look as busy as the maids.

Nick walked with Leah through the gardens, knowing he had to deal with his marriage and the unexpected turn of his emotions for his new wife, but knowing as well, resolving that situation was beyond him until his father's death rituals were complete. For now, Leah at his side and in his arms was too great a comfort to give up.

He knew he was in particularly dangerous waters when he woke up in the middle of the night, wrapped around her and content simply to stay that way.

"Go back to sleep, lovey." He kissed her neck and tucked her against him.

"Did everybody else trundle off to bed when you told them to?" Leah asked, her lips brushing his forearm where it lay across her collarbone.

"I made sure Nita got to bed," Nick replied. "And Ethan has sought his bed. The rest of them are in need of a good visit without the elders around."

"You're an elder?"

"Head of the family, God help me."

Leah scooted over to her back and considered him by the waning firelight. To accommodate her change in position, Nick threaded her arm under his neck, hiked one of Leah's legs over his hips, and shifted up to prop his head on his palm.

"You have been head of this family for several years." She brushed his hair back from his forehead. "You will have to give the eulogy."

"I've worked on it some." Nick's hand smoothed down her sternum and rested on her belly. So smooth, her skin, such a delight to stroke. "It doesn't seem natural, to publicly praise a man who was in truth very private, but I suppose it's expected."

"There are the rituals, and then there is the grieving, the real mourning, which is God-awfully miserable work."

"We'll mourn." Nick leaned down and kissed her shoulder. "Nita said it was Papa's wish we not observe deep mourning for more than six months, and then only on formal occasions. He'd buried two wives, two mistresses, and two babies, and didn't see the sense in all the ritual and display."

"Two children?" Leah's hand drifted up the column of Nick's throat. The touch was soothing and quite... personal.

"Between George and Della," Nick said. "A boy and a girl, both of whom died in infancy. He wanted to stop trying at that point, but my stepmother was desperate for more babies. They had spectacular rows before Della showed up."

"Everybody grieves differently," Leah said. "Why don't you want children, Nicholas? The real reason, if you please."

Nick rolled slightly and buried his face against Leah's neck. He had not seen this coming, not now. "There is risk to you, Leah. Honest to God risk, no matter what medical assurances are given, no matter how safely you bore your son."

"You still think you killed your mother? I was certain you were bruiting that about as a mean sort of jest."

"I would never jest about a woman's death, much less my mother's," Nick said, his words muffled against Leah's neck. His tongue slipped softly along her jaw, just taking a taste of female sweetness and warmth—to distract her, to comfort him.

"But you had nothing to do with your mother's death, Nicholas. If anybody was to blame, it was your father."

"I respectfully disagree." Nick's hand slid over Leah's stomach, coming to rest on her opposite hip. "He was a third son inheriting a title later in life, and intent on doing his duty, and he succeeded, as yours truly lives and breathes."

"But you were being weaned," Leah said. "It was your father's fixation on producing a spare that cost your mother her life."

Nick pulled back and stared down at her. "I have the sense we are talking at cross purposes."

"As do I."

"My mother died as a result of complications following childbirth, and I am the only child she bore." He knew this; he'd known it all his life.

"You were shy of a year old, Nick," Leah said gently. "Lady Warne told me her daughter had conceived again and was weaning you at your father's insistence. Losing that second child late in the pregnancy is what led to her eventual death."

Silence, filled only by the hiss of the last of the embers in the fireplace.

"Nana told you this?" Nick said slowly, rolling to his back.

"She most assuredly did." Leah propped herself on his chest and peered at him. "You had nothing to do with your mother's death. Not. One. Thing."

He stared at the shadows flickering on the ceiling and tried to fathom the sense of her words. There was loss in what Leah said, but loss of a burden as well as loss of a dearly held belief. Leah folded herself down over his chest and slid an arm behind his neck.

Did she seek to anchor him physically while his entire world went tumbling?

"You honestly thought you killed your own mother. Oh, Nicholas..."

His arms came around her, carefully, slowly. "How did Lady Warne convey this information?"

"We'd finished fitting my wedding dress," Leah said, "and I asked her if you'd killed your mother."

"You were afraid?" Of course she'd be afraid. Nick was afraid.

"Curious," Leah clarified, her cheek over his heart. "Your heart-beat is steadier than the beat of a clock. I love that you are so tall that your heart lies right under my ear when you hold me."

That simple little compliment, coming on the heels of unexpected absolution for his mother's death, sliced at Nick's soul. Leah thought he was handsome, when most women of her station thought he was a freak. She was protective of him—all seventeen damned stone of him—when by any sane lights, protecting ought to be his exclusive domain.

"Leah..." But he had no words, so he kissed her. He meant to express things beyond words— gratitude, wonder, relief, and tender-ness—but Leah surprised him. When his lips pressed against hers, she groaned softly and fitted her mouth over his. Tentatively, her tongue seamed his lips, asking entrance even as her hand moved over the contours of Nick's shoulders.

He let her tempt him, assuring himself he was equal to the self-restraint needed to enjoy the kiss without letting it go too far. In careful increments, Nick felt Leah exploring the limits of a passionate kiss between spouses naked, in bed, in the privacy of deepest night. She sampled the heat of his mouth, the pleasures and textures of his tongue, and the soft fullness of his lips. Without Nick wanting it or willing it, his wife was also learning how easily a well-kissed man became aroused.

"Lovey, we have to slow down."

"You're wrong," Leah muttered, taking his hand and fitting it over her breast. "You were wrong about your mother, and you're wrong about this too, Husband." She closed his fingers over the fullness of her breast.

Leah's head fell back, and her back arched, begging him to repeat the caress.

She had every right to expect pleasure of him. Nick marshaled his self-discipline, despite the hard throbbing in his cock. He brought his free hand up, framed Leah's other breast with it, and urged her closer to his mouth.

"Nicholas..." His name was a hiss of pleasure and longing, and Leah's nails digging into Nick's forearm only confirmed the intensity of her passion. Gently, he laved her nipple with his tongue, knowing he could not deny her satisfaction, not on one of the last nights they would spend together. He was condemned to please, and take little for himself, just as he had been so often condemned in the past.

Leah didn't know of his devil's bargain, though, and when her fingers feathered over Nick's nipples, pleasure bucked through his body. His cock leaped at her sex, longing coursing through him with an ache he felt in his body and in his soul. The ache turned to torture when Leah eased her body over him, caressing his length with the slick heat of her sex.

"Leah..." Nick rasped, pressing his face to her chest. "You can't..."

She did it again, and desire coiled more tightly.

"We can," she retorted in a fierce whisper.

"No." Nick grabbed her wrists, but she used her body weight to push her hands apart and spread his arms out on the bed. With unerring instinct, she positioned herself so the head of Nick's cock was nudging at the opening in her body.

"Leah... you must not."

"You did not kill your mother, your reservations are groundless, and I need you." As she captured him with her body and shifted that first, exquisite half inch downward, Nick went utterly still. Leah's head dropped forward on a gusty exhale, and she eased her hips forward.

"Easy," Nick cautioned, resigned to yet greater self-restraint. "Don't let me hurt you."

"You couldn't," she whispered, rocking her hips in a small, slow pattern of thrust and retreat. "You feel wonderful to me, absolutely, gloriously... Ah, Nicholas..." He lay beneath her, letting her have complete control as she took him more and more deeply into her body. His hands eased away from her wrists and moved gently over her face, then her neck and shoulders. He stroked her breasts, her belly, and her arms, and all the while watched her expression in the last of the firelight.

"I want..." Leah opened her eyes to plead with him silently.

He wanted to cry, to weep with the knowledge of what could not be his.

"I know," Nick replied. "But slowly, Leah, and gently. I will not forgive myself if I hurt you."

She shook her head. "You are lovely inside me, so sweet and full and unbearably... God... All I want is more of you. More and more..."

Her words hammered at him, hammered at the place inside him that said he was not entitled to take pleasure from a woman, not ever, for surely it pleased him to hear her sighs and her lavish compliments. It pleased him, warmed his soul, and aroused his body. He was already fighting the tightening up behind his balls that signaled his own impending satisfaction, and the feel of Leah slowly hilting him in her body pushed his control to the limit.

"Nicholas?" Leah settled herself slowly and completely onto him then folded down onto his chest. "You aren't moving with me."

"I don't dare," he whispered, finding her mouth with his. "But you can move, Leah." His hands caressed her back then gripped her hips, encouraging her into a slow, languorous rhythm. "Come like this for me." He trailed one hand up to cup her breast and tease her nipple. "Take your pleasure of me."

Torture me so this one memory, at least, will be mine.

He intended that his voice, his hands, his kisses, the throbbing fullness of his cock lodged deep in her body all conspire to give her pleasure. As soon as Leah withdrew and pressed forward again, he felt her silently shatter.

Nick did move then; he rocked himself inside her, prolonging and intensifying her pleasure with slow undulations of his hips and glancing caresses to her breasts. When her passion ebbed, Nick brushed his thumb against the top of her sex and drove her up again.

"Nicholas... Nicholas..." She breathed his name so softly Nick felt it more as exhalations against his chest than words. His arousal clawed at him, and yet he let his hips fall still and cradled Leah against his body.

"You are all right?" he whispered.

"I am utterly replete," Leah whispered back. "But you are not. You touch me so carefully, Nicholas, so caringly, but you haven't found your pleasure."

"Leah, I can't..." He didn't know how to tell her what he needed, but any minute—any second—it would be too late. With a soft groan, he rolled them and lifted himself out of her body, then lay himself over her, tightly seaming his wet cock between them. "I'm sorry," he rasped, thrusting against her belly until pleasure radiated through him and he spent his seed between their bodies. "I'm just so... damnably sorry."

He lay between her legs, physical repletion warring with self-disgust, while Leah's arms went around him and her hands threaded through the hair at his nape.

The haven she offered was precious and never to be his. If he allowed the embrace, then he might allow the confidences such embraces engendered. The thought inspired him to lever up, taking his weight on his forearms and knees.

"Don't go." Leah tightened her grip. "I like your weight on me."

Confound the woman. "You can't breathe," Nick answered, more harshly than he'd intended. "And I've made a mess of you. Let me go, Leah. Please."

Her arms slid from his neck, and she let her legs fall open. Nick extricated himself, crossed the room, and fetched the basin and towel kept near the hearth. As he sopped one end of the towel in the water then rubbed it briskly over his stomach and his genitals, all he could think was: *What have I done? What have I done?*

"Say something," Leah prompted, her voice catching, as if tears threatened.

"I'm sorry," Nick said flatly. "That should never have happened." He used the towel on her as impersonally as he could, when what he wanted was to bury himself in her again and again and again.

"Why shouldn't it have happened?" Leah asked, bewilderment coming to the fore. "It was beautiful, and ordained by God, and one of the few pleasures any married person is entitled to expect of his or her mate."

Beautiful—and potentially tragic.

"But not us," Nick said, firing the towel across the room with unnecessary force. "We're not entitled to that. I am not entitled to that."

"But, Nicholas, why not?"

"I could get you with child, even if I don't spend inside your body," Nick said wearily. "I wish it were not so, Leah. I desperately wish it were not so, but I was honest about my terms when you agreed to marry me. I am profoundly sorry to have breached my word to you as far as I have, and I can only hope there won't be consequences we both regret."

"I do not understand you," Leah said in quiet misery. "You are a sumptuous lover, Nicholas, and I will not, not ever, regret what has passed between us here tonight. I will instead resent until my last day that you deny us both what is our right."

She flopped back down to the bed and pulled the covers up to her chin.

He had hurt her, hurt her in the one area a spouse's trust and protection ought to be inviolate, and the need to comfort her was a living, writhing misery in Nick's soul.

He hadn't the right. He also hadn't the right to stalk from the bed and leave her even more alone than she felt now.

And he hadn't the courage to ask her if she wanted him to leave.

So he waited until Leah fell asleep then carefully folded himself around her once more, and like a thief in the night stole what consolation from her he could, while darkness hid his anguish.

~

"IS IT TIME TO RISE?" Leah asked, blinking.

"Not yet," Nick said. "There's tea on the hearth. Shall I fetch you a cup?"

He was polite, at least. They'd spent the previous day being so polite Leah's teeth nigh ached with it, and then last night in his sleep, Nick had held her desperately close.

"Fetch us both a cup." Leah pushed her braid over her shoulder and wrestled the pillows behind her back. "How are you on this day, Nicholas?"

He rose from the bed, naked—at least he wouldn't deny her that much. "I feel like I felt when Ethan was sent north to school: bewildered, powerless to stop someone I love and rely on from being taken away." He brought the whole tray to the bedside table and sat on the mattress, his back to Leah.

"You have known a bucketload of loss," Leah said. She wrestled the bedclothes aside and knee-walked over to Nick, wrapping her arms around his shoulders for a brief hug. He tolerated it, closing his eyes on a sigh.

"Let's drink this in bed," Nick suggested, maybe by way of an olive branch. "Soon enough we'll be up and about, dressed in sobriety and grief."

"Maybe at first, but you grieve in proportion to how you loved, and eventually, the love pushes through the loss." She knew this. If it was all he'd allow her to give him, she'd offer it freely.

Nick settled back against his pillows and sipped his tea.

"You speak such eloquent words, Wife. Nonetheless, I am royally out of charity with my papa, and that is hardly worthy of me or the life he lived."

Of course he'd be angry, and Nick was not comfortable with anger in any sense.

"You think I wasn't wroth with my mother for leaving me so soon after my child died? It frightens us to be without our parents, whether they were doing much parenting before they died or not. Nicholas?"

"Wife?"

Wife—that was something. "For today, don't shut me out. I know you are displeased and upset over what passed between us in this bed, but you bury your father today, and that must take precedence over our troubles. Your family will need to lean on you, and..." She looked away, self-conscious, yet unwilling to back down. "I am inviting you to lean on me."

"I have leaned on you." Nick reached out a long arm and let the backs of his fingers drift over her cheek. "And, Leah, I am so damned sorry about the way I spoke to you the other night. You are not to blame."

And then she was angry. Angry at the big, noisy family who assumed Nick would take on every difficulty and see to every problem. Angry at the mother who'd died and left him with such a load of guilt, even his broad shoulders should not have to bear it alone.

And she was angry at him, so stubbornly determined to keep every burden ever thrust upon him.

"We can deal with all that later, Nicholas, agreed?" She studied her teacup lest she start shouting at him. "We'll deal with it later, and you have my thanks for your understanding. I am your wife, and I would be your friend."

Nick turned to set his teacup aside and spoke to Leah over his shoulder. "Will you let me hold you? I know I should not ask this of you, but I can behave, Leah. I promise you that, it's just..."

"Of course." Leah passed him her teacup and scooted over. She settled against his side, where she fit as if God had made her just for that cozy location. Nick's hand fell to her shoulder, brushed her braid aside, and began drawing slow patterns on her arm and her back, until she was dozing contently in his arms, his chin resting on her temple.

A soft tap on the door heralded the arrival of breakfast. Nick brought the covers up to Leah's chin and bade the serving maid enter, then dismissed her after she'd built up the fire.

Before he could leave the bed, Leah climbed over to straddle Nick's lap. There were mounds of bed covers between them, softly compressed between their bodies. She batted them aside until she got her arms around Nick's neck, hugging him close at the start of this most trying day.

"I know, Nicholas, we have dreadful difficulties ahead, sad things to say to each other, but one grief at a time is more than enough. For today, I am your devoted wife, if you'll allow it."

"I'll allow it." Nick pressed his face to her throat. "I don't deserve it, but I'll allow it."

Unspoken between them hung two words that held back a wealth of foreboding and misery. Nick would allow her support—*for now*. Only for now.

∾

"LEAH?" Nick poked his head into the ladies' parlor—the Squealery, according to the late earl—the day after the burial in the late afternoon, and found his wife surrounded by all of his sisters, addressing replies to cards of condolence. "Nicholas?"

"A word with you, if you can spare me a moment," Nick said, purposely not letting even one sister catch his eye. "I'll meet you in the gardens."

Nick waited for Leah on the same bench they'd occupied after the viewing, feeling more solemn than even at the burial.

"You look very serious, Nicholas." Leah took her seat beside him, her fingers twining with his. In just a few short days, this had become their habit—to hold hands, regardless of the company or the hour.

"I am serious," he said, his gaze tracing over each of her features. She was tired and probably didn't even realize it. "I asked you out here to let you know I have considered your suggestion that we separate, and find myself agreeing to it."

Leah's fingers went limp in his. Nick had never hated himself more.

"I see." Leah's voice held no more life than her fingers. "Is this to be a permanent separation?"

"If I were less selfish," Nick said, "I would tell you that yes, this is permanent, except for those unavoidable family occasions when we must be seen together, or the periodic meetings we schedule for business purposes. Then too, you'll be expected to attend my investiture. But I am selfish, Leah, and so I will say I do not know how long we will need to live apart, and I regret this development, because it hurts you."

"What about you, Nicholas?" She withdrew her hand from his and regarded him with an appearance of dispassion. "Does this development hurt you as well, or will you be relieved to be shut of me?"

"It is not what I'd wish for either of us," Nick said. "Particularly not what I'd wish for you. You have to know, Leah..." He raised a hand to touch her face, but at her utterly contained expression, he never connected with her cheek.

"Know what?"

"I cannot trust myself to behave around you as I promised I would, and I can see no other means of keeping my word," Nick offered stiffly. "You deserve better, but I cannot undo our marriage, and for the sake of your safety, I will not even try."

"My safety?" Leah hissed incredulously. "I wish..." She rose as tears gathered in her eyes. "I wish I could hate you, Nicholas. I cannot understand this decision you've made, to dwell in the loneliest form of hell imaginable, and to fashion a cell for me there as well. You are a lovable man, intelligent, kind, and decent. Your decision makes no sense to me, not now, when I see what potential we have together."

She stalked off, skirts swishing madly, leaving Nick to sit in the dying sun and curse his fate.

When he came to bed that night, Nick found Leah doing a cred-ible impersonation of sound sleep, though she was given away by the speed with which the pulse in her throat leaped and the fact that her mouth was closed. In sleep, Leah's lips parted the barest fraction of an inch. Still, Nick didn't blame her for avoiding him. He shifted and climbed naked onto the mattress, hating the ache in his chest and knowing she likely felt something similar.

Which was entirely his arrogant, presumptuous fault. He'd thought he could be a sexual convenience for her, within the limits of his self-imposed marital celibacy. He'd planned on being her, what? Her sexual friend, as he'd been to so many other women. And her husband, entitled and bound to protect her, and her social escort when duty required it.

He'd never, ever planned on seeing the depths of her courage, her humor, her tenacity, her loyalty to family. Her passion for him, and not just for the pleasure he could give her.

On a sigh, he shifted across the bed and reached for her. She surprised him by meeting him and cuddling into his arms as if they'd been married for twenty good, happy years. But when Nick leaned down to rest his cheek against hers, he felt the lingering dampness of her tears.

"I'm sorry," he whispered. Leah said nothing, but laced her fingers through his, and drew his arm securely about her waist.

Which left him feeling, as impossible as it seemed, yet sorrier still.

CHAPTER FIFTEEN

"So how do we do this, Nicholas?" Leah was sharing a glass of brandy with Nick in the Clover Down library, their evening meal concluded and the rain a steady, battering downpour against the mullioned windows.

"How would it be least trying for you?" Nick asked, staring at his drink. Leah had chosen to sit beside him on the sofa, a generosity on her part he both treasured and detested.

She should hate him, for he most assuredly did hate himself, and his life.

"I found my years in Italy were made bearable by my brother's companionship, and that of the people who lived around me. But I had the anticipation of Charles's birth, and then his presence, to bring cheer to the whole experience."

Nick closed his eyes at the practical way she delivered that blow.

"Shall we hire you a companion?"

"We shall not. I've made do without before, but I would like a riding horse of my own."

"That's easy enough to accomplish, but, Leah"— Nick risked a glance at her—"I don't want you to feel you're confined here. If you want to spend time at Belle Maison, or if you need the town house, send word. I've a number of places I can stay."

Leah's hands tightened on her glass, and Nick realized she was likely tormenting herself with thoughts of all the beds he'd be welcome in.

"Is there something wrong with me, Nicholas?"

"Wrong with you?" He speared her with a puzzled look. "Of course not. Why would you think that?"

"You are a man who enjoys the ladies. You made that plain when I accepted your proposal, but now, it seems of all the ladies in all the beds in all the towns of England, mine is the one bed you won't share. I must conclude the fault lies with me."

Nick felt gut-punched as he saw the flickering uncertainty behind the studied composure in Leah's eyes, and yet, she had her finger on the difficulty: the difficulty was that she was his wife, his countess, and the only woman who could bear his legitimate heirs.

"The problem is that I do not want to have children with you, Leah," Nick said slowly, staring at his glass. "I've been honest about that much from the start."

"Do you dislike children, Nicholas?"

"I love children," Nick said on a harsh exhalation. He wouldn't lie to her about that, but the truth had him so frustrated, he had to set his drink down before he hurled it at the hearth with all the considerable strength in him.

They sipped their brandy in miserable, jagged silence, until Leah laid a hand over Nick's.

"I have an imposition to ask of you, Husband."

Nick's relief that she was changing the subject was pathetic. "Ask," Nick said, meeting her eyes. "Ask anything."

"You have offered to pleasure me," Leah said, a blush heating her cheeks as she spoke. "I would avail myself of your kindness in this regard."

"My kindness..." Nick closed his eyes. He would love to pleasure her, love it. If she'd allow him that... Even this one last time, he would adore the privilege and pain of it. But he'd proven unequal to the necessary restraint, and so her imposition was an accurately aimed dagger thrust into his floundering self-respect.

"We will not share a roof again," Leah said, "and you cannot think to leave for London in this downpour, at this hour. Stay with me tonight, Nicholas, please."

That last word, offered with such longing and sadness, *please*, it stole past Nick's defenses, tempted him to folly, and brushed aside rational processes.

Nick was an expert on good-bye sex and the comfort and condolence it could offer. He knew about the tenderness and gratitude an intimate parting could convey, and he knew how to make the experience dear and memorable, and the very best way to slip away from a liaison. He knew all of that only because, in the past, he'd been the one to decide the timing of each final encounter, and now Leah had taken the initiative from him.

Leah deserved that at least. She deserved to torture him, and she deserved to have her pleasure of him. Within reason.

"I will need some privacy first, Leah."

She started to nod, then her eyes narrowed. "Oh, no, you don't," she said with soft menace. "You will not ease yourself in private then come to me spent and safe, Nicholas. You will show me how to pleasure you and what you had envisioned for us were we not to part. That, or we sleep apart."

She had him, and Nick knew it. He surrendered with good grace. "Come to bed then. It shall be as you wish."

The nights at Belle Maison had given them a certain practical ease with each other that served well when they'd closed the bedroom door. Nick unfastened Leah's dress; Leah relieved him of cravat pin, watch, and boots. He took down her hair; she untied his cravat and fetched his robe while he stripped off his riding attire. She brushed out and rebraided her hair while he used the wash water, then he took Leah's robe from her so she could follow suit.

The only variation in their nocturnal routine was that Nick

tossed the used wash water out a window then refilled the basin and set it on the night table. He also put both of his handkerchiefs on the table beside the basin and towel.

"You won't blow out the candles?" Leah asked, climbing across the bed before taking her robe off.

"Soon," Nick said, shrugging out of his robe and settling on the bed, his back against the pillows. Leah drew the covers up to her chin and only then eased off her robe. "You are having a sudden attack of modesty, Wife? Not five minutes ago, you were naked and washing between your legs."

Leah scowled at him and tugged the covers up higher. "Five minutes ago you were not naked or regarding me with that anticipatory look in your eyes, and I was behind a privacy screen."

He would miss her until his dying day. "So I am naked, and you must cover up. Interesting."

A silence fell while Nick considered his next step. Just watching Leah disappear behind the screen with the basin and towel, knowing she'd invited him to be intimate with her, had set his blood galloping in low places.

"Maybe this wasn't a good idea," Leah muttered, flopping over onto her side, her back to Nick.

"It was a fine idea," Nick said, "one of your best, but you must come here, Leah, for matters to get under way."

"Oh, very well." Leah tossed the covers up and scooted closer to Nick, then settled back down on the pillows. "Now what?"

"I think we need to talk a little more," Nick said, revising his first set of plans for the evening.

"Talk?" The notion apparently did not comport with her plans. "About what?"

"Come here, lovey." Nick held out an arm. "And I'll tell you."

Leah visually measured the distance to him, her frown deepening. Then she seemed to come to some internal decision and laid herself down along Nick's side, letting his arm encircle her shoulders.

"I'm here."

"I rejoice," Nick said, not even half teasing despite the lightness of his tone. His hand came to rest on her shoulders, where he traced the pattern of her bones until he felt Leah's weight relaxing against him. "We must give some thought to your finances."

"Finances?" Leah's brows went up, as Nick's choice of pillow topics was clearly unexpected.

"I want you to be able to function independently of me," Nick said. "Nothing aggravates me more than husbands who control their wives through the purse strings but ignore them otherwise. You need to know there's a strongbox in the bottom drawer of the library desk, with a considerable sum of cash in it. The key is on the mantel under the lathed candlestick on the left. Are you paying attention?"

"Of course," Leah said, snatching her hand from Nick's chest as if caught stealing an extra tea cake.

"So where is the key to your strongbox, Wife?"

"Under the candlestick on the left side of the mantel," Leah repeated, though Nick suspected she was half guessing. "What else would you tell me about finances?"

"I'll forward to you a quarterly sum adequate for your personal needs," Nick said, "and fill out some bank drafts as well, so you'll have them in an emergency. If you want some excitement, I suggest you apply to David, Lord Fairly, to invest your excess funds for you. The man is beyond canny about mercantile matters, and he has a way of discussing business that is very unlike his titled peers."

"Your titled peers," Leah corrected him, her hand smoothing over his belly again.

"My peers?" Nick sucked in a breath as Leah's thumb traced his navel.

"You're Bellefonte." Leah yawned and snuggled closer. "You outrank most of the friends who showed up at your father's funeral." She circled his navel lazily again. "Greymoor is an earl, but Lady Warne told me yours is the older title."

Nick marshaled his scattered thoughts. "In any case, you will not be in need of funds. Would you like to manage Clover Down?"

That stopped her hand from wandering any lower, much to Nick's relief. His cock was throbbing to life and would soon be pointing due north if he couldn't distract Leah and her infernally busy hand.

"Would you like to manage this place?" Nick asked again. "It's in tidy shape as we speak, and I can add it to your dower estate so it will pass to you upon my death."

"I have no dower estate."

No dower estate, no husband worth the name, no children. Hurt for her would crush him.

"Lady Warne would have it otherwise," Nick said. "I don't know all the details, for she deals with her own solicitors, but she put a nest egg aside for you, and at the time, I had no authority to comment on it or disclose it to you."

"Do my brothers know?"

She didn't even ask how much. "I doubt Nana consulted anybody, save the Almighty and her own conscience, not in that order," Nick replied. "I'll have her man of business send you the particulars."

"Nicholas?"

"Lovey?"

"Are you finished discussing finances with me?"

"I suppose." Nick nearly gulped as he felt Leah's hand brush across the head of his cock. "There's nothing that won't keep if you'd like to discuss something else."

"Good." Leah nodded complacently but then nearly caused Nick to vault off the bed as her hand closed around his shaft. "I find I'd like to change the subject." She flipped the covers back and frankly surveyed Nick's erection. "In fact, I know I would."

❦

MORNING ARRIVED for Leah with an abrupt awareness of brilliant sunshine and Nick's warmth swaddling her right side. Pleasurable sensations piled upon one another from there—his sandalwood scent washing through the crisp air, a slight soreness between Leah's thighs from where Nick's beard had rasped against her skin, an awareness low inside her body in a place Leah hadn't thought of since she'd realized she was carrying a child.

One more thing to miss into a healthy old age.

He leaves me today, was her first fully formed thought, and it pierced the haze of physical pleasure and emotional lassitude like a javelin hurled with deadly intent.

"I leave you this day." Nick lay facing her, his hand cradling her jaw. "But you will not leave my protection, Leah, or my heart. If you need me, I will come, and I will come gladly and quickly. Agreed?"

A little palliative tossed to the part of Leah that feared she would never see him again, a kindness in the midst of a cruel undertaking. She nodded, turned her face into Nick's palm, and closed her eyes. Immediately, she felt him shift on the bed and cover her with his body.

Not again, Leah thought as she clung and let the tears seep from her eyes. Nick held her—as he had last night after bringing her such unbelievable pleasure—and let her cry and silently curse and rail against this decision; but ultimately, now as then, her arms loosened their hold, and her tears ceased.

"You will be all right, Leah," Nick assured her, raising his body up but crouching over her. "A few weeks ago, we hadn't met, and you were managing well enough. A few weeks from now, you'll be settled in here, and you will be managing well again. I'm really not worth missing for long. You'll see." He kissed her eyes and tucked her face into the crook of his neck.

"You are wrong," Leah said, forcing her hands to her sides. "I will miss you and miss you, Nicholas. You are wrong to leave me, and you are wrong to think I won't miss you."

"I meant what I said, Leah," Nick rumbled against her neck. "If you have need of my protection, my funds, my name, my houses, anything, send word to me, and the matter will have my most prompt attention. Promise me you will."

"I will, Nicholas." She kissed his cheek. Her only alternative would be her brothers, and she was no longer their affair to worry about. "I promise."

Some tension went out of him at her words, maybe some guilt and shame as well. Nicholas was stubborn and wrongheaded, but Leah was in no doubt that he suffered with his decision as much as she did.

"We have things to do this morning," Nick said, easing back a few inches. "I'll leave after luncheon, if the roads dry out. I want to introduce you to the steward who takes care of this estate and some other holdings for me. I also want to introduce you to the tenants and make sure you know how to reach my solicitors, Ethan, and Beckman." He shifted back farther, then straightened his arms, so he was looking down at her broodingly.

"I'll also want you to have the directions of several others," Nick informed her. "Matthew Belmont; Andrew, Lord Greymoor; and Valentine Windham, of course. You already know how to reach Lady Warne and my sisters. If all else fails, apply to Gareth, Marquess of Heathgate. He lacks charm, but he's hell in a fast chariot if he thinks women and children are in harm's way. Then too..."

"Nicholas." Leah smoothed his blond hair back from his forehead, loving him, hating him, and heart breaking for him.

"Yes, lovey?"

"It's time to get up."

Nick swallowed, nodded, and remained right where he was, staring down at her as if to memorize the feel of her naked beneath him, her hand in his hair, her breathing against his body. Last night, they'd shared pleasure upon pleasure—everything but the act most likely to result in conception—as if this morning wouldn't come.

Oh, but it had come.

"Please," Leah added softly. "You aren't leaving for hours yet, and it's time to get out of this bed."

He cradled her against him for one brief, fierce hug, then hoisted himself off of her and off the bed. As Leah followed, Nick stretched out a hand and brought her to her feet to stand naked in his embrace. They remained thus for just an instant, and then Nick was handing her a dressing gown and shrugging into his own.

A knock on the door, followed by Nick's permission to enter, began the next step of their parting. A maid wheeled in a tea cart and quietly departed after building up the fire.

"For June, it's remarkably chilly this morning." Or maybe the chill was only in Leah's heart.

"I refuse to discuss the weather, Wife. Come have some sustenance, and let us continue planning the day."

"Let you continue your lecture, more like." Leah offered him a wan smile. "Can't you just enjoy the meal, Nicholas, and send me the rest of your admonitions and instructions in some epistle?" She took a seat on the sofa by the hearth and surveyed the selections on the tea cart.

Tea, she was up to; food was too much of an effort.

"Eat something." Nick lowered himself beside her. "Share a slice of buttered toast with me, at least."

It seemed important to him that she eat, so Leah accepted the food from his hand after he'd slathered her portion with butter. Nick took his to the window and parted the curtain to eye the weather.

"Quite cool," he said, "but sunny and breezy. The roads will dry easily."

"And you will go," Leah added, forcing herself to take a small bite.

"I will go." Nick said, still staring out the window. "But not far, and I will come back if you sense any mischief afoot whatsoever. I'll also let Darius know you are in residence here, and Trenton as well."

He turned to face her again, and there was an intensity to his blue-eyed gaze Leah could not decipher, as if he were trying to discern her internal workings by visual inspection of her outer attributes.

"I'll also call on Lady Warne. The funeral distracted me from asking her about something that's been plaguing me."

"Burying one's father is distracting," Leah agreed, taking another bite of toast, though it tasted like so much buttered sawdust.

"I want to know who the seconds were at the duel where Frommer lost his life. It's a detail, but I can't shake the sense it's an important detail."

"You still think it matters?" Leah asked, putting down the rest of her toast.

"I think you are absolutely safe here," Nick said. "I also think there are questions to which you still deserve an answer. You assume your father killed Frommer in a fair fight, but I'm not so sure. And if it's not the case, then somebody can bring your father to justice."

Leah didn't argue that the matter should drop, largely because Nick seemed intent on pursuing it regardless of its seeming irrelevance. He would not be deterred, and it gave her a sense that his caring about her was genuine and not just a function of guilt.

So she capitulated—something she'd long ago grown adept at.

"You're not eating much," Nick said, eyeing her half-eaten toast.

"Not much appetite, I'm afraid."

"Of course not," Nick said, but to Leah's relief he kept his one thousand and seventeenth apology behind his teeth. "May I help you dress?"

She nodded and rose, and again they fell into the intimate, casual ritual of spouses attending each other's mundane needs. To Leah, though, it seemed Nick's touch on her hair and skin lingered, and he stood rather nearer than he needed to. And instead of letting her assist him, he brushed out and re-pinned her hair first, taking extraordinary care with the task, until Leah wanted to weep with frustration at the tenderness he showed her.

When they were both dressed and presentable, Leah could not manage to sashay through their bedroom door.

"I don't want to leave this room," she said, the dread she'd held at bay congealing in her chest.

"There's nothing out there I'd allow to hurt you," Nick said, obliquely admitting he was the cause of her pain. "And I cannot depart until after luncheon. Let's find your farmers and your steward, Lady Bellefonte, and stroll in your garden."

That feeling of dread inside Leah's body sank down to her vitals and spread, like an illness taking over, until Nick's proffered arm was not merely a courtesy but a real support.

The morning went, as Nick intended, with them trotting briskly from one farmstead to the next and spending more than an hour with the steward, reviewing the progress of the newly planted crops, the livestock, and the upcoming harvest of hay.

Luncheon arrived, and Nick suggested they take their meal in the garden. They dined sheltered from the breeze by the high walls near the house, if pushing food around and nibbling the occasional bite could be called dining.

Nick called for his horse when the luncheon teacart was wheeled back into the house. He remained sitting beside Leah on her stone bench, his hand linked with hers.

"I don't want you to go," Leah said finally. She wasn't crying—yet —but her chest ached terribly, and she had the feeling she was burying her marriage and any hope for her long-term happiness with it.

"But I leave because I care about you," Nick said, "at least in part, and I can only urge you to be as happy as you can, Leah. That is what I want for you, though it might not seem like it."

Leah looked at him curiously. "And for yourself? What do you want for yourself, Nicholas?"

"Honor would be nice," Nick said, staring at their joined hands, "but not likely possible. Peace, perhaps. Mostly, I want the happiness of those I love."

His tacit admission hung in the air between them a moment longer, then he rose to take her in his arms when Leah said nothing in reply.

"I am intent on my course, though I regret deeply its consequences to you," Nick said by way of one thousand and eighteenth apology.

"Perhaps time will create greater understanding for us," Leah offered, and in her words, she intended that he hear both acceptance and hope.

"Walk me to my horse?"

"Of course." Leah slipped her hand into his and tugged him in the direction of the stables when he seemed content to remain rooted in the fragrant, flowery garden where the summer blooms were making a good effort. As they walked past a bed of forget-me-nots, Nick fished for a handkerchief and silently passed it to her.

Dratted man. Dear, dear, dratted man.

His mare was waiting, saddled and patient at the mounting block, a groom at her head. Nick turned again to Leah and drew her against him.

"If you need anything," he said against her hair, "if you sense any danger or anything amiss..."

"I promise," Leah said around the painful ache in her throat. *I need you, I need you, I need you.* "And you—you must let me know how you go on from time to time."

"Always," Nick murmured then stepped away.

He seized her in his arms again though, thoroughly kissing her despite the waiting groom and the myriad eyes no doubt peering out from the manor and stables.

"Always," Nick repeated as he let her go. He swung up, and without turning to face Leah again, touched his crop to his forehead and sent his horse cantering down the drive.

While Leah subsided unceremoniously onto the mounting block, her eyes trained on his retreating figure, his sandalwood-scented handkerchief pressed to her nose. When he reached the foot of the drive, Nick turned the horse not left, toward London, but right, toward the estate where the blond young lady no doubt awaited his visit.

In the mare's retreating hoofbeats, Leah heard the sound of her marriage and her heart shattering into a thousand miserable pieces.

∾

NICK LEFT Clover Down intent on ending the misery of parting for Leah. On the short journey to Darius Lindsey's estate, he assured himself he'd done the only thing he could under the circumstances, and Leah would be much, much happier without her sorry excuse for a husband lurking about, lusting for her, and resenting—for the first time in his life—the burden of desiring a lovely woman.

When he reached the Lindsey holding, he was in a foul mood, ready to frighten small animals and intimidate the hell out of anybody who crossed him. Darius himself met him at the door, the creaky butler nowhere in evidence.

Nick nodded curtly, scowling down at Leah's brother. "Lindsey."

"Reston." Darius stepped back. "Or it's Bellefonte now. My profound condolences. May I offer you a drink?"

"You may." Nick stepped over the threshold and saw no footman at attention in the front foyer. "Was that Lady Blanche Cowell's carriage I passed on your driveway?"

"Yes." Darius ran a hand through his hair. "If you're about to lecture me about the company I keep, why aren't you keeping company with my sister?"

Well, damn. Lindsey had obviously eyed the saddlebags on Nick's mare as she'd been led away, and realized this was not strictly a social call.

"That drink?" Nick arched an eyebrow, unwilling to confess his sins in the foyer. And come to that, Lindsey looked like he could use a drink too. "Though I don't promise you won't get a lecture as well," Nick went on as Darius led the way through the house. "What can you possibly see in that woman?"

"My bloody miserable fate," Darius said. "Brandy or whiskey?"

"Whiskey." Nick decided on the libation that suited his harsh, volatile mood. "I've left your sister."

Darius went still in the act of removing a glass stopper from a decanter, but then carefully set the stopper down

on the sideboard. "Did she send you away?"

"She did not, and she has not in any way displeased me, nor does she deserve the talk that will undoubtedly ensue in time."

"I see." Lindsey poured one drink, very rudely tossed it back before pouring another for himself, then pouring a third and passing it to his guest. "Shall I call you out, Bellefonte?"

"Don't call me that." Nick accepted the drink, downed it, and passed his glass back for a refill.

"What shall I call you?" Darius inquired in lethally soft tones. Nick surveyed him and saw a man who was several inches shorter than he, a few years younger, and decades better acquainted with bitterness.

"Leah would kill us both for dueling," Nick said as he accepted the second drink from his host and tossed that one back as well.

"I will not suffer my sister to be hurt," Darius said, "but losing one of us in a duel would no doubt hurt more than weathering some gossip. So..." He looked around the room. "Shall we sit and blast away at each other with civilized insults and veiled threats, or can you tell me why you're being such an ass?"

If Nick hadn't liked Lindsey before, and respected him for his championing of Leah, Nick liked him thoroughly in that moment.

"We sit and enjoy your surprisingly fine spirits."

Darius gestured to the couch for Nick, and took a well-cushioned chair for himself, letting silence stretch while Nick took a seat.

"You will look in on Leah?" Nick set his empty glass down on the table, wondering if Lindsey possessed enough decent spirits to get them both drunk.

"Of course," Darius replied. "But why are you doing this, if you can tell me? I suspected your affection for Leah was genuine." There was a hint of sympathy in Darius's tone, and Nick dropped his gaze to his empty glass rather than face compassion head on.

"My affection for your sister is genuine," Nick said, "but have you never made a decision, Lindsey, that rippled out across your life, having repercussions you could not possibly have foreseen? Have you never given a promise in good faith you lived to regret?"

"I don't promise anybody much of anything," Darius replied with a snort of humorless laughter. "I have regrets, though. I most assuredly do have substantial, relentless regrets." He lifted his drink to sip, when the door to the library burst open, and a little boy came barreling straight for Darius. Darius quickly set the drink down and caught the child up in his arms.

"Dare!" the child cried. "She's gone! I can come out now, and we can go for a ride!" Darius's arms tightened around the squirming boy, and his gaze over the child's shoulder became so fierce Nick felt relief they wouldn't meet over pistols or swords.

Darius Lindsey's gaze promised death to Nick, right then and there, should Nick offer any hurt or insult to the child.

"She is gone," Darius said quietly to the child in his lap, "but we have another guest, John, so why don't you make your bow?"

The bottom of Nick's stomach dropped out as he gazed into young eyes so like Leah's.

"John Cowperthwaite Lindsey," the child piped cheerfully as he scrambled to his feet and bowed to Nick. "At your service, good sir."

Nick rose and bowed to the child. "Bellefonte. Pleased to make your acquaintance." Then he squatted when he saw wee John's stunned reaction to his great height. "But you can call me Nick, with mine host's permission, as Bellefonte is not so friendly, young John, and I should like to make a new friend today."

"Are you a giant?"

"Of course not," Nick scoffed, still hunkered at the child's eye level. "I am merely a fellow who ate all his vegetables, went to bed without a fuss every night, and bathed when nurse said I must.

Darius was not quite as well behaved as I, at least when he was a boy."

John eyed Darius, who was sitting as still and attentive as a hungry papa wolf. "Is that why Dare isn't so big as you?"

"Quite possibly, though as grown fellows go, he's on the tall side," Nick said. "We mustn't hurt his feelings when it's too late for him to grow any more. Sit you down, John, and we will impress Darius with our conversation." Nick hoisted the child onto his lap. "Now, my good fellow, tell me about your pony."

John chattered on with the bright, happy oblivion of a well-loved child before a new audience, and Nick let go of some anxiety. Every child deserved to be loved, and this one had at least that in his favor.

Nick interrupted John's description of his latest tumble from his pony. "Don't you suppose if you're to go riding, you'd best don appropriate attire?"

John looked for a translation from Darius, who'd been silent and watchful throughout the entire exchange.

"Put on your boots and breeches," Darius said, "and grab a carrot or two from Cook, but take a proper leave of Lord Bellefonte first." John executed a perfect little bow of parting and scampered off, leaving an enormous silence in his wake.

"It seems we have more to discuss than I thought, Lindsey." For a wretched, uncomfortable suspicion had bloomed in the back of Nick's mind.

"Leah will kill us both if you call me out," Darius said with bitter humor. "There is an explanation for why matters stand as they do, but I've been trying to convince Trent that because Leah's circumstances have changed, perhaps it's time to change John's circumstances as well."

"No perhaps about it," Nick shot back. "That boy deserves his mother's love, to say nothing of what Leah deserves."

Surprise crossed Darius's features, surprise he made no effort to mask. "You and the rest of Polite Society are supposed to conclude John is my by-blow."

"He has eyes like yours, Lindsey. Beelzebub's hairy balls, you can't—"

Lindsey held up a hand. "John is my paternal half-brother, our paternal half-brother. His mother was a maid at Wilton Acres who walked here from the Lindsey family seat in Hampshire to seek my aid. Wilton had discarded her when she couldn't hide her condition any longer and scoffed at the notion she might be carrying his child. If Wilton knew the boy dwelled here, the consequences to the child would be unthinkable. Leah doesn't know of him. She's had enough to deal with, and the time was never right."

Another secret kept from Leah, by another man who professed to love her. The idea should have assuaged Nick's guilt, when in fact it did the opposite.

"You won't tell Leah?" Darius asked, his manner softening a little.

"I won't tell Leah, yet," Nick said, "but she will know soon, and you'd best use the time to make sure John is prepared for that day. She lost a child, Lindsey, and her marriage will not provide any opportunities to replace that loss with joy. I will be very surprised if she doesn't snatch the boy from you the moment she learns of him."

Rather than rant and rail to the contrary—and wouldn't a rousing argument suit Nick's mood wonderfully?—Darius's gaze turned pensive.

"You're an earl now, Wilton's peer," he said. "Leah would dote on the boy."

Behind dark eyes, the millwheel of Lindsey's brain was turning at a great rate, and Nick suspected he knew exactly the direction of Lindsey's thoughts.

"You and John can ride a few miles with me in the direction of town. We'll talk."

And talk they did.

CHAPTER SIXTEEN

Leah took a dinner tray to the back garden, trying to make sense of her husband's flight. As the day had worn on, she'd concluded it had made little sense to Nick himself.

As Leah's thoughts continued to ramble, she noticed a groom on a lathered horse trotting up the drive. A stable boy took the horse to walk it out, the groom slipped off, and Leah went back to her musings. Her mind was functioning on two levels, as she knew it would for some time.

Part of her could rationally process information and plan the next day to write to her sister or to Lady Nita, to map out a little ride around the neighborhood, to draft a note to send to the local vicar's wife.

Another part of her mind wailed in silent, passionate grief for the loss of her husband. That part of her was on its feet and heading for the library in search of an illicit tumbler of brandy when a footman approached in the waning evening light.

"Letter for you, your ladyship, from his lordship." The footman offered a sealed epistle on a salver.

She took the letter and, with a pounding heart, continued her progress toward the library. Something had to be wrong for Nick to be communicating with her so soon after leaving her side. Something had to be terribly wrong.

Several minutes later, Leah stared at Nick's missive, puzzled but a little cheered as well.

DEAREST LOVEY WIFE,

Because you might need to contact me, please be informed I will breakfast with Hazlit tomorrow, then call on Lady Warne. The solicitors have told me they will read Papa's will at noon, and Beck and Ethan will be on hand for that as well. I expect we will dine at my club, after which I must closet myself with my man of business to make further inroads on the reams of correspondence that arrived while I was at Belle Maison. I am looking into a polyglot amanuensis, for your suggestion has increasing merit.

I hope this finds you well and apologize for the manner of my leave-taking earlier this day. There is no pleasant way to part from one's dear spouse, regardless that the whole sorry business is my doing. Forgive me, though, as I am blundering close to another apology, which you've told me I must not do as long as I will not also explain.

I miss you, Wife, and require your assurances you need nothing from me but perhaps a little silence. Tell me how you go on, or I shall fret unbecomingly.

Nicholas, Bellefonte

NICHOLAS HAD an odd way of going about an estrangement, but then, he was kind, and perhaps he was merely easing her into their separation, using the little courtesy of a note to reinforce his willingness to remain cordial. The next evening, however, Leah received another evening epistle, hurried out from Town on a lathered horse.

LOVEY MINE,

You will be surprised to learn my papa left a contribution to your dower estate sizeable enough to make my untimely demise loom before you with some appeal. The details will be forwarded by the weasels swarming over the will, no doubt in language it will take an Oxford don to decipher. Lady Warne has threatened to disown me for our estrangement, and I cut my visit to her short lest she do herself an injury boxing my ears.

Tomorrow I call upon your late Frommer's oldest brother, who had the great misfortune to have inherited the marquessate two years ago. Because I've recently inherited my own father's title, he and I can perhaps commiserate. Hazlit claims the man acted as Aaron's second, and from him, I am hoping to learn who seconded Wilton. Lord Valentine has managed the domestics here in my absence, and while he sympathizes with my loss, he is playing rather a lot of finger exercises when I'm underfoot. He claims I try his patience, if you can imagine such a thing.

I slept badly last night, tired though I was.

Perhaps you are faring better?

Yours, Nicholas, Bellefonte

WHEN LEAH also received an epistle on the third night following Nick's departure, she considered that maybe Nick would not be quite as successful at being estranged as he might have hoped.

MOST STUBBORN LOVEY and Dear Wife,

Your silence conveys a hint of the anger at me to which you are entitled. Either that, or you have broken your hand, for I have had no word from you to indicate you yet breathe. You will please provide same, post haste. Lady Warne is no ally to me, as she is not speaking to the "henwitted, clodpated embarrassment of a grandson of whom she used to be so proud." I am lucky I am still quick enough to keep my backside from her reach—mostly. The first swat caught me unaware.

I was astonished to learn from Frommer the Eldest that Hellerington seconded your father. Somebody fired too early, but as our man was tossing his accounts into the bushes at the precise moment when bullets flew, only Hellerington can attest for a certainty to the identity of the bad sport—or murderer—who fired early. Bad business, my dear, and I am sorry, because either way, somebody close to you behaved poorly.

I am pining for the want of you, of course, and doing an abysmal job of keeping my temper. Beck and Ethan are leaving tomorrow in disgust. I've drunk all the good liquor, and my staff is too piqued with me to set much of a table. My horse is not speaking to me either, and her conversation is a real loss.

Valentine has condemned me to prancing little Haydn sonatas until I, in his words, "Come to my feeble senses." So you really must write to me, love, truly you must.

Your Nicholas, Bellefonte

WHAT TO WRITE in response to that blather/love letter/letter from school? Leah pared the tip of a pen and stared at the foolscap before her. She stared for a full fifteen minutes before deciding that "Dear Nicholas," would do as a place to start. To reach that brilliant conclusion, she'd discarded a list of possibilities... Dearest Nicholas, Nicholas, Spouse, Errant Spouse, Henwitted Clodpate, Bellefonte, Dearest Clodpate...

"There you are." Ethan's voice sounded from the doorway, and Leah looked up to find him and Beckman smiling at her tentatively, two men who looked a good deal like Nick without quite matching him for handsomeness, charm, or—she was angry with her spouse—clodpatedness either.

"Gentlemen." Leah rose, her own smile tentative as well. They looked so like Nick and they'd just been with him and they were so dear to call on her and her eyes were stinging.

"Oh, ye gods." Beckman stepped around Ethan and enveloped Leah in a hug. He wasn't as large as his oldest brother, but he was big enough and had the same muscular, masculine feel to his embrace, and he knew enough to carry a handkerchief into battle.

Though his scent was all wrong. Bergamot, like a cup of doctored tea.

"Now we've done it," Ethan muttered, closing the door. "Nick won't like this one bit, making his countess cry."

"As if," Beck said over the top of Leah's head, "himself didn't see to that first. She's entitled to cry, after all, if not for lack of Nick, then for his lack of sense."

Ethan nattered on in agreement, probably to give Leah time to compose herself.

"Shall I ring for tea?" Leah suggested as she stepped out of Beck's arms. "Or a late luncheon, perhaps?"

"Both," Ethan said. "Beck wants to push south before nightfall, and I must hie back to London. Some sustenance and company would be appreciated. Now that Beckman has surrendered his white flag, how fare you?"

"Miserably," Leah said, sensing honesty was the norm among Nick's family. "I miss him, I don't know why he does what he does, and though I am hurt and angry, I still worry that he is..."

"He's what?"

"He's doing what he must," Leah said. "He can't see another option. But tell me, did Nick put you up to this spying?"

"He's too clever for that," Ethan said. "Lady Warne put us up to spying, and Nick will grill me when I get back to Town. The sisters will no doubt grill Beck by letter, about you, Nick, and myself."

"Poor Beck," Leah said. "Shall we sit?"

Her brothers-in-law charmed her, entertained her, and consumed great quantities of food, leaving Leah feeling a little breathless but pleased at the distraction they offered. When they rose to leave,

Ethan wandered around the room far enough to see the paper still on the escritoire by the window.

"Did we interrupt your effort to pen some remonstrance to Nick?" Ethan asked, eyeing the two words on the page.

"I was just getting started, but I doubt anything will come of it," Leah said. "I seem to have too much to say, and nothing to say of merit."

"Nonsense," Beck corrected her gently. "Your dimwitted spouse wants merely to see your hand, Leah. Describe which rose looks like it will bloom first, and he'll be pleased—assuming you want to please him?"

"I honestly don't know."

"Why don't we see to our horses," Ethan said, "and you can jot a few choice imprecations in the meanwhile. I'll be happy to deliver your epistle, and this way, I can report to Lady Warne that you and Nick are at least corresponding."

Leah shifted her gaze from one brother to the other. They would be terribly disappointed if she did not write at least a few words.

Disappointed and worried. "I think kindness runs in the Haddonfield family."

"Kindness." Beck rolled his eyes. "I'm guessing you'd rather have us offer more practical emotions right about now."

"Let her write her epistle while we saddle up."

So they left, and Leah was faced again with the challenge of communicating in writing with her spouse.

DEAR NICHOLAS,

You are a devoted correspondent for an estranged husband, but I will bow to your greater wisdom regarding the particulars of our situation, for I myself am quite at sea. I have kept busy, riding out on Casper when the weather permits, devising some changes to the cutting gardens—I've pulled up the bed of forget-me-nots, for example

—and replying to the many letters coming at me from your sisters at Belle Maison.

Then too, your solicitors forwarded a description of my bequest from your father, and that has, indeed, taken a lexicon and a quizzing glass to decipher. Rest assured, I am not at this point inspired by financial considerations to hasten your demise. Not yet.

Please give my very best to your grandmother, a woman whose sense and wisdom impressed me almost as much as her swift right hand no doubt impressed your fundament.

Your brothers have promised to spread all manner of gossip regarding the goings on here at Clover Down, though their account of your life in Town is suspiciously dull and devoid of fraternal barbs. You must commend them for their loyalty when next you interrogate them.

I hope you fare well, dear Husband, though I hesitate to further burden you with excessive correspondence when I know how great your distaste for same can be.

Your wife,

Leah

SHE READ and reread the note, not sure what she wanted it to say or not say. In the end, she added a four-word postscript in the spirit of gracious honesty Nick had set in his own epistles. She didn't know if the addition was a kindness or not, didn't know if Nick would appreciate or resent it. She knew only that what she had written was the truth.

∾

ETHAN WATCHED as Nick tore open Leah's note and scanned its contents. His expression was fierce, then interrupted by a bark of laughter, then fierce again. Before he folded up the note, his brows rose in surprise, then his face took on a pained, thoughtful expression as he refolded the note.

"She says she misses me. In a postscript. She didn't mean to be anything save honest, Ethan, but those four words—*I do miss you*—make me feel like an ass."

"You are not an ass, exactly." Ethan crossed Nick's study to the decanter and lifted the stopper with a questioning gesture. "You are navigating uncharted waters and doing the best you can, with questionable results."

"Help yourself," Nick said. "None for me. I am off to grovel before Lady Warne."

"Groveling won't help," Ethan said, pouring himself a single finger of liquor. "She doesn't understand what you're about Nick, separating from your wife not a month after the wedding, especially when it's clear you and Leah adore each other."

"But that's the problem, Ethan." Nick's eyes were bleak. "I do adore her, with all the love and lust in me, which is considerable. Sooner or later..."

"Sooner or later you would have children," Ethan finished for him softly. "And like any other pair of loving parents, you would cope, Nick. You would."

"We would, for as long as the Lord granted us breath and sense to cope, but then what, Ethan?"

"You don't think the family would help? Our sister Della is fifteen years your junior, and she'd be aunt to any offspring of yours. You need to rethink this, Nick, and before Leah gives up on you."

Nick merely shook his head, a determined man whose commitment to a particular course would not falter because that course was difficult, lonely, and costly.

"Go see Nana," Ethan said gently. "Maybe she can talk some sense into you."

~

LADY WARNE WAS NOT HOME to Nick, which hurt more than it should. She was given to fits and starts, but not cruel, so Nick decided to test her resolve by going around back to the kitchen and invading by stealth. He found his quarry enjoying a cup of tea with old Magda.

"You!" Lady Warne snorted at him from her perch at the worktable. "You are not welcome until you behave as a proper earl to your countess."

"My lady..." Magda's voice bore the reproach of somebody who'd known her employer since girlhood.

Lady Warne turned her glower on the older woman. "Don't you take up for this scamp, Magda Spencer. I held my tongue while he swived the indecent half of London for years on end, and I held my tongue when his misguided papa let him hare off to Sussex. I held my tongue when he married that poor woman as if he were some knight on a white charger, and I held my tongue—"

"So hold your tongue now," Magda interrupted her, rising and gesturing for Nick to sit. "The boy needs understanding now, and you are the only one who can provide it. Who else will he talk to? Those brothers of his? His sisters? His married friends are all over the Home Counties, and their wives likely to skewer them for taking his part. Pour the lad some tea, and let him say his piece. And you"— Magda jerked her chin at Nick—"I told you to sit and let your grandmother pour you some tea."

Nick sat. Lady Warne smirked—and poured him tea.

"So wiggle your handsome way out of this one, Nicholas." Lady Warne pushed his tea at him. "You leave a wonderful woman to rusticate less than a month after the wedding, your father is barely cold in the ground, and you seek to resume your wenching already?"

"My wen—" Nick's eyebrows rose then crashed down as he stared at the ridiculously delicate teacup in his hand. "I can say with all certainty Leah has ruined me for wenching, Nana. Of that you may be sure."

"The bordellos should hang their windows with black crepe," the marchioness retorted. "So what are you about, Nicholas, to abandon your wife to gossip and scorn this way? Don't you think she had enough of that with young Frommer? Or with her own father?"

"The gossip will eventually die down, but what if we have children, Nana? What in God's name will we do if we have children?" He sat forward abruptly, his face in his hands, abruptly sympathetic to the demented creatures who howled their despair at the full moon.

"If you have children," Lady Warne said carefully, "you will love them."

"God in heaven, Nana." Nick rose abruptly to his full height. "What if my heir turns out like Leonie? She can barely read, she must print her letters, she trusts everyone who smiles at her, she wants me to read fairytales to her when I visit, and she will be playing with dolls until I'm an old man. Bad enough my children will be taunted for their height and size. Bad enough they'll be assumed to be stupid oafs good only for hitching to the plough, bad enough they'll never feel they fit in..."

He spun on his heel and went to the window, shoulders heaving with emotion before gathering his composure and continuing more softly.

"I cannot consign Leah to mothering a brood of oversized idiots," Nick informed them. "Worse by far, I will not consign my children to the ridicule and cruelties that would have been Leonie's lot had I not intervened. Bastards may enjoy a certain anonymity, but not the heirs of a belted earl. Though you may cease your tantrums and lectures, for I have at least resolved to explain to Leah why ours must be a chaste marriage. She deserves the truth, and I deserve her undying enmity for not having shared it with her sooner."

He regarded two old women who'd loved him since he'd first drawn breath, both looking at him with such... such compassion. Who would regard his children like this when he was dead and buried? Leah, perhaps. His entire future hung on that possibility.

"I will explain to Leah what we'd risk were we to have children, and if she leaves me once and for all, I will accept her decision."

Silence. Dumbstruck, dismayed silence, and Nick realized he'd shouted at his grandmother and his old nurse. "My apologies, ladies." He bowed. "You can appreciate my concern."

Magda's lips were pursed in thought, while Lady Warne rose and pushed Nick back toward the table.

"Sit, you," she said. "You are under a misapprehension I would relieve you of. Magda?"

Magda nodded and slid down beside Lady Warne.

"You believe Leonie's limitations are a function of her parentage," the marchioness began briskly. "They are not."

"But Papa had a brother..."

"Who fell from his damned horse as a lad," her ladyship snapped. "There are many traits that run in the Haddonfield and Harper lines, Nick, but madness and mental impairment are not among them."

"But how did Leonie come to be as she is?" Nick asked. "She has been simple since I've known her."

"Fevers," Magda supplied. "You didn't meet the girl until she was well past two years of age, and until that winter, she'd been just another darling, happy child. She walked by one year, began speaking about the same time, and put her sentences together the same as any other child."

"So what happened?"

"Leonie fell ill with the same influenza that took her mother," Lady Warne said. "But Leonie eventually recovered. Magda noticed the child wasn't coming along as she had before, though physically, Leonie has always been vigorous enough."

Nick's mind could not absorb all that Lady Warne said, but he could comprehend that last. "She's been healthy as a horse, except for that flu."

"I thought we might lose her," Magda said. "She shook with the fevers and shook with them, night after night, and grew so tiny it's a wonder she lived."

Another silence fell, as Nick began to consider the information the old women had just imparted. He ran his finger around the rim of his teacup.

"You are saying Leonie was not born simple."

"No more than any other child," Lady Warne said. "No more than you were, Nicholas."

"So I've put aside my wife for nothing?" Nick asked the room in general.

"You put her aside to try to protect her," Lady Warne replied, "and to protect your unborn children from what you thought would be a life of ridicule and judgment."

"God help me. Ladies, you will excuse me. I have another call to make."

Nick stumbled out of the kitchen, not even hearing what they might have said to him in parting.

～

NICK HADN'T LIED; he did have another appointment. But it wasn't for another hour, and he needed that hour to put his world back on its axis. He found himself in the park by the duck pond, his little scrappy friend nowhere to be seen.

The day was pleasant, the breeze soft, the sunshine warm on Nick's face. Just another pretty afternoon in the park, though Nick felt as if his whole life was shifting.

He'd been so wrong for so long, and so sure of himself in his wrongheadedness. He didn't know whether to cry with relief or cry with sorrow for the damage his misjudgments were still causing even as he sat in the afternoon breeze and listened to the laughter of children. Normal children, like little John. Children who could learn cursive writing and Latin, do sums and see malice and contempt when it came at them.

A loud quacking disturbed his musings, and Nick looked up to see an indignant young drake flapping and hissing at him. His friend, well on the way to growing up, though a yellowish cast to his plumage betrayed his identity. Nick fished a tea biscuit left over from breakfast out of his pocket and tossed it at the young duck. The tea biscuit disappeared, and the duck waddled down to the water to join his fellows.

They grew up—John and Leonie and children everywhere. They grew up, and their families shouldn't miss the short window of childhood. God above, Leah would be reeling to find herself possessed of a half-brother who'd been kept from her.

And then, when she'd recovered from that blow, or maybe before she sustained it, Nick would have to tell her about Leonie.

~

LEAH HAD NEVER HAD such a sociable week.

Ethan and Beck came on Thursday. On Friday, David Worthington, Viscount Fairly, appeared and took her to visit with his wife and children. On Saturday, more of Nicholas's friends, Lord and Lady Greymoor, showed up, with his lordship ponying a pretty mare behind his great black gelding, a wedding present to Leah. They stayed for luncheon before removing to Fairly's, and while Lady Greymoor admired Leah's gardens, she also admonished her hostess to bring that lackwitted Nicholas to heel.

Sunday saw a lull in the traffic, with Darius offering to escort Leah to services at the local church. It was a pretty day, and an innocuous way to meet her neighbors, so she went.

"I'm off to Town tomorrow," Darius said as he handed Leah down from his coach when he saw her home. "I should be back by nightfall."

"You'll give my regards to Trent and the children?" Leah asked, searching her brother's face.

"Of course, if I have time to stop by. I've a few appointments to see to first, and I thought checking in on Emily might be the higher priority."

Leah regarded him sternly. "You are not to make her into your next damsel in distress. Wilton dotes on her, and her letters suggest she is enjoying the patronage of Lady Warne. She'll be all right, as I am all right."

"Give Nick some time," Darius said. "I like him, and I'm not easily impressed. What seems so insurmountable one day can often be managed the next."

Leah glanced at him, wondering where such an encouraging sentiment came from, particularly as she needed to hear it—badly.

"Travel safely." She kissed his cheek again, touched and a little surprised when he hugged her tightly, kissed her back, and then hugged her again before hopping up onto the box with his coachman.

"I'll see you later in the week, Leah," he called down. "Save some time for me."

"Of course." She waved him on his way, wondering what that was all about. She'd no sooner given the order for tea to be served in the garden when she saw the now-familiar groom trotting up the drive. Leah waved him over so they might dispense with formalities, and took the letter directly from his hand.

As she caught a whiff of Nick's scent on the sealed missive, she felt a pang of longing for her husband—for his smile, his embrace, the sound of his voice, the feel of him shifting on the mattress beside her at night.

She cut those thoughts off and made her way to the back gardens, Nick's latest letter in hand.

BELOVED WIFE,

If you will receive me, I will call upon you Monday afternoon. We have matters to discuss. I continue to miss you, and though it flatters me not, I am cheered to learn you miss me as well.

Your Nicholas, Bellefonte

LEAH SCANNED those three sentences several times before it sank in that Nick was coming back to Clover Down, the very next day. She set the letter aside and reached for the teapot, thinking to pour herself a cup to steady her nerves.

Except her hands shook too badly to manage even that, so she simply went inside, jotted off a reply, and settled down to await her fate.

~

"WELL?" Nick's eyes bored into the hapless groom who'd pulled the duty of delivering Nick's Sunday epistle to Leah.

"She seemed quite well, my lord," the man said, handing over the reply. "But I met her brother, Mr. Lindsey, at the foot of the drive, and he bade me pass along another message."

"Go on." Nick did not tear open Leah's reply, not while the groom was still in the same room.

"He said he would expect you and your lady on Tuesday for luncheon."

"Thank you." Nick nodded in curt dismissal. "But Druckman?"

"My lord?"

"Tell the lads I'll be sending another note out to Kent tomorrow, this one to Blossom Court," Nick said, his fingers itching to open the letter.

Druckman nodded resignedly. "Aye, my lord."

When he'd taken his leave, Nick crossed to the brandy decanter, eyeing Leah's reply like a squirming sack. It could hold the key to his future, but was it snakes or kittens? Condemnation or happiness? Nick tossed back a brandy, marshaled his courage, and opened the letter.

HUSBAND,
 It will be my pleasure to receive you tomorrow afternoon.
Leah

NICK STARED AT THE LETTER, trying to will insight from a mere handful of words. She would receive him— that was good—but that was all. No hint of concern for him, no admission that she missed him, no humor. Nick frowned and looked closer, thinking her handwriting was maybe not so tidy as usual.

Ah, well, tomorrow would come, and it would go, perhaps taking Nick's last chance at happiness with it. Where were his friends when there was a brandy decanter and a long night to get through?

CHAPTER SEVENTEEN

"I never anticipated how tiring separation from one's husband would be," Leah said as Buttercup was led off to the stables, "nor how many people call you friend, Nicholas."

Leah sank onto the front steps leading to the Clover Down front door, and Nick realized his wife was delaying the moment when they were private. Well, to hell with that. He moved up a couple of steps and sat behind her so one of his legs was on either side of her. When Leah only watched him with veiled caution, he wrapped his arms around her and propped his chin on her crown.

"I love you," Nick said. "I need to get that out, before any of my well-meaning, infernal friends come trotting up that drive, your brother drops by, one of my brothers drops by, or some servant comes around to eavesdrop."

"I beg your pardon?" Leah's cheek was resting against his chest, her ear over his heart, where she'd once told him she liked to have it.

Nick pulled her away from him enough that their gazes could meet. "I love you, Leah Haddonfield. I hope it matters."

He folded her back against him, unwilling to see her reaction in her eyes. What if he'd left it too late? What if he'd been too ridiculous, separating from a perfectly luscious wife because she was perfectly luscious? What if she laughed at him?

"I love you too," Leah murmured against his chest.

Relief leavened his anxiety. At least she wasn't laughing. All she'd said was... His hand in her hair went still, and he stopped nuzzling her temple.

"I'm not sure I heard you aright, Wife."

Leah peeled back, met his gaze squarely, and pronounced sentence on him slowly. "I love you, Nicholas Haddonfield," she said, "but that is only a start. Why are you here today with me when you left a week ago, hell-bent on separation?"

"You love me?" Nick took visual inventory of the front court of his favorite little estate, then took a deep breath through his nose. Leah's scent filled his awareness, assuring him he hadn't fallen asleep on his horse, only to dream this moment.

"I love you." Leah smiled, but there was sadness in that smile, and Nick's initial bubble of joy began to drift away.

"I've hurt you," Nick said, "and I am sorry. I'd like to show you how sorry." He rose, drew her to her feet, and laced his fingers through hers, tugging her into the house and toward the staircase.

Leah tugged back, bringing him to a halt. "Nicholas?"

"Come upstairs with me, please?" He wouldn't resort to overt groveling. Not yet.

"I cannot." She dropped his hand, and it might as well have been Nick's heart she cast aside. "I cannot bear for you to leave me again, Nicholas. If you take me up those stairs, you must promise you will not leave me, not for some wrongheaded notion, not for some other woman. I know you are a man with needs, but I am your wife, and I will try... No." She stopped herself. "I will not beg. I will not."

"I will not leave you." Nick drew her into his arms. "Not ever, though you might send me away. I don't just love you, Wife, I am in love with you, and I can promise you I've never said those words to a woman before, not a human woman anyway."

Leah frowned up at him.

"I might have said them to my horse," Nick amended hastily, "but you mustn't worry I'll leave you or be tempted to mischief or ever want another in my bed. We have much to discuss, more than you know, in fact, but please for the love of God, Leah, let me love you now."

She searched his face then nodded once. Nick swept her up in his arms and all but ran for the bedroom.

Thank you; thank you, Jesus; thank you, God; thank you, Leah. This wasn't what he'd intended when he'd cantered his mare up the drive. He'd intended to sit Leah down in his study with a tumbler of spirits, and clear the air between them of all the mistakes and deceptions. He should stop and do just that, because she might not be amenable to this reconciliation once she knew what he'd withheld.

That thought, however, made him only more desperate to seize his first and possibly last opportunity to be truly intimate with her.

He stood her on her feet rather than toss her on the bed, ruck up her skirts, and have at it. This had to be right for her, in every detail, for he might never have another chance to be his wife's lover in fact.

So he turned her by the shoulders and carefully undid the hooks running down the back of her dress. He untied the bows of her chemise then drew her to sit at the vanity, where he took the pins from her hair and finger-combed the mahogany silk of it over her shoulders.

"We usually undress at night," Leah said, catching Nick's gaze in the mirror. "By candlelight."

"You are glorious in any light." Nick bent to kiss the juncture of her shoulder and her neck, to inhale her, to feast on her. "And you smell of spring and sunshine." He nuzzled and nibbled lazily before raising up to regard her in the mirror. "And you taste of warmth and willingness and every man's fondest desire."

"I want only to taste of your fondest desire," Leah replied, almost sternly. She rose and inspected her fully dressed husband, a wealth of meaning conveying itself in her single arched eyebrow.

Nick was naked in seconds.

"Come here." He held out his arm the very next instant and beckoned with one hand toward his wife. "Come here, please."

That word, Nick was finding, had a magical effect on his countess. She liked to hear him ask politely for what wasn't polite at all. When she was standing next to him in her chemise and stockings, Nick perused her with such intensity she blushed.

"I don't deserve you," he said at length. "I don't deserve what we're about to share, and I don't deserve your forgiveness, but I'll presume on it anyway."

As puzzlement at his words clouded Leah's eyes, Nick distracted her by pushing her chemise off her shoulders and down over her hips. He knelt to step her out of it and to untie her garters and roll down her stockings, leaving her utterly naked in the soft afternoon sunshine.

When Leah would have turned to climb onto the bed, Nick gathered her into his arms, her skin warm and smooth against his. He was already aroused, the evidence of his desire arrowing up between their bodies and pressing against Leah's abdomen.

"God, how I want you," he murmured against her neck. "To think..."

"I missed you," Leah whispered, turning her face to his chest. "I wanted to ride into London and clobber you soundly on your handsome, stubborn, addled blond head."

"I know," Nick said, pushing her back so she sat on the high bed. "I deserved to be coshed. I am addled."

"And you should be spanked." Leah hiked back on her elbows and then must have noted a gleam in Nick's eyes. "Oh, no, Husband. It's daylight, for the love of God..."

"All the better to see you." Nick snatched a pillow from the bed, tossed it at his feet, and knelt between Leah's legs. "And pleasure you, and make you scream and beg and promise never to leave me." When she would have squirmed back in protest, he wrapped an arm around each of her thighs and tugged her bottom to the edge of the mattress.

"And taste you," he added, swiping the flat of his tongue right up the crease of her sex.

He tormented, teased, and suckled until Leah was whimpering and undulating with frustration. When he deigned to slip two fingers into her damp heat, she convulsed around them hard, long, and loudly, much to Nick's satisfaction.

"Tell me again that you missed me." Nick smiled down at her as he stood beside the bed and took a sip of water. She was on her back, forearm shielding her eyes, her legs splayed in the most lovely testament to satiety Nick had ever seen.

Leah opened her eyes. "I still miss you. Inside me, here." She slid her hand over her mons. "I miss you. I grieve for the lack of you inside me."

Grief. He'd caused his beloved wife not just heartache and disappointment, but grief. Nick set the water glass down and slipped his arms under Leah's shoulders and knees, to arrange her on the mattress so her head was on the pillows.

"I miss you, too," he said, coming down beside her and pushing her hair back from her forehead. "In here." He took her hand and laid it over his heart. "And here," his belly. "And here." He wrapped her fingers around his cock and rolled to his back so Leah was the one on her side, regarding him as she stroked her fingers over his shaft.

"You are uncomfortable?" she asked, sleeving him in a long, easy stroke.

"I ache," Nick said, opening his eyes to meet hers. "I ache for you, for the sensation of being inside you and over you and... Merciful... Eternal... Leah."

She bent and tongued him, a soft, hot swipe of dampness followed by gentle suction applied just under the tip.

"Lovey." It came out "looovveeey." Nick closed his eyes and cupped the back of her head gently. "I'll spend."

She ignored him, much as he'd ignored her earlier. Her fingers found the soft weight of his testes then eased up to stroke his shaft while her mouth tended to the velvety head of his cock.

"Please, lovey," Nick whispered. "This time, I want to be inside you."

Leah sat back and regarded him as he lay back against the pillows. "What has changed, Nicholas?"

He was glad she realized that something was different, that *he* was different, and that he wanted today to be a beginning for them.

"Everything," he said, pushing up off the pillows and gently urging her down on her back. "Let me love you, please. I'll be careful, I promise. I'll go slowly, and I won't hurt you."

"You couldn't hurt me."

"I have hurt you," Nick corrected her, easing his body over hers. "I hurt the heart you gave into my keeping, and... ah, God, Leah." He fastened his mouth over hers and slowly plundered his way past her lips. The great length of his cock lay heavily on Leah's stomach, hot, and still wet from her loving. She arched up against it and pushed her tongue into Nick's mouth.

"Shame on you," Nick whispered, arching away from her. "I intend to make a proper job of this, Wife, and you will not rush me."

"Hah." Leah wrapped her legs around his flanks and pressed her wet sex to his shaft.

"You do not play fair, my lady. And I adored you before you started breaking the rules."

"I'm merely making a proper job of it," Leah whispered just as her thumbs glossed over his nipples.

Holy everlasting... He loved his wife, loved this mischievous, tantalizing, playful, inventive side to her. Her mouth brushed over one of his nipples, while her hand slid down, down the length of his back to grip his fundament. Nick fought a moment's panic as his arousal threatened his control.

Proper job or not, he would not last much longer, not with his she-devil wife intent on her own goals. With unerring instinct, he pressed the tip of his cock against Leah's sex and succeeded in distracting her from her various plots against his sanity.

"Nicholas?"

"Let me," he whispered, sensing the question in her body and in her heart. "I love you, and I would give you this. Give us both this, if you're willing."

He slipped his forearms under her neck and cradled the back of her head in one hand. She curled up against his chest, so he felt more than saw her single nod. She laid her cheek against his chest in a gesture of surrender, and Nick felt his cock leap in response.

They weren't even joined yet, he'd merely seated himself snugly against the opening to her body, and already, his arousal strained at the leash of his control. So he distracted himself, kissing her forehead, her eyes, her cheeks. He softly scraped her earlobe with his teeth and slipped one hand down to cup and knead a full breast and tug at a ruched nipple.

All the while, he pressed forward slowly with his cock, until Leah's sex eased around him and teasing became the start of penetration. She exhaled, and Nick glided forward the first full inch.

"Steady," Nick rasped when he felt her gather herself to roll her hips. "We're just getting started."

Started, indeed, Leah's sex convulsed around him, though she held completely still otherwise, as did he.

"Oh, my... Nicholas..."

The sensations went on so long Nick thought he might expire from the frustration of holding still. He contented himself with tucking her face against his throat and synchronizing his breathing with hers, then counting the tight, murderously pleasurable spasms as they passed through her to him.

She held still through it all, then pulled herself up to him in a snug embrace when the aftershocks had faded.

"You're all right?" Nick asked, resting his cheek against her temple.

"That was wonderful. You are wonderful, but I want more, now, Nicholas, not in five minutes."

Her voice had a purring quality that resonated through Nick bodily.

"You'll have more," he assured her, tentatively retreating from even the shallow ground he'd gained, then advancing again.

"Please, Nicholas." She clutched at him with her legs around his flanks. "I need..."

"I know," Nick replied softly, reassuring her with the beginning of a rhythm. "I know, lovey. I need, too."

He plied her with more patience than he'd laid claim to in his entire life, easing forward, easing back, listening for the telltale hitch in breathing that might suggest he was moving too deeply, too quickly.

It never came. Instead, in the waiting stillness he heard the gradual acceleration of Leah's breathing, the little sighs of pleasure and satisfaction, the soft groan of encouragement as she felt him stroking in and out of her body. When he was moving easily to her depths and back out again, Nick tightened his hold around Leah's shoulders.

"Move with me," he urged at last. "Love me back, lamb. Let me bring you pleasure."

She lasted four well-coordinated strokes before her body gave itself up again to ecstatic contractions around his swollen cock. He thought he might outlast this onslaught as well, but then Leah added some little internal *something* to the thrust and buck of her pleasure.

Be gentle with her, for the love of God, be gentle...

"Nicholas!" Leah heaved up against him in a mighty shove of her hips, and gentleness was obliterated by mutual passion. Leah's ankles locked at the small of Nick's back, and she rode him in a hard resurgence of her pleasure. He met her thrusts with firm, measured strokes of his own, feeling pleasure bloom in every particle of his being.

As his body surrendered to the ecstasy of an intimate joining, Nick felt at once the profound pleasure of genuine sexual gratification, and the profound bond forged with his wife. The moment was erotic, spiritual, passionate, and tender, all the wonderful things he'd thought to deny himself joined in a single, perfect procession of instants.

And the perfection did not end, though his sexual pleasure eventually spent itself in Leah's body. Afterward, he took some of his weight on his forearms but kept his torso laid along hers, his arms snug around her.

Peace settled around him—peace and gratitude and a comprehension of the great depths to which love might grow with the woman sharing his bed.

Sharing his life, his heart.

"I could not love you more," Nick whispered against Leah's neck. He shifted to kiss her cheek, finding the dampness of her tears with his lips. "Lovey? Did I hurt you?"

Leah shook her head and found his hands on the pillow with her own. Lacing her fingers through his, she strained up to be closer to him.

"Love you, too, Husband," she whispered. "So very much."

She was as shaken as he, Nick concluded, reassured and moved beyond measure. He gathered her close and rolled to his back, so she could rest on him and he could keep his arms around her. His hands traced lazy patterns on her back, and a sweet, wondering silence came down on the sunbeams around them.

"Tell me again," Leah said on a soft sigh.

"I love you. I love you. I love you," Nick obliged, reveling in the words.

"The other, too," Leah instructed, her tongue grazing the pulse at his throat.

The other... Nick cast around, distracted by that hot, pink little tongue, then his mind seized on its quarry.

"I will never, ever leave you again," he said, "unless you cast me from your side, and then I will importune you the livelong day to forgive me and take me back and let me sit penitently at your feet, gazing worshipfully at the hem of your gown."

Leah's nose wrinkled. "What if I'm not wearing a gown? My husband likes us to sleep as God made us."

"I'll gaze at your toes." He wanted to put off what came next, and he needed to get it behind them, regardless of the consequences. "Seriously, Leah, there are things we need to discuss that will put you out of charity with me."

Leah sighed mightily and rubbed her cheek against his chest. "Must we discuss them now?"

"To be honest, I would rather order us a bath, work my wiles on you, and keep you naked for the next week, at least. But, lovey, I am in earnest when I say there are matters we have yet to deal with."

Leah peered up at him. "Such as why you took it into your head that we should not consummate our marriage?"

"Such as that very thing." His countess was both bright and brave. "Much as I'd like to dodge that issue, I will not. I owe you the truth."

"You do. I'm not up to a recitation of your paramours, Nicholas. Not now, not ever. I promise in return not to bore you with tales of my blessedly forgettable experiences with poor Aaron."

"We have a bargain on that score, but there's more to be resolved than our respective amorous pasts, Leah."

"You are sounding oppressively serious, Nicholas. Why must you go hunting serpents in paradise now that we've finally found our way here?"

"Because we cannot stay in paradise, my love." Nick's hands shifted up to cradle her jaw. "Not with anything less than complete trust between us."

"I trust you, Nicholas." Leah spoke with her lips against his palm, and they were sweet, sweet words. He wanted to close them in his fist and hold them tightly.

"And I am humbled to agree, though it is I who must demonstrate my trust in you."

"Isn't that what you just did?"

In her words, Nick heard a whole separate universe of reasons to love her—not just for the passion and ferocity of her sexual loving, but also for the feminine wisdom and generosity that sustained her regard for him when he was too unworthy. Too pigheaded, too stubborn, too...

"Nicholas." Leah shifted up on his chest and regarded him steadily. "Whatever it is, you must not fret. We'll deal with it together. I'll not abandon you just when you've found me."

He closed his eyes and held her fiercely as she put her dainty finger on his most dreaded fear and his most carefully treasured hope.

CHAPTER 18

"So where are we off to?" Leah asked her oddly silent husband while they waited for their horses. He'd held her and cuddled her and rubbed her back and murmured all manner of sweet nothings, but the restlessness had been upon him again, and Leah had suggested they rise as the afternoon began to shift toward evening.

"We will have a late tea with the neighbors," Nick said, his tone was evasive.

"Any particular neighbors?" Leah pressed as Nick gave her a leg up onto Casper.

"Neighbors at Blossom Court," Nick said, swinging onto Buttercup. They turned their horses down the drive, and for many minutes, Leah was silent as they cantered along.

"I've seen them," she said as they approached the Blossom Court drive. "Two ladies, one quite a bit younger than the other."

Nick kept his gaze on the lane before them. "Where have you seen them?"

"In their own garden, as I walked up among the trees on the hilltop. You were visiting with the blond."

"It isn't what you think, Leah, though that will hardly reassure you, I know."

"You love her," Leah said, unable to keep bewilderment from her tone, "or you at least care a great deal for her."

"I love her. It isn't a love you need to fear, Leah—or I hope it won't be."

Now Leah was the one staring at the lane. "Can't you just explain this situation in the King's English?"

"If words were easy, I would have found the right ones weeks ago, maybe even years ago."

Leah stopped interrogating him after that, not sure she'd be able to bear the answers he gave her.

A groom trotted out from the stables when they arrived to Blossom Court, and waited while Nick assisted Leah from her horse.

"Loosen the girths," Nick said. "Put them up with some hay and water, but don't take off the saddles. I don't know how long we'll be."

"Aye, guv." The man disappeared with the horses.

"We'll probably find our hostess in the garden at this time of day," Nick said. "The older woman is Mrs. Waverly and the younger I usually address simply as Leonie."

And he didn't say more, so Leah didn't press him. She did, however, note that for once, Nick had not taken her arm or her hand or in any way made an effort to touch her. That rattled her, and the closer they came to this introduction to the neighbors, the more quiet and distant Nick became.

On instinct, Leah slid her hand through his. Nick looked up, startled, but closed his fingers around hers.

"Mrs. Waverly," Nick called as they passed through a rose arbor. "I believe you might be expecting us?"

"Indeed, my lord." The woman rose from her bench, but the tall blond lady beside her rocketed across the garden with a shriek of glee.

"Nickie!" Oblivious to Leah's presence, she flung her arms around Nick's neck. "Oh, Nick! You came, you came. I am ever so glad to see you, and you brought your wife to see me too. Good day."

She paused in her chatter and flung a curtsy at Leah. "I am Leonie, and you are Nick's wife. Will you have tea with us?"

Leah stopped short as she surveyed the little table set up before the bench where Leonie had been sitting. A doll and a stuffed horse were seated at the table. Both were well worn, veterans of long years of service.

"Tea would be delightful," Leah replied, studying Leonie carefully. Her age was hard to determine. She was tall and possessed of womanly curves, though her movements were coltish and her hair up in a simple knot, as if she were a young girl. Her complexion was lovely, also like a young girl, and her movements were somehow unrestrained as she gamboled along on Nick's other side.

"Nick has to sit on the bench," Leonie explained to Leah. "He is very, very tall, like me, but taller. You may have the rocking chair because you are his wife, and I will sit on the little chair. Mrs. W says I am getting too grown-up for the little chair, but I still fit, don't I?" She turned huge blue eyes on Nick, and Leah was pained to see a wealth of tenderness in Nick's gaze.

"You are becoming quite grown-up, Leonie mine," Nick said. "I think you might consider inviting another friend to your tea parties, say that furry little cat who sleeps on your pillow."

"Mr. Cat will not sit at table with Mrs. Crumpet," Leonie reminded Nick. "Though he will share a brandy with Lord Steed when the weather is nippy."

Leonie chattered on, her prattle confirming Leah's growing suspicion that though Leonie had the appearance of a young lady, she was a child still in her mind, and likely in her heart as well.

But what was she to Leah's husband? Nick loved this Leonie, and Leonie obviously loved her Nick.

"How do you take your tea?" Leonie asked very properly. Leah glanced over at Nick, but his expression was watchful, giving nothing away.

"I am rather spoiled in this regard," Leah said. "I like plenty of cream and at least two lumps of sugar."

"Papa has a sweet tooth as well," Leonie confided, beaming at Nick. "Don't you?"

"I have a sweet tooth in proportion to the rest of me," Nick admitted, his guarded eyes belying his easy tone. "What about Lord Steed? I've known others of his ilk to be fond of sugar."

Leonie turned to the stuffed horse. "He says we can't very well put carrots in his tea."

As the sun set slowly, tea passed in a pleasant childish amalgam of make-believe, let's pretend, and social banter. Leonie was peculiarly intuitive, sensing currents around her more accurately than would others her age.

And yet... As Leah watched Nick taking tea with his daughter and her stuffed animals, saw the fathomless love and concern for her in his eyes, Leah realized that here was the reason Nick Haddonfield still had a capacity for whimsy.

Leonie was the reason Nick was so affectionate, so devoted to his family, so tenderhearted, protective, and responsible—Leonie and her need for him. When another in Nick's position might have become just one more strutting young lordling, Leonie had instead given Nick the impetus to turn himself into a man anyone would be proud to call friend.

As Leah took in blond hair, blue eyes, significant height, and a host of mannerisms shared between parent and child, she tried to absorb the fact this lovely, fey, childlike young woman was Nick's very own daughter. Nick had loved her for her entire life and would love her until his dying breath and beyond.

And that love only enhanced the regard Leah felt for her husband.

"As it is nigh dark," Mrs. Waverly said, "we'd best be retiring, Miss Leonie. I'm sure your papa needs to seek his own bed."

Leonie shook her head vigorously, which had a few more tendrils of blond hair tumbling loose. "Not Papa. He's allowed to stay up late."

"That I am, Leonie mine." Nick rose and drew Leonie to her feet with a flourishy bow. "But young ladies need their rest."

"Good night, Papa." Leonie flung her arms around Nick's waist and hugged him tightly. He bent over her, wrapping his arms around her gently and kissing her crown. "Will you come see me again soon?"

Nick smiled down at her. "As soon as I can, princess."

"Will you bring Mrs. Nick? May we have another tea party in the garden?"

Nick's smile became subtly pained. "Perhaps. If one plans a tea party, that has a tendency to provoke the heavens into raining, but we'll see."

"Of course we'll come for another tea party," Leah interjected, smiling at Leonie. "I am new to the neighborhood, so I will be out making calls, and it will be nice to share a cup with some friendly faces. Perhaps next time I can meet Mr. Cat?"

"He should love to meet you," Leonie assured her earnestly, disentangling herself from Nick's embrace. "Good night, Mrs. Nick." She startled Leah no end by flinging her arms around Leah's neck as well, a dicey proposition, when Leonie had two inches of height over Leah and was an enthusiastic hugger.

"Off to bed with you, favorite brat," Nick chided playfully. "Set a good example for Lord Steed and Mrs. Crumpet."

"Yes, Papa." Leonie beamed at them in the waning light, blew Nick a noisy kiss good night, then turned and scampered into the house.

Or scampered as well as someone could who was nearly six feet tall.

Nick offered Leah his arm and escorted her to the stables in complete silence. The horses were brought out, and when Nick would have boosted Leah into the saddle, she leaned in close to read his expression.

Nothing. Nick's face gave away not one thing. Not relief, not fatigue, not resignation, nothing.

"Do you mind if we walk back to Clover Down?" Leah suggested on impulse. She wanted to be touching Nick when they finally got around to discussing his daughter, not stealing glances at him from atop her horse.

"It's a pleasant night." Nick handed the reins to the groom, who led the horses off without a word. Leah accompanied her husband to the foot of the lane before Nick's voice pierced the gathering gloom.

"For God's sake, Leah, say something."

CHAPTER 19

"That Mrs. Crumpet is rather a dull thing," Leah managed. "Makes you wonder upon whom Leonie modeled her."

"Her previous companion," Nick replied. "I took nearly a year to comprehend that the dratted woman threatened to hide Leonie's stuffed animals if Leonie complained to me of anything."

"How old is your daughter?"

"She just turned sixteen," Nick said on a soft exhalation. "Physically she's sixteen, but mentally..."

"I'm not sure mentally matters a great deal. We can all be reduced to mewling infancy under the wrong circumstances. Tell me about her, Nicholas. You are clearly a devoted papa, and she adores you."

"She adores anyone," Nick said, wearily to Leah's ears, maybe guardedly as well. "Her affectionate nature scares the hell out of me, if you want the truth. Someday, some bloody young swain will come along, delivering the eggs, and walk off with her heart if not her virtue."

He went on, pouring out a litany of every father's hopes and fears for his daughter, his fondest memories and most harrowing moments.

Leah listened, leading Nick around to the back gardens at Clover Down as the words continued to flow from him, haltingly at first, but then more steadily, until his voice was a rumbling torrent of paternal devotion.

When it had been full dark for more than an hour and the crickets were chirping at the moon, Leah sat beside Nick among the newly blooming roses, holding his hand and hoping she was reading the situation correctly.

"So how did she come to be as she is?"

"Fevers, though I didn't realize it until my old nurse informed me of it this week. I thought Leonie was born that way."

"It must have been quite a shock," Leah said, "to be what, fifteen years old, and a father?"

"It was a shock. I didn't find out about Leonie until I was seventeen. I'd been dallying for several years at that point and had come to comprehend the precautions that must be taken. As a very young fellow, though, I was heedless."

"You got somebody with child. I can't understand why the young lady didn't simply apply to you for support."

"She was a relation of Magda's," Nick said. "Daughter to a tenant, and she went to Magda first, thinking to rid herself of the child. Even the heir to an earldom is a poor bet for one's future when he's fifteen years of age."

"Your father pensioned her off?" Leah suggested, drawing Nick's hand through hers.

"Magda sent the girl to live with cousins here in Kent," Nick said. "Then announced her own retirement about a year later. No one thought anything of it, given that Magda is older than dirt."

"And you would have been sixteen when your nurse left Belle Maison."

"Sixteen, and as is the case at that age, a very different heir than I would have been at fourteen or fifteen. I charged off to university, full of my considerable self, ready to have at adult life."

"What happened?"

"When I was seventeen, Leonie's mother died," Nick said, his arm stealing around Leah's waist. "Of influenza or high fevers, I'm not sure exactly what, but Magda thought at that point I was old enough to intervene. Her own little pension would not suffice to raise an earl's by-blow, and I had grown up enough in her opinion to do the right thing. Magda is, after all, elderly, and she didn't want Leonie getting attached to her just as her own health failed—or worse."

In other words, Magda had not wanted Leonie embarking on the series of losses that had marked Nick's early upbringing.

"You became Papa to a two-year-old at seventeen."

"Nearer three," Nick recalled, "and she was gorgeous, all blond curls, smiles, and big blue eyes. I understood when I first held her what it was that drove my father to be so fierce sometimes, so irrationally protective. Leonie is the most tenderhearted, dear person..."

"Like her papa." Leah laid her head on Nick's shoulder and heard a great, heartfelt sigh go out of him. "Nicholas, did you really think I would censure you or your daughter because she hasn't the same kind of intelligence as the empty-headed twits you danced with all spring?"

"I was cautious," Nick said slowly, resting his cheek against Leah's temple, "but I'm trying to tell myself it wasn't without some reason."

Leah waited, sensing they were reaching the most difficult part for Nicholas.

"I mentioned I did not know Leonie's ailment was caused by fevers until recently," Nick said. "I assumed she was born simple, that it was tainted blood causing her mind to remain that of a child. I had an uncle who was the same way, and we never talked about him, but he was still sailing boats and climbing trees as his hair turned gray."

"You probably got on well with him."

"The few times I met him, yes, but he was kept hidden away on some little estate in Shropshire, and I understand why."

"He was an embarrassment?"

"I honestly don't think so. I think it was the only way Grandpapa could protect his son from ridicule. Leonie could play with children her own age when she was very young, but even then, she was taunted for her height. Children being what they are, the taunts soon included her mental abilities, and she withdrew to her dolls and toys, and storybooks."

"So she can read a little. Reading has always been one of my secret comforts."

Nick's hand began the gentle caress along the length of her spine Leah loved. Leonie taught him that gentleness, too. Leah had observed it in his every interaction with his daughter.

"I am so lucky Leonie's a female, a creature who can dwell in peace at home. If my heir had been similarly afflicted, a young man who'd be forced to socialize and be seen—I cannot bear to see Leonie cry. How could I have kept the next Viscount Reston safe and happy?"

$\sim$

THAT QUESTION HAD HAUNTED Nick for years, for as long as he'd known he had a daughter. How would he keep an heir to an earldom safe? Who would love his children, should they all turn out to have Leonie's limitations?

Except, he knew the answers to those questions now, or knew enough of them. With the Countess of Bellefonte snuggled in his arms, Nick knew she would have managed those difficulties with him and made it look easy.

Nick went silent, trying to find a name for the feeling that was expanding his heart. He felt more than relief at Leah's reaction, more than gratitude to be able to envision a future that included his wife and his daughter. He turned to straddle the bench and drew Leah against his chest.

Hope, he thought with a flash of insight. Hope that set tears trickling from his closed eyes, and joy singing through him in the very coursing of his life's blood.

"I was afraid," he finally got out. "I was afraid for my children, for my brothers and sisters, afraid for you. I was afraid..." He'd been terrified, and he was still daunted, but his fears would no longer to dictate the limits of his happiness or those of the people he loved.

"Any father would be concerned," Leah said against his chest. "But you've kept Leonie safe, and she's happy, too. She has her papa's love, and that has been enough."

"Enough." Nick nodded against Leah's hair. "Enough for my youthful by-blow, but I could not see how to protect my heir had he similarly been afflicted, or my legitimate daughters, who would be expected to make come outs and good matches, and bear children of their own. Society is so..."

"Mean," Leah interjected. "Judgmental, petty, spiteful, and in the end, stupid. You know this, because you are so wonderfully grand in your proportions, including the proportions of your heart."

"I'm too damned big," Nick corrected her tersely. "Which has resulted in my being a freak, albeit one popular with the ladies."

"Ladies can be discerning. This explains why you were willing to nip off to the shires for a few years and forgo your place in Society."

"And travel frequently," Nick said, "and bury myself in commerce before my father's demise, and trot from one family holding to another. My idea of hell is to endure Polite Society for any length of time, and then too, moving around so much allows me to drop in on Leonie frequently."

"Well, that will have to stop," Leah said sternly.

Cold dread seeped down Nick's spine. Surely Leah wouldn't deny him time with his daughter? "What do you mean?"

Leah pushed off his chest to regard him in the moonlight. "You love that child with your whole soul, Nicholas Haddonfield, and it breaks your heart to have to part from her, never knowing when you can steal another little visit, never seeing her day to day as all parents can see their children. You missed her first two years, and it simply won't do for you to miss any more. She's clever enough to try to extract promises from you regarding your next visit, and she wants to be with you more as well."

Nick buried his face against Leah's neck, his throat constricting. "She's difficult, she has a temper, she's loud, and she can be clumsy when she's happy—also when she isn't."

"I have a temper when my courses are near," Leah said. "I hate needlepoint, and I will hoard chocolates if left to my own devices. Leonie is your daughter, and of all people, Nicholas, of all *women*, I cannot stand by and watch another young lady fret that her papa doesn't love her, doesn't want to be with her, isn't proud of her. I will argue with you on this and not give up."

"She knows I love her," Nick said roughly. "She has to know that."

"Of course she does, but it's the sort of thing that can be doubted even while one knows it." Leah folded herself back against him, wrapped her arms around his waist, and tucked in close. "She's your daughter. She should live with her papa."

And now what Nick felt was beyond words, beyond even the concepts of hope, joy, and gratitude. It made him humble and invincible, determined and at peace. It gave him the strength to cry and the courage to accept the miracle he held in his arms.

Sitting on the stone bench in the moonlight, his backside going numb, his wife in his arms, Nicholas Haddonfield knew he was absolutely and unshakably, unequivocally and eternally loved.

～

"I BELIEVE you have something that belongs to my wife." Nick glowered at his father-in-law, though he relished those two little words: *my wife.*

"Why would I retain any evidence of the blight she embodied under my own roof?" Wilton replied mildly.

Nick braced himself on his fists and leaned over Wilton's ornate desk. "Because at some point," he replied in equally unimpressed tones, "you considered it might gain you leverage, with someone, somewhere, to be able to prove her marriage to Frommer was legal, and to conceal such evidence in the meanwhile."

"How do you reach such an absurd conclusion?" Wilton rose and turned his back on Nick, his posture suggesting he was absorbed in the study of the gardens behind the Wilton town house.

"Hellerington was forthcoming," Nick said. And Nick had been inclined to believe the old reprobate, even when he claimed to have had nothing to do with an attempted abduction from the park. "Seems while taking the waters in Bath, your old friend got some enterprising little shop girl with child. He no longer pants after Leah, which, under the circumstances, is most wise of him, albeit inconvenient for you."

"Hellerington's doings are no concern of mine."

"Not now," Nick said, "but you saved those marriage lines in case you needed to convince Hellerington you could not keep your promise to him, that you had no authority to promise your widowed daughter's hand to anyone."

"Widowed..." Wilton did turn then, and though he hid it well, Nick saw the fear behind the calculation in the older man's eyes.

"Widowed," Nick said. "Widowed, entitled to both her portion and her inheritance from her mother, which—alas we will find mysteriously plundered by none other than my father-in-law."

"You are making wild accusations against a peer of the realm," Wilton spat.

"Peer being the operative word," Nick retorted, "when I now enjoy that status myself. Did you really think Hellerington would keep his mouth shut forever? You promised him a wife if he kept the details of the duel to himself. You reneged on your promise, and now he neither needs nor wants the only wife you could have procured for him."

"He doesn't know the details of any duel," Wilton shot back, his voice rising.

"One can hardly call it a duel when a young man trips before the count is done and his pistol discharges while he yet faces away from his opponent, and that opponent turns, sees the young man on the ground, and shoots him in the back. I agree with you, it doesn't qualify as a duel, but it bears an exact resemblance to murder."

"You don't know that's what happened," Wilton hissed. "You can't know that."

"First hand? Perhaps not, but I have Lord Hellerington's sworn affidavit, and that will do to get things started."

"You would not dare," Wilton retorted, desperation ruining his attempt at indignation.

"I might not, but Frommer's brother heard the same tale from young Frommer on that unfortunate man's deathbed. Because the Marquess was himself not an eyewitness, he did not feel he could come forth with the tale, his inattentiveness at the scene reflecting further dishonor on the proceedings, and on himself. In short, Wilton, you got lucky. But deathbed confessions are admissible hearsay in a court of law."

Nick let that sink in and felt a petty gratification as he watched the color leach from Wilton's face. A silence spread through the room, full of satisfaction on Nick's part, no doubt full of dread on Wilton's.

"What will you do, Bellefonte?"

"Don't know." Nick's tone was jaunty to the point of nastiness. "I know what you will do, though."

"What?"

"You will retire to Wilton Acres," Nick said, "where you will attend your estate in such a manner as to ensure a reasonable profit. You will sell the town house you purchased for that viperous little mistress of yours, and you will lease out this property, should your sons not be interested in its use. With those proceeds and the profits off Wilton Acres, you will repay your children what you've stolen from them, with reasonable interest. You will not circulate in Society at any level, not for at least five years."

He was banishing his father-in-law, as Leah had been banished, but Wilton had the grace to at least ask one question. "Emily?"

"She will enjoy my grandmother's hospitality," Nick said, "and that of her sister's household, under my protection, and that of her brothers. They are aware of your situation, by the way, and agree that short of causing the scandal you deserve and they do not, this is the best course."

Wilton sat heavily in one of the delicate, expensive chairs, staring at Nick mutely.

"I suggest you start packing," Nick said, tapping his hat onto his head and pulling on his gloves.

Wilton addressed the carpet before Nick could move to the door. "It was an accident—with Frommer. I wanted to scare him off, of course. He could have taken Leah's portion, and there was none to be had, but when his gun went off..." Wilton shook his head. "I panicked. It was an accident, I swear. I hate the girl on some level, hate that her mother did what she did, hate that I couldn't... But I just wanted Frommer intimidated enough to never ask the wrong questions. About dowries, of course, but also about inheritances. I made a mistake."

"As perhaps the girl's mother made a mistake, when she married you."

Wilton nodded miserably but said nothing further.

"Wilton," Nick said before his compassion evaporated in the heat of his contempt, "I believe you did not premeditate murder. You will live out your days in the country anyway, because what you did before and after that accident was deliberate cruelty toward those you should have protected."

Another nod, and then Wilton seemed to shrink and draw in on himself, a physical metaphor for the shriveling of his soul.

If indeed he still possessed one.

～

"I DON'T UNDERSTAND," Leah muttered, glancing over at Nick as their coach rumbled off toward Darius's estate. "You called on Wilton?"

"I am your husband." Nick took pleasure in reminding them both of that happy fact, though his errand with Wilton had meant Leah had awoken alone in their bed. "Your battles are mine to fight."

"You beat him?" Leah's tone bore equal hints of relish and dismay.

"Figuratively. You and Frommer were legally married, Leah. Your father encouraged the elopement to explain the lack of dowry, but he'd forgotten you also had inheritances—funds he'd stolen several years before—of which Frommer might have got wind. Those funds were to go to you in trust upon your marriage, a hedge against your father's embezzlement of your dowry."

The coach slowed to make the turn from the lane, shifting Leah's weight more snugly against Nick's side. "Mother mentioned something about that, though she was very ill at the time, and I didn't know if she was speaking factually or in terms of unmet wishes."

"Factually," Nick said, settling his arm around Leah's shoulder. Her scent was particularly luscious, and to his eyes, she looked subtly radiant. "Embezzlement left your father with a need to put a good scare into any notions Frommer might have had about poking into your finances. As the son of a Marquess, Frommer could have seen it done."

Leah turned to gaze out the window, which meant Nick's fingers could caress the curve of her cheek. "But Wilton killed Aaron before any awkward questions were asked?"

"Wilton claims it was an accident," Nick said, "and the circumstances don't particularly contradict him." Hellerington did, of course, but his account was not entirely unbiased, and Nick could easily see Wilton panicking in a crisis. "The upshot is your father will make financial reparation to his children and behave himself in Hampshire for the foreseeable future."

She nuzzled his hand, which was enough to make Nick wish the coach were headed back toward Clover Down. "You're sure?"

"The statute of limitations on murder does not toll," Nick replied. "Wilton probably doesn't have that many years left on this earth, given the weight of his sins."

"The wicked put off meeting their fate as long as they can," Leah observed. "What do my brothers think of this?"

Their reactions didn't matter to Nick, provided his countess was happy. "I don't know. I sent messages to them this morning, summarizing my actions, and set off before they could reply. I gave Wilton to understand we are a united front, of course, because scandal would serve no one. Did you know I am an uncle?"

She shot him a glance at the abrupt change in topic. Her father's perfidy would no doubt take time to ponder—and recover from.

"Ethan has children?"

"Two little boys whom I've not yet met," Nick replied, though given Ethan's proportions, they were probably big little boys. "I can't wait to chase them through our orchard."

He waited while Leah digested that, but when his wife—his countess, his Leah, his lovey—made no comment, Nick abandoned half measures and scooped her onto his lap.

"Better," he pronounced. "I should not have left you alone in our bed this morning. A woman dealing with a pilfered inheritance, purloined marriage lines, a surprise, mostly grown stepdaughter, and a clodpated husband should not be waking all on her lonesome."

"A comfortable, clodpated husband," Leah allowed, relaxing against him. "There's more, though, isn't there? You haven't taken a sudden notion to go calling on Darius today, of all days, because you've tired of my charms already—I've not tired of yours, in case you were wondering."

Nick brushed his lips against her ear. "I was wondering if you were sore, lovey. My countess is a passionate lady." And wasn't that a fine, fine thing?

"Blame me for provoking you to protracted displays of virility, will you?" She sounded wonderfully disgruntled as she kissed his jaw. "If this is your version of flirting, Nicholas, you are in sad want of direction. It shall be my pleasure to provide it to you upon our return to Clover Down."

"And it will be my duty..." The rest of the blather flew out of his head as Leah bit his earlobe. The coach rumbled along, the earl and his countess kissing all the while, until Nick caught a glimpse through the window of Darius's gateposts.

"Lovey?"

She struggled to sit up, which allowed Nick to notice that their spate of kissing had taken a toll on her coiffure.

"That is not a dignified endearment, Nicholas. I am a countess, soon to be the guiding female influence on your only daughter, and I will not allow—"

Nick allowed himself one more little kiss, to stop his lovey's verbal frolicking. "What would you think about becoming the sole female influence on Leonie and a somewhat younger child, a boy who bears a particular resemblance to your brother Darius?"

She went silent, shifted off his lap, and tucked the stray lock of hair behind her ear, all vestiges of frolic and flirtation gone from her expression.

"We have another secret, don't we, Nicholas?"

"Please don't look so worried, wife of mine. This is a happy secret, a joyous secret that need not be kept secret much longer."

The silly woman tried to scoot away from him. Nick hauled her back against his side. "Shortly after you returned from Italy, a young woman presented herself to your brother, claiming that Wilton had ruined her. Your brother took her in, passed her child off as his own, and has kept the pleasure of raising the boy to himself these past few years. This struck him as the best way to keep the boy safe from Wilton, and in this instance—in this one instance—I will allow I agree with Darius."

When Leah would have worried a fingernail, Nick took her fingers in his hand and kissed them.

The worry remained in her gaze. "I have a brother."

"A busy little fellow named John. We're to meet him, assuming he hasn't run off and joined the Navy." Nick tried for humor, tried for a lightness he didn't feel as he watched anxiety cloud his wife's face. "Darius has asked us to add the boy to our household for a bit, in fact. He wants to put the lad even farther from Wilton's reach, at least for a time."

The coach swung past a hedge of blooming honeysuckle, the sweet, soothing scent at odds with the tension Nick felt radiating from his wife. She started blinking, slowly, then more quickly.

"Lovey, we don't have to take the boy in. I'm sure Darius would understand. I did not promise we would, and you've dealt with enough upheaval." Belatedly it occurred to Nick that a woman who'd lost a son might not be keen on raising a half sibling for the convenience of others. He'd bungled—

"He looks like Darius? He has dark hair?"

What had that to do with anything? "Sable, I'd say. And his manners are impressive for such a wee lad." A tear slipped down Leah's cheek, and Nick nearly bellowed for the coachy to turn the damned vehicle around.

"My Charles had sable hair," Leah said, taking the handkerchief Nick stuffed into her hand. "Charles and Darius were very alike, the same smile, the same eyes. Charles loved his uncle, and I believe Darius would have died for that child."

Nick could not tell if this was a good thing, given some of dear Darius's other antics. "Darius loves this little fellow, Leah, clearly." He brushed a tear from her cheek. "I was hoping you might love him too. We're the boy's family, you see, and he hasn't had an easy time of it with only your brother to raise him."

"Of course."

Of course—what? What did "of course" mean, muttered in near strangled terms?

"Lovey?" Nick bent nearer, close enough to catch the fragrance of lilies of the valley, near enough to recall the flower symbolized the return of happiness. "Of course, what? I can make excuses to your brother, and you need not leave the coach. I can understand that you're dealing with a lot, and I may have misjudged—"

He shifted back just in time to avoid her elbow as she twisted sharply and flung her arms around his neck. "Nicholas, I love you. I love you so. I love you until I ache with it, and then I love you even more."

"I love you too." His arms came around her and held her tight, not for her, but for him—because he needed to hold her when she was upset. "But please don't cry. I cannot abide it when you cry, Leah."

And yet, these tears did not strike him as tears of misery.

"You don't even know this boy, and you must scheme with my brother for the child's safety," Leah wailed. "You didn't know me, and you m... married me, and made me your countess. You trust me with Leonie, and your own sisters don't know her, and my brother is an idiot to keep this from me, but you're making him tell me, aren't you?"

She kissed Nick before he could answer, and the kiss told him what the words and the tears had not: Leah was happy. She was pleased to have another sibling—which certainly made matters easier —and she was also pleased with him. With Nicholas Haddonfield, her husband, which made Nick happy too.

"I did not make Darius do anything."

"Yes, you did." Another kiss, this one damp and salty with her tears. "You threatened to treat Darius to some fisticuffs if he didn't allow us to help him, all in aid of preserving his pride, I'm sure, because Darius is quite fierce, but oh, Nicholas..."

She subsided to the seat beside him, which was fortunate, because the coach had been standing still for some moments.

Nick took his thoroughly wrinkled handkerchief from her grasp and blotted her tears. "I did not want to upset you, Wife. This should be a happy day." He took her hand in his, the better to comprehend the emotions rioting through her. "Why the tears, Leah? Is John to come stay with us at Belle Maison? Leonie alone will create a commotion. Two children at once, children who are strangers to each other and strangers to you, is hardly how I wanted you to begin your duties as my countess."

～

LEAH COULD HARDLY SPEAK for the feelings thundering inside her.

"Nicholas." She clutched his hand, trying to find words. "I want to call you lovey, too. Did you know that? It's such a wonderful endearment."

He smiled, a man purely indulging a daft female. "I would be honored to be your lovey, but that's not what you wanted to tell me, is it?"

She shook her head. "For years—years—I was alone. I was barely tolerated. My father called me a walking disgrace to English womanhood and worse. My brothers did what they could for me, but that just made me feel worse, more ashamed. You have given me your daughter, and that... that..."

Leah bit her lip, trying not to let more tears fall, because Nick looked nigh to panic when she cried. She tried again, before the urge to kiss her husband could overtake the need to find the words.

"You assumed I would make a place for John in our household. You faced down my father and exiled him to Hampshire. You've recruited Lady Warne to look after Emily's come out, you, you..."

"I love you," Nick said, sounding bewildered. "Of course I will do those things. It's my privilege and honor to do them, because you are my wife and my countess, and I pray to Almighty God we have decades upon decades to raise our children, love our family, and love each other in every possible sense of the word."

He understood. He understood what she'd been trying to say, the magnitude of the bounty she'd acquired when he'd taken her to wife.

"Yes, and when you are clodpated, I will love you, and when I am wrong-headed, you will love me."

Nick's smile was tender and luminous. In her heart, Leah said a prayer that he'd always have that smile for her, even when they were old and gray.

She made the acquaintance of her very small brother John, and she agreed with Nick that the boy should join their household at Belle Maison. When she offered John her hand, that he might drag her off to the stables and introduce her to his pony, Leah caught Nick giving her that same tender, indulgent smile again.

As it turned out, even after they'd had decades upon decades to raise their many delightful children, love their family, and love each other in every possible sense of the word, Nicholas still smiled at Leah—his wife, his countess, his lovey—like that.

Just exactly, wonderfully like that.

TO MY DEAR READERS

To my dear readers,

Nicholas is an old friend, originally published in 2013. I'd met Nick several manuscripts earlier, in Thomas and Matthew's stories, and then he also popped up in **The Virtuoso**. Busy guy!

The version you've just read is slightly updated and revised, because publishing rights have reverted to me and I have that latitude. I love this book and hope you enjoyed it too. The rest of the **Lonely Lords**, starting with Ethan's story, will also be reverting to me for updating and reissuing.

And I have new titles coming out, as follows:

April 28, 2020, saw the release of my fourth **Rogues to Riches story**, **A Duke by Any Other Name**. Lady Althea Wentworth has retreated to the wilds of Yorkshire after failing miserably in one London Season after another. She's determined to fit in with rural society, but realizes she will need the *entrée* that only her neighbor, Nathaniel, the reclusive Duke of Rothhaven, can provide. His Grace is sympathetic to her situation, but family secrets have rendered him more prisoner than recluse. She longs for acceptance and social cachet, he needs to be left alone... or so he claims.

Silly duke. Excerpt below.

And June (May in the **web store**) will see the publication of my next **True Gentlemen**, *A Lady's Dream Come True*. Oak Dorning is off to the bright lights of London, where he will finally, finally begin establishing himself as a professional portraitist. A temporary job in the wilds of Hampshire restoring some paintings for the widowed Mrs. Verity Channing is simply a means to earn the blunt that a London lifestyle requires. Verity was married to a successful artist, and she has no interest whatsoever in the small minds and endless gossip she endured in Town.

And then... well, you can read the excerpt below. Here there be smoochies!

I am also nibbling away at organizing my backlist and re-releasing some other novellas that have been de-published for various reasons. *The Windham Ducal Duet* (The Courtship/The Duke and His Duchess) is already on the shelves, as is *A Lady Without Peer*, and *A Duke Walked into a House Party*.

If you'd like to stay up to date with all of these illustrious doin's, the easiest way to do that is to follow me on **Bookbub**. They never spam you, and only send alerts when there's a new release, discount, or pre-order on the horizon. You might also keep an eye on my **Deals** page, because every month, I have either an early release or a discount happening somewhere. Then there's always my **news-letter**, if you'd like more of the details and kitten pictures.

Happy reading!

Grace Burrowes

Read on for an excerpt from *A Duke by Any Other Name*!

EXCERPT—A DUKE BY ANY OTHER NAME

The usual polite means of gaining an introduction to Nathaniel, Duke of Rothmere, have failed Lady Althea Wentworth utterly. Being a resourceful woman, she's turned to unusual measures to achieve her goal...

Althea heard her guest before she saw him. Rothhaven's arrival was presaged by a rapid beat of hooves coming not up her drive, but rather, directly across the park that surrounded Lynley Vale manor.

A large horse created that kind of thunder, one disdaining the genteel canter for a hellbent gallop. From her parlor window Althea could see the beast approaching, and her first thought was that only a terrified animal traveled at such speed.

But no. Horse and rider cleared the wall beside the drive in perfect rhythm, swerved onto the verge, and continued right up—good God, they aimed straight for the fountain. Althea could not look away as the black horse drew closer and closer to unforgiving marble and splashing water.

"Mary, Mother of God."

Another smooth leap—the fountain was five feet high if it was an inch—and a foot-perfect landing, followed by an immediate check of the horse's speed. The gelding came down to a frisking, capering trot, clearly proud of himself and ready for even greater challenges.

The rider stroked the horse's neck, and the beast calmed and hung his head, sides heaving. A treat was offered and another pat, before one of Althea's grooms bestirred himself to take the horse. Rothhaven—for that could only be the dread duke himself—paused on the front steps long enough to remove his spurs, whip off his hat, and run a black-gloved hand through hair as dark as hell's tarpit.

"The rumors are true," Althea murmured. Rothhaven was built on the proportions of the Vikings of old, but their fair coloring and blue eyes had been denied him. He glanced up, as if he knew Althea would be spying, and she drew back.

His gaze was colder than a Yorkshire night in January, which fit exactly with what Althea had heard of him.

She moved from the window and took the wingchair by the hearth, opening a book chosen for this singular occasion. She had dressed carefully—elegantly but without too much fuss—and styled her hair with similar consideration. Rothhaven gave very few people the chance to make even a first impression on him, a feat Althea admired.

Voices drifted up from the foyer, followed by the tread of boots on the stair. Rothhaven moved lightly for such a grand specimen, and his voice rumbled like distant cannon. A soft tap on the door, then Strensall was announcing Nathaniel, His Grace of Rothhaven. The duke did not have to duck to come through the doorway, but it was a near thing.

Althea set aside her book, rose, and curtsied to a precisely deferential depth and not one inch lower.

"Welcome to Lynley Vale, Your Grace. A pleasure to meet you. Strensall, the tea, and don't spare the trimmings."

Strensall bolted for the door.

"I do not break bread with mine enemy." Rothhaven stalked over to Althea and swept her with a glower. "No damned tea."

His eyes were a startling green, set against swooping dark brows and features as angular as the crags and tors of Yorkshire's moors. He brought with him the scents of heather and horse, a lovely combination. His cravat remained neatly pinned with a single bar of gleaming gold despite his mad dash across the countryside.

"I will attribute Your Grace's lack of manners to the peckishness that can follow exertion. A tray, Strensall."

The duke leaned nearer. "Shall I threaten to curse poor Strensall with nightmares, should he bring a tray?"

"That would be unsporting." Althea sent her goggling butler a glance, and he scampered off. "You are reputed to have a temper, but then, if folk claimed that my mere passing caused milk to curdle and babies to colic, I'd be a tad testy myself. No one has ever accused you of dishonorable behavior."

"Nor will they, while you, my lady, have stooped so low as to unleash the hogs of war upon my hapless estate." He backed away not one inch, and this close Althea caught a more subtle fragrance. Lily of the valley or jasmine. Very faint, elegant, and unexpected, like the moss-green of his eyes.

"You cannot read, perhaps," he went on, "else you'd grasp that 'we will not be entertaining for the foreseeable future' means neither you nor your livestock are welcome at Rothhaven Hall."

"Hosting a short call from your nearest neighbor would hardly be entertaining," Althea countered. "Shall we be seated?"

"I will not be seated," he retorted. "Retrieve your damned pigs from my orchard, madam, or I will send them to slaughter before the week is out."

"Is that where my naughty ladies got off to?" Althea took her wing chair. "They haven't been on an outing in ages. I suppose the spring air inspired them to seeing the sights. Last autumn they took a notion to inspect the market, and in summer they decided to attend Sunday services. Most of our neighbors find my herd's social inclinations amusing."

"I might be amused, were your herd not at the moment rooting through my orchard uninvited. To allow stock of those dimensions to wander is irresponsible, and why a duke's sister is raising hogs entirely defeats my powers of imagination."

Because Rothhaven had never been poor and never would be. "Do have a seat, Your Grace. I'm told only the ill-mannered pace the parlor like a house tabby who needs to visit the garden."

He turned his back to Althea—very rude of him—though he appeared to require a moment to marshal his composure. She counted that a small victory, for she had needed many such moments since acquiring a title, and her composure yet remained as unruly as her sows on a pretty spring day.

Though truth be told, the lady swine had had some *encouragement* regarding the direction of their latest outing.

Rothhaven turned to face Althea, the fire in his gaze banked to burning disdain. "Will you or will you not retrieve your wayward pigs from my land?"

"I refuse to discuss this with a man who cannot observe the simplest conversational courtesy." She waved a hand at the opposite wingchair, and when that provoked a drawing up of the magnificent ducal height, she feared His Grace would stalk from the room.

Instead he took the chair, whipping out the tails of his riding jacket like Lucifer arranging his coronation robes.

"Thank you," Althea said. "When you march about like that, you give a lady a crick in her neck. Your orchard is at least a mile from my home farm."

"And downwind, more's the pity. Perhaps you raise pigs to perfume the neighborhood with their scent?"

"No more than you keep horses, sheep, or cows for the same purpose, Your Grace. Or maybe your livestock hides the pervasive odor of brimstone hanging about Rothhaven Hall?"

A muscle twitched in the duke's jaw.

The tea tray arrived before Althea could further provoke her guest, and in keeping with standing instructions, the kitchen had exerted its skills to the utmost. Strensall placed an enormous silver tray before Althea—the good silver, not the fancy silver—bowed, and withdrew.

"How do you take your tea, Your Grace?"

"Plain, except I won't be staying for tea. Assure me that you'll send your swineherd over to collect your sows in the next twenty-four hours and I will take my leave of you."

Not so fast. Having coaxed Rothhaven into making a call, Althea wasn't about to let him win free so easily.

"I cannot give you those assurances, Your Grace, much as I'd like to. I'm very fond of those ladies and they are quite valuable. They are also particular."

Rothhaven straightened a crease in his breeches. They fit him exquisitely, though Althea had never before seen black riding attire.

"The whims of your livestock are no affair of mine, Lady Althea." His tone said that Althea's whims were a matter of equal indifference to him. "You either retrieve them or the entire shire will be redolent of smoking bacon."

He was bluffing, albeit convincingly. "Do you know what my sows are worth?"

He quoted a price per pound for pork on the hoof that was accurate to the penny.

"Wrong," Althea said, pouring him a cup of tea and holding it out to him. "Those are my best breeders. I chose their grandmamas and mamas for hardiness and the ability to produce sizable, healthy litters. A pig in the garden can be the difference between a family surviving through a hard winter or starving, if that pig can also produce large, thriving litters. She can live on scraps, she needs very little care, and she will see a dozen piglets raised to weaning twice a year without putting any additional strain on the family budget."

The duke looked at the steaming cup of tea, then at Althea, then back at the cup. This was the best China black she could offer, served on the good porcelain in her personal parlor. If he disdained her hospitality now, she might...cry?

He would not be swayed by tears, but he apparently could be tempted by a perfect cup of tea.

"You raise hogs as a charitable undertaking?" he asked.

"I raise them for all sorts of reasons, and I donate many to the poor of the parish."

"Why not donate money?" He took a cautious sip of his tea. "One can spend coin on what's most necessary, and many of the poor have no gardens."

"If they lack a garden, they can send the children into the countryside to gather rocks and build drystone walls, can't they? After a season or two, the pig will have rendered the soil of its enclosure very fertile indeed, and the enclosure can be moved. Coin, by contrast, can be stolen."

Another sip. "From the poor box?"

"Of course from the poor box. Or that money can be wasted on Bibles while children go hungry."

This was the wrong conversational direction, too close to Althea's heart, too far from her dreams.

"My neighbor is a radical," Rothhaven mused. "And she conquers poverty and ducal privacy alike with an army of sows. Nonetheless, those hogs are where they don't belong, and possession is nine-tenths of the law. Move them or I will do as I see fit with them."

"If you harm my pigs or disperse that herd for sale, I will sue you for conversion. You gained control of my property legally—pigs will wander—but if you waste those pigs or convert my herd for your own gain, I will take you to court."

Althea put three sandwiches on a plate and offered it to him. She'd lose her suit for conversion, not because she was wrong on the law—she was correct—but because he was a duke, and not just any duke. He was the much-treasured dread duke of Rothhaven Hall, a local fixture of pride. The squires in the area were more protective of Rothhaven's consequence than they were of their own.

Lawsuits were scandalous, however, especially between neighbors or family members. They were also messy, involving appearances in court and meetings with solicitors and barristers. A man who seldom left his property and refused to receive callers would avoid those tribulations at all costs.

Rothhaven set down the plate. "What must I do to inspire you to retrieve your *valuable* sows? I have my own swineherd, you know. A capable old fellow who has been wrangling hogs for more than half a century. He can move your livestock to the king's highway."

Althea hadn't considered this possibility, but she dared not blow retreat. "My sows are partial to their own swineherd. They'll follow him anywhere, though after rioting about the neighborhood on their own, they will require time to recover. They've been out dancing all night, so to speak, and must have a lie-in."

Althea could not fathom why any sensible female would comport herself thus, but every spring she dragged herself south, and subjected herself to the same inanity for the duration of the London Season.

This year would be different.

"So send your swineherd to fetch them tomorrow," Rothhaven said, taking a bite of a beef sandwich. "My swineherd will assist, and I need never darken your door again—nor you, mine." He sent her a pointed look, one that scolded without saying a word.

"I cannot oblige you, Your Grace," Althea said. "My swineherd is visiting his sister in York and won't be back until week's end. I do apologize for the delay, though if turning my pigs loose in your orchard has occasioned this introduction, then I'm glad for it. I value my privacy too, but I am at my wit's end and must consult you on a matter of some delicacy."

He gestured with half a sandwich. "All the way at your wit's end? What has caused you to travel that long and arduous trail?"

Polite Society. Wealth. Standing. All the great boons Althea had once envied and had so little ability to manage.

"I want a baby," she said, not at all how she'd planned to state her situation.

Rothhaven put down his plate slowly, as if a wild creature had come snorting and snapping into the parlor. "Are you utterly demented? One doesn't announce such a thing, and I am in no position to..." He stood, his height once again creating an impression of towering disdain. "I will see myself out."

Althea rose as well, and though Rothhaven could toss her behind the sofa one-handed, she made her words count.

"Do not flatter yourself, Your Grace. Only a fool would seek to procreate with a petulant, moody, withdrawn, arrogant specimen such as you. I want a family, exactly the goal every girl is raised to treasure. There's nothing shameful or inappropriate about that. Until I learn to comport myself as the sister of a duke ought, I have no hope of making an acceptable match. You are a duke. If anybody understands the challenge I face, you do. You have five hundred years of breeding and family history to call upon, while I..."

Oh, this was not the eloquent explanation she'd rehearsed, and Rothhaven's expression had become unreadable.

He gestured with a large hand. "While you...?"

Althea had tried inviting him to tea, then to dinner. She'd tried calling upon him. She'd ridden the bridle paths for hours in hopes of meeting him by chance, only to see him galloping over the moors, heedless of anything so tame as a bridle path.

She'd called on him twice, only to be turned away at the door and chided by letter twice for presuming even that much. Althea had only a single weapon left in her arsenal, a lone arrow in her quiver of strategies, the one least likely to yield the desired result.

She had the truth. "I need your help," she said, subsiding into her chair. "I haven't anywhere else to turn. If I'm not to spend the rest of my life as a laughingstock, if I'm to have a prayer of finding a suitable match, I very much need your help."

Order your copy of *A Duke by Any Other Name,* and read on for an excerpt from *A Lady's Dream Come True*!

EXCERPT—A LADY'S DREAM
COME TRUE

Oak Dorning and his temporary employer are having an interesting discussion...

Mrs. Channing swept past Oak into the gloom of the attic, her faint floral fragrance blending with the scents of dust and old wood.

"I don't go around kissing strange men, Mr. Dorning," she said, facing away from him. "You were kind to Catherine, and that touched me, and I still should not have... I should not have kissed you. Not even on the cheek."

So they were to have a *discussion*. Very well. "Why not?" Oak asked. "Kissing is enjoyable, provided all parties to the activity are consenting adults."

"Because..." She turned slowly. "One shouldn't kiss strangers, in the first place."

"One should not *be caught* kissing strangers, perhaps. What's in the second place?"

She drew a finger across the shelf of a sconce that held an empty oil lamp. "I haven't wanted to. Kiss any strangers, that is. Kiss anybody."

Oak pushed the door closed. "You have been in mourning." He took out a handkerchief, dusted off the top of a sea trunk, and gestured for the lady to take a seat, which she did. "Might I have the place beside you?"

"We're discussing kisses, Mr. Dorning. You need not stand on ceremony."

"And yet, you call me Mr. Dorning." Vera Channing was pretty, and she was more than pretty. She was sensible, devoted to her children, no stranger to grief, and she had a fine sense of humor. Oak wanted to capture the *more* on canvas, not simply the lovely face and gracefully curved figure.

He also wanted to kiss her, and not only on the cheek.

"Who do you think did that landscape?" she said, frowning at a canvas resting against the far wall.

Oak rose from the trunk and forced himself to consider the sheep, the clouds, and the little stream running diagonally through the scene.

"This might be the work of Hanscomb Detwiler. He's quick, accurate, and a good mimic, but he lacks a sense of adventure when it comes to brush work." The painting held other clues to the artist's identity—the specific blue of the sky, the manner in which sunlight was flatly reflected from the cottage windows—but Oak wasn't particularly interested in the painting.

He was interested in the woman wearing the old dress as she sat on the dusty trunk. "Will you kiss me again?" he asked.

"I want to, but I'm trying to determine my motivations. Behaving impulsively is the province of artists, not their widows."

Oak resumed the place beside her. "I cannot afford to behave impulsively. I know what I want: a career as a respected painter. That has been my ambition from earliest youth and remains the objective I will pursue when I've restored your paintings."

"Honest," she said. "I appreciate honesty."

"I thought you might. I certainly hope to be dealt with honestly." And that seemed to settle the matter. Neither of them was looking for a permanent attachment, and neither of them wanted a mindless indulgence.

"Would you like to kiss me?" Vera asked.

"Very much." More than kiss her too. She had to know that.

She rose and twisted the lock on the doorlatch. "Why don't we give it a try and see how it goes?"

Oak remained seated, the better to ignore the evidence of arousal this conversation was inspiring. "Will you regret this?"

"Will you?"

Oak considered that question, or tried to, as Vera stood before him. He would leave Merlin Hall in the autumn, and whether he painted her portrait or not, he'd have canvases for Sycamore to hang in his club. He would travel to London to deliver those paintings in person, and to embark on his activities as a professional portraitist. Nothing on that schedule precluded a few friendly interludes with a willing widow.

"No regrets," Oak said. "No expectations and no regrets."

Vera stepped between his legs and looped her arms around his shoulders. "This is an experiment, Mr. Dorning. You will in some ways be my first. Moderate your expectations accordingly."

"Oak." He took her by the hips and drew her closer. "An experiment then."

She pressed a luscious, lingering kiss on his mouth, and desire reverberated through Oak like a thunderclap. Her hands winnowed through his hair and he rose, the better to gather her in his arms and lose himself in her embrace.

Coherent thoughts tried to swim against the tide of pleasurable sensation. Some notions were irrational. *I've missed you*, for example, made no sense at all, though missing the voluptuous joy of an erotic kiss made all the sense in the world.

And other thoughts were howlingly inconvenient: Oak would be Vera's first, as she'd said. Her first affair, her first intimacy as a widow, her first foray into non-marital overtures. She'd waited several years to take this step and chosen him from among many options.

Oak was mindful of the honor she did him and he offered her respect, liking, and desire in return. Even so, he could not ignore the plaintive, *foolish* voice in his head that admitted to envying the man who could take a permanent place at her side.

Vera made a soft, yearning noise in her throat, and a final conclusion managed to coalesce in Oak's mind: The experiment was a success. If the hypothesis had been that he and Vera could enjoy a shared kiss, the hypothesis had been proved gloriously true.

Order your copy ***A Lady's Dream Come True***!

CPSIA information can be obtained
at www.ICGtesting.com
Printed in the USA
LVHW031017110720
660407LV00004B/1181

9 781952 443077